J. J. Connington and The Murder Room

››› This title is part of The Murder Room, our series dedicated to making available out-of-print or hard-to-find titles by classic crime writers.

Crime fiction has always held up a mirror to society. The Victorians were fascinated by sensational murder and the emerging science of detection; now we are obsessed with the forensic detail of violent death. And no other genre has so captivated and enthralled readers.

Vast troves of classic crime writing have for a long time been unavailable to all but the most dedicated frequenters of second-hand bookshops. The advent of digital publishing means that we are now able to bring you the backlists of a huge range of titles by classic and contemporary crime writers, some of which have been out of print for decades.

From the genteel amateur private eyes of the Golden Age and the femmes fatales of pulp fiction, to the morally ambiguous hard-boiled detectives of mid twentieth-century America and their descendants who walk our twenty-first century streets, The Murder Room has it all. ›››

The Murder Room
Where Criminal Minds Meet

themurderroom.com

J. J. Connington (1880–1947)

Alfred Walter Stewart, who wrote under the pen name J. J. Connington, was born in Glasgow, the youngest of three sons of Reverend Dr Stewart. He graduated from Glasgow University and pursued an academic career as a chemistry professor, working for the Admiralty during the First World War. Known for his ingenious and carefully worked-out puzzles and in-depth character development, he was admired by a host of his better-known contemporaries, including Dorothy L. Sayers and John Dickson Carr, who both paid tribute to his influence on their work. He married Jessie Lily Courts in 1916 and they had one daughter.

By J. J. Connington

Sir Clinton Driffield Mysteries

Murder in the Maze (1927)
Tragedy at Ravensthorpe (1927)
The Case with Nine Solutions (1928)
Mystery at Lynden Sands (1928)
Nemesis at Raynham Parva (1929) (a.k.a. *Grim Vengenace*)
The Boathouse Riddle (1931)
The Sweepstake Murders (1931)
The Castleford Conundrum (1932)
The Ha-Ha Case (1934) (a.k.a. *The Brandon Case*)
In Whose Dim Shadow (1935) (a.k.a. *The Tau Cross Mystery*)
A Minor Operation (1937)
Murder Will Speak (1938)
Truth Comes Limping (1938)
The Twenty-One Clues (1941)
No Past is Dead (1942)
Jack-in-the-Box (1944)
Common Sense Is All You Need (1947)

Supt Ross Mysteries

The Eye in the Museum (1929)
The Two Tickets Puzzle (1930)

Novels

Death at Swaythling Court (1926)
The Dangerfield Talisman (1926)
Tom Tiddler's Island (1933) (a.k.a. *Gold Brick Island*)
The Counsellor (1939)
The Four Defences (1940)

A Minor Operation

J. J. Connington

An Orion book

This edition published by
The Orion Publishing Group Ltd
Orion House
5 Upper St Martin's Lane
London WC2H 9EA

An Hachette UK company
A CIP catalogue record for this book is available from the British Library

ISBN 978 1 4719 0613 8

All characters and events in this publication are fictitious and any resemblance to real people, living or dead, is purely coincidental.

www.orionbooks.co.uk

CONTENTS

Introduction
by
Curtis Evans

During the Golden Age of the detective novel, in the 1920s and 1930s, J. J. Connington stood with fellow crime writers R. Austin Freeman, Cecil John Charles Street and Freeman Wills Crofts as the foremost practitioner in British mystery fiction of the science of pure detection. I use the word 'science' advisedly, for the man behind J. J. Connington, Alfred Walter Stewart, was an esteemed Scottish-born scientist. A 'small, unassuming, moustached polymath', Stewart was 'a strikingly effective lecturer with an excellent sense of humour, fertile imagination and fantastically retentive memory', qualities that also served him well in his fiction. He held the Chair of Chemistry at Queens University, Belfast for twenty-five years, from 1919 until his retirement in 1944.

During roughly this period, the busy Professor Stewart found time to author a remarkable apocalyptic science fiction tale, *Nordenholt's Million* (1923), a mainstream novel, *Almighty Gold* (1924), a collection of essays, *Alias J. J. Connington* (1947), and, between 1926 and 1947, twenty-four mysteries (all but one tales of detection), many of them sterling examples of the Golden Age puzzle-oriented detective novel at its considerable best. 'For those who ask first of all in a detective story for exact and mathematical accuracy in the construction of the plot', avowed a contemporary *London Daily Mail* reviewer, 'there is no author to equal the distinguished scientist who writes under the name of J. J. Connington.'[1]

Alfred Stewart's background as a man of science is reflected in his fiction, not only in the impressive puzzle plot mechanics he devised for his mysteries but in his choices of themes and depictions of characters. Along with Stanley Nordenholt of *Nordenholt's Million*, a novel about a plutocrat's pitiless efforts to preserve a ruthlessly remolded remnant of human life after a global environmental calamity, Stewart's most notable character is Chief Constable Sir Clinton Driffield, the detective in seventeen of the twenty-four Connington crime novels. Driffield is one of crime fiction's most highhanded investigators, occasionally taking on the functions of judge and jury as well as chief of police.

Absent from Stewart's fiction is the hail-fellow-well-met quality found in John Street's works or the religious ethos suffusing those of Freeman Wills Crofts, not to mention the effervescent novel-of-manners style of the British Golden Age Crime Queens Dorothy L. Sayers, Margery Allingham and Ngaio Marsh. Instead we see an often disdainful cynicism about the human animal and a marked admiration for detached supermen with superior intellects. For this reason, reading a Connington novel can be a challenging experience for modern readers inculcated in gentler social beliefs. Yet Alfred Stewart produced a classic apocalyptic science fiction tale in *Nordenholt's Million* (justly dubbed 'exciting and terrifying reading' by the *Spectator*) as well as superb detective novels boasting well-wrought puzzles, bracing characterization and an occasional leavening of dry humour. Not long after Stewart's death in 1947, the Connington novels fell entirely out of print. The recent embrace of Stewart's fiction by Orion's Murder Room imprint is a welcome event indeed, correcting as it does over sixty years of underserved neglect of an accomplished genre writer.

Born in Glasgow on 5 September 1880, Alfred Stewart had significant exposure to religion in his earlier life. His father was William Stewart, longtime Professor of Divinity and Biblical Criticism at Glasgow University, and he married Lily Coats, a daughter of the Reverend Jervis Coats and member of one of

Scotland's preeminent Baptist families. Religious sensibility is entirely absent from the Connington corpus, however. A confirmed secularist, Stewart once referred to one of his wife's brothers, the Reverend William Holms Coats (1881–1954), principal of the Scottish Baptist College, as his 'mental and spiritual antithesis', bemusedly adding: 'It's quite an education to see what one would look like if one were turned into one's mirror-image.'

Stewart's J. J. Connington pseudonym was derived from a nineteenth-century Oxford Professor of Latin and translator of Horace, indicating that Stewart's literary interests lay not in pietistic writing but rather in the pre-Christian classics ('I prefer the *Odyssey* to *Paradise Lost*,' the author once avowed). Possessing an inquisitive and expansive mind, Stewart was in fact an uncommonly well-read individual, freely ranging over a variety of literary genres. His deep immersion in French literature and supernatural horror fiction, for example, is documented in his lively correspondence with the noted horologist Rupert Thomas Gould.[2]

It thus is not surprising that in the 1920s the intellectually restless Stewart, having achieved a distinguished middle age as a highly regarded man of science, decided to apply his creative energy to a new endeavour, the writing of fiction. After several years he settled, like other gifted men and women of his generation, on the wildly popular mystery genre. Stewart was modest about his accomplishments in this particular field of light fiction, telling Rupert Gould later in life that 'I write these things [what Stewart called tec yarns] because they amuse me in parts when I am putting them together and because they are the only writings of mine that the public will look at. Also, in a minor degree, because I like to think some people get pleasure out of them.' No doubt Stewart's single most impressive literary accomplishment is *Nordenholt's Million*, yet in their time the two dozen J. J. Connington mysteries did indeed give readers in Great Britain, the United States and other countries much diversionary reading pleasure. Today these works constitute an estimable addition to British crime fiction.

After his 'prentice pastiche mystery, *Death at Swaythling Court* (1926), a rural English country-house tale set in the highly traditional village of Fernhurst Parva, Stewart published another, superior country-house affair, *The Dangerfield Talisman* (1926), a novel about the baffling theft of a precious family heirloom, an ancient, jewel-encrusted armlet. This clever, murderless tale, which likely is the one that the author told Rupert Gould he wrote in under six weeks, was praised in *The Bookman* as 'continuously exciting and interesting' and in the *New York Times Book Review* as 'ingeniously fitted together and, what is more, written with a deal of real literary charm'. Despite its virtues, however, *The Dangerfield Talisman* is not fully characteristic of mature Connington detective fiction. The author needed a memorable series sleuth, more representative of his own forceful personality.

It was the next year, 1927, that saw J. J. Connington make his break to the front of the murdermongerer's pack with a third country-house mystery, *Murder in the Maze*, wherein debuted as the author's great series detective the assertive and acerbic Sir Clinton Driffield, along with Sir Clinton's neighbour and 'Watson', the more genial (if much less astute) Squire Wendover. In this much-praised novel, Stewart's detective duo confronts some truly diabolical doings, including slayings by means of curare-tipped darts in the double-centered hedge maze at a country estate, Whistlefield. No less a fan of the genre than T. S. Eliot praised *Murder in the Maze* for its construction ('we are provided early in the story with all the clues which guide the detective') and its liveliness ('The very idea of murder in a box-hedge labyrinth does the author great credit, and he makes full use of its possibilities'). The delighted Eliot concluded that

Murder in the Maze was 'a really first-rate detective story'. For his part, the critic H. C. Harwood declared in *The Outlook* that with the publication of *Murder in the Maze* Connington demanded and deserved 'comparison with the masters'. 'Buy, borrow, or – anyhow – get hold of it', he amusingly advised. Two decades later, in his 1946 critical essay 'The Grandest Game in the World', the great locked-room detective novelist John Dickson Carr echoed Eliot's assessment of the novel's virtuoso setting, writing: 'These 1920s [. . .] thronged with sheer brains. What would be one of the best possible settings for violent death? J. J. Connington found the answer, with *Murder in the Maze*.' Certainly in retrospect *Murder in the Maze* stands as one of the finest English country-house mysteries of the 1920s, cleverly yet fairly clued, imaginatively detailed and often grimly suspenseful. As the great American true-crime writer Edmund Lester Pearson noted in his review of *Murder in the Maze* in *The Outlook*, this Connington novel had everything that one could desire in a detective story: 'A shrubbery maze, a hot day, and somebody potting at you with an air gun loaded with darts covered with a deadly South-American arrow-poison – *there* is a situation to wheedle two dollars out of anybody's pocket.'[3]

Staying with what had worked so well for him to date, Stewart the same year produced yet another country-house mystery, *Tragedy at Ravensthorpe*, an ingenious tale of murders and thefts at the ancestral home of the Chacewaters, old family friends of Sir Clinton Driffield. There is much clever matter in *Ravensthorpe*. Especially fascinating is the author's inspired integration of faerie folklore into his plot. Stewart, who had a lifelong – though skeptical – interest in paranormal phenomena, probably was inspired in this instance by the recent hubbub over the Cottingly Faeries photographs that in the early 1920s had famously duped, among other individuals, Arthur Conan Doyle.[4] As with *Murder in the Maze*, critics raved about this new Connington mystery. In the *Spectator*, for example, a reviewer hailed *Tragedy at Ravensthorpe* in the strongest terms, declaring of the novel: 'This is more than a good detective tale. Alike in plot, characterization, and literary style, it is a work of art.'

In 1928 there appeared two additional Sir Clinton Driffield detective novels, *Mystery at Lynden Sands* and *The Case with Nine Solutions*. Once again there was great praise for the latest Conningtons. H. C. Harwood, the critic who had so much admired *Murder in the Maze*, opined of *Mystery at Lynden Sands* that it 'may just fail of being the detective story of the century', while in the United States author and book reviewer Frederic F. Van de Water expressed nearly as high an opinion of *The Case with Nine Solutions*. 'This book is a thoroughbred of a distinguished lineage that runs back to "The Gold Bug" of [Edgar Allan] Poe,' he avowed. 'It represents the highest type of detective fiction.' In both of these Connington novels, Stewart moved away from his customary country-house milieu, setting *Lynden Sands* at a fashionable beach resort and *Nine Solutions* at a scientific research institute. *Nine Solutions* is of particular interest today, I think, for its relatively frank sexual subject matter and its modern urban setting among science professionals, which rather resembles the locales found in P. D. James' classic detective novels *A Mind to Murder* (1963) and *Shroud for a Nightingale* (1971).

By the end of the 1920s, J. J. Connington's critical reputation had achieved enviable heights indeed. At this time Stewart became one of the charter members of the Detection Club, an assemblage of the finest writers of British detective fiction that included, among other distinguished individuals, Agatha Christie, Dorothy L. Sayers and G. K. Chesterton. Certainly Victor Gollancz, the British publisher of the J. J. Connington mysteries, did not stint praise for the author, informing readers that 'J. J. Connington is now established as, in the opinion of many, the greatest living master of the story of pure detection. He is one of those who, discarding all the superfluities, has made of deductive fiction a genuine minor art, with its own laws and its own conventions.'

Such warm praise for J. J. Connington makes it all the more surprising that at this juncture the esteemed author tinkered with his successful formula by dispensing with his original series detective. In the fifth Clinton Driffield detective novel, *Nemesis at Raynham Parva* (1929), Alfred Walter Stewart, rather like Arthur Conan Doyle before him, seemed with a dramatic dénouement to have devised his popular series detective's permanent exit from the fictional stage (read it and see for yourself). The next two Connington detective novels, *The Eye in the Museum* (1929) and *The Two Tickets Puzzle* (1930), have a different series detective, Superintendent Ross, a rather dull dog of a policeman. While both these mysteries are competently done – the railway material in *The Two Tickets Puzzle* is particularly effective and should have appeal today – the presence of Sir Clinton Driffield (no superfluity he!) is missed.

Probably Stewart detected that the public minded the absence of the brilliant and biting Sir Clinton, for the Chief Constable – accompanied, naturally, by his friend Squire Wendover – triumphantly returned in 1931 in *The Boathouse Riddle*, another well-constructed criminous country-house affair. Later in the year came *The Sweepstake Murders*, which boasts the perennially popular tontine multiple-murder plot, in this case a rapid succession of puzzling suspicious deaths afflicting the members of a sweepstake syndicate that has just won nearly £250,000.[5] Adding piquancy to this plot is the fact that Wendover is one of the imperiled syndicate members. Altogether the novel is, as the late Jacques Barzun and his colleague Wendell Hertig Taylor put it in *A Catalogue of Crime* (1971, 1989), their magisterial survey of detective fiction, 'one of Connington's best conceptions'.

Stewart's productivity as a fiction writer slowed in the 1930s, so that, barring the year 1938, at most only one new Connington appeared annually. However, in 1932 Stewart produced one of the best Connington mysteries, *The Castleford Conundrum*. A classic country-house detective novel, Castleford introduces to readers Stewart's most delightfully unpleasant set of greedy relations and one of his most deserving murderees, Winifred Castleford. Stewart also fashions a wonderfully rich puzzle plot, full of meaty material clues for the reader's delectation. *Castleford* presented critics with no conundrum over its quality. 'In *The Castleford Conundrum* Mr Connington goes to work like an accomplished chess player. The moves in the games his detectives are called on to play are a delight to watch,' raved the reviewer for the *Sunday Times*, adding that 'the clues would have rejoiced Mr. Holmes' heart.' For its part, the *Spectator* concurred in the *Sunday Times*' assessment of the novel's masterfully constructed plot: 'Few detective stories show such sound reasoning as that by which the Chief Constable brings the crime home to the culprit.' Additionally, E. C. Bentley, much admired himself as the author of the landmark detective novel *Trent's Last Case*, took time to praise Connington's purely literary virtues, noting: 'Mr Connington has never written better, or drawn characters more full of life.'

With *Tom Tiddler's Island* in 1933 Stewart produced a different sort of Connington, a criminal-gang mystery in the rather more breathless style of such hugely popular English thriller writers as Sapper, Sax Rohmer, John Buchan and Edgar Wallace (in violation of the strict detective fiction rules of Ronald Knox, there is even a secret passage in the novel). Detailing the startling discoveries made by a newlywed couple honeymooning on a remote Scottish island, *Tom Tiddler's Island* is an atmospheric and entertaining tale, though it is not as mentally stimulating for armchair sleuths as Stewart's true detective novels. The title, incidentally, refers to an ancient British children's game, 'Tom Tiddler's Ground', in which one child tries to hold a height against other children.

After his fictional Scottish excursion into thrillerdom, Stewart returned the next year to his English country-house roots with *The Ha-Ha Case* (1934), his last masterwork in this classicmystery setting (for elucidation of non-British readers, a ha-ha is a sunken wall, placed so as to delineate property boundaries while not obstructing views). Although *The Ha-Ha Case* is not set in Scotland, Stewart drew inspiration for the novel from a notorious Scottish true crime, the 1893 Ardlamont murder case. From the facts of the Ardlamont affair Stewart drew several of the key characters in *The Ha-Ha Case*, as well as the circumstances of the novel's murder (a shooting 'accident' while hunting), though he added complications that take the tale in a new direction.[6]

In newspaper reviews both Dorothy L. Sayers and 'Francis Iles' (crime novelist Anthony Berkeley Cox) highly praised this latest mystery by 'The Clever Mr Connington', as he was now dubbed on book jackets by his new English publisher, Hodder & Stoughton. Sayers particularly noted the effective characterisation in *The Ha-Ha Case*: 'There is no need to say that Mr Connington has given us a sound and interesting plot, very carefully and ingeniously worked out. In addition, there are the three portraits of the three brothers, cleverly and rather subtly characterised, of the [governess], and of Inspector Hinton, whose admirable qualities are counteracted by that besetting sin of the man who has made his own way: a jealousy of delegating responsibility.' The reviewer for the *Times Literary Supplement* detected signs that the sardonic Sir Clinton Driffield had begun mellowing with age: 'Those who have never really liked Sir Clinton's perhaps excessively soldierly manner will be surprised to find that he makes his discovery not only by the pure light of intelligence, but partly as a reward for amiability and tact, qualities in which the Inspector [Hinton] was strikingly deficient.' This is true enough, although the classic Sir Clinton emerges a number of times in the novel, as in his subtly sarcastic recurrent backhanded praise of Inspector Hinton: 'He writes a first class report.'

Clinton Driffield returned the next year in the detective novel *In Whose Dim Shadow* (1935), a tale set in a recently erected English suburb, the denizens of which seem to have committed an impressive number of indiscretions, including sexual ones. The intriguing title of the British edition of the novel is drawn from a poem by the British historian Thomas Babington Macaulay: 'Those trees in whose dim shadow/The ghastly priest doth reign/The priest who slew the slayer/And shall himself be slain.' Stewart's puzzle plot in *In Whose Dim Shadow* is well clued and compelling, the kicker of a closing paragraph is a classic of its kind and, additionally, the author paints some excellent character portraits. I fully concur with the *Sunday Times*' assessment of the tale: 'Quiet domestic murder, full of the neatest detective points [. . .] These are not the detective's stock figures, but fully realised human beings.'[7]

Uncharacteristically for Stewart, nearly twenty months elapsed between the publication of *In Whose Dim Shadow* and his next book, *A Minor Operation* (1937). The reason for the author's delay in production was the onset in 1935–36 of the afflictions of cataracts and heart disease (Stewart ultimately succumbed to heart disease in 1947). Despite these grave health complications, Stewart in late 1936 was able to complete *A Minor Operation*, a first-rate Clinton Driffield story of murder and a most baffling disappearance. A *Times Literary Supplement* reviewer found that *A Minor Operation* treated the reader 'to exactly the right mixture of mystification and clue' and that, in addition to its impressive construction, the novel boasted 'character-drawing above the average' for a detective novel.

Alfred Stewart's final eight mysteries, which appeared between 1938 and 1947, the year of the author's death, are, on the whole, a somewhat weaker group of tales than the sixteen that appeared between 1926 and 1937, yet they are not without interest. In 1938 Stewart for the last time managed to publish two detective novels, *Truth Comes Limping* and *For Murder Will Speak* (also published as *Murder Will Speak*). The latter tale is much the superior of the two, having an interesting suburban setting and a bevy of female characters found to have motives when a contemptible philandering businessman meets with foul play. Sexual neurosis plays a major role in *For Murder Will Speak*, the ever-thorough Stewart obviously having made a study of the subject when writing the novel. The somewhat squeamish reviewer for *Scribner's Magazine* considered the subject matter of *For Murder Will Speak* 'rather unsavoury at times', yet this individual conceded that the novel nevertheless made 'first-class reading for those who enjoy a good puzzle intricately worked out'. 'Judge Lynch' in the *Saturday Review* apparently had no such moral reservations about the latest Clinton Driffield murder case, avowing simply of the novel: 'They don't come any better'.

Over the next couple of years Stewart again sent Sir Clinton Driffield temporarily packing, replacing him with a new series detective, a brash radio personality named Mark Brand, in *The Counsellor* (1939) and *The Four Defences* (1940). The better of these two novels is *The Four Defences*, which Stewart based on another notorious British true-crime case, the Alfred Rouse blazing-car murder. (Rouse is believed to have fabricated his death by murdering an unknown man, placing the dead man's body in his car and setting the car on fire, in the hope that the murdered man's body would be taken for his.) Though admittedly a thinly characterised academic exercise in ratiocination, Stewart's *Four Defences* surely is also one of the most complexly plotted Golden Age detective novels and should delight devotees of classical detection. Taking the Rouse blazing-car affair as his theme, Stewart composes from it a stunning set of diabolically ingenious criminal variations. 'This is in the cold-blooded category which [. . .] excites a crossword puzzle kind of interest,' the reviewer for the *Times Literary Supplement* acutely noted of the novel. 'Nothing in the Rouse case would prepare you for these complications upon complications [. . .] What they prove is that Mr Connington has the power of penetrating into the puzzle-corner of the brain. He leaves it dazedly wondering whether in the records of actual crime there can be any dark deed to equal this in its planned convolutions.'

Sir Clinton Driffield returned to action in the remaining four detective novels in the Connington oeuvre, *The Twenty-One Clues* (1941), *No Past is Dead* (1942), *Jack-in-the-Box* (1944) and *Commonsense is All You Need* (1947), all of which were written as Stewart's heart disease steadily worsened and reflect to some extent his diminishing physical and mental energy. Although *The Twenty-One Clues* was inspired by the notorious Hall-Mills double murder case – probably the most publicised murder case in the United States in the 1920s – and the American critic and novelist Anthony Boucher commended *Jack-in-the-Box*, I believe the best of these later mysteries is *No Past Is Dead*, which Stewart partly based on a bizarre French true-crime affair, the 1891 Achet-Lepine murder case.[8] Besides providing an interesting background for the tale, the ailing author managed some virtuoso plot twists, of the sort most associated today with that ingenious Golden Age Queen of Crime, Agatha Christie.

What Stewart with characteristic bluntness referred to as 'my complete crack-up' forced his retirement from Queen's University in 1944. 'I am afraid,' Stewart wrote a friend, the chemist and forensic scientist F. Gerald Tryhorn, in August 1946, eleven months before his death, 'that I shall never be much use again. Very stupidly, I tried for a session to combine a full course of lecturing with angina pectoris; and ended up by establishing that the two are immiscible.' He added that since retiring in 1944, he had been physically 'limited to my house, since even a fifty-yard crawl brings on the usual cramps'. Stewart completed his essay collection and a final novel before he died at his study desk in his Belfast home on 1 July 1947, at the age of sixty-six. When death came to the author he was busy at work, writing.

More than six decades after Alfred Walter Stewart's death, his J. J. Connington fiction is again available to a wider audience of classic-mystery fans, rather than strictly limited to a select company of rare-book collectors with deep pockets. This is fitting for an individual who was one of the finest writers of British genre fiction between the two world wars. 'Heaven forfend that you should imagine I take myself for anything out of the common in the tec yarn stuff,' Stewart once self-deprecatingly declared in a letter to Rupert Gould. Yet, as contemporary critics recognised, as a writer of detective and science fiction Stewart indeed was something out of the common. Now more modern readers can find this out for themselves. They have much good sleuthing in store.

1. For more on Street, Crofts and particularly Stewart, see Curtis Evans, *Masters of the 'Humdrum' Mystery: Cecil John Charles Street, Freeman Wills Crofts, Alfred Walter Stewart and the British Detective Novel, 1920–1961* (Jefferson, NC: McFarland, 2012). On the academic career of Alfred Walter Stewart, see his entry in *Oxford Dictionary of National Biography* (London and New York: Oxford University Press, 2004), vol. 52, 627–628.
2. The Gould-Stewart correspondence is discussed in considerable detail in *Masters of the 'Humdrum' Mystery*. For more on the life of the fascinating Rupert Thomas Gould, see Jonathan Betts, *Time Restored: The Harrison Timekeepers and R. T. Gould, the*

Man Who Knew (Almost) Everything (London and New York: Oxford University Press, 2006) and *Longitude,* the 2000 British film adaptation of Dava Sobel's book *Longitude: The True Story of a Lone Genius Who Solved the Greatest Scientific Problem of His Time* (London: Harper Collins, 1995), which details Gould's restoration of the marine chronometers built by in the eighteenth century by the clockmaker John Harrison.

3. Potential purchasers of *Murder in the Maze* should keep in mind that $2 in 1927 is worth over $26 today.
4. In a 1920 article in *The Strand Magazine,* Arthur Conan Doyle endorsed as real prank photographs of purported fairies taken by two English girls in the garden of a house in the village of Cottingley. In the aftermath of the Great War Doyle had become a fervent believer in Spiritualism and other paranormal phenomena. Especially embarrassing to Doyle's admirers today, he also published *The Coming of the Faeries* (1922), wherein he argued that these mystical creatures genuinely existed. 'When the spirits came in, the common sense oozed out,' Stewart once wrote bluntly to his friend Rupert Gould of the creator of Sherlock Holmes. Like Gould, however, Stewart had an intense interest in the subject of the Loch Ness Monster, believing that he, his wife and daughter had sighted a large marine creature of some sort in Loch Ness in 1935. A year earlier Gould had authored *The Loch Ness Monster and Others*, and it was this book that led Stewart, after he made his 'Nessie' sighting, to initiate correspondence with Gould.
5. A tontine is a financial arrangement wherein shareowners in a common fund receive annuities that increase in value with the death of each participant, with the entire amount of the fund going to the last survivor. The impetus that the tontine provided to the deadly creative imaginations of Golden Age mystery writers should be sufficiently obvious.
6. At Ardlamont, a large country estate in Argyll, Cecil Hambrough died from a gunshot wound while hunting. Cecil's tutor, Alfred John Monson, and another man, both of whom were out hunting with Cecil, claimed that Cecil had accidentally shot himself, but Monson was arrested and tried for Cecil's murder. The verdict delivered was 'not proven', but Monson was then – and is today – considered almost certain to have been guilty of the murder. On the Ardlamont case, see William Roughead, *Classic Crimes* (1951; repr., New York: New York Review Books Classics, 2000), 378–464.
7. For the genesis of the title, see Macaulay's 'The Battle of the Lake

Regillus', from his narrative poem collection *Lays of Ancient Rome*. In this poem Macaulay alludes to the ancient cult of Diana Nemorensis, which elevated its priests through trial by combat. Study of the practices of the Diana Nemorensis cult influenced Sir James George Frazer's cultural interpretation of religion in his most renowned work, *The Golden Bough: A Study in Magic and Religion*. As with *Tom Tiddler's Island* and *The Ha-Ha Case* the title *In Whose Dim Shadow* proved too esoteric for Connington's American publishers, Little, Brown and Co., who altered it to the more prosaic *The Tau Cross Mystery*.

8. Stewart analysed the Achet-Lepine case in detail in 'The Mystery of Chantelle', one of the best essays in his 1947 collection *Alias J. J. Connington*.

Reguiller, remains the native poem [illegible] In this poem 'Mazama' [illegible] attacked [illegible] which [illegible] its poets through [illegible] portraits of the [illegible] Frazer's [illegible] interpretation of [illegible] most [illegible] work. The [illegible] Sun [illegible] and [illegible] with *Tom* [illegible] *Island* and *The* [illegible] *Mountain* [illegible] proved too esoteric for [illegible] Little, Brown and Co., [illegible] *The* [illegible] *Goes* [illegible]

4. Stewart analysed the [illegible] epic case in detail in 'The [illegible] of Chaucer' [illegible] one of his best essays in his [illegible] collection [illegible] *E.J.* [illegible]

CHAPTER I

THREE MEN ON TICKET-OF-LEAVE

NICHOLAS ADENEY reached over and took a cigarette from the box which stood on the garden-table beside his chair. For a moment or two he examined it abstractedly before screwing it into his holder and striking a match.

" It's queer, Hazel, how much one misses little things when one can't get them," he said ruminatively, after he had got it well alight. " Cocktails and a good cigarette were what I felt the lack of most, at the beginning. I used to find my hand going round in search of my case. And now, somehow, a good brand of tobacco doesn't seem to taste as well as it used to do. I suppose I must have exaggerated its charm when I had to go without it so long."

He drooped his wrists between his knees and stared blankly over the garden. Though barely thirty, he looked five years older. His cousin glanced at him with pity in the eyes from whose colour she had got her name. They were expressive eyes, large, long-lashed under arched brows ; and in them there seemed always to be a faint suggestion of weariness which belied the rest of her looks.

" It must have seemed terribly long," she said, with ready sympathy.

" Long ? " echoed Nicholas bitterly. " I never knew what time meant, before then. Five years ! They knock off a quarter if you behave yourself. That leaves three years and nine months of it. And, of course, you're full of resolutions about good conduct, at the start. When they put you in at first, you work it out in days. You haven't much else to think about. Saves you from brooding over what a fool you were, at any rate; and that's something gained. Three years and nine months. That's 365 multiplied by three and three-quarters. You don't know how much that is, Hazel?"

The girl shook her head, It was rarely that Nick spoke of his imprisonment; but she could feel that when his feelings welled up it did him some good to voice them, and she had no wish to steer him away from the subject.

"I know," Nicholas continued. "I've gone over it often enough. It's 1,369 days, less six hours. That's how you begin. Then, after a bit, you wonder if it works out any shorter, taking it month by month, since the months aren't all the same length. Three times 365 is 1,095; and when you tot up the days from 17th January to 17th October, it comes to 273. Total only 1,368 instead of 1,369. But after a bit you remember that 1932 is a Leap Year, which adds on an extra day. That was a nasty jar to me, when I thought of it. When you get up to figures like these, 1,368 doesn't look much different from 1,369 to the man in the street; but it's different when each day seems to take an eternity to go past."

"I've got some sort of idea of what it's like," Hazel said gently. "I did the same thing when I was in hospital with scarlet fever when I was a child, you remember, Nick. That was six weeks' treatment, and I used to work it out in hours, trying to make it seem shorter. Only I was no good at mental arithmetic, and the answer came out different almost every time, which made it worse."

"After the first month, it isn't so bad," Nicholas went on. "Then you reckon in months and the figures get more bearable. Only forty-five."

He fell silent, as though going over his experiences in his mind. Hazel, with perfect understanding, made no attempt to interrupt the chain of his thoughts. At last he looked up again.

"And when it came near the tail-end, it was almost as bad," he confessed. "I used to lie awake at nights and wonder how I'd be received by the old lot when I got out again. Would they be the same as before the smash? I wasn't over-optimistic about that. Just as well, in most cases. Only one or two of them were actually rude. But the rest of them made it pretty plain that they didn't want a jail-bird about the house. And even with the best of them I was completely out of touch. Births, marriages and deaths had happened in between and I knew nothing about them. I put my foot in it again and again; and every blunder reminded them of where I'd been, all these years. Even with the decent ones I felt awkward. . . ."

He reflected for a while, with an ugly expression about his lips. Then his face cleared, and he added:

"You never let me down, Hazel. You're about the only one who took me back on exactly the old footing—as if the thing had never happened. It meant a lot to me, that. I know I snarl a good deal at times. I'm snarling now. But don't take any notice of it."

"Snarl away, Nick," Hazel advised, with a smile which had no mockery in it. "Of course I understand. Don't worry about that."

"I hate to sponge on you the way I'm doing," Nicholas went on in a dogged tone. "You've kept me going for nine months now. And I seem no nearer a job than when I started. Nobody wants a jail-bird on their salary list any more than they want him as a friend of their sons and daughters. Especially daughters. I don't blame them. In their shoes, I expect I'd feel much the same. One must make allowances."

" Don't talk about the money, Nick," Hazel interrupted. " You know you're welcome to it, and I'd give you more if you'd take it. Money's nothing between the two of us. What you might do, if you want to please me, is to come and live here. I hate to think of you in that awful little place you stay in. Why won't you come here ? There's a room waiting for you. You've only to walk in."

Nicholas Adeney frowned at the proposal, then his features relaxed again in a grateful smile.

" Just like you, Hazel," he said, with a quiver in his voice. " It's not that I don't appreciate it. But it would never do, you know. I'm experienced enough to know what would happen. 'Oh, yes, Mrs. Deerhurst is a friend of ours, but it's awkward, now. If one goes to see her, there's that jail-bird cousin of hers always hanging about the place. One can't ignore him altogether. And one doesn't care to sit down at a bridge-table with a convicted embezzler—or was it fraud, or something ? Besides, if one asks her to dinner, can one leave him out ? It looks pointed, if one does. And if one doesn't, what about one's other guests ? It's really a very troublesome problem, my dear.' That's what they'd feel, even if the decent ones didn't actually say it. No, no, Hazel. If I camped out on the premises it would make things very awkward for you socially. It's bad enough as it is, and I'm not going to make it worse."

" I don't know that I'd miss them much, if that's the sort of people they are," Hazel asserted. " Besides, I'm sure you're wrong, Nick. People as a whole aren't like that."

" No, but most of them are," Nicholas returned gloomily. " I've had experience, you know. And, after all, why make it awkward for your friends ? There's no need to put them in a hole. Let things stay as they are. Then they can come here or invite you without running risks of meeting me. It's just common sense."

A thought seemed to strike him and he went on again after a brief pause.

"That reminds me of one thing, Hazel. I don't much care about this system of yours of being alone in the house at night. Can't you get maids who'll stay on the premises?"

Hazel shook her head decidedly.

"It's just a fancy of mine," she explained. "I like to feel I have the place entirely to myself sometimes. What's the good of being one's own mistress if one can't do exactly as one chooses? It's my way of doing things. I've done it for years and I'd hate to change now."

"Another sound reason for my not shifting camp, then," Nicholas retorted, with a laugh. "Seriously, though," he said, with a change in tone, "I don't quite like the idea of your being all alone at night. There's been a sort of wave of burglaries lately, you know."

"I'm insured," Hazel declared lightly. "I'm not sentimentally attached to anything valuable in the house. If I hear any burglar on the premises, I'll lock my bedroom door, go to sleep if I can, and ring up the police next morning. No harm will come to me. Don't worry about that, Nick, unless you'll look on it as an argument for coming to stay with me here."

"Well," Nicholas conceded reluctantly, "what you say goes, so far as I'm concerned. The last thing I want is to worry you. You've been too good to me over my own affairs. And, Lord knows, you've had troubles enough of your own on your shoulders without sharing mine. It was a bad day for us when Uncle brought Len Deerhurst into the business."

Hazel made a gesture as though to sweep away something disagreeable.

"It's no use blaming father, Nick. You and I were just as much taken in as he was, in different ways. Of the three, I think I made the biggest mistake."

Nicholas assented with a nod. He was grateful to Hazel for putting it in that way. So like her, he reflected, to refrain from any reproach; for in his own mind he never ceased to blame himself for not seeing through Deerhurst before the damage was done. If he had exerted himself, if he had kept his eyes open, things would never have got to this pass.

"That's another thing that's worrying me," he said slowly. "That swine's due to get out in a day or two, isn't he? He got a year more than I did. That's nine months extra, deducting the quarter for good conduct. Has he written to you, or anything?"

"He gets out on the 17th." Hazel said, with a little shudder. "He wrote to tell me. Of course I didn't answer him."

"Of course not. But what are you going to do about it? I haven't bothered you with questions, Hazel. I know it's too sore a business to talk much about, so I've left it alone. But now it's coming to a head, anyhow, and I want to know how you stand. You're not thinking of taking him back, are you?"

Hazel's eyes dilated at the question, and she gripped one hand with the other till her knuckles whitened under the unconscious effort. The slight movement made Nicholas glance at her, and the expression on her face carried him back twenty years. His memory threw up a picture of himself, a boy just into his teens, confronting a little fury, flushed with rage, tight-lipped, with blazing eyes all the brighter for unshed tears. Then she had sprung at him, her whole strength concentrated on hurting him as he had just hurt her kitten.

Only Hazel herself knew what unceasing effort had been needed through the years to bring that volcanic temper into control. She had disciplined herself, painfully and steadfastly, into equability, ever on her guard against that slumbering demon. Her closest friends looked on her as a model of serenity and Nicholas was probably the only person who could now recognise the danger-signal when he saw it.

With a manifest effort she relaxed into a normal attitude.

"Take him back?" she said, with a shrug which pointed the absurdity of the suggestion. "Hardly that, Nick. What right has he here? This house is mine, bought with my own money, not his. There's not a thing belonging to him on the premises. And there are no children to give him a hold over me. No, I'm not thinking of starting life afresh with *him*. Still . . ."

She broke off, as though in doubt whether to say more or not.

"Still . . . ?" queried Nicholas, watching her intently.

Hazel leaned back in the garden-chair and let her hands clasp lightly in her lap. Evidently she had fought down her demon once again.

"I want to be done with him, once for all," she said deliberately. "A divorce would be the real solution, but I can't get it. So it will have to be the next best thing: a judicial separation. I've gone into that with my solicitors, and the grounds are adultery, desertion or cruelty. The first's no good; he's not such a fool as that. As for desertion, all he wants is to settle down here and live on my money. He'll never desert me, so long as I've got an income. So that leaves cruelty as the only shot in the locker, you see."

Nicholas's face grew grave, but he made no attempt to interrupt her.

"There are two kinds of cruelty, it seems," Hazel went on in the tone of one discussing a well-worn subject. "There's what they call persistent cruelty which forces a wife to live apart from her husband. But that would entail living with him, first of all, for some considerable time. I couldn't do it. It would be like finding a slug or a snail on the table-cloth at dinner, or a frog in the bathroom, or a worm in the salad. Ugh! You see, that's no good, Nick, don't you?"

Nicholas made a gesture of agreement.

"But what's the alternative?" he demanded, doubtfully.

"This," said Hazel, with sudden vehemence. "If a husband is convicted of an aggravated assault on his wife, then she can get a separation with no more ado. That's the way out, Nick. Now do you see why it's perhaps as well that you're not coming to stay here? Once he's released, he'll come back here. He'll try to force himself on me, if I know anything about him. The rest won't be difficult to manage. I've worked it out to the last detail, Nick. I've thought of little else for the last few months. And I'm going to get clear of him, if it can be done at the cost of a little pain. That's nothing, compared with the relief of being rid of him for good."

Nicholas sat up suddenly.

"That alters things a bit," he said brusquely. "You don't expect me to stand by and let you be manhandled by Len, do you? I'll shift my traps up here to-night."

"No, Nick, you won't," Hazel said decisively. "You had the offer, and you know what it must have cost me to make it, with this idea in my mind. You turned it down. It's finished. I'm taking my own way now. Do you think I've plotted and schemed through all these months simply to let you blunder in at the last moment with chivalrous ideas? And spoil the whole affair? We'll quarrel, if you talk like that. I mean it."

A glance at her face showed Nicholas the danger-signal flaming in her eyes. He turned away, elbow on knee and chin in hand, staring across the garden, an obvious prey to indecision.

"It's no good, Nick, old boy," Hazel continued in a gentler tone. "This is the only way out. It is, really. After all, it's my own affair. I must get rid of him legally, so that I can snap my fingers at him. If I don't, he'll hang about and make life unbearable. Fancy sitting waiting every day to see if he turns up to make himself unpleasant. I simply won't go through that; and you've no right to ask me to risk it, merely to spare your feelings now. I was a fool even to mention it to you, but I never thought you'd take this line. Do be sensible, Nick."

Nicholas had always been the weaker character; and now, though he evaded a direct promise, he surrendered by changing the subject.

"If only you and Ferrestone hadn't got across each other," he said despondently, "things would have been different."

Hazel winced as though he had put a heavy finger on a bruise.

"Don't remind me of that," she said abruptly. "I think about it enough already."

"I suppose you do. A good sort, Ferrestone," he went on with unconscious cruelty. "At the time of the trial he was one of the few men who took the trouble to treat me as if I wasn't a pariah. I thought of writing to him, sometime, just to let him know I'm still grateful."

"I shouldn't if I were you," Hazel advised rather hurriedly. "He might not reply; and that would hurt, wouldn't it? Better leave well alone, Nick."

"Something in that, perhaps," Nicholas conceded, after a pause. "Things do change, when one's been under lock and key for years. I might be an embarrassing ghost from the past, eh? I think I'll leave him alone. Is he doing much with his painting?"

"He made a success; but he hasn't painted anything for a year or two now," Hazel explained. "Let's not talk about him, Nick."

Nicholas seemed to realise that he had been less than tactful in his absorption in his own affairs.

"What made you take on this secretaryship to old Mandrell?" he demanded, to change the subject. "You don't need the money, and it must be a bit of a drag on you."

Hazel seemed to welcome the new topic, possibly as a sure escape from more awkward ones.

"Mutual benefit," she said lightly. "Mr. Mandrell wanted a girl who could be trusted to keep her tongue still, both inside and outside his office. I don't know what other inventors are like, but he's the limit in untidiness where papers are concerned; so it's convenient for him to have someone he can trust with anything. I have to type out all his odd notes and jottings, you know, besides doing his ordinary correspondence work; and there's a good deal of his stuff which would be very useful to his commercial rivals, if they could lay hands on it before it gets the length of the Patent Office."

"He's safe enough with you, then. But what do you get out of the job?"

"I wanted something to do, Nick. I can't hang about at a loose end all the time. It's not my way."

Nicholas admitted this with a gesture.

"That's so. Even in your teens you were all for making yourself useful. Do you remember the row Uncle made when you went off for that training of yours?"

" Father didn't care about my leaving home," Hazel admitted. " Still that sort of experience sometimes comes in useful. One never can tell."

She turned away her head to hide a smile at something which crossed her mind at the moment and which she had no wish, apparently, to share with her cousin.

" As to Mr. Mandrell," she went on, " he doesn't take up much of my time, only the mornings. I'm free from lunch-time onwards. That reminds me, my holiday's due in a few days. Quite an event, that! Think of being able to lie in bed in the mornings if I want to! Not that I really want to; but still it's pleasant to know one can do it if one chooses, while the holiday lasts. You see that going to business has its advantages, Nick. Gives a touch of spice to things that would be uninteresting if one were quite one's own mistress."

Nicholas was relieved to find her smiling at the conceit.

" You're right there," he agreed, reaching over for a fresh cigarette.

" I must be off now and change," Hazel announced, pushing the cigarettes towards him as she rose to her feet. " Some people are coming in to play bridge to-night. You're staying to keep me company at dinner, Nick. Just the two of us, so you needn't bother to change."

Nicholas pondered for a moment, but her oblique reference to his lounge suit reassured him.

" I'll clear out before they turn up," he stipulated.

Hazel made no protest.

" I shan't be long," she assured him. " Bring that cigarette box into the house when you come, will you ? "

And with a slight affectionate gesture and a smile, she turned away and went off towards one of the open french windows behind them.

Left to himself, Nicholas grew restless. A picture of Deerhurst appeared on his mental screen : a big, bullying fellow, always loud-voiced in argument, a great shouter-down of more diffident opponents. Coupled with an overweening belief in his own cleverness, there was something indefinable in his make-up : oiliness, slyness—hard to give it a precise name. He had seen his chance with Hazel and caught her on the rebound after that trouble with Ferrestone. But for that, he'd never have got round her. Not her sort, really. And how she must have despised him after the smash, when all his trickery came out in court. One could gauge something of that from the feeling she had betrayed a few minutes ago.

Nicholas rose from his chair, as though he felt he could sit still no longer. This scheme of Hazel's went against the grain with him ; and the more he thought of it the less he liked it. "Aggravated assault"? That meant she would need to have something to show : bruises on her wrists or probably something more serious. No doubt she would be able to goad him into a passion with her tongue ; she'd had long enough to ponder over the exact phrases that would lash him into fury. But then . . . And Nicholas winced at the picture of Hazel in the grip of that brute.

He ought to have insisted on coming to stay with her, he reflected sourly. And yet, from her point of view, she was quite right in refusing to have him on the premises, once she had made up her mind. It might salve his conscience to be there as a watchdog ; but it would cost her that complete freedom on which her mind was set, and he could hardly put his own feelings in front of hers, after what she had said.

Then an idea crossed his mind, and his face lightened a little.

"After all," he mused, "there's nothing to hinder

me keeping a look-out on the premises at night, after the maids have gone. She won't know I'm doing it; and I'll always be handy to interfere if necessary."

Then, as his idea expanded, the cloud cleared from his brow.

"If he does try any of his cave-man stuff, I'll be there to see the start of it, and I'll be a good enough witness to call, if they want a third party's evidence. That's the notion!"

Much relieved in his mind by this development, he wandered aimlessly about the garden, thinking out further details of his scheme. His eyes took in nothing of his surroundings, so engrossed was he in his thoughts; but when at last he had got his plan into shape, he woke up to find that he had sauntered down to the gate, which was screened from the house by clumps of rhododendrons. He paused for a moment before turning back, and glanced mechanically up and down the avenue on which the house stood. Then, suddenly, he grew alert and, shading his eyes with his hand from the low-hanging sun, he stared intently, while annoyance and disgust mingled in his expression.

Along the pavement, with a peculiar short-stepping gait, tripped a little figure. As it drew nearer, Nicholas recognised the bulbous forehead, the round eyes, and the weak, ugly mouth with its half-grown moustache.

"Sturge!" he ejaculated under his breath when mistake became impossible.

This was something he had not counted upon, and a qualm of apprehension took him as he realised the possibilities which lay behind this unwelcome visitation. The man had been one of the gang in which Nicholas had worked at one time while serving his sentence. He remembered him well enough: an habitual criminal with many convictions on his record, and a bad prison reputation.

For a moment Nicholas clutched at the idea that the appearance of this ill-omened visitant was due to pure ill-chance. The creature might have drifted into this locality by the merest accident, and there might be nothing in it. Coincidences of that kind were continually occurring in the ordinary affairs of life. But even as he framed the hypothesis in his mind, he ceased to believe in it. There was more than mere ill-luck in the business. To put the matter to the proof at once, he turned away from the gate, pretending that he had not recognised the man. Sturge saw the movement, quickened his pace, and called out in a high, disagreeable voice:

"Hi! I'm wantin' to talk to you, Adeney."

Smothering a curse, Nicholas turned back to face his undesired visitor.

"Well, what is it?" he demanded curtly.

"Not so hard on the old college chum," protested Sturge. "You and me's got to have a little chat, Adeney. I always aims to please, so you can have it friendly, if you like, or you can have it t'other way, if you like that better."

"When did you get out?" Nicholas demanded.

"Best part o' four months ago," Sturge declared.

Nicholas drew a breath of relief. If the ex-burglar had left him alone for four months, he could hardly mean real mischief at this moment. And yet why had he turned up at all?

"And what do you want, now you're here?"

Sturge seemed to think it best to postpone this for the moment.

"Didn't see a visitor in your mornin' cup o' tea, did you? No? Well, that's nothin' agin' fortune-tellin'. For why? 'Cause I didn't come here for to call on you, see? Your bein' here's just a gift o' fortune, in a manner o' speakin'. All I want's a bit o' information, an' you can give me it as well's the next man, without no fuss over it."

Nicholas breathed a sigh of relief. What the man wanted he could not conjecture; but on the face of things he had no intention of giving trouble.

"You wouldn't be thinkin' of askin' me into the house, would you—so we could talk it over private-like?" Sturge suggested.

Nicholas shook his head decisively.

"And let you have a look round the premises for professional purposes?" he retorted. "It doesn't appeal to me. Besides, it's not my house. I don't live here."

"I wouldn't be thinkin' o' such a thing, Adeney," Sturge protested with not too well-feigned asperity. "It's just I don't like standin' here on the door-step, so to say, with the flattie lookin' cross-eyed at me if he passes, 'cause he finds me back in bad company again."

The joke was not to Nicholas's taste. Its point reminded him that he was still on ticket-of-leave himself.

"Well, what is it you want?" he demanded. "Out with it."

"Just a bit o' news, that's all."

"Did you know I was here?" Nicholas asked, as a fresh thought occurred to him.

"I did not," Sturge explained. "I was comin' for to ask at the house here."

Nicholas had a vision of Hazel confronted by this unsavoury specimen; and he was glad that he had been there to intercept the ex-convict.

"Well, what is it?"

"It's just this," Sturge confided. "Me an' one or two others has a wish for to see Deerhurst. We know he's due out in a day or two. So I'm lookin' for information about him, see?"

A flicker of malevolence crossed the ugly face, and the uneven teeth showed for a moment under the scrubby moustache. Nicholas saw at once that here was something worth probing further, if he could manage it without exciting Sturge's suspicions.

"Oh—Deerhurst? He gets out on the 17th. But you won't find him here."

Sturge's face showed more than a trace of scepticism.

"I won't, you say, Adeney? Queer, that is. Here's a wife, and a nice house, an' lots o' money—by the look o' the place—all ready waitin' for him; an' you say he won't be here? What're you givin' me, eh? Tryin' for to put me off with that yarn, are you? You'll have to go for to think of a better one."

He pondered for a moment, and then seemed to see more light.

"Oh, yes, Adeney. You're a relation o' Deerhurst's, now I come to think of it. And you won't want any truck with the old college pals, eh? That's it, I see," he drawled with an effort at irony in his tone. "I see. 'T won't wash, Adeney."

Nicholas saw that he might have to put some of his cards on the table. He could not afford to have this creature hanging about the place, giving Hazel annoyance. He made up his mind swiftly.

"Whether you annoy Deerhurst or not, it's all one to me," he said. "I'm not his keeper. But if you want him, you'd better look elsewhere. He won't be here."

His tone seemed to carry conviction. Sturge paused for a moment in reflection; then he remembered something which made his doubt fade away.

"O' course," he admitted. "You was the mug in that business, now I come to think of it. I've heard some crack about your affairs once on a time. Deerhurst, he let you in, didn't he? That puts a new light on the biz., so to say. It would hardly be just a happy family party with you waitin' here on the doorstep to receive him, would it? I see. Somethin' in that, perhaps. Aye, he was a dirty dog, was Deerhurst."

Nicholas restrained himself from asking a direct question.

"Think so?" he asked, with as much apparent indifference as he could muster.

Sturge inspected him calculatingly.

"Think so?" he echoed. "Sure, I do. Lookee here. You're a gent, Adeney, and I'd just like your opinion on your dear relation. This is how it was. Some of us—no names, no pack-drill—some of us had drawed up a little scheme for to save His Majesty from the cost of our keep——"

"Meaning prison-breaking?"

"Well, we had a scheme," Sturge persisted, avoiding the plainer language, "and a good scheme, too, give you my word. But somehow or other Deerhurst, he got wind of it. Must have heard some of my pals discussin' it. He's got sharp ears, if you remember, Adeney. Anyways, he got on to our game. And what d'you think he did? He went and *squeaked*, he did! That ditched it. And it didn't make life any happier for me an' my pals, give you my word."

"I never heard about it," Nicholas objected.

"Oh, you wouldn't hear about it," Sturge explained. "They hushed it up, o' course. Bad for dis-*sip*-line, that, if it had o' come out. Make other people restless. Put bad notions in their heads, an' what not. No, Adeney, they didn't bring out no special editions over it. But we found out who'd given us away. We did that."

Prison-life had given Nicholas some sympathy with the convict's outlook; and to him this latest episode in Deerhurst's career seemed especially mean. Betraying men simply to curry favour with the authorities. Just what one might expect, of course.

"And so you want to get hold of him and beat him up? Is that it?"

Sturge's ugly teeth showed in a grin, but his eyes were full of suspicion.

"No, no!" he said, but his denial was unconvincing. "We just want to have a bit of a chat with him, like. Mebbe we could bring him for to see that he owes us a bit of financial compensation over it, that's all."

Nicholas laughed unaffectedly at the idea.

"You can't get blood out of a stone," he said tritely. "Deerhurst hasn't a stiver in the world. It all went in the smash."

"Don't you believe it," Sturge retorted. "You were the mug in that affair, an' I expect you lost everything. But Deerhurst has a bit tucked away somewheres or another. I can't put my claws on it, nor could you either. But we know Deerhurst, we do. He's not the kind to come out into a cold, hard world, without knowin' where to look for a bit of silver linin waitin' for him in a safish place. Not him. Them bone-selfish ones always looks after Number One, whoever else loses. An' I'm a man with a wife and three kids to fend for—one of 'em half-blind, poor little devil," he ended passionately.

"What's wrong?" Nicholas asked sympathetically.

"Somethin' wrong with what they calls the cornea," Sturge explained without hesitation. "There's glasses would put it right, the doctor at the Eye Hospital says. Not specs. Somethin' fresh. But they cost a God's amount o' money. More'n a fiver, anyways. I can't rise to it just now, with all the rest ot 'em to keep. It fair tears the heart out o' me, times, when she says: 'Oh, Daddy, if only I could *see*, like you!' That's what she says, Adeney. Pitiful, it is."

He broke off with a gesture which said more than words.

Nicholas nodded sympathetically, and then stared

at the ground for a moment or two without replying. This was the sort of case which would appeal to Hazel, he felt sure. It was genuine enough. Sturge's tone had made that plain to him; and in any case they could satisfy themselves fully by communicating with the hospital, wherever it was, if things got that length. A tenne r would probbly cover the cost and give the child back her sight. But he shrank from saying anything to Sturge until Hazel made her decision, since the matter lay with her. He could only raise a tenner himself by spending the money she gave him as an allowance.

He pulled out a notebook and passed it to the ticket-of-leave man.

"Write down your address, will you?"

Sturge seemed a shade suspicious, but after a slight hesitation he jotted down something.

"That'll find me any time," he said, handing back the notebook. "I know you ain't like Deerhurst. You wouldn't give me away with this, if there was any trouble."

He halted for a moment, his face a mask of bitterness and anxiety.

"I've just got to get that money somehow," he declared.

"Wish you luck," said Nicholas cordially. "Now I must go."

Sturge made no pretence of formal leave-taking. He nodded absently and then moved off down the avenue, his shoulders hunched, his whole attitude betraying dejection. Nicholas gazed after him and saw him once cast a glance over the hedge, an appraising glance which seemed to take in the lawns, the flower-beds, the car by the garage door, and the spick-and-span house among the greenery.

"Poor devil!" he reflected as he walked back towards the front door. "It must make him rage to see people with houses like this, when he's at his wits' end for enough to cure his kid's sight. 'More'n a fiver'! He talks as if it were all the money in the world! H'm! I'm sorry for him, though he's anything but an attractive creature. We've all got our troubles."

CHAPTER II

AN UNACCREDITED EMISSARY

"A DISASTROUS evening!" said old Mr. Calbourne in a mock-despondent tone as he finished totting up the score. "I owe you nine and six, Marjorie. This is what comes of taking up Contract on the edge of my second childhood."

He drew an assortment of silver coins from his trouser pocket, and selected from them three-half crowns and a florin. Stacking them into a neat pile, he pushed them over to his daughter with his forefinger.

No one would have identified him as a solicitor from his outward appearance. With his stiff white hair, his keen blue eyes, and his white torpedo beard, he might easily have been taken for a retired skipper who had perhaps done well in the China trade in the days when captains made their own opportunities.

He had been the junior partner in a firm of solicitors employed by Hazel's father, and had risen to the head of it some time before Adeney & Co. had collapsed. Nicholas, who trusted the old man implicitly, had put his affairs into his hands at the time of the trial; and it was one of his few comforting reflections that Calbourne, knowing the whole business, had never wavered in his friendship for the convicted man.

On retiring from active practice with a comfortable income, Mr. Calbourne migrated to a new neighbourhood; and, as he was alone, his daughter Marjorie—a young widow—came to keep house for him. The Adeneys and the Calbournes had been intimate for years. Hazel and Marjorie were playfellows in their earliest days and, rather unusually, they remained inseparables even when they grew up and married. Thus it was natural enough that, when the Adeney crash made her native town distasteful to Hazel in some ways, she bought a house not far from the Calbournes, to be near Marjorie. She had a fair fortune of her own and could afford to pay for her fancies.

"Every little helps," Marjorie declared cheerfully, as she transferred her winnings to her bag. "If I could only play against you often enough, Father, I'd come out square in my bridge at the end of the month. Which reminds me, Hazel. Will you and Nick come round to us next Wednesday evening? Or Thursday, if that suits better?

Hazel laughed as she picked up the cards to put them away. For some reason which Mr. Calbourne could not fathom, she seemed to be in a peculiar frame of mind that evening, passing swiftly from one mood to another.

"Tact was always your long suit, Marjorie," she retorted. "But this time the answer's 'No!' in two letters with a dot after them. I'm on holiday now, and I'm making no engagements for a week or two."

"You do seem a bit above yourself," Marjorie admitted critically. "If the prospect of seven days at Shrimpton-on-Sea can excite you as much as this, there's something to be said for the treatment."

Marjorie had been watching Hazel closely. Long intimacy made it easy enough to read the signs; and she had a feeling, vague but uncomfortable, that something was further amiss than appeared on the surface. These alternate moods of liveliness and depression, succeeding each other swiftly as they had done this evening, were quite foreign to Hazel's normal behaviour. It reminded Marjorie of something far back in the past. . . .

Then she recalled what had eluded her for a moment or two. The old nursery at home, with rain beating on its windows from a sullen sky and forbidding any thought of the garden. Hazel and herself perched on chairs at the table, their feet dangling, busy with a much be-fingered old pack, engrossed in the only card-game they could understand at their age : Beggar-my-Neighbour. She could see Hazel's face, eager, flushed, excited, as card after card came fumblingly from their hands. She remembered that pause of almost anguished hesitation before a player dared turn her card and learn her fate. A King ! Then, one card . . . two cards . . . and hope was almost gone. Would the third be a court card ? What a thrill of expectation. What a faltering in fear lest the revelation of the next card's face should be fatal to one's hopes.

It was the same situation that she sensed to-night in Hazel's changes of mood. At one moment it was : "Things will be all right" ; and then soon after : "One can't be sure of anything." And behind it all, Marjorie imagined that same hesitation before putting matters to the touch, though the move was inevitable in the end. It was useless to question Hazel, she knew. Hazel had a way of carrying her own troubles, a spice of the pride of Lucifer in her make-up. It was that, as much as anything, which had let her hold her head high in the Adeney crash. Of course, this time, it was Deerhurst again, Marjorie reflected. It couldn't be anything else ; and that was bad enough in all conscience. But if it was Deerhurst, these alternations of mood seemed beyond interpretation. How could Hazel see any gleam of hope in that affair ? No answer to that enigma.

Nicholas had pushed the card-table aside and ranged the arm-chairs hospitably. He made a gesture inviting the guests to sit down, but Mr. Calbourne glanced at his watch.

" After ten," he said hesitatingly. " I hate to seem ungracious, but you know what an early bird I am in these days, Nick. We really ought to be thinking of moving."

Then he altered his mind suddenly.

" Well, just for a few minutes, then," he conceded, taking a seat as he spoke. " But you know how it is with you people. One sits down with the best resolutions, and then, before one knows how time's gone, it's after midnight."

" I suppose that's a compliment," Hazel retorted. " But it might mean that our conversation puts you into a doze."

Mr. Calbourne seemed in no mood for persiflage.

" There's one thing I've in mind to say to you, Hazel ; but my memory's not so good as it used to be, and I've forgotten it, time and again. I may as well say it now and be done with it," he said seriously. " You ought to make a will."

" Think you see signs of an early break-up ? " Hazel inquired, with pretended seriousness. " I don't feel it coming on."

" Oh, I don't suppose you're likely to die to-morrow," Mr. Calbourne answered. " *Absit omen!* Though when I see you scorching in that car of yours, I sometimes think a fatal accident's merely a matter of time. Short of that, you're good for a half-a-century yet, I hope. But," he continued in a graver tone, " we lawyers like to have things ship-shape. I don't think you realise that if you died to-morrow, Deerhurst would come into every penny you left. You don't want that to happen, I take it ? "

" It's the last thing I want to happen," Hazel confirmed, with a frown. " Is that really how things are ? Then the sooner I make a will, the better. I'll come around to see you and talk it over to-morrow morning, if that won't put you out."

"Certainly, if you wish. And then you can put the thing into the firm's hands, to get it knocked into proper shape so that you can sign it."

The sharp ring of the telephone bell interrupted him. Hazel went across the room and picked up the receiver.

"Yes. She's speaking. . . . Who? . . . Oh, yes, of course. I remember now. . . . Yes. If you wish it. No, not to-morrow night. . . . No, I shan't be here. . . . To-morrow morning would do. . . .To-night? . . . Is it very urgent? . . . Very well, then. That will do. Good-bye."

Hazel put down the instrument and turned back to the others with a puzzled and faintly apprehensive expression on her face.

"That was Mr. Granfield—you remember? Len's solicitor. He wants to see me to-night, I can't think why."

Evidently she augured no good from the proposed visit. Anything even indirectly concerned with her husband was likely to be unpleasant.

Had anyone suggested to Marjorie that she was super-sensitive to "atmosphere," she would have laughed. But that evening, even she had detected an unwonted tension in the air. For four years Deerhurst had been no better than a phantom, a Presence in the far background of Hazel's life, ill-omened, but safely barred off from any direct influence upon her. Now that phantom was taking flesh again, drawing nearer in time and space, solidifying as it came. Marjorie could almost feel that sinister approach. Yesterday the prison gates had restrained it. This morning they had swung ajar to leave a passage. Somewhere, in the unknown, Deerhurst was free once more, preparing for his descent which would rob Hazel of her tranquillity. And this telephone call implied that his arrival was imminent. How else came his solicitor to intervene thus urgently?

At the name of Granfield, Mr. Calbourne pricked up his ears. He glanced at the clock on the mantelpiece and pursed his lips when he saw the hour. Apparently he thought it was over-late for a professional call. But there was something further in his mind which he put into words.

" See what comes of breaking good resolutions," he said with a pretence of self-condemnation. " I should have been on the way home to bed, long ago, and out of temptation. Still, since I am here . . ."

He turned directly to his hostess.

" This man Granfield wants to see you this evening, Hazel, and can't wait until to-morrow morning ? His business must be urgent, then, I take it. He's not a personal friend of yours, I believe ? No, I thought not. So his excuse for calling at this hour must be professional. Something to do with Deerhurst, one may guess."

" I suppose so. He didn't say why he wanted to see me," Hazel explained rather apathetically.

" In that case," Mr. Calbourne pursued, " I think I should point out to you that it's not expedient for you to see him alone, with no one to advise you. This man Granfield is a sharp fellow—too sharp for my taste, in some ways. If he's here on Deerhurst's behalf, you ought to be careful. A smooth-tongued fellow like that might get round you and let you commit yourself without your quite seeing what you were doing."

Hazel saw the kindly intention behind his words.

" You mean you'll stay and see what he's after ? That's good of you, if you'll do it. I quite see what you mean, and it's on the cards that I might make a mess of it by myself. I don't understand much about legal affairs."

" That's made my mind easier," Mr. Calbourne confessed. " Between ourselves, this fellow Granfield

—though he's smart enough—is not one of the leading lights in our profession hereabouts. I admit his cleverness. But he gambles. I can't stand a gambling solicitor, and still less can I stand a gambling solicitor who brags about his winnings . . . and says precious little about his losses. I'm old-fashioned and all that, but it's not my idea of the profession. So I don't like this fellow."

"Should Marjorie and I go into another room and leave you two to tackle him?" Nicholas inquired.

Mr. Calbourne shook his head, after a moment's thought.

"No," he decided. "If by any chance he's come on a piece of straight business, there's no harm in our hearing it—unless Hazel objects. On the other hand, if he's coming with some underhand dodge or other, then the more witnesses the better."

"Of course I don't object," Hazel acquiesced. "If there's some scheme of Len's behind this, then the more we all know about it the better. We'd be talking it over afterwards, anyhow."

"Of course we should," said Marjorie, "and most likely we'd get it all mixed up amongst us, with repeating it to each other. Far better get it straight out of the tap, once for all."

"Whatever it is," added Nicholas.

"That's a problem on which it is fruitless to speculate at present," Mr. Calbourne pointed out. "It will be safer to talk about something else just now, so as to keep our minds free for the thing when it comes. How is the writing business prospering, Nicholas?"

On his release Nicholas had hit upon authorship as a possible source of income. In that field, at least, his past record would not go against him, if he adopted a pseudonym. He had stuck to his self-imposed task with more industry than his friends had expected when he started ; but he was inclined to conceal any slight success under a cloak of irony.

" Prospering ? " he answered. " It depends which side of the business you look at, you know. The output's considerable ; the expenses are steady ; but the profits are miserable. I don't seem to have the right knack, somehow."

" Have you taken one of these courses they advertise ? " Marjorie demanded. " The advertisements speak very highly of them, I see."

" No, I haven't," retorted Nicholas. " I've gone to the very root of things. At first I found I'd no vocabulary to speak of. So I bought a Concise Oxford Dictionary and read through it, a letter a day. It's not a work of art. The stories are too short, for one thing ; and they lack human interest, somehow. I was pretty weary when I came to 'zymotic' and I breathed a sigh of relief. But then I found they spring a whole set of Addenda on you, and I had to start all over again at the " A's "—'Aasvogel' and such-like, down to 'Zulu.' And after that I bought a Thesaurus to look up synonyms in. The Compleat Author, in fact, except for the cheques."

" Perhaps you send your things in hand-written," Marjorie suggested. " I've heard editors don't like that."

" I haven't even that excuse," Nicholas explained gloomily. " Where are the cigarettes ? Oh, over there ? Thanks. No, it's not my hand-writing that stands in the way. Hazel lent me her typewriter, and all my stuff's typed. It's just that I haven't the knack of the thing. Still, it fills in the time, and that's always something."

" Talking of writing, Nick," Hazel broke in. " Have you got that affair fixed up yet ? The case of the little girl, you know."

" Sturge's kiddie ? Yes, It's quite genuine. I

wrote to the mother and got the address of the Eye Hospital. The specialist who examined the kid says these contact glasses, as he calls them, would make a vast improvement in her sight. He'll see to the business if you send him a cheque. I forget exactly what they cost." He felt in his pocket and produced an envelope. "Here's his letter. You can see what it amounts to yourself."

Hazel took the letter, and after a gesture to ask permission from the others, read it through carefully.

"I'll give you the cheque now," she said, sitting down at an escritoire and taking a cheque-book from a drawer. "There it is, Nick. Now please send it off as soon as you can, will you? I hate to think of that poor mite losing even a day before getting fit to see better."

She handed over the slip of paper and turned to Mr. Calbourne.

"Somehow, anything wrong with sight seems to me a dreadful thing. It must be terrifying to find that something's gone wrong with one's eyes."

She shivered slightly as though in apprehension that she herself might suffer from eye-trouble.

"Not much wrong with you in that way," Marjorie commented. "I'd sooner have you than anyone as a partner in a foursome when I've lost the ball. And my own sight's none so dusty."

"I wasn't thinking of myself," Marjorie began, and then stopped abruptly, biting her lip.

"This child, eh?" inquired Mr. Calbourne. "What's the matter with her?"

Nicholas interposed and gave him some account of the case, but before he had got to the end of his story, an electric bell trilled in the back premises of the house.

"That's your visitor, I expect, Hazel. The maids have gone, I suppose? You'd better go to the door yourself and show him in. Don't tell him we're here;

it'll be amusing to see his face when he finds us waiting for him."

Hazel nodded and left the room. They heard her admit the visitor and a few moments later, she ushered him in.

The first thing noticeable in Louis Granfield was his heavy face: the great thick nose, the full, compressed lips, the two straight furrows slanting to the corners of the ruthless mouth, and the deep-sunk eyes. In comparison with that massive head, the rest of his physique seemed dwarfed, though actually he was only an inch or two below average height. At the first glance, the immobile features suggested a certain dullness of mind, but this was belied by the quickness and keenness of the pale blue eyes in their deep sockets.

"A born poker-player," Mr. Calbourne reflected, not for the first time. "With a face like that, nobody could guess whether one had a pair or a straight flush in one's hand."

If Granfield was taken aback to find others visitors present, not a quiver of his features betrayed it. He greeted them courteously in turn, since none of them was a complete stranger to him. Then, seeming to ignore the object of his call, he remained silent, leaving the opening move to one of the others. By a quick, significant glance, Mr. Calbourne signalled to Hazel that she had better begin.

"You wanted to see me about something?"

Her tone was almost perfunctory, and Mr. Calbourne gave her a good mark for her opening. She was obviously on her guard and meant to say as little as possible.

For a moment or two Granfield made no response. He was evidently one of those people who knew the effectiveness of a pause. His quick eyes glanced from one to the other of the faces in front of him, as though he were classifying the various members of the group and assessing their relative importance to him at the moment. Marjorie he seemed to dismiss instanter, Nicholas got a swift scrutiny, Hazel appeared to have been considered already, but he dwelt longer on Mr. Calbourne than on any of the others. It was all over almost before it had begun.

"I'd no idea I was breaking in on you while you were entertaining your friends," he said with a shade of apology in his tone. "I imagined you were quite free, when you asked me to come in. I've come on a matter of business, rather delicate business."

He paused again, and his unspoken meaning was perfectly clear. "I've said my say. You're all well-bred people and can take a hint. I'm giving you the chance to say good-night and take yourselves off. After you've gone, Mrs. Deerhurst and I can discuss things."

No one moved, however, and Hazel motioned him to a chair. She chose a seat near Mr. Calbourne and sat down, her elbow on the chair-arm, her chin in her hand. Granfield had suffered a first defeat, but nothing in his face betrayed it.

"What is this business?" Hazel asked in a tone which simulated only a natural interest.

Despite his facial immobility, Granfield was no bad actor. By his manner, he suggested a slight embarrassment due to his unexpected surroundings.

"It's a private matter, rather difficult," he explained with apparent candour. "Perhaps if we . . ."

His gesture suggested that the two of them might retire to another room where they could thrash it out between themselves. He had an air of wishing to spare her any unnecessary publicity.

"You can speak quite freely, Mr. Granfield," Hazel assured him pleasantly. "These are very old friends, you know. I've nothing to conceal from them."

Granfield was too astute to pursue what was evidently a losing game. By another gesture, he conceded the point without more ado.

" Well, since you insist," he said. " Mr. Deerhurst has just been released. . . . Have you had any communication from him ? "

Hazel shook her head.

" Ah," Granfield said softly, but it was impossible to gather from his tone whether he was surprised or not. Without the usual pause he continued : " I'm his solicitor. But, of course, you know that."

Hazel nodded, keeping her eyes fixed on Granfield's face, as a fencer watches his opponent's eyes.

" A bad business, the whole thing, a very bad business," Granfield continued as though he was musing aloud. Then his tone grew more practical. " I've seen him, once or twice, in prison. Once, quite recently. Naturally he discussed things frankly with me, various things, and he showed me some letters you'd written to him."

He paused again as though to let the implications of this sink well home.

" Yes ? " prompted Hazel in a neutral tone.

Granfield leaned slightly forward in his chair with a movement which suggested a confidential communication.

" I needn't go into details," he went on. " I think we can take some things for granted. It's sufficient to say that the future relations between yourself and Mr. Deerhurst are . . . h'm ! . . . fraught with difficulty in some respects. He showed me the letters he had received from you," he concluded in a tone which showed that he felt he had driven a nail home.

" Indeed ? " Hazel's tone showed no resentment at this invasion of her private correspondence. " That saves me explaining my sentiments in the matter. But I don't quite see why you've come to see me."

Again Granfield hitched himself a little forward in his chair.

"I'll be quite frank with you," he said. "I've come to see if some *modus vivendi* can't be arrived at. With a little goodwill on each side, it might be possible, I believe."

"Are you suggesting that I should take him back?" Hazel demanded, and Nicholas saw the danger-signal flash out in her eyes at the idea.

"That would be in the nature of a final settlement," Granfield pointed out. "What I meant was merely something in the way of a temporary arrangement which might give time for both parties to reach a definite settlement. I think something of the sort could be contrived."

Again the usual pause.

"In fact, I am pretty certain I could arrange it."

Mr. Calbourne intervened swiftly before Hazel could reply.

"In other words, Mr. Granfield, Deerhurst has some proposals to make, and you're his accredited ambassador?"

Granfield swung his head slowly round to face his new interrogator.

"Hardly an accredited *ambassador*," he said, as though he deprecated the grandiloquence of the phraseology.

But Mr. Calbourne was not deceived by the accentuation.

"Accredited, though, of course?" he demanded, with a wintry smile.

"I know Deerhurst's views," Granfield countered.

Mr. Calbourne's smile grew a shade bleaker.

"Ah, now I understand. An unaccredited emissary, eh?"

"Call it that, if you choose," Granfield conceded indifferently.

Mr. Calbourne paused in his turn before speaking.

" I'm not mistaken, I think," he said, as if summing up the result of reflection. " You've come here to get Mrs. Deerhurst to give you some idea of her point of view, her terms, in fact. And then you mean to present these to Deerhurst, who himself has made no move in the matter. In other words, you're playing honest broker, acting for both sides? Hardly professional, as you know well enough."

" I'm sorry you look on it like that," Granfield answered with a graven face. " My real object was to arrive as quickly as possible at some *modus vivendi*, as I explained before, for the sake of both parties. Time is rather important, if unnecessary friction is to be avoided. One can easily foresee incidents which might make a final settlement more difficult if they are allowed to occur."

A thought seemed to strike him and he turned to Hazel.

" Have you Mr. Deerhurst's present address? He didn't give me it, as I believe he proposed to come here shortly. If you have it, I could perhaps . . . Well, you don't want him here, and I might manage to keep him away till we came to some arrangement."

Hazel shook her head.

" I know nothing about his whereabouts since he left prison."

Granfield rubbed his chin, as though vexed by an unexpected hindrance to his scheme.

" That's a nuisance," he said, with the first departure from impassivity. Then he turned to Mr. Calbourne. " I see your point," he admitted. " I hadn't looked at it in that way. If I can get hold of Deerhurst I'll find out the terms he proposes for a settlement, or, rather, I'll try to dissuade him from his present plan, which is to come back here. If I succeed I'll take the matter up with Mrs. Deerhurst's solicitors. My only object is to get some arrangement made which will be satisfactory to both parties. I'm sure you see that."

" So long as the business is done in business-like fashion, I've no criticism to make," Mr. Calbourne conceded, though his tone was far from cordial. " In the meantime, Hazel, I think we may wish Mr. Granfield good night."

Granfield ignored the implied sneer and rose to his feet.

" You've nothing further to say, Mrs. Deerhurst ? Then I must be going. I've a long drive home, you know. Oh, by the way, you'll be in to-morrow evening, if I happen to ring up ? I might have further news."

Hazel hesitated for a moment, then shook her head.

" I doubt if it's worth troubling. You'd better write to Mr. Calbourne, I think," she decided. " I agree with him about business methods."

If Granfield felt the cut, he did not show it. He took his leave with punctilious courtesy and Nicholas showed him out.

Mr. Calbourne glanced at his watch with something more than a pretence of dismay.

" Good heavens ! As late as this ? " He turned to Hazel with a smile. " Your late visitor has one characteristic of a gentleman : he never shows a wound. Still, I think it's just as well we were here to-night. ' Accredited ambassador ! ' I don't wonder he jibbed at that. ' Busybody ' comes nearer the mark. Have nothing to do with fishers in troubled waters, Hazel."

He held out his hand in farewell.

" I'll come and see you to-morrow morning," Hazel reminded him. " To talk over this will of mine, you remember. Would eleven o'clock do ? "

CHAPTER III

A SHOCK FOR MRS. BUTTERSWICK

HAZEL'S housekeeper, Mrs. Butterswick, was middle-aged, placid, comfortably stout, and gifted with a store of maternal feeling which had found no direct outlet. She and her late husband had been childless, and the niece with whom she lodged was but newly-married. Diverted from their normal channel, her feelings found expression in an unobtrusive attempt to mother Hazel, so far as her employer's independent character would permit.

Though not addicted to malicious gossip, Mrs. Butterswick had not failed to learn all that was publicly known about the Adeney-Deerhurst trial ; and her privileged position had supplied her with further facts gleaned from her observations of Hazel's moods and from chance scraps of conversations between Hazel and Nicholas which she had overheard. Pondering over these data in her respectful sympathy, Mrs. Butterswick had arrived at two clean-cut opinions : that Hazel was an angel in adversity and that Deerhurst was a devil in human form. There were no greys in Mrs. Butterwick's moral paint-box : white was white and black was black to her, stark and unqualified.

She knew the date of Deerhurst's release, and for the last month she had been counting the days and feeling a heavier cloud settle about her as each one passed. Scanning her mistress with deferential affection, she had grieved over Hazel's increasing disquiet as the fatal date drew nearer and nearer. Deerhurst she had never seen in the flesh. She had to picture him for herself. And her imagination could conjure up only a dim, sinister figure, incredibly malign, menacing the peace of her adored mistress.

And then the fateful day had come . . . and no bolt had fallen from the sky. Another day passed in quietness. Still no sign. At the end of it, Mrs. Butterswick began to wish that the monster would come, come quickly, if merely to get the thing over. She was feeling the strain almost as much as Hazel, since her loyalty forbade her to discuss the matter with anyone, whereas Hazel had her own confidants.

Mrs. Butterswick ranked punctuality among the cardinal virtues. Shortly after seven o'clock each morning she left her lodgings, walked briskly up the hill to Cedar Avenue, and at a couple of minutes before the half-hour she was on the doorstep of Norwood House, inserting her latch-key in the door. The maid, whom Mrs. Butterswick did not trust with a key except on special occasions, was due to arrive a few minutes later.

The housekeeper had gone tobed, oppressed by her forebodings ; but she was one of those people who are always at their best in the morning, and as she turned into Cedar Avenue she was in an almost optimistic frame of mind. The new day itself seemed bent on raising her spirits, with its fresh still air, its brilliant sun, and its cotton-wool clouds lazily adrift in the overhead blue. She hastened along the broad pavement, with a passing glance over the hedges at the trim silent villas in their spacious gardens. She seemed to have this part of the world to herself. When she reached the gate of Norwood House she glanced approvingly over the shaven lawns and neat flower-beds. Oakley, the handy-man who tended the garden and cleaned the car, took some pride in his work, as one could see by the results. Mrs. Butterswick put it down to Hazel's character. Anyone would work himself to the bone to please a lady like that. She glanced at her watch, saw that it was just two minutes before the half-hour, and inserted her key in the front door. Then, with a perfunctory glance up the Avenue in case the maid was in sight, she went in and closed the door softly behind her.

She turned to slide the knob of the Yale lock so that the maid might enter in her turn. But the catch was already in place, the Yale was out of action, and the door could have been opened merely by turning the outer handle. Mrs. Butterswick found nothing amiss in this. Hazel occasionally forgot to secure the Yale lock at night before she went to bed. Apparently she had overlooked it this time. Mrs. Butterswick gave no thought to the matter but pursued her daily routine. She went first to take off her hat and coat. Then she began the round of the rooms, to draw aside the curtains, and open the windows.

The drawing-room door was shut, and when she pushed it open, her nostrils caught a heavy odour of tobacco in the air. Hazel smoked Virginia cigarettes herself, but she kept a Turkish brand for guests who preferred it; and Mrs. Butterswick inferred that someone had been paying a visit late on the previous evening. Idly wondering about this person's identity, she stepped into the dim lit room, moving gently so that her steps on the parquet should not disturb her mistress in the bedroom overhead. She crossed to the nearest window, parted the curtains cautiously, and threw open the casements to air the room.

Then, as she turned to go to the next window, her eye caught a dark patch on the smooth surface of the floor near the centre of the room. She went over and examined it, and as she saw what it was her heart gave a painful leap. Even her inexperienced eye had no difficulty in recognising that little pool of sticky blood.

Mrs. Butterswick was not a swift thinker, but if her mental processes were on the slow side, at least they generally yielded some definite results. Her first reflection was rather comforting. There was very little blood, perhaps about as much as one saw in a bad case of nose-bleeding. She had a vision of Hazel, alone in the house, slipping on the smooth parquet, coming down on her face, and bleeding for some seconds before she could pull herself together to get to her feet again. Then, probably, she had dragged herself up to bed. Mrs. Butterswick tried to persuade herself that this explanation was sound, but something at the back of her mind insisted on suggesting ominous doubts.

She stepped past the little pool and regained the threshold. As she did so, the front door opened and Evie Sutton, the maid, came into the hall. Acting on impulse Mrs. Butterswick closed the door of the drawing-room behind her, turned the key, took it from the lock, and kept it in her palm. She regarded Evie as too young and light-minded to be trusted with serious matters. Until she knew how things actually were, Evie had better be kept in the dark.

"Get Mrs. Deerhurst's tea, Evie, will you? I've got something I want to do, just now. And then you can set the breakfast-table."

Evie set off to the back premises to rid herself of her outdoor things; and as soon as she had vanished Mrs. Butterswick went upstairs. She tapped at the door of her mistress's bedroom, softly at first, then with increasing disquiet, more loudly. No reply. Mrs. Butterswick, her mind picturing a variety of disasters, turned the handle and pushed open the door. The drawn curtains made the room dim, but she needed no second glance to see that the bed was unoccupied; had not been slept in that night.

The thing Mrs. Butterswick had kept at the back of her mind now sprang into the foreground of her thoughts, dominating and sinister. She tottered to the nearest chair, sank into it, and for a moment almost lost control of herself. The whole affair pieced itself together in an instant: that unusual tobacco smoke, the unlatched door, the blood on the parquet, and Hazel's disappearance.

"Deerhurst!"

That was the keyword to the riddle. Mrs. Butterswick did not speculate further. For weeks the return of 'that scoundrel' had tinged her thoughts. She had known all along that his reappearance would bring tragedy in its train. But not this kind of tragedy. Fuss, disturbance of the even tenor of life at Norwood House, "scenes," perhaps. That was what she had expected. But not blood. Not this kind of thing. Not . . .?

And then Mrs. Butterswick, with her face in her hands, began to think what might lie behind that ominous mark of interrogation. Deerhurst had returned, secured an entrance, found Hazel alone. Then . . . Mrs. Butterswick forced herself to face it . . . then there had been bloodshed. No getting over that fact, with the thing staring at one from the floor down below. But whose blood was it? Mrs. Butterswick mentally stepped round that question, as she had stepped round the pool of blood itself. But no sooner had she evaded it than something almost as grim appeared in its place. *Someone* had been wounded—she avoided the uglier word even in her mind—and that person must be somewhere on the premises, surely.

Mrs Butterswick's first inclination was to pull herself together and ring up the police; but her level-headedness overcame this. The police would take their time, and even if they hurried, it would be long enough before they came on the premises. Meanwhile the victim might be bleeding to death somewhere in the house. It might be Hazel; it was almost certain to be Hazel. . . .

And at that Mrs. Butterswick was galvanised into action. She got to her feet, somehow, and with tottering steps began to search from room to room. She drew blank on the upper floor, though she peeped under the beds and opened cupboards and wardrobes. Downstairs she could hear Evie moving to and fro as she laid the breakfast-table while waiting for the kettle to boil. That left only one small sitting-room unvisited. Mrs. Butterswick ran heavily downstairs, hurried to the sitting-room door, flung it open, peered about—and discovered nothing. Except for herself and Evie, the house was untenanted.

Mrs. Butterswick had never seen that danger-signal flaming in Hazel's eyes. To her, Hazel was the adored mistress, so considerate, so thoughtful, so slow to find fault even when it was deserved. And as she stood there on the threshold of the sitting-room, she had a waking nightmare.

In her mind's eye she saw the drawing-room, the slender figure of Hazel—that was clear and sharp—confronting a bigger, shadowy form; then a blow from the misty figure, a fall, a trickle of blood; and then the horrid shape bending over Hazel, picking her up in its arms, and carrying her out into the dark. Beyond this point, Mrs. Butterswick refused to follow. But that was how it had happened, of that she felt assured. And with that vivid picture in her mind, and her blood pulsing angrily at the thought of Hazel having suffered at the hands of "that scoundrel" she hastened to the telephone in the cloak-room, shut the door behind her, and rang up the nearest police station. It might be too late to help her mistress now, but at least the avengers should be set forthright upon the track of that midnight assassin.

She replaced the receiver with a hand which trembled with rage now as much as with horror. Somehow, the unleashing of the sleuth-hounds (as she found comfort in describing it) calmed her a little. She could think clearly again. And the first problem to present itself was that of Evie, the housemaid. Evie, Mrs. Butterswick reflected, was a bit high-strung and nervous. Like enough, she might go off the handle, get hysterical and silly, if she found herself in a "murder house" with only Mrs. Butterswick for company and support. Better let her learn of the tragedy after the police had arrived, with their re-assuring masculinity.

She opened the door of the cloak-room and emerged to find Evie, tray in hand, about to mount the stairs.

"Here! Stop a minute, Evie. Give me that tray. I've something for you to do. Put on your things and go down to Mr. Adeney's place. Tell him he's wanted here immediately. Don't waste a minute, do you hear?"

Evie stared at her in unconcealed surprise as she handed over the tea-tray.

"Is she ill?"—she nodded towards the upper flat. "Is it anything catching?"

"It isn't catching," Mrs. Butterswick answered, tactfully ignoring the first question. "Now you get along at once and bring Mr. Adeney back with you. Hurry, now!"

Evie, somewhat disconcerted by the expression on Mrs. Butterswick's face, scurried away to put on her hat and coat. The housekeeper watched her go, and then, to maintain the deception, mounted the stairs, with the tray in her hands. She listened on the landing till she heard Evie let herself out of the front door.

Some subconscious guidance led her to Hazel's room. Mechanically she pushed open the door, and looked in. Then, at the sight of the unused bed and the embroidered gossamer nightdress unfolded on it, Mrs. Butterswick's self-restraint broke down. The glimpse of these familiar things had more effect upon her than that grim sticky patch on the parquet below. She set the tray down on the bedside table, sat down on the bed, covered her face with her hands and fell into a storm of weeping for her lost mistress. When she opened her eyes again, she caught sight of the filmy nightdress.

" She'll never wear it again ! " sobbed Mrs. Butterswick, with a fresh realisation of the tragedy.

It was long before she could bring herself back under control. Then she rubbed her tear-reddened eyes, got up from the bed without a glance about her, and went downstairs again just in time to admit the police.

CHAPTER IV

AN INSPECTOR AND SOME OTHERS

WHEN Mrs. Butterswick opened the front door, she was confronted by a tall man in plain clothes, with two uniformed figures in the immediate background.

"I'm Detective-Inspector Dornfell," the tall man explained.

He had a kind voice, Mrs. Butterswick noted, and the crows-feet at his eye-corners seemed to suggest that in his leisure moments he might be an amusing companion. She felt reassured by the look of him.

"Will you come in, please?" she said, standing aside so that he might enter. Then she added: "I'm so glad you've come."

The trite phrase seemed to amuse the inspector, for his eyes twinkled.

"Some people aren't so pleased to see us," he commented solemnly. "Now what's the trouble? And what's your name, by the way?"

"Butterswick—Mrs. Butterswick. Letitia's my first name."

Rather to her relief, he did not immediately pluck a notebook from his pocket and jot down this information. Mrs. Butterswick's conception of senior police officials was rather vague, but she had an idea that they noted down everything you said and then told you it would be used in evidence against you. Compared with her ideal, Inspector Dornfell seemed a friendly person, and she was correspondingly relieved.

" Now, Mrs. Butterswick," explained the inspector, " when I was called in they told me that Mrs. Deerhurst, of Norwood House, Cedar Avenue, had disappeared under suspicious circumstances. That's all I know about this affair. You'll have to tell me the rest. What's Mrs. Deerhurst's full name, by the way ? "

" Hazel's her first name."

" Deerhurst . . . ? " mused Dornfell, half aloud.

Mrs. Butterswick rose to the bait.

" I know what you're thinking," she broke in. " Yes, it's him—the man who was sent to prison. He's at the bottom of this. They've just let him out, you know, and he must have come here last night. She was expecting him to come, afraid of him turning up, I know. She hated him, and no wonder, after what happened."

Inspector Dornfell nodded. The Deerhurst case was an old story now, and it had been a complex financial trial in which he had taken little interest at the time. For the present, it was enough to know that Deerhurst was a convict released on licence. With this information, they could lay their hands on him if they wanted to. The inspector dismissed that side of the matter for the present.

" What is Mrs. Deerhurst like to look at ? " he inquired.

Mrs. Butterswick hesitated for a moment or two. When one has lived in daily contact with a person and seen her in all sorts of dresses and with her hair done in different ways, one's impressions are apt to be somewhat blurred, she found.

" She's got lovely fair hair," she began, " and brownish eyes—hazel, you know—and her eyebrows are a shade darker than her hair. She's as pretty as a picture."

" Have you got a photograph of her ? " demanded

the inspector, who seemed dissatisfied with this last descriptive touch.

" No, there isn't one in the house," Mrs. Butterswick explained. " I can't think why she never got her picture taken, with looks like hers. But she never did, that I know of."

" What height was she ? "

" Not tall. An inch or so taller than myself, I'd say, if we were both in our stockings."

" About five feet six or so, then. Anything more ? Hands, figure, feet and ankles—the way she walked ? These are the things people notice, you know."

This lead assisted Mrs. Butterswick to add some further items to her description.

" Small hands and pretty nails—she kept them beautifully. She'd a lovely figure—slim ; and you'd have looked at her twice in the street, she'd such a nice walk, quick somehow and not hurried either. Fours were what she took in shoes, and she'd the neatest ankles. And she'd perfect teeth and such a lovely smile."

The inspector took out his notebook and made a few notes, which seemed brief compared with Mrs. Butterswick's verbal description.

" Now the next thing," he said, stowing away his pencil. " Begin at the beginning. When did you see Mrs. Deerhurst last ? "

" Lunch-time yesterday," Mrs. Butterswick explained. " It was my afternoon off and I went out after lunch, about half-past two."

" Anyone left in the house with Mrs. Deerhurst ? "

" Evie Sutton, the maid. I'm the housekeeper."

" Any more on the staff ? "

" There's Oakley. He's the gardener and cleans the car, too. But he doesn't come into the house."

" You didn't see Mrs. Deerhurst when you came back last night ? "

" I don't come back," Mrs. Butterswick explained. " Evie and I sleep out. Mrs. Deerhurst's alone in the house at night. Often I've thought it wasn't safe."

" Where's Evie Sutton just now ? "

" I sent her out, to bring Mr. Adeney—Mrs. Deerhurst's brother. He lives quite close here."

" Nicholas Adeney ? " Dornfell amplified. " Oh, yes, I know about him. I'll see him when he comes. Now the next thing. When did you get here this morning ? "

" Half-past seven, exact. I looked at my watch. Evie came in a few minutes after me."

" You've got a latch-key ? Has Evie Sutton got one too ? "

Mrs. Butterswick was reminded of the unlocked door.

" I've got a key, but Evie hasn't. But when I came this morning the front door was open. I mean it wasn't locked. Anyone could get in by just turning the handle. Sometimes Mrs. Deerhurst forgets to lock up at night, so I didn't think anything of it at the time."

" Well, go on, now. Tell me what you did after you arrived here."

Mrs. Butterswick had kept her head wonderfully well, and she was able to give the inspector a fairly accurate narrative of her doings up to the time he himself came upon the scene. He had only to put three or four questions, none of which elicited anything of special importance. In the end, he read over his notes to her and got her to sign them.

" Now I'd better have a look at the drawing-room," he suggested. " Which is it ? "

Mrs. Butterswick still had the key clutched in her hand. She opened the door for him.

" You noticed a smell of strong tobacco when you came in, you said, didn't you ? " the inspector demanded, sniffing, as he entered the room. " There's a whiff of it still about, in spite of the window being opened. No cigarette left that reek."

He went over, knelt down and examined the patch of coagulated blood on the carpet.

"It's been there some hours, but that's all it tells me," he admitted, as he stood up again. "There's not much of it, is there?"

There had been quite enough for Mrs. Butterswick, as she was quick to inform him. Now that she had grown accustomed to the inspector, she found herself a little disappointed in him. Anyone could come and ask a few questions and then stare at some blood on the floor. He didn't seem to have found out anything, for all the time he'd taken over it.

Dornfell, unaware of this adverse verdict, began to examine the room. So far as the chairs went, there were no signs of any struggle having taken place, and the rugs had not been ruffled up.

"Any of the furniture been shifted, do you notice?" he asked over his shoulder.

Mrs. Butterswick glanced about the room to verify her impressions before replying.

"Nothing that I can see. The chairs usually got shifted about a bit when people came in and sat down to suit themselves. I've seen them like this dozens of times."

Then her over-wrought nerves found an outlet in querulousness.

"Aren't you going to find out something?" she demanded irritably. "I've had to show you everything myself. Why don't you *do* something—find a clue, or——"

"—or a mare's nest, eh?" said Dornfell, quite unperturbed. "And if it turned out to be a mare's nest from start to finish, we'd all be happier, wouldn't we? But I know what you're expecting. Cigar ash, like Sherlock Holmes. Well, here's your cigar ash."

He pointed to a grey smear on one arm of a big chair. " And that means there must have been an ash-tray somewhere about. Just let's see."

He lay down on the floor and peered over the parquet in various directions.

" Ah! There it is! "

He drew a pair of rubber gloves from his pocket, slipped them on, and then, reaching under an arm-chair carefully, he brought out a silver ash-tray. Putting it down on an occasional table, he held his rubber-covered hands behind his back and sniffed at the silver.

" Cigar, right enough," he commented.

Again he lay down on the floor and scanned its surface in all directions.

" Not there," he confessed, giving up his search for the anonymous object. Then as he rose to his feet, his eye fell upon the fire-place, and a fresh thought seemed to strike him. " Might be there, perhaps? " he suggested to himself; and after a moment or two he extracted from the back of the coals the smoked-out stub of a cigar, which he examined thoughtfully before stowing it away in an envelope.

" Doing a little better with practice, aren't I? " he said with a quizzical smile. Then his face grew grave again. " Now, Mrs. Butterswick, anyone can see this is a well-run house. So that cigar must have been smoked—since when? When do you dust this room? "

" Before breakfast, every morning. That's why I came in here first thing: to open the windows and air the room before starting to dust it."

" So that cigar was smoked in here since yesterday morning, some time," Dornfell commented with a nod. " Now tell me, which of Mrs. Deerhurst's friends smokes cigars? You must know that, from clearing up ash-trays after their visits."

Mrs. Butterswick's opinion of the detective had been rising a little. This was what she had really been expecting: finding clues and making something out of them.

" Mr. Calbourne's the only one. But you needn't think Mr. Calbourne has anything to do with this—this business. He's one of Mrs. Deerhurst's oldest friends. He wouldn't hurt a hair of her head. His daughter's in and out of the house all the time."

" Mr. Calbourne the solicitor? Looks like a retired sea-captain, doesn't he? I know him," the inspector admitted. Then, after a momentary hesitation, he added: " The point is, Mr. Calbourne may have dropped in, early on in the evening, to see Mrs. Deerhurst. If he did, then he must be able to tell us when he left here. And that gives us the time when she was last seen alive and well. See it? That's the time we want to establish as near as may be."

Mrs. Butterswick was obviously relieved by this statement, and also slightly flattered by being taken into the inspector's condence.

" I see that now," she assured him. " And Mr. Calbourne would do anything to help, I'm sure. He's that fond of Mrs. Deerhurst, he'll be dreadfully put about when he hears what's happened. And so will Mrs. Latchmere. That's his daughter. She's Mrs. Deerhurst's best friend. They've known each other since they were babies."

The inspector seemed hardly to attend to what she was saying. Something on the parquet had caught his eye, and he stooped down near the ash-smeared arm-chair, intent upon some small object. With a gesture warning Mrs. Butterswick to keep back, he moved over to the writing-desk and picked out a sheet of writing-paper. A search in his pocket brought to view a small camel's-hair brush. Then he knelt on the floor and began, with fastidious care, to sweep something from the parquet on to the sheet of paper. Mrs. Butterswick could see that it was a red powder. There was little more than a pinch of it, and it seemed to have accumulated in a tiny pile.

Mrs. Butterswick's opinion of the police rose still further. This was detection according to the best standards, in her view. She gave a sigh of relief as the inspector rose delicately to his feet and proceeded to fold up the paper, druggist-fashion. He was just stowing it away in his waistcoat pocket, when there came a sudden sound of raised voices at the front door. The maid had returned, bringing Nicholas Adeney with her, and evidently there had been some difficulty with the constables on the doorstep. Inspector Dornfell cocked his ears at the noise. He moved across the room and closed the casements; then, motioning Mrs. Butterswick out of the drawing-room, he followed her and turned to lock the door behind him.

"Let them in," he called to his subordinates.

Nicholas passed the constables who had barred his way, and came up to Dornfell. The inspector looked him up and down in a swift scrutiny.

"You're Nicholas Adeney, on ticket-of-leave? Let's have a look at your licence," he demanded brusquely.

Nicholas thrust his hands into his trouser pockets.

"I don't need one," he retorted with an angry frown "My sentence expired on the 17th."

That sharp exchange came as a shock to Mrs. Butterswick. She knew, of course, that Nicholas had been a convict; but somehow she had always taken it for granted that he must have been some very special kind of convict, a superior article entirely. She had never imagined Hazel's cousin being treated as anything but a gentleman, and it would have been beyond her to picture him as mixed up with low criminals of the kind that are sent to Dartmoor. In connection with him, the word " prison " had always had a tinge of make-believe about it for her. And now here was a policeman treating him like this. " As if he was an old lag," she phrased it to herself, from some recollection of a crime novel she had read.

Nicholas thrust his hands still deeper into his pockets and regarded the inspector with increased hostility.

" Question for question," he said curtly. " What are you people doing on these premises ? Has there been a burglary, or what ? "

Mrs. Butterswick was momentarily surprised by this question. Then she remembered that Evie had been sent off on her errand in complete ignorance of the true state of affairs. Of course it must have been a surprise to Mr. Adeney to find constables on the door-step. And no wonder he was short with the police. Look at what they had done to him—put him in prison for years.

" We received information that Mrs. Deerhurst had disappeared," Dornfell explained.

Nicholas paused for a moment before speaking again.

" Disappeared ? What do you mean by *disappeared* ? " he asked with very evident sarcasm.

Inspector Dornfell was for a moment at a loss.

" She was here yesterday and she isn't here now," he said in a slightly defensive tone. " She left no message to say she was going away——"

Nicholas interrupted him in the middle of the sentence. His tone seemed to indicate a rising temper, as though a weak man were lashing himself into a rage to cover his timidity.

" Does she need to report her movements to the police, if she chooses to leave home for a day or two ? She's not on ticket-of-leave, is she ? No ? Well, she's gone away. Why not ? "

The inspector looked just a shade uncomfortable at this. Then his face cleared.

"She's gone away, you say? Where's she gone to?"

Nicholas shrugged his shoulders contemptuously. "That's her business, I think."

But Dornfell was not to be put off with this.

"You say she's gone away. How do you know?"

Nicholas's shrug was slightly emphasised.

"Because she told me so."

The inspector was plainly disconcerted. He threw an ugly look at Mrs. Butterswick. Had that silly old fool of a woman led him up the garden with this tale of hers? If so, things might be awkward, with this obviously vindictive fellow Adeney only too anxious to give trouble. Then the facts of the case reassured him, and he put a further question.

"When did she tell you that?"

Nicholas stared at him with well-simulated surprise.

"That's *my* business," he replied bluntly. "Do you think I'm going to retail private conversations with my cousin to the first flattie that chooses to push his way into her house? Think again."

Inspector Dornfell had a sense of humour, but it stopped short of seeing any joke in his being called a "flattie" especially by a fellow who had every reason to know the difference between an inspector and a mere constable.

Nicholas's temper appeared to get the better of him.

"Enough of this foolery," he said with a tinge of malevolence. "I'm in charge, here, in my cousin's absence. You'd better get off the premises, and quick about it."

"Not *quite* so fast," the inspector countered. "There's a thing or two needs explanation. A patch of blood, for one."

"In the drawing-room?" Nicholas began and then stopped himself suddenly as though he had made a slip.

"How do you know it's in the drawing-room?"

broke in the inspector swiftly. " Tell me that, please."

Nicholas hesitated for a moment and seemed to reflect at lightning speed.

" Because I saw you coming out of the drawing-room and locking the door behind you as I came in," he said, with a stiff smile. " Very simple bit of deduction. Even the police might have made it."

But his face had gone a shade whiter, and the inspector saw it.

" I suppose you heard about it in one of these private conversations," he said with assumed politeness. " Did you learn how it came to be there ? "

Nicholas had regained his calmness by an obvious effort.

" Somebody's nose been bleeding, perhaps," he suggested, unconsciously echoing Mrs. Butterswick's own original explanation to herself.

" Ah ! So you know what size it is, eh ? " commented the inspector meaningly. " Very interesting, that."

Nicholas apparently resolved to try a fresh line of argument. He modified his tone to correspond.

" Look here, Inspector, take my advice and drop it. You're after a mare's nest ; and you'll find trouble in it when you light on it. It's no affair of mine to keep you from burning your fingers, but naturally I object to my cousin being made the centre of a lot of foolish gossip, which it's sure to be if you fuss about any more. She'll be anything but pleased when she comes back and finds you've been poking your nose into her affairs in this fashion. You've tried to browbeat me because I'm an ex-convict. But she's a fairly wealthy woman with powerful friends—quite a different sort of person. If you raise a storm in a tea-cup, she'll raise something bigger about your ears. I'm saying that for your own good, and I know what I'm talking about."

Unfortunately for Nicholas, Inspector Dornfell was not amenable to threats, no matter how they were veiled. His suspicions were merely intensified by this treatment.

"I'll talk to you afterwards," he decided, curtly. "Just now, I want to ask that girl a few questions."

Nicholas fell back with a troubled expression which the inspector did not fail to note.

"You name's Evie Sutton, isn't it?" Dornfell began, turning to the maid. "When did you last see Mrs. Deerhurst?"

Evie was more than a little confused in her mind. To find the constables on the doorstep had been a shock to her, and the hints she had gathered from the inspector's examination of Nicholas had raised qualms in her mind, though she could not quite see her way through the affair yet. However, this first question was easy enough to answer.

"About half-past two, yesterday afternoon," she said, with a slight hesitation. "At least, it was just a bit after Mrs. Butterswick went away for her afternoon off. Between half-past two and three, wouldn't it be?" she appealed to the housekeeper.

"I went out myself about half-past two," Mrs. Butterswick confirmed.

"Well, just shortly after that, Mrs. Deerhurst rang for me and said it was such a nice day I might as well get some fresh air, so if I'd set out a cold supper in the dining-room it would do for her as she wasn't very anxious for dinner seeing the weather was so hot, so I set the supper and then I got myself ready and went out, and that was the last time I saw her."

"Supper for her alone?" interjected the inspector. "She wasn't expecting visitors?"

"No, just for herself."

"And you didn't come back again later?"

Evie shook her head.

" But she had her supper," she volunteered, " for when I went into the dining-room this morning the plates had been used."

" She wouldn't be likely to take supper before seven, I suppose ? " inquired the inspector, turning to Mrs. Butterswick, who gave a confirmative nod.

" Any messenger-boys likely to have called at the house in the afternoon, or evening ? "

" No, not that I can think of," Mrs. Butterswick answered after a moment's consideration.

" She said nothing to you, either of you, about going away ? " queried Dornfell. " No ? H'm. Had she ever gone off like this before ? Without saying a word to you, I mean ? "

" She very seldom went away from home, except on holiday," Mrs. Butterswick declared, " and then she always told us she was going and told us she didn't need us. The house was always shut up while she was away, and we just come back in time to get it ready for her."

" Who has a key to the front door ? "

" Mrs. Deerhurst has one," Mrs. Butterswick explained. " And I have one. And I think Mr. Adeney has one, haven't you, sir ? "

Nicholas evidently was taken aback by this revelation, but he nodded to admit that he had a key.

Dornfell, however, did not pursue the subject at the moment. He apparently wished to finish with the maids first. He turned back to Evie.

" What did you do, after you left here yesterday afternoon ? "

" I did a bit of shopping down town, and I rang up a friend and we had tea together at the Bonne Bouche in Glasford Street—you know where it is ? —and then she and I went to the pictures—at the Imperial—and then I went home to supper, and after supper I went for a walk with my sister and then came home to bed."

"What about this friend of yours?"

"She's Miss Worland; lives at 7, Palatine Road, three doors along from where I live myself."

"And you, Mrs. Butterswick?" asked Dornfell.

Mrs. Butterswick was sharper than Evie.

"You're not thinking I've anything to do with the thing, are you?" she challenged the inspector. "I wasn't even in town. When I left here, I met my niece, Mrs. Gratton, of 54, Stanway Street—I live with her—at the bus stop in Frome Road, and we went into the country together to see a relation of ours at Tracey Abbas. We stayed there till it was time for the last bus home, and then we went straight off to bed."

"One has to ask these things," Dornfell explained with a hint of apology. "No one minds questions of that sort when they've got a clear conscience, eh? I may have to make another inquiry or two of you later on, but that's all I want just now," he said, with a gesture of dismissal. Then he turned to Nicholas. "Now I think you and I had better have a talk, quietly, by ourselves."

Nicholas shrugged his shoulders as though he took no responsibility for anything further, since his warnings had been disregarded.

"Very well. Try the dining-room—in here," he and the inspector followed him in, closing the door behind him.

When they were alone, Dornfell dropped the faintly official manner which he had hitherto maintained and spoke in a friendly tone.

"Now look here," he began. "You know something about this. You've made a slip or two that gave the show away, as you recognised yourself the moment you'd made 'em. Now why not come clean? Put the cards on the table? I can quite see there are things one doesn't talk about before the maids ; and most likely it's something of that sort that made you keep quiet when they were there. One doesn't want all one's family troubles dragged out for public inspection, naturally."

His pause was an invitation to Nicholas, but it produced no response. Inspector Dornfell's face hardened slightly.

" Got nothing to say ? H'm ! You needn't think we don't know about your Deerhurst."

He watched the effect of this shot in the dark, and caught a momentary flicker in Nicholas's eyes at the name. Getting no verbal answer, he began to grope after something more definite, keeping his keen eyes on Nicholas.

" Released on the 17th, wasn't he ? "

Nicholas nodded, rather indifferently. Dornfell guessed that he was on the wrong line, so he tried again.

" Mrs. Deerhurst wasn't very eager to see him back ? "

Nicholas seemed roused by this. His mouth twisted into a mirthless sardonic smile as he replied.

" Been gossiping with the servants, eh ? Well, it's not a matter I care to discuss with most people, but since you're such an old friend of the family, I don't mind saying that you're not far off the mark."

" She may have cleared out to avoid him, perhaps ? " Dornfell ventured.

" It's not impossible," Nicholas concurred, rather impatiently.

" You didn't like him yourself ? " the inspector continued.

" Why should I ? He swindled me out of my money and got me five years by his lying. That's more or less public property."

Dornfell was puzzled. There had been no mistaking that flicker of uneasiness at the first mention of

Deerhurst, and yet his further probing seemed, if anything, to be off the sore spot. And then that impatient acceptance of a motive for Mrs. Deerhurst's disappearance seemed as though there might be something simple enough behind the whole affair. But that didn't account for the little pool of blood on the floor of the next room. There would have to be some explanation of that, before things were clear. His manner stiffened as he put his next question.

"Where were you last night?"

Nicholas smiled the same twisted smile, but this time it seemed to blend malice with an ugly amusement.

"Sounds like a head-line from an old-fashioned tract, doesn't it? And a bit further down the page it used to say cheerily: '*To-morrow you may be in hell.*' They're cleverer at the business nowadays. At the prison gate, when I came out, some old chap was handing out leaflets headed: '*Safety, Certainty and Enjoyment.*' Some of the men began to read 'em. Thought they were advertisements—you know the sort? It made me smile to see 'em when they realised what they'd really got. First smile I'd had for a long time."

"You haven't answered my question," Dornfell interrupted.

"I noted it, never fear," Nicholas assured him with a sneer. "'Where was I last night?' Well, at 7 p.m. or a minute or two earlier I was in my humble lodgings, 19, Parkdale Lane, dressed in a short coat and black tie. As I went out, I mentioned to my landlady that I was going out to dinner and would probably be late. Not that it mattered, since I have a latch-key. I then walked by the shortest route to Domira, Stanmore Drive, where Mr. Calbourne lives, now that he's retired from the firm of Calbourne, Willoughby and Blunt, who happen to be my solicitors. I dined with Mr. Calbourne and his daughter, Mrs. Latchmere;

and I spent the evening with them. Mr. Calbourne went to bed about eleven p.m., as he usually does. Mrs. Latchmere and I sat up talking until about half-past twelve. To save you hunting up another mare's nest, I may tell you that she and I played together as children. At half-past twelve I left Domira and walked home by the shortest route. As I was going into my lodgings, the flattie on the beatcame up and I had a few minutes' chat with him about his eldest boy, who's sick. That flattie and I are quite old friends. He's a decent fellow. And then he moved on, and I went into the house and retired to bed. And this morning I was waked up by the young maid here, with a message to say I was wanted at once. That covers the ground, I think. You won't take my word for it, of course. You'll go and bother all these people, to check what I've given you. You're welcome, so far as I'm concerned, though they may not like it much, you know. Any other questions ? "

Dornfell had listened intently to the details of the narrative, but what had struck him most was the tone in which they were delivered. It reminded him, vaguely, of a beginner at his chess club who could never say " Check ! " without letting a tinge of exultation into his voice. It might quite well mean that Adeney was laughing at the ease with which he had produced an easily-confirmed account of his movements last night. But, it might mean something quite different : that he had laid a trap and thought Dornfell must inevitably fall into it. In either case, the inspector felt sure, this tale would turn out to be accurate when it was tested.

CHAPTER V

THE MACHINE

"YOU'VE asked me a fair number of questions, Inspector," Nicholas pointed out, with a spice of derision in his tone. "My turn now, I think. How does it feel to be a trespasser on enclosed premises? For that's what you are, at present."

"Not a bit of it," Dornfell denied with a snap. "I was called in by Mrs. Butterswick, who was in charge of the premises."

"That may be," retorted Nicholas coolly. "But I happen to be in charge now, in the absence of my cousin; and I have the pleasure of ordering you to remove yourself and your pals outside, without more ado. Or, in plain language: 'Get out!'"

This put Dornfell into a difficulty. He did not profess to know precisely how the law stood in these peculiar circumstances, and he had the uncomfortable knowledge that Adeney meant to make trouble if there were any slip. And behind Adeney loomed the figure of Mr. Calbourne, who had the reputation of being a remarkably astute legal adviser. Once, when in a very junior position, Dornfell had made a mistake, and the reprimand which ensued was still one of his more vivid recollections. As a matter of fact, he had little tangible evidence to prove that a crime had actually been perpetrated. Some cigar smoke, an upset ashtray, and a spot of blood on the floor: that was all he had to set against Adeney's very definite statements. He might be on the verge of what he termed " a most unholy bloomer."

On the other hand, suppose he backed out and then later on it transpired that some crime had really been committed. Where would he be then ? In a much worse hole, obviously.

Risk being over-zealous, or play for safety : these were the alternatives. What turned the scale in Dornfell's mind was not reason but that indefinable sixth sense which insists on signalling " Something wrong here."

" I'm going to search these premises," he announced curtly.

" You are, are you ? " Nicholas replied in an intentionally colourless tone. " At your own risk, then, remember that. And, naturally, as I'm in charge here, I shall oversee your doings."

The inspector bit his lip at this announcement. If there was anything fishy in the business, then Adeney was in it. Of that he was convinced. And the idea of conducting a search with a suspect at his elbow had no attraction for him. But if he refused, he had an uncomfortable certainty that Mr. Calbourne would have something to say on the subject. Short of putting Adeney under arrest, it was impossible to prevent him moving about as he chose in his sister's house, even if he insisted on making his movements coincide wfth those of the inspector.

" Do as you like, " he conceded. " You may be able to give some information as we go along."

" I can see that you do your job tidily, which is more to the point," Nicholas growled.

Evidently he was smarting under his defeat.

" I'll begin upstairs," the inspector said, after a moment's reflection.

He went to the door, summoned one of his men and sent him in search of Mrs. Butterswick.

" Tell her I'm upstairs," he directed.

The housekeeper joined them as they stood on the landing, and Dornfell turned to her with an unexpected question.

" Was Mrs. Deerhurst a nervous person ? "

" Nervous ? " echoed Mrs. Butterswick in a tone of contempt. " She was quite the other way. Many's the time I've wondered at her being able to stay in this house all alone at night, with never a thought of what might happen if a burglar got in. Nervous ! The only thing she *was* afraid of was fire, and that's something anyone might be scared of."

" Afraid of fire, was she ? " Dornfell queried, evidently with his mind on other things.

" Yes, she was always more than a bit afraid of fire," Mrs. Butterswick went on. " She had a special switch in her bedroom, so that when she went to bed she could switch off the current all over the house, and feel sure that it didn't make a short-circuit in the night and set the place ablaze. And very wise, too, I think."

" Very wise," agreed the inspector absently. " This is her room, is it ? "

He pushed open the door and went in, followed by the others.

" That's the switch there, beside her bed, so that she could pull it out last thing before she went to sleep," Mrs. Butterswick explained.

But the inspector seemed to have no interest in the switch. He glanced at the unslept-in bed with the filmy nightdress stretched on it.

" If she was going away, why is this bed made ready ? " he asked Nicholas.

Mrs. Butterswick hastily intervened. She had a feeling that it was next-door to profanation that this man from the police-station should be feasting his eyes on Hazel's night attire.

" Evie made down the bed before she left yesterday.

She always does that before going off for the day, unless it's her day off, and then I do it myself. You don't suppose Mrs. Deerhurst makes down her own bed, do you? " she ended scornfully.

"I see," Dornfell admitted, unperturbed. "You can leave things as they are. Now what I want to know is: what clothes are missing. That's what I needed you for, Mrs. Butterswick. You're bound to know what dresses, and so forth, she had. Go through the wardrobes and drawers and tell me what's missing."

Mrs. Butterswick, relieved to find that alien hands were not to profane her mistress's "pretties," as she put it, began her search by counting the various dresses and frocks which hung from their pegs. Hazel had a fairly extensive outfit, and when Mrs. Butterswick had gone through the whole series she looked a trifle puzzled. She began at the beginning once more, and repeated her search with greater care and deliberation. Then she turned to the two men with an expression of bewilderment through which a shade of fear showed itself.

"There's nothing missing here," she said in a curious voice. "Twice I've been over them, and there's nothing missing. Here's the one she was wearing when I left the house yesterday. That's funny."

"Go on with the other things—dressing-gowns and so forth," ordered the inspector.

As Mrs. Butterswick made her announcement, he had glanced at Nicholas's face and seen an unmistakable expression of surprise flit across it for an instant. Then the mask had come down again.

Mrs. Butterswick pursued her researches into the drawers of the tallboys, with results which evidently puzzled her as she went on. Finally she announced her conclusions, which the inspector took down in his notebook. He pondered over his list for a few moments, then turned to Nicholas with a rather unpleasant smile.

" Mrs. Deerhurst has gone away from home for a day or two, you told me ? Her choice in clothes rather surprises me. She was wearing corsets, a brassiere, a silk vest, ditto petticoat and knickers. She had two pairs of stockings on, and apparently a pair of bedroom slippers over a pair of walking shoes. She had no hat, though she carried a handbag with half a dozen handkerchiefs in it. And her outer garment was a bright silk kimono-dressing-gown. If she's abroad in that outfit, we shall hear of her very shortly, no doubt. It seems likely to cause comment, surely."

He stared intently at Nicholas, hoping to read something in his face. The mask seemed to have got slightly askew, and the inspector thought he saw perplexity mingled with a growing misgiving. Then Nicholas regained his control.

" Some dirty work here, that's plain," concluded the inspector. " I'm on velvet, after all. He won't talk so gay about mares' nests now, I guess."

If Nicholas concealed his thoughts, Mrs. Butterswick had less reticence. Concentrated on the task of noting the missing garments, item by item, she had not considered the list as a whole until Dornfell strung it together. Then, all in a moment, she seemed to see what lay behind that catalogue.

" Oh ! " she cried agitatedly. " I see what's happened. It's dreadful, sir ! Oh, poor thing ! She forgot to lock the door when she came upstairs for the night. She came up to this room and took off her frock and hung it up on its peg. Then she put on her dressing-gown and her bedroom slippers. And just then that scoundrel came to the front-door and found it open—unlocked, I mean. He must have got in and come upstairs, slinking up quietly so that she didn't hear him. Then he must have fallen on her.

She couldn't make any sort of struggle against a great brute like that. And he tied her hands and ankles with a pair of silk stockings from the drawer. It's the only thing he could use. And then he must have carried her downstairs and taken her away. In the car, perhaps. Goodness knows what he may have done to her, the brute. Or where he's taken her to. Oh, I can't bear to think of it!"

She gave every sign of a collapse of her nerves at the picture she had conjured up. The inspector hastened to throw cold water on her explanation, as the easiest way of bringing her back to normal.

"No good, I'm afraid, Mrs. Butterswick," he said kindly. "First, there's not the least sign of a struggle here. Everything's in apple-pie order. Second, your tale doesn't account for her walking shoes being missing. And her handbag. No, it won't do. Not that it isn't neat as far as it goes. But she'd have screamed, you know, and someone would have heard her, one would think."

He glanced at Nicholas's impassive face, and then added:

"Who do you mean by 'that scoundrel,' by the way?"

"Her husband, of course," Mrs. Butterswick declared. "You really don't think that's what happened?" she demanded anxiously, as though only too eager to have her theory dismissed. "You don't think he's taken her off somewhere, to a quiet place, where he could . . . kill her . . . without anyone hearing?"

Dornfell had reconsidered his last objection almost as he put it into words. Of course the girl might have been choked, so that she could not cry out. But he had seen enough of the state of Mrs. Butterswick's nerves to keep this to himself.

"You can't think of any reason why he should

take the outdoor shoes and the handbag?" he inquired.

"He might have taken them to make marks on the ground with, to pretend she'd gone away last night," Mrs. Butterswick suggested. "And she may have had money in her handbag that he needed."

Dornfell shook his head reassuringly.

"No good. All the garden paths are hard-rolled. You couldn't make an impression on them if you tried with a shoe. And if he needed money he'd have taken it and left the bag. No, it won't wash."

He considered for a moment, and then continued:

"You've got a box-room, I suppose? Some place where you keep trunks and suit-cases? Let's see if anything's missing from it."

But after examination, so far as Mrs. Butterswick could tell them, no suit-case or trunk was missing from the store. Dornfell made a search through the other rooms on that flat, but discovered nothing which seemed suspicious. Nor could he find anything worth noting in the ground-floor rooms which he had not hitherto entered. When he had finished this survey, he went to the telephone and rang up the police-station.

"The photographer and the finger-print man will be here in a little while," he explained as he came back into the hall. "In the meanwhile, I'm going to look through the drawing-room again."

Nicholas seemed to have resigned himself to allowing the search to proceed, though he made no pretence of liking it. He watched the inspector unlock the drawing-room door. Then he made a significant gesture to the housekeeper.

"You'd better come with us, Mrs. Butterswick," he suggested. "There's no harm in having an extra witness, in case anything turns up. No objection to that, Inspector, I suppose? Mrs. Butterswick will be useful, since she knows the lie of the land even better than I do."

Dornfell made no overt objection. Obviously there was something in Nicholas's suggestion. They entered the drawing-room, Mrs. Butterswick in the rear, with her eyes steadfastly averted from the smear of blood on the parquet. Nicholas stepped forward, examined it for a moment or two without comment, and then stood aside.

Dornfell had given a casual glance at the clock on the mantelpiece, and seemed surprised at the hour it marked. He compared it with his wrist-watch, and Nicholas, catching the movement, consulted his own watch.

" A bit slow, isn't it ? " he commented.

" Nearly four hours behind time," the inspector agreed. " Three hours forty-four minutes, to be exact." He went over to the mantelpiece and examined it. " Mains-controlled electric ? That's funny."

Mrs. Butterswick was completely surprised by this incident.

" I've never known that clock go wrong before," she said, in a puzzled tone. " It's a special clock. It was a present to Mrs. Deerhurst from Mr. Mandrell—one of his own inventions, she told me. She's his secretary, you know. Some of these clocks need to be twirled at the back to make them start, but this one's a self-starter. It stopped at night when the current went off, and we had to set it right in the morning by the wireless. Elsewise, it kept time to a second."

Some recollection of the fate of " My Grandfather's Clock " seemed to flit across her mind and increase her trepidation.

" I wonder now," she began. " ' *For it stopped short, never to go again* . . .' Mrs. Deerhurst thought a lot of that clock," she interrupted herself suddenly.

"Well, it's going again, all right," Dornfell pointed out, not unsympathetically. "It only wants re-setting. But don't touch it, Mrs. Butterswick. Nothing must be shifted, you understand?"

Though ostensibly he addressed the housekeeper, it was really Adeney whom he meant to warn, and he glanced at him as he spoke. For the first time he caught Nicholas completely off his guard. He was biting his lip in obviously genuine perplexity, and staring at the clock dial as though it had set him some riddle which he could not solve. Then he shook his head as though dismissing the problem, whatever it was.

"A slip in the cogs somewhere," he suggested in what was meant to be a light tone. "Wants oil, perhaps, or something like that."

"Probably," Dornfell concurred. "Three hours forty-four minutes," he said half aloud as he jotted down a note in his book.

Then he went to the door and called one of the constables.

"Teale! Get a newspaper and unbuild this fire set in the grate here. See if you find anything amongst the coals."

The constable procured a paper, spread it on the floor, and began to remove the coals and sticks from the hearth piecemeal, examining each fragment as he placed it on the paper. The inspector watched for a few moments to make sure he was doing his task properly. Then he turned away.

"When does the postman come round, by the way?" he asked Mrs. Butterswick.

"He ought to be here very shortly," the housekeeper explained. "Nothing came by the first delivery this morning, but he'll be here soon on his second round, I expect."

Again the inspector went to the door to give instructions.

"Hamsell! When the postman comes round, I want to see him. Keep your eye on the road and call him in, if he doesn't come up to the door."

Dornfell came back into the drawing-room, and seemed to hesitate before setting definitely to work.

"Care to smoke a cigar?" he suggested to Nicholas, as though to take the edge off the formality of the proceedings.

Nicholas shook his head.

"I thought you might offer me one," Dornfell hinted awkwardly.

"Sorry it didn't occur to me," Nicholas apologised in obvious irony. "You see, I don't smoke cigars, do I, Mrs. Butterswick?"

"Oh, no, sir," Mrs. Butterswick confirmed. "Cigarettes a-plenty; but I've never seen you with a cigar."

Her testimony convinced Dornfell that he would have to look elsewhere for the cigar-smoker of the night before. He did his best to cover his *faux pas* by stepping over to the little escritoire, pulling out the chair and sitting down, preparatorily to beginning his search. As he did so, his foot touched something in the well of the desk, and he stooped down to remove the obstruction. It was a brown millboard box with a white label stuck on the lid.

"*Library Books,*" read the inspector from the label. "Addressed to *The Times* Book Club. *From Mrs. H. Deerhurst. Subscriber's Number:* GN. 7079. Empty"—he weighed it in his hand and shook it as he spoke. "Is this name and number in Mrs. Deerhurst's handwriting?"

"Oh, no," Mrs. Butterswick explained. "That's a label they send in the parcel with the books. You just stick it on the box when you want to post them back to London. It's the library people who write that.

You have to send the books back in that box when the next lot comes."

The inspector nodded and laid the box on the floor beside him, after opening it and glancing inside to see that it was really empty. He made a rapid inspection of the pigeon-holes above the writing-desk, noting the tidy stacking of envelopes, private letter-paper, post-cards, letter-cards, and other odds and ends, including a pink packet of application cards and return slips from *The Times* Book Club. One compartment held a bundle of neatly-docketed unpaid accounts in a rubber strap and a corresponding one of receipted bills. Evidently Mrs. Deerhurst was more than usually methodical in her business affairs, and the inspector noticed that the last receipt was dated on the previous day. In another division were a few letters, also docketed.

The desk itself was almost bare. There was a small twine-box, a fountain-pen, a little letter-balance, and a rocker-blotter with a silver mounting. Dornfell picked this up and examined the absorbent surface, but it was a mere blotch of overlaid impressions, quite indecipherable.

The inspector deferred an examination of the docketed letters, and continued his search by pulling open the top drawer of the escritoire. And here he came upon something which completely baffled him.

It was some sort of machine, mounted upon an aluminium baseboard about fourteen inches long and eleven broad. The base-board was hinged in the middle, like an ordinary chess-board, and at each side, an inch or so from the edge, it was pierced by a line of eighteen holes about a quarter of an inch in diameter. At one end was a peculiar arrangement which Dornfell finally decided was a clip of some sort, though its precise purpose escaped him. At the other end was a curious piece of mechanism mounted on a rack. Three levers ending in keys like those of a typewriter extended to right and left ; and an oval plate at the extreme right was also apparently a key of some kind, so that the control mechanism was spaced thus :

```
*           *
  *       *    0
    *   *
```

Dornfell stared at his find uncomprehendingly for a moment, then turned to Mrs. Butterswick for enlightenment.

" What's this ? " he demanded.

But Mrs. Butterswick quite obviously had never seen the machine before.

" I couldn't tell you," she admitted at once. " I never set eyes on it till this minute. I never pry into Mrs. Deerhurst's desk," she added with a shade of indignation in her tone. " It's no business of mine."

The inspector ignored the implied criticism.

" It looks almost new," he ruminated aloud. " No sign of much use about it."

He slipped on his rubber gloves and was about to begin a closer examination of the machine when Mrs. Butterswick had a bright idea.

" It'll be one of Mr. Mandrell's inventions, maybe," she suggested. " Something he's wanted to get tried. And he's given it to Mrs. Deerhurst to test for him. I know he once lent her an adding-machine or whatever they call them—things that do sums for you and all that kind of work."

" No dials on it," Dornfell pointed out conclusively. " It's not anything of that sort."

He glanced covertly at Nicholas to see if he recognised the thing, but quite plainly Nicholas had never seen the instrument before and knew no more about its purpose than Dornfell himself.

The inspector set to work to examine the mysterious machine more closely. He was not mechanically-minded, but the thing seemed very simple when one looked at it. Gingerly he put his finger on one of the levers, avoiding the keys for fear of destroying finger-prints, and depressing it gently. As he pushed it down, the " key-board " moved one space along the rack, just as a typewriter carriage moves when a key is depressed.

Emboldened by this success, Dornfell tried the lever supporting the oval plate, and again the " carriage " travelled one space along the rack. Then, more by accident than design, he depressed two of the key-levers simultaneously. Instead of jamming, as a typewriter would do under this treatment, the little machine moved as before. He repeated his operations several times, and at last, as the carriage came near the end of its line of travel, a little bell went " ting ! " like the warning bell of a typewriter.

" A typewriter of sorts, seemingly," mused Dornfell. " But where's the type ? And why has it only six keys and a space-bar ? "

" Perhaps it's meant to write in some foreign language," suggested Mrs. Butterswick hopefully.

The inspector grunted for all reply and then proceeded to lift the carriage and rack completely off the base-board and turn it upside down to examine the place where he expected the type to be. But when he did so, he found merely a smooth plate, faintly engraved with tiny circles arranged in sets of six.

" Like the pattern of a six-blank at dominoes," he commented to himself. " Thirty-seven of 'em, side by side. Something to do with the six keys, evidently. But it beats me what happens when you press these keys. Barring the carriage moving, I don't see any results."

He replaced the carriage, discovering as he did

so that it had two pegs on its underside which fitted into the holes on either side of the base-board. Then he lifted the little machine and put it back into the drawer, which he closed.

" What has Mrs. Deerhurst got to do with Mr. Mandrell ? " he asked, turning to Mrs. Butterswick.

" She's a sort of private secretary to him," Mrs. Butterswick explained. " I don't know exactly what she does, but it's something like that, very confidential, for she never mentions him to me, one way or another."

" The inventing man ? " queried the inspector.

Mrs. Butterswick nodded. An idea seemed to cross Dornfell's mind.

" She'll know what new inventions he has in hand, perhaps ? " he said, half to himself. " I wonder, now."

But what he wondered, he kept to himself.

Before he could continue there came an interruption. The police surgeon was ushered into the room by Constable Hamsell. The inspector rose to greet him.

" Nothing much for you to do, doctor," he admitted, " but I'd like you to have a look at that patch of blood and see if you make anything of it. Perhaps you could give us an idea how long it's been there."

Dr. Bonchurch was a man of few words. He knelt down on the floor and examined the dark spot on the parquet for a few moments. Then he rose to his feet again.

" Might as well ask me to tell your fortune," he said gruffly. " It's coagulated. Could have happened any time in the last few hours. Nothing to go on, there. You noticed the threads of some stuff in it, cotton-wool by the look of them ? "

Dornfell had missed this, but he was too wise to admit his oversight. Instead he made a non-committal gesture and passed to a fresh point.

" Nothing peculiar about it, I suppose ? "

"Nothing to see. You'd better give me a sample, though. The Chief Constable likes to know which brand of blood turns up in a case. He's made it pay in one or two cases before now. You know what I want ?"

"I'll see to it," the inspector assured him. "Sorry to have bothered you, doctor, but I just wanted to be quite sure."

Dr. Bonchurch was evidently a busy man. He wasted no time in farewells but went off immediately. As he closed the door behind him, Constable Teale made a movement to attract the inspector's attention.

"I've been through all this stuff, sir, and the only thing in it is a cigar-band."

He handed it over as he spoke, and Dornfell, after a glance at it, stowed it in an envelope which he put in his pocket.

"You can put all that stuff back into the fireplace again," he ordered.

He reseated himself at the escritoire and pulled open another drawer. As he did so, a faint ejaculation escaped him. The drawer contained a roll of cotton-wool, wrapped in blue paper, and it was plain that some of the cotton-wool had been torn away.

"What did Mrs. Deerhurst want this for," demanded Dornfell, indicating the roll to Mrs. Butterswick.

"Oh, that ? I once burned my wrist, with some boiling water," Mrs. Butterswick explained. "It made a big blister—sore, it was—and the bandages in the First Aid case weren't quite big enough. So after that Mrs. Deerhurst got this big roll of cottonwool, to keep just in case of accidents."

"Has it ever been used ?" inquired the inspector in a casual tone.

"Only once," Mrs. Butterswick explained. "At least, only once that I know of. Oakley cut his hand

—the gardener, I mean—and Mr. Adeney tied it up for him with some of this cottonwool. That's the only time I ever knew it to be used."

The inspector threw a shrewd glance at Nicholas to see how he took this evidence. Cottonwool fibres in the blood-patch, cottonwool in the drawer, whose presence could be known only to people about the house. And Adeney had actually used some of this cottonwool to patch up the gardener's hand, which made it fairly certain that he knew where to lay his hands on the roll at a moment's notice.

Dornfell turned back to the escritoire, closed the drawer and opened another. This contained an almost complete ream of typewriting paper, quarto size, neatly stacked in a pile. The inspector turned round to Mrs. Butterswick.

"Has Mrs. Deerhurst a typewriter ?"

"Yes, she has," Mrs. Butterswick declared. "Or rather, she hasn't just now. She's lent it to Mr. Adeney for the present. He has it."

"Quite so," Nicholas broke in, with a barely-suppressed sneer on his face. "I do some writing. '*How I Enjoyed Prison*,' and that kind of thing. Snappy articles like that. Naturally my cousin lent me her typewriter, since she could get along without it. Any comments on that ?"

Instead of answering, the inspector pulled the drawer still further out. Behind the block of typewriting paper was a pile of other sheets, one of which Dornfell drew out to examine. It was stiff yellow-brown wrapping-paper, apparently, and the sheet measured about twenty inches by fifteen—"a bit small for wrapping up anything but the smallest parcel," as Dornfell commented to himself. It occurred to him that it might serve to wrap up a book for the post. But to judge by the height of the pile, there was enough paper there to wrap up half-a-gross of volumes;

and that seemed a bigger store than anyone could need for current use.

"Any notion what this was used for?" he demanded from Mrs. Butterswick.

"I never saw it before," she declared, with a puzzled look.

The inspector's eye caught the brown millboard box beside his feet and that gave him a fresh idea.

"Perhaps she used it to wrap up single volumes to post back to this circulating library?"

Mrs. Butterswick shook her head emphatically.

"No, you have to send the books back in these boxes they supply," she explained. "That's their rule."

"But suppose you want to keep a volume back to read at leisure?"

"Then you've got to send another in its place from the three they've just sent you," Mrs. Butterswick asserted.

"Oh, you can send back a single volume if you want to," Nicholas broke in. "They don't mind, so long as you don't have more than three books at a time and if you return their box honestly some time or other."

The inspector nodded non-committally, replaced the wrapping-paper on the top ot its pile, and closed the drawer. He had now completed his examination of one tier of the drawers, so he began on the other side of the desk. The top drawer contained merely an assortment of packs of playing cards, some bridge-markers, pencils, and one or two boxes of cigarettes, and three cheque-book stubs held together by a ribbon band. A cursory examination satisfied Dornfell and he passed to the next drawer. Here, at the front, he found some boxes of private notepaper and envelopes to match, neatly packed. Behind them was an empty space which seemed to have been deliberately kept clear, since the boxes did not encroach upon it. And at one corner of this space the inspector noticed a small fragment of wrapping-paper like that in the other drawer. He took it out to examine it and found that it was apparently a corner which had been produced by some error in the cutting-machine. Evidently it had been left adhering to a sheet and had become detached in handling. The vacant space in the drawer corresponded roughly to the size of the complete sheets of brown paper. Dornfell tucked the fragment into an envelope and added it to his store. Then, opening the last drawer in the desk, he discovered that it held merely some unfinished embroidery work, with hanks of silk, and a needle-case.

As he reclosed this drawer, Constable Hamsell admitted three officials: the finger-print expert and the photographers. They needed no instructions except on one point.

"Take a photograph of that clock," Dornfell directed. "Get the hands sharp--make a snapshot of it. And note the exact time when you make the exposure. We may as well have a definite record of how much it's behind time. And, by the way, Hamsell, go and ring up the power-station and find out if there's been any breakdown in the lighting cables in this district within the last twenty-four hours."

Then a thought seemed to strike him and he turned to Mrs. Butterswick.

"Have you any notion when this clock was at the right time?"

Mrs. Butterswick pondered for a few moments, and then her face brightened.

"It was all right yesterday morning," she explained. "The night before last I forgot to wind up my watch, and it stopped just after breakfast time, in the middle of my work. So I came in here and set it by the clock when I wound it up again. It's at the right time now, so the clock must have been right yesterday morning."

The inspector verified her statement by a glance at her watch. Then he turned back to the desk and took from its pigeon-hole the bundle of docketed letters.

"We'll have to go into another room," he pointed out. "We'd be in the photographer's way here."

"What are you doing with these letters?" Nicholas demanded as Dornfell rose from his chair with the packet in his hand.

"Going to read through them in case there's anything useful in them."

Nicholas obviously resented this invasion of his sister's private affairs, but a glance about him showed that he was in presence of *force majeure*, and that no protest could be effective.

"Very well," he agreed in a sullen tone. "Have it your own way. Thank the Lord I'm not a policeman."

CHAPTER VI

THE REGISTERED LETTER

AS they were leaving the drawing-room, Constable Hamsell came up with the news that no electrical trouble had been reported in the district during the previous night. All cables were in perfect order. The inspector showed no particular satisfaction at the message. Clearly it had not helped him much. He went into the dining-room, sat down at the breakfast-table, and slipped the rubber band from the packet of letters. Then he glanced up at Nicholas, who was watching him jealously.

"I don't like this any more than you do," Dornfell said in a semi-apologetic tone, which he evidently meant to be conciliatory. "But——"

He spread out his hands as though to indicate that he could not help himself. Nicholas made no answer. Obviously he was not placated by the inspector's plea of duty.

The packet was a small one, and Dornfell soon finished his examination. The documents were of the most ordinary description: an estimate from a decorator, a note about an erroneous bill from a tradesman, a request for a pass-book from the bank, and half-a-dozen private letters from friends and acquaintances, none of which threw the least light upon Hazel's disappearance. The inspector shuffled them together automatically, snapped the rubber band round the packet, and offered it to Nicholas.

"You'd better keep them," he suggested. "There's nothing there that's of any use to us."

As Nicholas took the documents, Dornfell swung round in his chair to face him squarely.

"You know," he said in a kindlier tone than he had hitherto used, "you're making a mistake over this affair. You've not been exactly helpful. You've got a grudge against the police. Anyone can see that, and I don't altogether wonder at it. But I want to put it this way to you. Mrs. Deerhurst has disappeared and I don't mind telling you that I'm not very easy in my mind as to what's happened to her. For all I can tell, she may be in danger . . . perhaps in very grave danger. It's on the cards, anyhow. And if she's in any danger, then it's our business—yours as well as mine—to get on the track immediately before anything worse happens. And if she's come to any harm, then it's our business—yours as well as mine—to see that somebody pays for it. That's how I look at it. That's how I put it to you. Anyone can see you're holding back something. You know something that you haven't told me. Now, I put it to you, why not lay the cards on the table and give us all the help you can? I don't mind telling you I'm worried about the business, and I want you to take a hand and let us get ahead as quick as may be."

Nicholas listened to this appeal with a darkening face.

"Soft sawder," was his brutal verdict, after a moment's thought. "Much encouragement you've given me, haven't you? When I gave you information, you as good as called me a liar. You can find things out for yourself—if you can."

The inspector's kindliness vanished suddenly.

"Very well," he said abruptly. "I'll make a note of that."

A knock at the door interrupted him, and Constable Hamsell appeared, ushering in a rather bewildered postman with his bundle of letters for delivery in his hand.

" I caught him in the road," the constable explained. " He had no letters for the house on this round."

" Nothing to worry about," the inspector reassured the rather scared man before him. " We're not after you for stealing letters or anything of that sort. All we want is some information. What's your name, by the way ? "

The postman, it appeared, was one of those people who cannot be content with merely answering the questions put to them.

" Fred Cutler's my name. I've been ten years on this round and nobody's ever had a complaint to make against me that I ever heard of."

" Nobody's making one now," said the inspector testily. " Do you bring letters here on the afternoon delivery ? "

" Yes. I have the first delivery and this one. Jerdan does the next, and then I do the last delivery in the afternoon."

" Then you delivered letters here yesterday afternoon ? "

Cutler reflected for a moment or two before replying.

" That's so. I remember now. I brought two circulars and a registered letter, a big fat one."

" What time was that ? " demanded the inspector.

" That would be about six o'clock, within a minute or two. It was just an average delivery, neither one thing nor another, so I was here at my usual time."

" Somebody signed for that registered letter, of course. Mrs. Deerhurst, was it ? "

" No, I didn't see her. It was this way. As I came up to the gate Mr. Adeney here was standing, looking up and down the road. So I just handed him the letters and got him to sign for the registered one. I know him as well as I know my own brother, so it was all right. The receipt's quite in order."

Nicholas broke in abruptly.

" That's quite correct. There was a long envelope, pretty bulky. It had an embossed stamp on the flap, only half-covered with the wax of the seal, and I happened to glance at it. The letter was from Elvaston and Fairlop, Mrs. Deerhurst's stockbrokers."

" Ah ? " said the inspector thoughtfully. " And what did you do with it after you got it from the postman ? "

" Brought it into the house, of course, and propped it up against the clock over there," explained Nicholas, nodding towards the mantelpiece.

" It's not there now," commented the inspector.

" No, Mrs. Deerhurst took it, I expect."

" And you put the circulars along with it ? "

" Yes."

The inspector glanced round the room and his eyes fell on a waste-paper basket in one corner. He got up and examined it, fishing out some crumpled papers which he unfolded. Two circulars and two envelopes rewarded his search. He smoothed out one of the envelopes and handed it to the postman, pointing to the postmark.

" Does that correspond to your delivery ? "

Cutler inspected the postmark and seemed to make a mental calculation.

" Yes, that would be about right," he admitted. " This was posted in town before midday, so it would be in the afternoon delivery, the six o'clock one. Besides, I seem to remember the envelope. It's got a picture on it."

" Very well," said the inspector. " Just remember that carefully, Cutler. By the way, you didn't see Mrs. Deerhurst anywhere about when you delivered the letters—in the garden or anywhere ? "

Cutler shook his head.

" No, I didn't see her then. There was nobody about barring Mr. Adeney here."

The inspector jotted a few lines in his notebook and then passed the book to Cutler.

"Just read over that and put your name to it, if it's correct," he ordered. "Then we won't need you any more just now."

Cutler read over the notes of his evidence, pulled out a stub of pencil and appended his signature, evidently relieved to be done with this affair. When he had handed back the book he looked interrogatively at Dornfell and retired, accompanied by the constable.

"I must telephone for a moment," the inspector said, by way of excusing himself.

"To Elvaston and Fairlop, I suppose?" inquired Nicholas with a smile which seemed to have gone awry.

"Yes, to Elvaston and Fairlop," confirmed Dornfell. "I didn't see any trace of that letter in the packet I examined," he added in a significant tone.

In a few minutes he came back with a sterner look on his face.

"That letter had bearer bonds in it; five bonds for one hundred pounds each. You've no idea where it's gone?"

"None whatever," Nicholas asserted coolly, but the inspector saw that he seemed worried by the news.

"Curious, keeping securities of that sort in the house when she hasn't a safe on the premises," said the inspector thoughtfully.

Nicholas volunteered an explanation, rather to Dornfell's surprise.

"She sends all her securities to her solicitors. They have a big fireproof strong-room."

"H'm!" commented the inspector. "Would she have had time to post them last night before the post offices shut? When did you leave here, by the way?"

"About six-fifteen," Nicholas answered, taken off his guard by the naturalness of the inspector's query.

"Ah! Six-fifteen? Then, apparently, you must

have been the last person who saw her before she disappeared. H'm! You won't reconsider things—tell me rather more than you've done so far? No? Then I'll put a straight question to you. Do you profit in any way if she happens to be dead?"

For just a moment Nicholas hesitated, and Dornfell noted that suspicious pause.

"I don't mind telling you how things stand," Nicholas explained as though he were picking his words. "Mr. Calbourne pressed Mrs. Deerhurst to make a will the other night. She'd made none, and he pointed out that if she died intestate, Deerhurst would get all her money, and I'd get nothing from her estate. So far as I know, she's made no will. That's the position."

He seemed to be eager to know how the inspector was affected by this information, for he watched Dornfell's face keenly as he made his statement.

"I can see as far through a stone wall as most," the inspector answered, without betraying anything in his expression. "What you mean to say is that Deerhurst is the only person financially interested in his wife's death, eh? And she was afraid of Deerhurst, eh? H'm! That's a point, certainly."

He reflected for a few moments. When he spoke again it was in the kindlier tone which he had used before.

"I don't know anything about your troubles. I didn't read the trial at the time. Too intricate for me, these financial affairs. But perhaps you can tell me this. Do you think Deerhurst, now that he's come out, has any financial resources? I'd like to know."

In his turn, Nicholas paused to reflect before answering.

"I don't know," he admitted. "If he had anything, it must have been fairly well stowed away.

They certainly left me with just what I stood up in by the time they'd finished—the creditors, I mean. But Deerhurst knew the smash was coming, long before; and he may have taken his precautions. He was just the sort that would," he ended, in a bitter tone.

On this subject, evidently, Nicholas had no feelings of reticence the inspector noted, and he followed up the line of inquiry at once.

"Had he any close friends, people likely to know more about his affairs?"

"Louis Granfield, the solicitor, was one. They were as thick as thieves, in the old days. One funny thing, I remember, which just shows it. Before our smash Granfield got rid of a lot of our shares which he'd been holding. I heard some talk about it at the time. Some people who took over the shares weren't too pleased, and there was a bit of gossip about it. Inside information, given by Deerhurst to his pal in time to let Granfield out. That's what was said at the time. By the way, Granfield came here the other night to see Mrs. Deerhurst. He'd some notion of playing honest broker, I gathered. Mr. Calbourne could explain it better than I can."

"We'll see about that," the inspector promised. "Now, had Deerhurst any other cronies—or relations?"

"I met a cousin of his once," Nicholas answered promptly. "But I don't think they were very thick. He came from a different part of the country, you know, and I really knew very little about his family affairs or any old friends he may have had before he came into the firm."

Dornfell congratulated himself on having worked Nicholas into a more communicative mood, and now he put his last question.

"You think Deerhurst had a hand in this business?"

To his surprise Nicholas froze immediately.

" You can form your own opinion on that, just as well as I can," he said sharply.

The inspector saw at a glance that he had failed, and he had the wit to refrain from probing further.

" Then there's nothing more to say," he said, keeping vexation out of his voice. " I've some other things to see about now."

He went out into the garden, leaving Nicholas behind. Oakley was stolidly rolling one of the lawns, as though nothing had happened that day. He seemed a bovine sort of man, with large unspeculative eyes which he turned on Dornfell as the inspector approached him.

" I want a word with you," the inspector began. " You know who I am ? "

Evidently Oakley had heard all about him, probably from the maid, for he nodded, leaning on the handle of his roller.

" You're employed by Mrs. Deerhurst ? "

Oakley nodded slowly, and then, with an evident effort, opened his mouth.

" Yes."

Clearly he was a taciturn personage, one of those people who yield information only in response to outer stimulus.

" You're gardener, and chauffeur, aren't you ? "

" I look after the garden and I clean the car," Oakley corrected him.

" When do you leave off work ? " Dornfell demanded.

" Five o'clock, weekdays ; one o'clock, Saturdays."

" When did you leave here yesterday ? "

" 'Bout three o'clock."

" What made you leave early ? " demanded the inspector.

" 'Cause Mr. Adeney told me to."

" Did he give you any reason ? "

" Told me Mrs. Deerhurst wanted me to go round to Brand's Nurseries and see them about a greenhouse she was thinking of putting up, and stuff to put into it."

" You didn't see Mrs. Deerhurst herself ? "

" No."

" When do you clean the car ? "

" First thing in the morning."

" Did you clean it this morning ? "

" No. One of your men stopped me."

" Have you a key of the garage ? "

Oakley fumbled in his waistcoat pocket and produced a Yale key.

" Let's see the car," the inspector ordered.

Oakley abandoned his roller and led the way to the garage which formed part of the structure of the house. He threw open the door and Dornfell saw a small navy-blue saloon inside. Some tins of petrol were ranged at the back of the garage, near a second door which gave direct access to the house. The inspector went up to the car and examined it.

" A new car ? " he asked.

" Bought 'bout three weeks ago," Oakley explained.

" It doesn't need much cleaning in this weather," commented Dornfell. " There's no mud on the roads, just dust in places."

Oakley nodded without comment.

" You have a key of this garage. Mrs. Deerhurst would have one. Anybody else ? " inquired the inspector.

" Mr. Adeney," replied Oakley with his usual laconism.

The inspector reflected that neither Adeney nor his cousin needed a key, since they could get into the garage through the house and could secure the outer door by merely closing it, since it had a Yale lock.

" Did you see Evie Sutton leave the premises before yon went off yesterday afternoon ? "

Oakley gave an affirmative nod.

"Where were you last night, by the way?"

"At home. Sitting up with my kid. He's ill. Doctor was in twice during the night."

"Hard lines," sympathised the inspector. "Is he any better this morning?"

"Doctor says he's round the turn now."

"That's good," said Dornfell heartily. "Who's your doctor, by the way?"

"Dr. Verran."

"Oh, you're in good hands then. That's something. I hope the youngster'll be all right again soon. And now that's all I want from you just now."

Oakley nodded and trudged off to his roller, recommencing his labour on the lawn as though it were the only thing that interested him. Dornfell, at the start of his interrogation, had been surprised by the gardener's detachment from the affairs of Norwood House; but evidently his child's illness was taking up his mind. The inspector stood for a moment or two watching the heavy figure dragging the roller backward and forward over the grass; then he turned his back and began to stroll aimlessly about the garden, reflecting on what he had learned since his arrival at Norwood House.

The obvious starting-point was Hazel Deerhurst's disappearance. Now disappearance of that sort may be either voluntary or involuntary. Dornfell had a systematic mind and he proceeded to tackle the two possibilities in turn.

Assume a voluntary disappearance, and what followed? Mrs. Butterswick was a transparently honest witness, with more in her than he had supposed at the first glance. By no means a fool, in fact. And if one thing was plain, it was that Mrs. Butterswick adored her mistress, and that she had been perturbed by the possible return of Deerhurst. But her views must be merely a fainter reflection of those of her mistress. Ergo, Hazel Deerhurst must have been extremely apprehensive about meeting her husband. That might account for a sudden decision to decamp, leaving no address.

But that, the inspector reflected, did not fit in with the impression he had formed of Hazel Deerhurst's character. She wasn't a nervous girl, or she would never have preferred to spend her nights all alone in a detached villa. Fire was the only thing she feared, it seemed. And she was business-like, as all her affairs showed ; and therefore she was likely to look ahead, rather than to act on mere impulse.

As to the peculiar selection shown in the missing garments, the inspector had his own solution. Mrs. Deerhurst might easily have bought a new dress which Mrs. Butterswick had never seen. A new suit-case, too, could have been bought, brought home in the car, and taken up to her room without anyone noticing it. Nothing in that side of the thing except that if the list really represented all that had been taken, then Hazel Deerhurst either meant to be away only for a day or two, or else she intended to buy other clothes as she needed them.

"I wonder how much money she had in hand," Dornfell reflected. "That might tell us something."

But when he turned to the arguments on the other side they seemed to put a voluntary disappearance out of the question.

First, Adeney was a rank bad witness, and Adeney had declared he knew that his cousin meant to decamp. His manner when he said it was enough to discredit any story. Therefore Adeney was lying ; and as he was supporting the suggestion of voluntary disappearance, that made the hypothesis less probable. But why should Adeney insist that his cousin had gone off entirely of her own accord ? That was a bit of a puzzle, the inspector admitted to himself. Adeney had laid himself out to convince the police that they were after a mare's nest and to get the whole affair hushed up. Why?

In the second place, the idea of voluntary disappearance did not square with the other facts. It didn't account for that patch of blood for one thing; or that self-starting mains-controlled clock being so far out of its reckoning; nor for that pinch or two of red powder on the floor. That was heavy stuff, as the inspector remembered, certainly not rouge or anything of that sort.

No, take it all in all, voluntary disappearance didn't fit the bill. Still, it would be as well to take precautions, have inquiries made on the bus routes and at the railway stations. To judge from Mrs. Butterswick's description, Hazel Deerhurst must have been the kind of girl that men would look twice at, and railway officials and bus conductors are human, like the rest of us.

Dornfell turned to the alternative hypothesis—foul play. And at once the figure of Deerhurst sprang into the foreground, dim and sinister, very much as it had loomed in Mrs. Butterswick's imagination. Deerhurst was out of prison just at the critical moment; some man—a cigar-smoker—had been in that drawing-room last night; and Deerhurst was the person who would profit directly by his wife's death, in hard cash. On the face of things, he was the only person who *would* profit by it.

There might be something in Mrs. Butterswick's theory after all, the inspector mused. If the fellow had arrive in a car, he might easily have overpowered his wife; carried her to the car, alive or dead; and disposed of her anywhere within a radius of a hundred miles. That would fit in with most of the facts, easily enough. It would account for her *déshabillé*, if he had made his way in through that unlocked front door just at the moment when she was undressing to go to bed. It would explain the presence of that blood-patch on the drawing-room parquet. It would fit the unslept-in bed, the cigar-reek, the overset ash-tray, provided he had got her down to the drawing-room on pretence that he wanted to talk over their affairs. It might even, in time, suggest something about that patch of red powder.

But most certainly it wouldn't square with Adeney's evidence. And with that, the inspector's thoughts turned to Adeney himself. What game was he playing? For Dornfell was convinced he was playing some crooked game of his own. On the face of things, he and his cousin were on the best of terms; the fact that he had a latchkey and a key of the garage proved that well enough, not to speak of her lending him her typewriter. Besides, anyone could see that Mrs. Butterswick was wholly on Hazel Deerhurst's side; and it was plain enough that she had a kindly feeling for Adeney. She wouldn't have had that if there had been friction between him and his cousin; and she had the best chance of noting any such friction if it had been there. Further, Adeney stood to gain nothing from his cousin's death, as things stood. There was not the shadow of a motive.

And yet one peculiar thing had struck the inspector. It was curious that, although Adeney seemed anxious to give Deerhurst a bad character, he hadn't supported the housekeeper's suggestions that Deerhurst was at the back of the affair. In fact, by his lies, he had gone out of his way to exclude Deerhurst's having any direct hand in his cousin's disappearance; certainly he had not given the least hint that Deerhurst had been mixed up in foul play in that connection. One would have imagined he would have caught at any straw in an attempt to incriminate Deerhurst, instead of ruling him out by these lies about Hazel Deerhurst's going off on private business of her own. On the face of it, why should Adeney be so anxious to hush the whole affair up, as he had striven to do at the very start? The inspector could find no answer to that riddle.

Then his thoughts turned to that mysterious machine which he had discovered in the drawer of the escritoire. Mrs. Deerhurst acted as Mandrell's secretary, according to Mrs. Butterswick. Dornfell knew little about the ways of inventors, but he felt fairly sure that they did not bruit their inventions abroad until the Patents Office had made things all right. Mandrell's inventions had brought him in pots of money, as the inspector phrased it to himself. All the more reason for him keeping them hush-hush till the time was ripe. *Ergo*, his private secretary would need to be a reliable, responsible person. And further, that private secretary might—in fact, would—know a good deal about the things he was working out at the moment. Mrs. Butterswick had mentioned some invention or other which Mandrell had lent to Mrs. Deerhurst so that she could try it out. That proved she was very much in the inventor's confidence. . . .

Suddenly the inspector saw the whole affair from a fresh viewpoint. That girl had valuable knowledge—information worth hundreds of thousands, perhaps, about Mandrell's latest inventions. Suppose someone had thought it worth while to get her kidnapped, and screw that information out of her. And with that, the inspector glimpsed something which would account for Adeney's behaviour. Suppose he were in the plot? He knew how much his cousin knew of Mandrell's affairs. He was the person who had got rid of Oakley before his normal hour. He could have got into the house without exciting his cousin's suspicions. He and his pals, whoever they were, could have kidnapped her.

And when they had got Mandrell's secrets out of her, they could have turned her loose. Would she have given away her brother, even after that? Adeney would be able to gauge that better than most. And *that* accounted neatly for his effort to burke the whole business at the very start, and for his lying to cover up the trail.

The only thing which deterred the inspector from whole-hearted acceptance of his hypothesis was the illogical feeling that "these things don't happen hereabouts." Reason, faint at the back of his mind, protested: "But they do happen elsewhere, so why not here?"

Then a fresh thought crossed his mind, and he made a tour of the garden, examining closely to see if any fresh digging had been done in the last twenty-four hours.

He finished with a sigh of relief.

"She's not *there*, anyhow."

Somehow, Mrs. Butterswick had given him an attractive picture of the missing girl. He hated to think that she might have been the source of that blood on the drawing-room parquet.

CHAPTER VII

THE ADENEY DISASTER

SIR CLINTON DRIFFIELD, Chief Constable of the county, had spent the day on a tour of inspection in a distant district. There had been a rather intricate inquiry into a discipline case at Ambledown, which had cost time. Chancing to pass Talgarth Grange on his way back, he dropped in for tea with his old friend Wendover, and the upshot had been that he brought Wendover home with him to spend a day or two. They were both chess enthusiasts, but, living so far apart, they had not many opportunities of facing each other across a board unless one paid a visit to the other. Nor was this the only taste they had in common. Wendover was an eager student of criminology, and prided himself on being something better than a mere Watson. He had built up at the Grange a collection of books on crime which rivalled that on the Chief Constable's shelves; and nothing gave him greater pleasure than to follow out any case which was engaging Sir Clinton's official attention.

Dinner over, they passed into Sir Clinton's library, where he busied himself with bringing out the chess-table.

" Which hand ? " he asked.

Wendover tapped one of the extended fists, and was rewarded by a white pawn when it unclenched.

" Your move," Sir Clinton confirmed. " Wait till the next game, and I'll show you a fresh variant of the Allgaier-Kieseritzki gambit which should give you food for thought in that rural fastness of yours for the next week or two."

Wendover smiled sceptically, and began to arrange the pieces. But before the board was set, the telephone rang on Sir Clinton's desk, and he rose to answer it impatiently.

"Yes, he's speaking. . . . H'm! Is it *very* urgent? . . . Oh, in that case, certainly. . . . No, I've been away all day. I've only had time to glance over the papers about it. . . . Very good, then. Good-bye."

He put down the receiver and turned to Wendover with some vexation showing itself on his face.

"Sorry, Squire, but we'll have to postpone our game for a while. Just shove the table aside, will you? We can start later on. By the way, do you know old Calbourne, by any chance?"

"Calbourne?" echoed Wendover, as he pushed the chess-table into a corner of the room without dismantling the board. "There was a Calbourne, a big solicitor, I remember. But I never met him personally, if he's the man you mean."

"That's the man," confirmed the Chief Constable. "He wants to see me just now about some affair that happened last night—or this morning, if you like that better. A young friend of his, a girl, has disappeared, leaving not a wrack behind. Shakespeare if not Bacon. Dornfell—one of my inspectors; you don't know him—sent me in a report, but I haven't read it carefully yet."

He turned back to the desk, searched through a packet of papers, and selected some sheets which he brought with him back to his chair.

"Here it is. I'll give you the gist of it as I go through it, and then you'll know as much about it as I do."

"From what I've heard of him, Calbourne isn't the sort of man to put himself out unless the thing's serious," Wendover said thoughtfully. "Was she a pretty girl?"

Sir Clinton smiled at the unexpectedness of the question. Wendover always had a protective feeling where good-looking girls were concerned.

"Nothing like getting a clear idea of the dramatis personæ, right at the start, is there?" he retorted sardonically. "Sorry I can't help. Her name's Hazel Deerhurst. She's married, if that damps you, Squire. And she may be cross-eyed, for all I know. Address further inquiries to Calbourne, when he comes. Now let's get this thing straightened out. He may be here in a quarter of an hour."

He read swiftly but carefully through the report in his hand, summarising it to Wendover as he went along.

"It sounds a bit fishy," he concluded, putting the documents back on his desk, "but we'd better wait to hear Calbourne's side of it before we start theory-building. This is evidently only a part of the whole story."

"Is Calbourne a friend of yours?" Wendover inquired.

"I've met him once or twice," Sir Clinton explained. "That's about as far as it goes. I've never been in his house, and this is the first time he's offered to visit me."

"He evidently believes in going straight to headquarters," commented Wendover in a meditative tone. "I wonder why? By his reputation, he's too smart a man to think he can pull wires with you over anything official. And I don't see what direct connection he has with that affair."

"Well, we'll know in a minute or two," Sir Clinton answered. "That's his car, I expect."

Almost immediately Mr. Calbourne was shown into the room. Sir Clinton greeted him, and then turned to introduce Wendover. Mr. Calbourne's swift, comprehensive glance of friendly inspection took in Wendover's grey hair, close-clipped moustache, open-air complexion, easy manner, and faintly consequential air. "The best brand of country gentleman, and no fool," was his unspoken verdict. Wendover, on the other hand, thought he had seldom seen anyone who differed more from the imaginary "lawyer type" than Mr. Calbourne.

"Now, Mr. Calbourne," Sir Clinton began, pushing forward an armchair for his guest, "Mr. Wendover is a J.P., a very old friend of mine, and I can answer for his discretion. Of course, if you'd rather . . ."

He paused, giving the solicitor a chance to take advantage of his deliberate aposiopesis.

Now Mr. Calbourne had come that evening with several projects in his mind, one of which was to repair as far as possible the effects of Nicholas Adeney's tactless handling of Inspector Dornfell. Looking at the two men before him, he decided that Wendover was the better type for his immediate purposes. The Chief Constable looked faintly cynical, whereas Wendover seemed, on the whole, more kindly and more likely to be moved by a "hard luck" story. These two would probably talk the matter over later on; and if he could convert Wendover, he would leave behind him an advocate who could speak after he himself had gone.

"Say no more," he broke in, before the silence had grown too long. "If Mr. Wendover will not be bored . . ."

In his turn he paused, apparently waiting for the reassuring gesture which Wendover immediately made.

"You know all about this difficulty, Sir Clinton," the solicitor resumed, "at least, I take it that you do. So I had better put it in a nutshell for Mr. Wendover."

He turned slightly in his chair so that he could address Wendover more directly, without losing sight of Sir Clinton's face.

" The fact is, a young friend of mine, Mrs. Deerhurst, has gone off on holiday rather unceremoniously. Her housekeeper, somewhat perturbed by this unheralded departure, immediately jumped to the conclusion that there was something wrong, and called in the police. Then, unfortunately, Mrs. Deerhurst's cousin—young Adeney—came on the scene and seems to have been rather rude to the inspector."

Wendover kept his face under control, but inwardly he was a little amused at the skilful way in which Mr. Calbourne passed lightly over the more suspicious details of the case.

" Young Adeney," Mr. Calbourne continued, " recognised very soon that he had made a fool of himself. He came to me shortly afterwards and asked me if I would do my best to smooth things over. I was an old friend of his father, so it was natural enough for him to turn to me for advice."

" And you advised . . . ? " interjected Sir Clinton.

" I advised him, of course, to go and make it up with the inspector. He refused, however; and I'm not sure that he wasn't right in that, considering the state of his nerves. He might easily have made things worse instead of better, I'm afraid."

" I'll speak to Inspector Dornfell about it," Sir Clinton promised, but Wendover noted that his tone was rather chilly. " Now, before we go further, I'd like to ask a question. You said that ' Mrs. Deerhurst has gone off on holiday.' Do you know that for a fact ? I mean, are you speaking from personal knowledge ? "

" To this extent," Mr. Calbourne replied at once, " that I know from her own lips that her holiday was due, just a day or so before she left home. Yes, and now I remember that I heard her tell Granfield on the 'phone that she wouldn't be at home on the night of the 18th. She acts as confidential secretary to Mr. Mandrell, whom you know, of course. And that brings me to my second reason for coming to see you this evening. Naturally, it would be awkward for Mrs. Deerhurst on her return if this affair gets into the newspapers in some exaggerated form. Very unpleasant for her, if she comes back to find that her name has been blazoned all over the county in that way, as I'm sure you'll appreciate. On that account, I'd like to see as little said about it as possible."

"With the best will in the world, I don't see how you can prevent it," Sir Clinton pointed out unsympathetically. "The neighbours know that the police have been called in. There's a constable on the premises at the present moment. You can't keep people from talking, you know."

"I suppose not," Mr. Calbourne admitted rather ruefully. "It's a pity, though, if it's going to make Mrs. Deerhurst uncomfortable when she gets back."

He seemed to ponder for a few moments, mechanically stroking that white torpedo beard which made him look so much like a sea-captain of the old school. Then he turned to the Chief Constable.

"Now I'm going to put my cards on the table, Sir Clinton. To you, and to Mr. Wendover also, I'm sure, Mrs. Deerhurst's behaviour must seem rather odd. Why should she disappear suddenly in this peculiar fashion? She gave me no hint of her intention, and I'm one of the oldest friends she has. I admit that on the surface it must seem *outré*, to say the least of it."

He turned to Wendover as though expecting an endorsement of this.

"It certainly sounds odd," Wendover agreed cautiously.

"It does," Mr. Calbourne confessed frankly. "But there's a good deal under the surface. Young Adeney could have told you something; but he's an interested party, and his evidence might have been regarded as *ex parte*. If he had volunteered it, very probably it would have been discounted, simply because it came from him. Now I have no axe to grind in the matter; my evidence is quite unbiased; and I happen to be in possession of all the facts. That's my main reason for coming here to-night. Unless you happen to know what's at the back of the business, you're almost bound to go off on the wrong track and make a mountain out of what is really a molehill."

He paused, and then added with a smile:

"I'm afraid I've got my metaphors mixed up, but at least my meaning's plain enough, I hope."

"Anything that tends to make things clearer will be a help to us," said Sir Clinton non-committally.

Wendover had not failed to note that so far the solicitor had avoided dealing with the really suspicious items in the evidence. Probably professional caution, he reflected. Mr. Calbourne was not the sort of person to blunder into unnecessary admissions, if one could judge from his looks. And probably he was reserving himself until he had paved the way for his story, whatever it might be.

"You may remember the Adeney-Deerhurst case, perhaps?" the solicitor queried.

Sir Clinton shook his head.

"Not in detail," he explained. "It was in the next county, outside my jurisdiction, so I had nothing to do with it. And I was on the Continent, on holiday, at the time of the trial, so I didn't follow it in the papers. If it comes in, you'd better take nothing for granted, so far as I'm concerned."

"This affair reaches back beyond the trial, a long way," Mr. Calbourne said, with a glance at his watch.

"It's not easy to say where it begins, really; and I've trespassed on your time already."

"We have the evening before us," Sir Clinton assured him, though there was a touch of formality in his voice. "Tell us whatever you think it right that we should know."

He mitigated the slight official stiffness of his tone by picking up the box of cigars from the table beside him and passing it to the solicitor.

"I'd rather take one of my own, thanks," Mr. Calbourne explained. "If I smoke anything but the brand I'm accustomed to, it seems to put me out, somehow."

He drew out his own case and selected a cigar, stripping off the band, and dropping it into the ash-tray which Sir Clinton put beside him. For a moment or two he busied himself with his cigar; then, when it was well alight, he settled himself comfortably in his chair and turned slightly towards Wendover.

"You know what a good many old-established firms are suffering from nowadays," he began. "The malady of the Third Generation, one might call it. A capable and energetic man founds a business; his son inherits enough capacity to keep it going; but the grandson has no commercial instinct whatever; and so the firm fails to keep abreast of the times and gets into a bad way."

Wendover, turning this proposition over in his mind and applying it to several cases known to him, had to admit to himself that there was something in the idea. He glanced at Mr. Calbourne with a more awakened interest.

"That was the history of the Adeneys," Mr. Calbourne continued. "Old John Adeney founded the business in early Victorian days. He was what our American friends would call a 'live wire,' though the phrase hadn't been invented then. He was shrewd, ambitious, forceful, quite ruthless, I should think, and untiring in his business. He was an old man when I was a boy, and I still remember him as a rather terrifying personage, with thatched brows and an eye that seemed to look clean through you. There was nothing of the 'too-old-at-forty' about him. He went to business up to the end and died in his office chair.

"Old John Adeney had two sons, Laurence and Philip. Philip was about my own age, and we were very good friends. Both brothers went into the Adeney business and eventually became partners in it. They were pale copies of their father, with none of the old man's dæmonic energy and swiftness to seize opportunities. Still, they were good business men of the jog-along sort; and if the firm gained no ground under their direction, yet it didn't fall back. They were cautious men in many ways, not inclined to take risks. Perhaps that was why they both married rather late in life.

"Laurence married an orphan girl with no relations that I ever heard about. Nicholas was the only child they had. When he was about ten years old, both his parents died while they were abroad on holiday. Typhoid, I believe. Luckily, Philip had married, too, by that time, and Hazel had been born, so there was a family circle ready to take Nicholas in. Philip took charge of him. Then Philip's wife died of pneumonia. They're an unfortunate family."

Wendover began to fear that Mr. Calbourne was that most irksome of all bores, the bore who insists on talking at length about unimportant people one never heard of before. He glanced covertly at Sir Clinton, but the Chief Constable's expression betrayed nothing of his feelings.

"The young Adeneys were about the same age as my youngest ones," Mr. Calbourne went on, "so they were a good deal about our house. Even as a boy,

Nicholas was something of a disappointment to his father. He had no application, no ambitions, no energy except for occasional bursts, and a marked bias for taking the easiest road, whatever it was. Hazel was different. She was a pretty little spitfire, with a temper that flashed up quite regardless of consequences. She's got it well in control nowadays, but it must have cost her something to suppress it. She had some of her grandfather's energy and always wanted to be up and doing. She took the notion of going in for nursing at one time, and had a violent quarrel with her father over it before she got her own way. But after a bit her health broke down and then she got the idea of being a secretary. That led to another family quarrel, because Philip Adeney prided himself on the idea that he could leave both his children well off and he saw no reason why Hazel should take a course of training which would, as he insisted, 'lead to nothing.' However, she got her way as usual."

"I understand," said Sir Clinton patiently. "That explains how she was able to take this secretaryship to Mr. Mandrell?"

"Oh, there was nothing of the dilettante about her," Mr. Calbourne declared emphatically. "Whatever she took up, she threw herself into it wholeheartedly, and she had plenty of wits to help her. If she and Nicholas could have changed places, Adeneys might be afloat to-day. But, of course, Nicholas was a man, and the business woman hadn't come to the forefront in those days, so Nicholas was made a partner when he came of age.

"Then the malady of the Third Generation got its footing in Adeneys in a worse form than the usual. My friend, Philip Adeney, began to crack up. I don't know what exactly was wrong with him; it may have been what they call softening of the brain or something like that. He began to lose his memory little by little, and that led to his losing his grip on the business. Things began to go wrong: little things at first and then rather bigger things, until at last Philip saw that something would have to be done. Nicholas had no turn for business at all. An excellent man for signing on the dotted line, when the paper was actually put on the desk in front of him; but quite incapable of directing a big business.

"Hazel might have stepped into the breach, perhaps; but by that time Hazel had got something else to think about. There was a young fellow, Duncan Ferrestone, an artist of sorts; in fact, rather a good man in his line, I believe. He made something of a name for himself later on, though I haven't seen much about him in the last two or three years. He and Hazel took a fancy to each other."

"A fortune-hunter?" interjected Wendover, suspiciously.

"Oh, no," Mr. Calbourne assured him. "Ferrestone wasn't that sort. I knew him fairly well. He was one of these rather dreamy creatures, the very antithesis of Hazel, without the faintest notion of the value of money. It simply meant nothing to him, apart from bread and cheese. And yet he was a likeable type, very likeable, and absolutely straight. Well, they got engaged, and seemed deliriously happy over it. We were all very pleased for they seemed to fit each other, though you might not think so from what I've said. So naturally Hazel was planning her life on lines well away from the offices of Adeney & Sons, even if there had been any idea of letting her try her hand at business. And, of course, that never crossed the minds of any of us."

Mr. Calbourne examined his cigar and then reluctantly knocked off the ash before continuing.

" By that time Philip Adeney had come to realise that something drastic must be done if the business was to be kept up to the mark. There was only one thing for it—bring in fresh blood from the outside. None of them liked the idea, I may say. Adeney & Sons had a history behind it. They were all very proud of the family business, with its record of honest dealing. There was a modest dignity in being one of *the* Adeneys, you understand, which had nothing to do with snobbishness or anything of that sort. Even Nicholas had a touch of it ; and Hazel, with more imagination, regarded the family business as a kind of trust handed down to them which must be cared for and transmitted to the next generation intact."

Wendover gave an understanding gesture. This was the kind of thing he could appreciate. An old-established business was like his own estate, something to watch over, improve if possible, and hand over to one's successors in good order, undiminished.

" Philip Adeney looked round for the fresh blood they needed. He was hardly the man for that, for his disease had got a firm hold on him by that time. But Nicholas was quite incapable of choosing a partner, so the old man had to do his best. He pitched on this fellow Deerhurst."

There was something in the intonation of the last three words which betrayed Mr. Calbourne's view of Deerhurst beyond mistake.

" They made him a partner, though they didn't put his name to the firm. He brought nothing in the way of cash ; energy and business acumen were supposed to be his contributions. I never liked him," Mr. Calbourne confessed frankly. " He had self-confidence without capacity on the same scale. One could see it in his face: that big nose which needs a chin to match, if it's to be any good ; only Deerhurst hadn't the right sort of jaw. He was good-looking, in a way, though. And he had that blustering manner which imposes on weaker people because they mistake it for strength of character. He was never afraid to tell people that they were fools if they didn't agree with him. I've a notion that he regarded himself as a kind of reincarnated buccaneer who had taken to business. 'The world's my oyster,' and so forth. There was always something of Ancient Pistol about him, to my mind.

"From the very start he imposed himself on the whole Adeney family. Philip Adeney was failing rapidly; his memory was going from bad to worse, so that he could keep no real grip on the affairs of the firm. He was only too glad to have younger shoulders there to take over the burden which had got beyond his powers. Nicholas left everything in Deerhurst's hands, and was only too glad to sign on the dotted line as before, if anyone would save him the trouble of thinking. As for Hazel, she looked on Deerhurst as a young giant who was going to lift the firm out of its rut and start it afresh on a new career of glory, so she was inclined to over-estimate him, in spite of her natural shrewdness."

Mr. Calbourne suppressed a sigh, apparently for some memories which he did not go into in detail.

"Up to that time Adeney & Sons had been a staunch old firm of the thoroughly reliable type. They turned out a good article at a fair price and were content with that. There's always a certain amount of forethought required in a business which needs raw materials which may fluctuate in price; but Adeney & Sons had kept their eyes on their own requirements and been quite satisfied with buying what they wanted at an economical cost. They were manufacturers, pure and simple.

"But with the advent of Deerhurst things changed.

Sources of supply had a fascination for him, and he brought off one or two successful deals in raw materials which put up the firm's profits for the year very nicely. The Adeney family congratulated themselves on the new recruit. He was a plausible fellow, and I don't think these minor triumphs lost anything in the telling when he came to talk about them."

Sir Clinton took a fresh cigar from the box, and Mr. Calbourne waited politely until he had lighted it.

"Everything seemed to be going well at that time. Hazel and Ferrestone were thinking of getting married shortly. Philip Adeney had offered his daughter an allowance that would make them comfortable enough; and Ferrestone's pictures were bringing in bigger sums each year. And then, almost on the edge of marriage, the two of them quarrelled about something. Goodness knows what it was; neither of them ever told me what they fell out over. Probably it was one of these unfortunate lovers' quarrels where one party lets slip some incautious words and the whole thing founders for no real reason at all and leaves bitterness on both sides.

"Whatever it was, it made a clean break between them. The engagement was broken off. Ferrestone betook himself elsewhere, hurt to the quick, apparently. If he'd stayed at hand, things might have come right eventually, as they generally do. But when two people are separated and each is too proud to make the first move by letter, it's unlikely that a quarrel of that sort will be patched up.

"Then Deerhurst, I suppose, saw a chance. He was always about the house. He was ready to play the sympathetic friend, and so forth. It's not so very hard to get into the good graces of a girl when she's suffering from a shock of that kind. And, of course, he was the brilliant fellow who was going to carry Adeney & Sons to fresh conquests, so there was a sentimental glamour about him for Hazel, with her pride in the Adeney history. I don't think she was in love with him. Ferrestone had got all that. But she admired him, and he took pains to make himself indispensable. To cut it short, he persuaded her to marry him."

"I've seen things of that kind happen," Wendover confirmed. "Loneliness, the feeling that the bottom's fallen out of the world, and that kind of thing: they throw a girl off her balance and often she's quite ready to take the second-best, just to fill the gap at any cost."

Mr. Calbourne nodded sombrely.

"It was a second-best in this case," he went on. "Up till then Deerhurst had been content to do a few speculations in futures directly connected with the firm's raw materials. Now he began to extend operations far outside the legitimate field. Soon he began to need a bigger capital to gamble with, and to get it he persuaded the two Adeneys to agree to the business being turned into a limited company. At that time, it was solvent enough; and the Adeney name was synonymous with good, sound, steady business. There was no difficulty; the issue was over-subscribed. Philip Adeney was chairman, Nicholas was a director, Deerhurst was managing director, and they had the legal number of others, who were merely dummies chosen by Deerhurst. My firm had nothing to do with it. Deerhurst picked out his own solicitor, a fellow called Granfield with whom he was very thick, and made him secretary for the company. And so the savings of thousands of decent people came under the control of Philip, who couldn't keep track of business, of Nicholas, who could do little more than sign on the dotted line, and of this fellow Deerhurst who was no better than a gambler with a wholly unjustified belief in his own smartness. And all on the strength of Adeney & Sons' past reputation."

Mr. Calbourne paused and made a wry face, as though even in retrospect the business pained him.

"You can guess what followed in the next few years. That fellow Granfield probably helped to draw up the original prospectus, and it gave the company power to deal in things far outside the legitimate scope of the business. Deerhurst dealt in a good many of them, not successfully. It culminated in a fraudulent balance-sheet, a riotous general meeting with poor Philip Adeney helpless in the chair, and a criminal trial. It killed poor Philip. He wasn't in the best of health when the storm broke, and he died of shame, I believe, before his case came on.

"The dummy directors were let off lightly. Deerhurst got six years in all. Nicholas got off with five. He'd been quite innocent in intention all the way through ; but he'd signed on the dotted line too often without looking to see what was above it, and the Judge made an example of him just to discourage that kind of easy-going method in business."

Mr. Calbourne stroked his beard reflectively for a moment or two as though puzzled by something.

"Nicholas Adeney might have stood a better chance but for his brother-in-law. Deerhurst did his level best to make a scapegoat of young Adeney, and to some extent he succeeded with the jury. Nicholas was a bad witness : not because he tried to wriggle, but simply because he was completely out of his depth. He didn't know this, and he couldn't remember that, and he had no recollection of something else. In fact, he left the impression of being a complete young twister. And, curiously enough, while Deerhurst did his best to cook young Adeney's goose for him, he took on his own shoulders a good deal of the blame which, to my mind, should have fallen on the company's secretary—Granfield. There were lots of things turned up in the trial which a solicitor must have known about ; and yet Deerhurst swore that Granfield had never had any cognisance of them.

" It was a frightful collapse. Money had been lost in this speculation and in that ; securities had been realised and the proceeds wasted ; there had been tricky work with loans and mortgages ; and a good round sum in cash had simply disappeared, no one knew where. The shareholders never saw a penny of their investments again. And the name of Adeney was dragged in the mud, after all these years.

" You can guess what it all meant to Hazel Deerhurst : her father killed by the shock, her brother in prison, the family name tarnished, and herself tied to the man who had brought the disaster upon them all. There was a completeness about that tragedy which luckily one doesn't often find in life. Fortunately for her, she was financially clear. When young Adeney was made a partner, Philip drew up a will in which he left his share in the business to Nicholas and his other property to Hazel. He'd been a saving man, and that left her with enough to yield quite a handsome income, after the smash, from money that had no taint attached to it. She spent some of it in relieving one or two of the hardest cases among the shareholders, little people who had lost everything. I did that for her, as she wouldn't let people know she was doing it. I leave you to imagine for yourself what her feelings towards her husband must have been. She didn't talk much on the subject, even to me.

" Nicholas, of course, had lost everything, and when he'd served his time, he came out into a difficult world. Some mud always sticks, and people looked askance at him, except his cousin and one or two more. He had no resources, and although his cousin was only too glad to finance him, he hated living at her expense. It's difficult for an ex-convict to get employment, especially if he's like young Adeney, with no capacity for business. He got out nine months ago, and he's been trying to make some sort of income by writing."

Mr. Calbourne straightened himself in his chair and regarded his audience rather apologetically.

"I've made a long tale of it," he admitted, "but I'm near the end now. Just try to picture to yourselves what Hazel Deerhurst's life has been for the last five years. Behind her she had the disgrace of the Adeney crash; before her she had the prospect of her husband's release and all the complications which it was sure to bring into her affairs. Those few years were just a breathing-space between the past humiliation and the coming one. You can imagine what it meant to a sensitive girl. One thing she resolved upon. Nothing should induce her to have the slightest dealing with her husband after he was released from prison."

"One can hardly be surprised by that," Wendover commented.

"Rather than see him, she told my daughter, she was ready to leave this district for a time and put into my hands any arrangements with her husband which would ensure his leaving her in peace permanently."

"Ah!" interjected Sir Clinton, with more interest than he had hitherto shown. "But apparently she didn't say that to you direct?"

"Not in so many words," Mr. Calbourne admitted. "But it was clear enough to me from things she said about him. I'll give you an example of her feelings. A night or two before she went away I pointed out to her that she had made no will, and that if she died intestate, Deerhurst would inherit her property. She was round at my house next morning to discuss the matter, and she asked me to draft a will for her which would cut Deerhurst out completely and leave her entire property to her cousin."

"Was that will signed?" demanded Sir Clinton.

Mr. Calbourne shook his head.

"No, she merely gave me verbal instructions to throw her wishes into proper form. She left her house that night."

"So that morning of the day of her disappearance was the last time when you set eyes on her?" inquired the Chief Constable.

Mr. Calbourne confirmed this with a nod.

"She gave you no inkling that she meant to leave her house?" Sir Clinton asked.

"None whatever."

"Did Deerhurst's name crop up in your conversation with her?"

"Naturally it did, in the course of our talk," Mr. Calbourne explained. "She mentioned that he had just been released from prison and she said, rather bitterly, that there had been quite enough scandals in the Adeney family and that she would take care that Deerhurst had no chance of raising any more."

"I don't wonder at that," Wendover declared. "It's been a dreadful affair for her altogether, poor girl."

Sir Clinton considered for a moment or two before putting his next question.

"You're a solicitor, Mr. Calbourne. Can you tell me exactly how things stand at present, if it should turn out that Mrs. Deerhurst is no longer alive? Who gets her property?"

Mr. Calbourne hesitated before replying.

"Technically," he said at last, "she would have died intestate and Deerhurst would inherit the residuary estate absolutely under the Administration of Estates Act, 1925. Actually, it might be possible that my evidence of her wishes and my notes of our conversation would be regarded as proof of her intentions in the matter, but I should not care to give an opinion on the point."

"And if Deerhurst had predeceased her ?"

"Then young Adeney would inherit everything, if my notes were taken as proof of her intentions."

"Ah," said Sir Clinton thoughtfully. "That's interesting. Merely as an hypothesis," he added, after a glance at Mr. Calbourne's face. "Did young Adeney know that she had made no will ?"

"Yes," said Mr. Calbourne reluctantly, "he was there when I spoke to her about it."

Sir Clinton changed the subject in his next question.

"By the way, I suppose you knew Deerhurst personally ?"

"Oh, yes," Mr. Calbourne confirmed. "I met him constantly in the days after he married Hazel Adeney. naturally."

Sir Clinton went to his desk, turned over some papers, and came back with an unmounted photograph.

"Do you recognise that ?" he asked passing it to the solicitor.

Mr. Calbourne fished out his spectacles, adjusted them deliberately and examined the print with a faint suggestion of incomprehension in his expression

"That's Deerhurst," he declared without hesitation. "But how do you happen to have his photograph ?"

Then a light seemed to dawn on him.

"Oh, of course, from the prison records, I suppose. But it looks as though he were in bed when it was taken. I don't quite understand that."

"I didn't take it," said Sir Clinton with a smile. "Let Mr. Wendover have a look at it."

Mr. Calbourne handed it across and Wendover examined it carefully, noting the big predatory nose, the thin lips, and the rather weak chin. He studied it thoughtfully, since it represented his first glimpse of the appearance of any of the actors in the drama which Mr. Calbourne had just described. Deerhurst, he decided, had good looks of a sort, but he wondered what sort of a husband he could have been for a sensitive girl, quite apart from the financial side of the affair. He passed the photograph back to Sir Clinton, who replaced it on his desk.

Mr. Calbourne rose to his feet.

" I've detained you too long already," he confessed, " and I hope you won't feel that I've altogether wasted your time. To be quite frank, I'm puzzled and perhaps a shade uneasy over this business, and I felt that you ought to have all the facts before you."

He hesitated for a moment, as though intending to ask something. Then, apparently, he thought better of it and held out his hand. Sir Clinton made no effort to detain him, nor did he give any indication of his own views.

" Thanks for giving us the information," he said politely. " It was kind of you to take so much trouble."

Mr. Calbourne seemed a shade disappointed by this non-committal attitude, but he wished Wendover good night pleasantly enough and then followed the Chief Constable to the door.

CHAPTER VIII

THE TOLL OF THE ROAD

WHEN Sir Clinton returned, after showing Mr. Calbourne out, his first move was to pick up the solicitor's cigar band which lay in the ash-tray.

" A Castañeda," he said, after a glance at it. " So it wasn't one of his cigars that was smoked in Mrs. Deerhurst's drawing-room on the night of her disappearance. Dornfell found the band belonging to that one, and it was a Flor de Naves. That's always something."

But Wendover was not particularly interested in this point.

" Where did you get the photo of Deerhurst ? " he demanded. " I know a record photograph when I see one, and that never came out of the office. There was something curious about it—the expression on the face, I mean. Old Calbourne saw that too, I'm sure, though you didn't give him a chance of commenting on it."

" One thing at a time and each in its turn," Sir Clinton said with wilful sententiousness, as he settled down in his chair again. " What did you make of friend Calbourne and his tale of woe ? "

" It was damned hard luck on the girl," Wendover declared with emphasis.

" Well, if you don't know your own mind, you suffer for it in this world," said Sir Clinton cynically. " I notice you don't drop a tear for Ferrestone's troubles in the same line."

"A girl's different," Wendover argued.

"Oh, quite, if you wish it," the Chief Constable admitted indifferently. "But I've no time to discuss the sex question in general, Squire. Go back three squares and start afresh. What do you make of Calbourne?"

"Well, he's an old friend of the Adeney family," Wendover began rather reluctantly, "and to that extent he's prejudiced, I suppose. Still, that tale of his seemed straight enough so far as the facts went. He rather puzzled me by coming here to tell you all about it. I mean, he blurted out things which he might quite well have kept his thumb on and yet told no lies. In fact, although I'd have admitted them under examination, if I'd been in his shoes, I don't know that I'd have volunteered them as he did."

"He's a fairly shrewd man," Sir Clinton pointed out. "And he did skate round an awkward corner or two rather gracefully, in spite of your criticisms. He began by a downright statement: that Mrs. Deerhurst had gone off on holiday rather unceremoniously. Obviously that was meant to make its mark on us right at the very start—creating the right attitude in our minds, and so forth. But when we went into the matter, it turned out that he'd no real basis for that story, you remember?"

"That's true," Wendover conceded. "He certainly did his best to create an atmosphere of sorts."

"Doesn't that throw some light on the rest of the business?"

"Not more than a glimmer," Wendover admitted.

Sir Clinton lit a cigarette, as though to give Wendover a chance of further consideration.

"Nothing further?" he inquired as he put down his extinguished match. "Well, I think you hit the mark in saying he was doing his best to create an atmosphere, and that accounts for his coming here to-night. Look at it this way, Squire, from his point of view. Here's a nice little family scandal in the Adeney-Deerhurst group. Old Calbourne knows all about it, and he knows that some of it has a bearing on this Norwood House affair. So, I take it, he put on his thinking-cap; and the result of his cogitation was something of this sort. 'When the police are called in they start on a basis of suspicion. They want to incriminate somebody, and as each thread of evidence comes to light, they fit it into its place in the web they're spinning. I can't burke their investigations; too many people know about the Adeney family troubles. But I can give Driffield the whole story, *en bloc*, and *from the Adeney point of view*. It'll be true enough to stand testing; but it'll throw a fresh atmosphere over the facts, and if I get in first with my tale, it may form the basis on which they'll work.' So he came along here, post-haste, to put his cards on the table, as he phrased it, with his 'hard luck' story."

"It certainly was a painful affair," Wendover commented.

Sir Clinton laughed, rather unfeelingly.

"Evidently the 'atmosphere' has affected you, Squire. A tribute to old Calbourne's powers, that. Now what caught my attention was something quite different. Old Calbourne comes here and does his level best to account for the girl's disappearance on quite normal lines, as part of the 'hard luck' story. But the blood-mark on the drawing-room floor doesn't fit in with that. And he avoided not only the blood-mark but everything connected with the girl's actual disappearance. And yet young Adeney had gone to him to-day and enlisted his help, so Calbourne ought to have known about these curious points."

"Calbourne was giving you first-hand evidence about the Adeney affairs," Wendover pointed out. "Anything he may have learned about the house was at second-hand, and, being a lawyer, he regarded it as 'not evidence' probably."

"Ingenious, Squire, but not good enough. He could have told us what he learned from young Adeney this morning, though he couldn't vouch for the truth of what young Adeney told him. But he never said a word about that interview. And that strikes me as . . . well . . . curious. You can take two views of it. Either young Adeney suppressed all the things that came to light at the house this morning, or else he told Calbourne about them, and Calbourne deliberately avoided mentioning them. Why? Does he guess at something behind all this, something far fishier than he cares to talk about to us?"

"Then why did he butt in at all?" Wendover demanded.

"Because he's an old friend of the Adeneys. He came here to produce that 'atmosphere' which affected you so strongly, Squire. He's done the Adeneys no harm by anything he said, and he might have done some good if I'd been susceptible to that kind of thing. Suppose he believes in the Adeneys and has convinced himself that they've got clean hands in the matter. Wouldn't he take just the course that he did take?"

"Well," retorted Wendover, "where's the evidence that their hands are anything but clean? Your man Dornfell has found a spot or two of blood on a parquet floor. It's no crime to have blood on the floor, is it?"

"No," admitted Sir Clinton with a twinkle in his eye. "I suppose you want a body or something of that sort, to make it interesting?"

"It would be more satisfactory than a mare's nest, certainly," Wendover agreed ironically.

"I can't produce a body at the moment," the Chief

Constable admitted, moving over to his desk, " but here's the photograph of one. Will that suit you ? "

He handed Wendover the print which he had brought out earlier in the evening.

" It was taken in a mortuary," he explained. " That accounts for the unusual position which struck our friend Calbourne, you remember. And now, Squire, doesn't it strike you that the Adeneys are in rather deeper water than old Calbourne would have had us believe ? "

He came back to his chair and watched Wendover studying the print.

" There's no doubt about the identity of the body. You saw that Calbourne recognised him at once, and there's even more convincing evidence on hand. That's Leonard Deerhurst, ex-convict, beyond a peradventure. The original of the photograph is forty or fifty miles away at present, waiting for the coroner's attention."

" It's been pretty quick work, finding the body and identifying it so soon," Wendover admitted.

" There was nothing much in finding him," Sir Clinton confessed. " He was left about in plain sight and couldn't be overlooked. And we had a stroke of luck in the identification business. Care to hear the whole story, Squire ? "

Wendover nodded and the Chief Constable, after a glance at his watch, began his tale.

" Do you remember a place called Six Road Ends, just beyond Hornadale ? " he asked.

" Fifty odd miles from here ? " Wendover queried to make sure of his ground. " Yes, I remember it fairly well. After Six Road Ends the road winds round under Sharpley's Hill, doesn't it ? "

" Yes, it's a lonely bit of country. After you leave Six Road Ends there isn't a single side-road till you get to the far side of Swallow Tail Copse, four miles or so along. Now on account of something which had nothing to do with this affair—a twenty-four hour traffic census—we happened to have a man on point duty all night at Six Road Ends, and another posted at Swallow Tail Copse cross roads. Is that all clear ? "

" I know the place," Wendover agreed. " What it amounts to is that you had a man on point at each end of the stretch between Six Road Ends and Swallow Tail Copse, and there isn't a side road between those two points."

" Exactly. Now it appears that a Dr. Stayton, a well-known local practitioner, was called out to an emergency case yesterday night ; and on his way home he passed the Swallow Tail Copse pointsman at about twenty past two, and took the road to Six Road Ends. About a mile on this side of Swallow Tail Copse he saw something on the road ahead, and on pulling up he found it was a body. Some well-dressed fellow had apparently been knocked down and killed by a car travelling towards Six Road Ends, since he was lying on the doctor's side of the road. Stayton had a look at him, found he was quite dead, and turned his car. He drove back to the man on point at Swallow Tail Copse cross roads, picked him up and took him back to the body."

" Quite safe to leave the body, in these circumstances," Wendover interjected. " It would be clear of traffic going towards the Copse. It's a wide road there, I remember. And Stayton could warn any car he met coming from the Copse direction."

" Exactly," Sir Clinton agreed. " It was the best he could do. Now, when the doctor told his story the constable recalled that just before one o'clock two cars passed him, going hell-for-leather towards Six Road Ends. The first of them had a merry bunch on board, singing and what not ; and the driving was nothing to praise. He guessed they had been to some spree or other. Just to be on the safe side, he made a note of the first car's number."

"Drunk, were they?" queried Wendover with a frown, for he had a well-founded prejudice against intoxicated motorists.

"They attracted the constable's attention, at any rate," Sir Clinton admitted.

"And I suppose they killed the poor devil and then made up their minds to keep it dark by simply driving on?"

"I know you can tell this tale better than I can, Squire," Sir Clinton confessed sardonically. "You're not hampered by the facts, and that's a great help. But just let me ramble along, will you? I'm doing my best."

Wendover grunted an acknowledgment of the touch.

"Stayton had the thoroughness to take the body's temperature," Sir Clinton pursued, "and from that he reckoned that death had occurred between two and three hours earlier – say round about midnight. But you know how variable that temperature business is, Squire."

Wendover contented himself with a nod of agreement.

"The next bit of the tale's merely how they got the body to the mortuary and raked out the police surgeon. Purely formal. But now the interest deepens; the plot expands. First of all, look at that photo of the dead man."

Wendover scanned the print again.

"If you mean his looks, I don't fancy them altogether. I know that type with the big nose and not enough chin to balance it. All the self-confidence of the big man and none of the big man's capacity."

"You mean the type that wants to boss everything and invariably makes a muddle of it eventually? They are a nuisance. But doesn't something else strike you ?"

Wendover made a further examination of the print, but except for a certain narrowness in the forehead he saw nothing in the face that struck him particularly.

"No, there's nothing out of the way, so far as I can see," he confessed, handing back the photograph.

"Curious that if he was hit by a fast-travelling car, his face should be completely free from scrapes and scratches, isn't it ?"

"He may have fallen on the back of his head," Wendover objected.

"And the car rolled over him without rolling him over ? It's possible, of course," Sir Clinton admitted, though in a tone which showed that he regarded the hypothesis as impossible. "However, let's get on with the tale. The constable went through his pockets to find out who he was. Love's labour lost at the first try. There were a few one-pound Bank of England notes in a note-case ; a few coins, copper and silver, in the trouser pockets ; a cigar-case ; a pen-knife ; and absolutely nothing else, not even a pocket handkerchief."

"No card-case or papers ?"

"Not so much as a book of stamps," Sir Clinton assured him. "But to continue : the police surgeon did a P.M. I spare you the technical details, Squire, as far as possible. He'd been rather squashed in parts. There was a bad bruise on the back of the head. . . ."

"Didn't I tell you ?" Wendover interjected. "And his skull was fractured, eh ?"

"No, there was no fracture, and no bleeding at either ear," Sir Clinton corrected, with an impish enjoyment.

"Oh, well, what does that matter ? The bruise shows he fell on the back of his head, just as I said."

"Wait for the next thrilling instalment," Sir Clinton cautioned him. "According to the surgeon, the bruise on the head differed from the bruises on the body. In the head bruise, blood had infiltrated among the tissues, whereas there was nothing of that sort to be seen in the body bruises. So the heart had been forcing blood into the bruised tissues on the head, but it had stopped beating when the other bruises were made. So the surgeon opines, at any rate."

"But in a motor smash all the damage is done in a split second," Wendover objected. "There's a screw loose, surely."

"Very loose, if you assume that the head bruise was made almost simultaneously with the body bruises. But why assume that? The screw's tight enough if you simply assume that the head bruise was made a good deal earlier than the body bruises, and that death occurred in between."

"You mean that death wasn't caused by the motor smash at all, that he was killed by a blow on the head, struck at an earlier time?"

"No, it wasn't," Sir Clinton contradicted, with unconcealed glee at having caught his friend out. "You're still at your old game of starting to reason before you've got enough facts, Squire. Now this is the really queer part of the business. Clean through the fellow's heart ran two punctured wounds made by something of the size and shape of a knitting-needle—a moderately thin one. That's what killed him, according to the surgeon."

"Wait a bit," begged Wendover. "What you mean is that he was first clubbed on the head, then stabbed while he was unconscious, and then thrown out on the road for the first car to run over him?"

"I shouldn't put it quite so definitely myself," Sir Clinton said cautiously. "I wasn't there at the moment, and I haven't your vivid imagination. But you seem to have caught the general idea certainly."

"He must have been tramping along the road,"

Wendover pursued incorrigibly, "and been set upon by roughs. Probably he put up a fight and they knocked him out. And stabbed him because he'd got a glimpse of their faces. Then they robbed the body and left it on the road to be run over. And then along came that crew of drunks and did the trick."

"You ought to be writing novels, Squire," Sir Clinton declared severely. "You've got the gift of romance, and you're letting it run to waste. I hate to knock the bottom out of your pretty story; but it won't hold water, anyhow, so there's no harm done. First of all, the moon's in its first quarter and it was a cloudy night; so I don't think he could have 'caught a glimpse of their faces.' Again, the body wasn't robbed. I told you there were several notes in the fellow's note-case."

"Perhaps they were interrupted before they could go through his pockets," Wendover suggested. "Or he may have had fivers as well as one-pound notes, and they took the fivers and left the others. . . ."

"To mislead the chuckle-headed police? Thank you. No, I hate to contradict you, Squire, but your way-worn wanderer is a myth. No pedestrian passed the men on point duty at either end of that strip of road after 10 p.m. Therefore, if any pedestrian did get on to it, even if he walked at a snail's pace, he'd have passed off it by 11.30 p.m.; and that's an hour and a half before the two cars were noted at Swallow Tail Copse. Further, the last pedestrian to pass in was twins, so to speak. At least they were two brothers going home together, both well known to the man on point duty. And they saw nothing suspicious on that stretch of road as they went over it."

"A road's got more sides than ends," Wendover pointed out. "He might have cut into it from the fields anywhere between Six Road Ends and Swallow Tail Copse."

" Ingenious but unconvincing," the chief constable retorted. " If he came through the fields, his shoes would have been soaked with the dew, which was fairly heavy last night up there. But actually the soles were as dry as a bone. No, Squire, it was simpler than that. These men on point duty were taking a census of the cars that used the roads that night. When their note-books were compared it was found that the fellow at Six Road Ends had two cars more in his total than the fellow at Swallow Tail Copse."

" You mean that one car had gone into that stretch of road and then turned and come back, without going the length of the Copse ? "

" You follow me like a bloodhound."

" I see what you mean," Wendover broke in. " Deerhurst was knocked on the head somewhere and then stabbed. That would be about midnight, from the doctor's guess. Then he was taken in a car into the Six Road Ends stretch and dumped overboard on the road. After that the car that brought him turned round and went back past Six Road Ends. And the first car that came along bumped into the body. The driver, thinking he'd killed the pedestrian, cleared off without informing anybody. It was that drunken lot, I suppose ? "

The Chief Constable shook his head.

" Neither a coconut nor a cigar this time, Squire. We've hunted out the driver and passengers on the second car, all of whom are sober and respectable persons. They were close behind the drunks' car throughout that strip of road, and they saw no accident, nor did they see any corpse."

" Oh, indeed ? " said Wendover, rather discomfited. " When did you say the drunks' car passed Swallow Tail Copse ? "

" Just before one o'clock."

" And the doctor went past the man on point duty

at 2.20 a.m. Did any car pass Swallow Tail Copse between those times ? "

" You're getting warm, Squire. No, no car entered that stretch of road between 1 a.m. and 2.20 a.m. from the Copse end."

" So the body must have been placed on the road after 1 a.m. and before 2.20 a.m. by a car coming from the Six Road Ends direction," inferred Wendover. " And what's more, the accident must have been a fake, made by the driver of that car after he had dumped the body on the road. He must have turned his car and run over the corpse on his way home."

" 'Q.E.D.,' as the friend of our youth used to say at the end of his propositions sometimes. I think you've come within a stone's throw of the truth, anyhow. Your notion fits in with the fact that the face of the body wasn't injured in any way. It wouldn't be if the body was lying on its back on the road and the car went slowly over its thorax, clear of the head. There would be no smash, no knocking of the man down, or anything of that sort."

" But just wait a moment," Wendover interrupted. " Your men were taking the numbers of all the cars that passed them, weren't they ? Then all you have to do is to go through the note-book of the constable at Six Road Ends and you'll find one number occurring twice. That'll be the number of the car that went into the Swallow Tail Copse stretch, turned, and came out again without passing Swallow Tail Copse."

" That didn't escape us, Squire. But, unfortunately, it won't work. As it happened, a big car with a caravan trailer came along one of the other routes at Six Road Ends and stopped right opposite the constable to ask the way to some place in the neighbourhood. It pulled up in such a position as to block the constable's view ; and while he was answering the driver's questions at least one car passed into the

Swallow Tail Copse stretch without his being able to see its number. By sheer ill-luck that seems to have been the very car we're hunting for, because the same number does *not* occur twice on the Six Road Ends list."

"But you can get at it another way," objected Wendover. "If you compare the list taken at Six Road Ends with the list taken at Swallow Tail Copse, then one number will appear on the Six Road Ends list and not on the Copse list, since it never passed the Copse pointsman."

"Alas! *Humanum est errare*, as it says at the end of the dictionary, among the foreign phrases. The fellow on duty at Six Road Ends was a new hand, and he took down four or five numbers all wrong. Possibly the tail-lamps were dim or the number-plates not as clean as they ought to have been; but the plain fact is that we can't rely on his list. We know that definitely, because at least two of his letter-combinations don't correspond to anything on the motor-car register. One can't blame him too much, Squire. Suppose—as he says happened once or twice—that two cars come along different roads and pass the Six Road Ends junction at about right-angles to each other. Each has got two letters and four figures in its number. Would you be very cross with yourself if you got a bit mixed in taking down these identification marks? That's what happened. And I must admit that this particular constable isn't too bright on the whole, for he made one or two other slips and jotted down numbers which were obviously wrong. We've traced the cars with these particular numbers, and they were nowhere near Six Road Ends that night."

"That's a pity," Wendover sympathised.

"It can't be helped. But the obvious result is that although we can take him as correct so far as the total number of cars that passed him is concerned, I shouldn't care to put him into the box to swear to the accuracy of his list of identification marks. It would be asking for trouble, with a sharp barrister against one."

"I'm afraid it would," Wendover agreed.

"Now let's continue," Sir Clinton pursued. "Like a good story-teller, I've kept a tit-bit or two for the final instalments. I gave you the result of the constable's searching of the corpse. When it got to the mortuary they were more thorough. They noticed the dryness of the shoes, for one thing. And they weren't content with merely looking at the outside of the cigar-case. They opened it and peeped inside, with interesting results. In the first place, they found three cigars, and the brand was Flor de Naves—the same as the cigar that was smoked last night in Mrs. Deerhurst's drawing-room."

"Not much in that," Wendover commented sceptically. "Plenty of people smoke that brand of cigar. It may be the merest coincidence."

"They also observed," Sir Clinton went on unperturbed, "that the weapon which made the heart-wounds on the body had gone clean through and made holes in the fabric of the victim's coat. And round these holes some shreds of cotton-wool were clinging. You recall that Dr. Bonchurch called Dornfell's attention to some shreds of cotton-wool in the patch of blood on the drawing-room parquet? Coincidence again, perhaps?"

"Certainly curious," Wendover admitted in a tone that showed he could no longer maintain his scepticism.

"And finally," the Chief Constable continued, "there was a folded sheet of paper in the cigar-case—an ordinary official telegram. It had been despatched from the G.P.O. here at 6.30 p.m. on the sixteenth, and it was addressed to Deerhurst at the prison from which he was released on the following day."

Sir Clinton went to his desk and brought back a slip of paper, evidently a copy of the wire.

"Here's the wording: '*Come here at* 11.30 *p.m. Wednesday. Don't advertise yourself. Don't reply. Hazel.*' That's to say, it summoned Deerhurst to an appointment—at Norwood House, presumably—at half-past eleven at night. He was to come secretly—'*Don't advertise yourself.*' And by midnight, or thereabouts, he was dead. And Mrs. Deerhurst has disappeared."

"It looks very black," Wendover admitted rather gloomily. "I suppose there's no doubt it *was* Deerhurst's body?"

"None whatever. His finger-prints were in the records, and we've had them looked up. This new system lets one check them over the phone. There's no doubt whatever that he's Deerhurst, quite apart from Calbourne's identification of the photograph. *But* . . . here's a rum thing. He's a convict released on licence, and he should have been carrying that licence in his pocket. There's no trace of it. It's gone, with all his other papers which might have identified him. The telegram escaped, evidently because whoever took the other documents never thought of looking inside his cigar-case."

"And what do you think?" demanded Wendover anxiously.

"I think it's a pity Dornfell didn't happen to put his hand on the radiator of the car when he looked at it in the garage," Sir Clinton answered, rather unexpectedly. "But perhaps we can find some other way of dealing with that."

Wendover digested this in silence for a moment; then he amplified his query.

"I mean, what's your view of the whole affair?"

"I? Oh, I think old Calbourne was well advised

to begin creating a favourable atmosphere at the earliest possible moment—from the Adeney point of view, of course."

"Oh, damn your fencing, Clinton!" Wendover exploded irascibly. "You know quite well what I mean."

Sir Clinton glanced at his watch.

"Not worth while troubling to-night," he said, as though answering some unspoken question he had put to himself. "Dornfell may as well get some sleep."

He took another cigarette from the box at his elbow, lighted it with exasperating deliberation, threw away the match, and then turned blandly to his guest.

"The night's still young. What you're asking for, Squire, is a lecture. I'll try to make it vest-pocket size. Title: 'MURDER AND ITS MOTIVES.' Admission Free. In the first place, I assume that Deerhurst was not done to death by a homicidal maniac. Therefore the person who killed him must have had some definite motive. It's a reflection on the limitations of the human mind that, speaking generally, there should be only three motives behind murder cases: hatred, money, and a woman. Now the trouble in this Deerhurst affair is that all three of them are possible, on the face of things. So that behind it there may lie one of these motives, or any pair of them, or all three together. That's seven possible cases, as your mathematical mind no doubt perceives *instanter*. A complex problem, in fact."

Evidently it proved no less complex on consideration, for Sir Clinton leaned back in his chair and pondered for the best part of a minute before speaking again.

"Hazel Deerhurst is the only woman in the case, so far as we've gone," he continued at last. "What do we know about her, Squire? If Calbourne told us the truth, she's rather a fine type: dead straight and anxious to be of some use in the world. She's business-like, or Mandrell would never employ her. She's fond of her cousin and she had more than a usual supply of family pride. She was in love with this man Ferrestone before Deerhurst stepped in. Now with a moral and mental outfit of that kind, what feelings could she have for Deerhurst except loathing and contempt? And we mustn't forget old Calbourne's description of her as a child: 'a pretty little spitfire with a temper that flashed up quite regardless of consequences.' She may have got that temper under control nowadays in normal circumstances. But things weren't normal last night at Norwood House."

"Evidently not," Wendover agreed dejectedly.

"Hazel Deerhurst's alone in that house," Sir Clinton continued. "Alone by choice, Squire, since she could have had her cousin staying there if she wished. Deerhurst arrives, long after any visitor is likely to interrupt them. Now what about Deerhurst? Here's a man who for over four years has been shut off completely from any association with women. His appetites must be all on edge, and from what we've heard of him he's apt to play the bully when he wants a thing. Hazel Deerhurst, one gathers, was a pretty girl."

"You needn't go on," said Wendover. "I see what you're driving at. You want to make out that she stabbed him when she was worked up by rage and panic. I shouldn't blame her if she did that. It would serve the brute right. If he found his way up to her room while she was in her dressing-gown, getting ready for bed . . ."

"That's one of the points that puzzle me in the affair," Sir Clinton interrupted. "On the evidence, one may assume that she was half-undressed and in her dressing-gown. But you're forgetting that Deerhurst came to Norwood House in answer to that wire which he got at the prison when he was released. If she was expecting him, would she not have been in an evening frock, unless . . ."

"A girl doesn't get into her dressing-gown and lingerie when she's going to interview a man she hates," interrupted Wendover impatiently. "There's a screw loose in the psychology of the affair."

"I'm not so sure about that," the Chief Constable objected. "There's the case of Judith in the Apocrypha, remember, who 'decked herself with her apparel and all her woman's attire' when she went to settle accounts with Holofernes. I don't say the cases are parallel; but one must remember that feminine psychology has resources beyond the limits of the mere male brand, Squire. I may as well admit frankly that this part of the affair puzzled me. Let's get to something where one can rely on logic.

"It's an established fact that Hazel Deerhurst has disappeared. She may have gone voluntarily, or she may have been kidnapped, or she may have been killed and the body removed by her murderer. These seem the three likeliest explanations."

"If she went voluntarily, it must have been late at night," Wendover pointed out. "After 11.30 p.m., at any rate, since she had made that appointment with Deerhurst for half-past eleven."

"She may have funked it at the last moment," the Chief Constable amended.

"But she wouldn't go abroad in a dressing-gown," objected Wendover. "By the way, have you made any inquiries at stations and on bus routes?"

"Oh, yes," Sir Clinton said indifferently. "The results were nil, as one might expect when we couldn't give a description of the dress she was wearing. Certainly no one saw her gadding about in her dressing-gown."

"Kidnapping's out of the question," Wendover pursued, with a certain reluctance in his tone. "No one had any motive for that, so far as I can see."

"Perhaps not," the Chief Constable conceded. "So

the choice is between flight and murder, eh? But who was likely to murder her? Deerhurst? But if that doctor was correct, Deerhurst was dead himself at midnight, roughly. How could he have met her, quarrelled with her, murdered her, and disposed of the body in a suburban district, and been murdered himself, all in well under an hour? It sounds a bit incredible, doesn't it?"

"There's the car," Wendover suggested in a half-hearted tone.

Sir Clinton's gesture disposed of that explanation, so far as he was concerned.

"No good, Squire. There simply isn't time for all that."

"Then, on your showing, it's a case of flight on her part?"

"It seems the likeliest solution," the Chief Constable said in a rather cautious tone. "That leaves us to find a motive for her vanishing; and that in turn demands a knowledge of the time when she left the house. And that we haven't got enough evidence to determine. Apparently, Squire, the Woman Motive seems to suggest more problems than it solves in this affair. Let's try Money next. The only money in the business was Mrs. Deerhurst's. She had made no will, so Deerhurst would come into it if she died. But did he know that?"

"I don't see how he could, unless she told him the facts when she met him," Wendover pointed out, "and she would hardly do that."

"Young Adeney knew," Sir Clinton recalled. "But he was fond of his cousin. Besides, he could only come in under this unmade will of hers. If Hazel Deerhurst died first, the money passed to Deerhurst automatically and would be allocated according to his will, if he had made one. Young Adeney wouldn't get a penny."

Wendover remained wrapt in reflection for some

moments ,evidently conning the matter over carefully. At last he looked up.

" No, it makes no sense, unless Deerhurst murdered his wife and then Adeney murdered him with the idea of interchanging the hours of death somehow, and so getting the money. But that won't work, for Adeney had a lock-fast alibi for the time of the murder of Deerhurst, if it happened at midnight."

" Then we can drop the money motive ? " inquired the Chief Constable. " That leaves hatred of one sort or another still on the list. Who hated Deerhurst ? A large assortment of people, I expect : shareholders who lost their money by his swindling. But I never yet heard of a defrauded shareholder feeling bitter enough to murder a fraudulent company director."

" You can leave them out," Wendover said impatiently.

" Then there's Mrs. Deerhurst," continued the Chief Constable. " She hated her husband, and she'd every reason for that, one must admit. Her family honour in the mud. Her cousin ruined and in jail. And her romance blighted. Admitted she'd herself to thank for that, still it probably rankled and added to her hatred of Deerhurst. And Mrs. Deerhurst had a temper which took very little note of consequences if it once got out of control. If hatred's to be the criterion, I should think Mrs. Deerhurst would be *hors concours.*"

" The fact that you hate a man doesn't prove that you'd go the length of murdering him," Wendover protested sulkily.

" Then there's young Adeney," Sir Clinton continued, ignoring Wendover's comment. " His life prospects have been shattered. His character's gone. He's a jail-bird. And he's fond of his cousin, so her troubles must have added some fuel to the fire. Against that, he seems to be a weak character."

"It's just these weak characters who get most embittered when they've had time to brood over their wrongs," Wendover pointed out.

"That's true. And some tough nuts are like them in that respect," Sir Clinton averred. "Curiously enough, some very tough nuts had a dislike for Deerhurst. Dornfell—very efficient fellow, Dornfell—got on to the prison over the phone and made inquiries about Deerhurst's record. It seems he was instrumental in foiling a neat little prison-breaking scheme. He overheard some of his fellow-convicts discussing their plans, and gave them away at once to the officials. No honour among thieves for Mr. Deerhurst, you see. Naturally these fellows don't love him; and some of them are pretty bad hats. One of them, a burglar called Sturge, is known to be actually in this neighbourhood at present. He had to report, being out on licence; so there's no question about his identity. I think these fellows might be considered, though there's nothing to connect them with the affair as yet."

"Oh," said Wendover uneasily, "that brings a fresh factor into the business. If these brutes followed Deerhurst to Norwood House last night and broke in while he was talking to his wife . . . They may have finished him and . . . Well, she'd be a witness against them, and they may have done anything to her to stop her mouth. I don't like that, Clinton. It's an ugly idea, and it sounds too likely to be comfortable. It fits so damnably neatly on the evidence."

"One hopes for the best," Sir Clinton said gravely. Then in a different tone he added, "but there's still another person who had every reason to hate Deerhurst. And, curiously enough, he's not been in the public eye lately."

"Who's that?" Wendover inquired, looking rather puzzled.

"Ferrestone," said the Chief Constable.

CHAPTER IX

MILES PER GALLON

ONE of Wendover's hobbies at Talgarth Grange was landscape gardening; and he was always alert to pick up hints on minor points of arrangement whenever he came upon fresh ground. As he walked up the short drive to Norwood House with the Chief Constable on the following morning he threw appraising glances to and fro.

"A roomier garden than one expects with a villa like this," he commented approvingly. "And whoever laid it out had some idea of how to make the best of it. I like that pergola."

Sir Clinton halted to give his friend time for examination.

"It certainly provides plenty of privacy for a suburban place," he said critically. "One could move about here and not be overlooked much by the neighbours or passers-by on the road. Nor even from the villa itself," he added, looking round. "That's clever."

"It must keep one gardener up to the collar in looking after it," reflected Wendover. "Especially if he has a car to clean as well. He must be a hard-working fellow. Everything's very spick and span. My own men don't keep things in better trim, and they're enthusiasts in their own lines."

"You can have a look round, afterwards," Sir Clinton suggested, moving on. "Business first, though, Squire. Ah! There's Dornfell waiting for us at the door. We'll hear if he's made any further progress."

After introducing Wendover, Sir Clinton wasted no time.

" Anything fresh, Inspector ? "

Dornfell's mouth drooped in humorous self-disparagement.

" Just one or two things, sir. Nothing that gets to the root of the business, I'm afraid."

" No trace of Mrs. Deerhurst then ? "

Dornfell shook his head seriously.

" You know how it is, sir. People never notice anything except what's a shade out of the ordinary. I questioned the station staff, of course. All they remembered, amongst them, was a cross old lady quarrelling with her taxi-driver over her change, a group of young fellows and girls skylarking on the platform, a woman with a fox-terrier on a lead, barking at everybody within range, a nurse with a suit-case helping an old woman into a third-class carriage, a couple of nuns, and a fussy dame who nearly took the wrong train by getting on to the up platform when she wanted the down one. Mrs. Deerhurst might have walked past in front of their noses and they'd never have looked at her."

" And the bus routes ? "

" Sergeant Lorrimore covered them, sir. Absolutely nothing to report, so far as usefulness goes. A complete wash-out. We've done our best and the result's nil."

" You've checked young Adeney's alibi story ? "

" Yes, sir. It's confirmed up to the hilt. Constable Goodrich met him outside his lodgings at a few minutes after half-past twelve and had a talk with him, just as Adeney told me. And the rest of the evening he spent at Calbourne's, just as he said."

" Finger-prints no use, I suppose ? "

" None whatever, sir. They found nothing barring those of the Norwood House people. Not a thing to go on."

" I suppose you got the name of these bearer bonds which came in the registered letter ? The stockbrokers would give you it."

" Yes, sir. Arctic and Frigidor Cold Storage Corporation. Five bonds of one hundred pounds each, paying five per cent, and numbered 515 to 519."

Sir Clinton hitherto had put his questions as though they were in the nature of formal inquiries. More interest came into his voice with his next query.

" And that red powder ? What did it turn out to be ? "

" Red lead, sir, the city analyst tells me. I asked him what it was used for, and he said that commercially it was employed in making paint and flint glass. That's not very helpful, I'm afraid, sir."

" Very dense," Sir Clinton said ruminatively.

" Do you mean me, sir ? " Dornfell asked suspiciously.

" I was speaking of the red lead," Sir Clinton assured him gravely, " but now you've got the hint, I think it will apply to you if you don't see how that stuff came to be where it was. But let's get on. What about the blood-tests ? "

" The pathologist has examined the samples from the floor here and from Deerhurst's body, sir, and he says they both belong to Group II."

" Forty per cent. of people hereabouts have Group II blood," the Chief Constable pointed out. " Still, taken along with the other evidence, it seems good enough. We may as well see if we can't find something further, since the blood itself has been examined. Where's the drawing-room in this place ? And you might borrow a sponge and some warm water from Mrs. Butterswick if she's on the premises still."

The constable on guard in the hall saluted as they passed and was despatched for the water and sponge while the inspector showed the way to the drawing-room.

"Nothing's been tampered with, I suppose?" demanded Sir Clinton as he glanced round the room.

"No, sir. I've had men on the premises ever since we were called in, with instructions to see that nothing was touched."

Wendover examined the drawing-room, but except for the dark stain on the floor he found nothing amiss. It was obvious at a glance that both taste and money had gone to the furnishing of it. Wendover prided himself on some knowledge of cloisonné ware, and he knew that the two examples of it on the mantelpiece were picked specimens, things which must have been sought after and not merely bought casually on a chance visit to a dealer's shop. So were the Persian rugs underfoot. But the scheme of the room as a whole was greater than any of its parts. Only a woman with an inborn sense of form and colour could have designed it; and Wendover suddenly found the explanation for the apparently incongruous choice which Hazel Adeney had made in her first love.

Only three pictures hung on the walls. They were plainly modern work, and just as plainly they had been painted by someone who knew his medium through and through. The style was unfamiliar to Wendover, and he moved over and examined the nearest one more closely in search of the artist's signature. There it was, in the corner, with the date below it:

Duncan Ferrestone
1931

Sir Clinton, noticing how Wendover was engaged, stepped across and looked over his shoulder.

"Nineteen-thirty-one," he said musingly. "H'm! What about the others?"

Followed by Wendover, he inspected the other two pictures, one of which was dated 1932, whilst the second had 1931, like the first.

"Deerhurst was gaoled in 1930," the Chief Constable said in a reflective tone. "And the series stops the year before last, though one could have put a couple more on the walls without spoiling the scheme by overcrowding. You remember that Calbourne dropped a hint, something about Ferrestone falling out of the race? There's some story or other behind this, I expect, if one could only see it. Any suggestions?"

But at this moment the constable arrived with the sponge and warm water. Sir Clinton turned away from the pictures and busied himself with his original object.

"Just wash away that blood, please," he directed the constable. "Don't rub it. Dab it gently with the sponge, so that it comes away easily."

Slowly the caked blood yielded to the treatment and left the parquet clean. Motioning the constable aside, Sir Clinton knelt down to examine the surface, while Wendover and Dornfell followed his example. Where the clot had been two slight indentations showed themselves in the wood, like the marks made by a fine punch. Sir Clinton rose to his feet again.

"They might have been made by the point of a kitchen skewer. Just about the same distance apart as the two wounds in Deerhurst's body, aren't they?" he asked Dornfell, who confirmed this with a nod.

"I think I see now, sir, why you talked about red lead being dense," the inspector volunteered. "You were thinking of something like a sandbag, weren't you? I mean, he was knocked out first by a blow on the head, and then stabbed while he was unconscious. If he was stabbed here, in this room, the chances are that he was knocked out here too. Red lead in a stocking would make a heavier 'cosh' than sand, and some of it might escape when the blow was struck. That's what you meant?"

"Not exactly," the Chief Constable explained, rather to Dornfell's vexation. "It struck me that with red lead instead of sand your 'cosh' could be made a good deal smaller and yet deal just as heavy a blow. A handier article, in fact, which wouldn't require a pocket Hercules to manœuvre it adroitly. Also, being smaller, it would be easier to conceal about one's person."

Wendover shuddered slightly. Behind the matter-of-fact words of the Chief Constable he perceived something left unspoken. Make the club handy enough, and a woman could use it with effect. At that suggestion a sinister moving picture rose in his imagination, vivid as Ferrestone's paintings on the walls of the room. He saw in his mind's eye Deerhurst, careless in his superior strength, sprawling at ease in that ash-smeared arm-chair with its low back which exposed his head. The slight figure of a girl passed behind the seated man on some excuse—perhaps crossing over to the escritoire, yonder—with that deadly little weapon in her hand. A raised arm, a set face, a blow delivered with all the force of long-pent anger—and the strong lay at the mercy of the weak. Then a horrid crouching over the helpless body on the floor, a fumbling at the breast to make sure of the right spot, and a deadly intent that was not satisfied with one stab, but must make sure work with a second. Wendover tried to banish that grim vision. Things like that didn't happen, he assured himself. But all the while he knew that sometimes they did.

Sir Clinton's voice, speaking to Dornfell, roused him to reality again.

"You might get that man Oakley, Inspector. I want to ask him a question or two. Round at the garage."

Dornfell left the room at once, but Sir Clinton lingered for a minute or two. He stood in front of each picture in turn, but Wendover surmised that the artistic merits of them had little to do with his apparent fascination. It was on the signatures and dates that he seemed to concentrate his attention, as if in the hope that the concrete symbols would suggest something to his mind. At last he turned away.

"There's something behind that," he repeated musingly, as he and Wendover made their way to the garage. "Deerhurst's no sooner in gaol than she begins to buy Ferrestone's work. Obviously she didn't care to buy it while her husband was on the premises."

"Or Ferrestone may have presented them to her," Wendover suggested. "He wouldn't care to do that while Deerhurst was about, perhaps."

"There might be something in that," Sir Clinton admitted in a doubtful tone. "But remember that Ferrestone depended on his art for a living—at least that's the impression I got—and from what we've heard of her, she'd insist on paying for any pictures she took. I'm more inclined to think that she bought them through a dealer or at one of Ferrestone's exhibitions. But why did she stop in 1932? It might be worth while putting someone on to look up Ferrestone's record. I hate to be puzzled."

When they reached the garage Dornfell and Oakley were there, and the doors had been thrown open. Wendover noticed that a thin film of dust was on the bonnet of the car. At the back of the garage stood a stack of petrol tins.

"Is this car's number on the Six Road Ends list?" Wendover asked the Chief Constable, and got a negative nod for answer.

Followed by Wendover and the inspector, Sir Clinton entered the garage and opened the driving-seat door. A twist of the ignition key set the petrol gauge in action, and Wendover noticed that the needle hovered just a shade below the five-gallon mark. When the tank was full it apparently held nine gallons, according to the dial. The Chief Constable inspected the milometer and the trip dial. Then he switched off the ignition.

" Now I want a few words with Oakley."

Though the gardener's professional skill had impressed Wendover favourably, he found little to attract him in Oakley's personal appearance.

" A blockish fellow, by the look of him," was his unspoken comment as he took in the man's outward characteristics.

" You look after this car ? " demanded the Chief Constable, turning to Oakley. " When was it out last, so far as you know ? "

" Forenoon, day before yesterday."

" Who was driving then ? " queried Sir Clinton, mindful of the fact that Nicholas Adeney had a key of the garage.

" Mrs. Deerhurst."

" Was she away long with it ? "

" Best part of the morning."

" You didn't clean it when she brought it back ? "

" No."

" Why not ? "

" Mrs. Deerhurst told me not to bother."

" When was the tank filled up last, do you know ? "

Instead of answering, Oakley slouched into the garage, felt in the pocket of the driving-seat, pulled out a penny notebook and began to leaf clumsily through the pages.

" Afternoon, day before yesterday, when I went off duty," he announced at length, beginning to replace the note-book in the door-pocket.

" Why couldn't you say that at once," the Chief Constable asked testily.

" 'Cause I didn't know if Mrs. Deerhurst had filled it up since," Oakley explained in an aggrieved tone.

" Let me see that book," Sir Clinton directed. " What is it ? "

Oakley passed it to him ; and Wendover, glancing over Sir Clinton's shoulder, saw a record of petrol supplies entered up in three different handwritings.

" It's a book Mrs. Deerhurst wanted kept," Oakley explained. " It's a new car, this. She wants to know how many miles per gallon she's getting with it. When she fills up from a pump she enters it up in the book. Same for Mr. Adeney. When I fill up from the tins here at night, after cleaning the car, I put down the figures too."

This unwontedly long speech seemed to have exhausted the gardener. Sir Clinton turned over the leaves of the book, made a short calculation on the back of an envelope and then handed the note-book to Dornfell.

" You'd better keep that. We'll probably need it."

The inspector stowed it carefully away in his pocket, and Sir Clinton continued.

" They didn't use the trip dial of the milometer, did they ? "

" Only now and again," Oakley explained. " Not regular."

" You're sure you filled the tank quite full the day before yesterday ? "

" It just came full with the last drops in the tin. There's the tin I filled it from," Oakley explained, giving one of the empty tins a kick with his toe.

" Then that's all I need you for just now," Sir Clinton said in a tone of dismissal.

When the gardener had gone out of earshot Sir Clinton turned to the inspector.

" The first entry in that note-book says that when the car was taken over the milometer stood at 243.

It's now standing at 1,328. That leaves 1,085 miles, corresponding to a total of forty-three gallons of petrol recorded in the book, or round about twenty-five miles per gallon if the tank had been completely emptied this time. If Oakley filled the tank full, as he says, and if no more petrol has been put in beyond what's entered up, then from the petrol gauge it appears that about four and a quarter gallons have been used. These gauges are never absolutely accurate, of course, but it may be near enough for our purposes. Four and a quarter at twenty-five miles per gallon is about equivalent to one hundred and six miles. The distance from here to the place where Deerhurst's body was found is fifty-two miles; I put a map measure over the map this morning. I think it's a fair inference that this was the car which passed twice through Six Road Ends that night."

Dornfell barely repressed a gesture of vexation.

"I ought to have thought of that myself, sir," he admitted.

"You've been fairly busy in other directions," Sir Clinton soothed him. "One can't think of everything. Now let's go back to the house. This door takes us through direct, doesn't it? I want to see the housekeeper, Inspector."

Mrs. Butterswick was produced, rather flustered by the prospect of being questioned by three interrogators.

"Now, Mrs. Butterswick," Sir Clinton began pleasantly. "I want one or two questions answered. First of all, had you a fire in your kitchen range on the day that Mrs. Deerhurst disappeared?"

This inquiry evidently took the housekeeper completely back by its unexpectedness.

"Oh, no, sir. We hardly ever have the range on in this weather. It makes the kitchen so hot. We do the cooking on a gas-stove."

" What about hot water for the house if the range is off ? "

" We have a circulator, sir, that heats the boiler supply."

Neither Wendover nor the inspector could make head or tail of these inquiries into the Norwood House economy, but Sir Clinton seemed satisfied with the answers he had got.

" Now another point," he went on. " During the last few days has any box been delivered here ? You know the kind of thing I mean, a cardboard box of the size that would hold a coat and skirt, or something like that."

Mrs. Butterswick shook her head decidedly.

" No, sir. I've seen nothing of the sort delivered. Nor has Evie either, or she'd have told me about it, for we're both very interested in anything new that Mrs. Deerhurst gets."

Sir Clinton nodded understandingly.

" And when you and Inspector Dornfell searched the house yesterday you didn't come across anything of the kind—any dress-box of that sort ? "

" Oh, no, sir. I'd have noticed it at once if we had."

" Well, we'll go upstairs and look at Mrs. Deerhurst's room for a moment. You come with me, please, Mrs. Butterswick."

When they reached the upper floor Sir Clinton and the inspector walked into Hazel Deerhurst's room. Wendover, with an old-fashioned scruple, remained on the threshold. He did not quite like the idea of prying into a girl's bedroom ; and as he was not there in any official capacity he was able to stand aside. The most he could force himself to do was to glance into the room. His eye took in the cheval mirror, the pedestal basin with its shining taps and glass shelf, the dressing-table strewn with silver knick-knacks, and the bedside table, with its reading-lamp, beside which a book was lying. Then, as his glance travelled round, it lighted on a picture hung on the wall facing the bed. The painter's technique was unmistakable ; but the picture, for some reason, appealed less to Wendover than the three in the drawing-room had done. Forgetting his scruples, he stepped into the room and examined the painting more closely. The signature was the same as before, but this time the date was 1933. Wendover scanned the canvas for the best part of a minute, trying to discover how it differed from the others.

Sir Clinton, noticing how he was employed, came over to his side and inspected the picture in his turn. Then he put into words the very thing Wendover had been trying to express to himself.

" Looks as if he'd taken to imitating Corot a bit, doesn't it ? I don't think it's an improvement."

The criticism crystallised the vague impression which Wendover had felt at the sight of the painting. It was not a direct imitation of Corot's technique. It was too individual for that. And yet, in some elusive way, it did recall Corot's treatment. Wendover gave the canvas another long scrutiny, and then turned away, feeling baffled by something which he could not even define to himself. Why should a man, with a talent of his own, deliberately change his style in this way ? And why had Hazel Deerhurst singled out this particular picture to hang in her bedroom ? Then it occurred to him that she might have put the best pictures where the ordinary visitor might see them, and kept this one out of the way just because it was not so good as the others.

Meanwhile, Sir Clinton had been more fruitfully occupied. Pulling open a drawer of the dressing-table, he unearthed two ladies' hair-brushes, a cloth brush and a hat-brush, silver-mounted, with initials, and part of the same set as the comb and mirror on the table top. The other drawers yielded nothing which seemed to interest him, and he transferred his attention to the glass shelf above the pedestal basin.

"I don't see a tooth-brush," he said, turning to Dornfell. "You haven't taken it, have you? And the nail-brush as well?"

The inspector shook his head.

"I don't remember seeing either of them, sir, now you mention it."

Sir Clinton addressed Mrs. Butterswick.

"I see a face-cloth here, but there's no bath sponge. Perhaps Mrs. Deerhurst kept that in the bathroom? She did? Then would you mind seeing if it's still there, Inspector? You know your way about the premises."

As Dornfell left the room Sir Clinton moved to the bedside table and picked up the volume which lay upon it. Wendover caught the name on the back.

"Axel Munthe's *Story of San Michele?*" he read out. "Oh, yes, I remember reading that. It was a best-seller when it came out."

The Chief Constable turned to the fly-leaf.

"It's her own copy," he said. "Her name's on it. By the way, Mrs. Butterswick, was Mrs. Deerhurst a reader? I mean, did she read regularly?"

"Oh, yes, sir. Every night she read herself to sleep. And she used to get a parcel of books from *The Times* Book Club once or twice a week. She was a great reader, sir."

Sir Clinton replaced the volume on the table as Dornfell came back into the room.

"Well?" he inquired.

"I can't find it, sir. No sign of it in the bathroom, anyhow."

"It isn't here," the Chief Constable said, with a final glance round the bedroom. "I think we'll go over the rooms downstairs now."

CHAPTER X

THE SECRET OF THE MACHINE

AT the foot of the stairs Sir Clinton hesitated for a moment and then went into the dining room, followed by the others. It presented nothing striking to Wendover's eye : a fine old dining table, a carving-table, and other furniture to match. Two or three etchings hung on the walls, and though the names of the artists were unfamiliar to Wendover, he recognised that their work was above the average. Evidently Hazel Deerhurst knew what she wanted and was not inclined to buy things merely because they had well known names attached.

The Chief Constable stepped over to the waste-paper basket by the fireside, extracted one or two envelopes containing circulars, and examined the post-marks.

" You'd better preserve these," he suggested to Dornfell. " One never knows what one may want."

Then he turned to the mantelpiece.

" It was here that Adeney said he's left that registered letter ? "

" Yes, sir. He said he propped it up against one of the ornaments."

Sir Clinton looked at Mrs. Butterswick, who was hovering in the doorway.

" Did Mrs. Deerhurst entertain much—dinner-parties and so on ? "

" Perhaps once or twice a week, sir. Mr. Calbourne

used to come quite often with his daughter, Mrs. Latchmere, and Mr. Adeney was generally here with them to make up a four for bridge afterwards. And often Mr. Adeney and Mrs. Deerhurst used to dine together, almost every night when Mrs. Deerhurst hadn't other engagements. And of course some neighbours used to be invited from time to time. Oh, yes, sir, Mrs. Deerhurst was very sociable."

"But on the night of her disappearance she was alone here? Nor even Mr. Adeney was invited, I gather?"

"No, sir. She ordered a cold supper instead of dinner, just for herself, that night."

"What about afternoon tea?"

"Well, sir, she sent Evie—that's the housemaid, sir—away about three o'clock. Evie set a tea-tray all ready before she left. And Mrs. Deerhurst must have made the tea herself, for we found the cups and things waiting to be washed up next morning."

"Cups?" queried Sir Clinton.

"Yes, sir. Two cups. That would be Mr. Adeney that was with her, sir, I expect."

"Very likely," Sir Clinton agreed. "Now I want to go back to the drawing-room."

Wendover had been fidgeting to go there. He had been disappointed on their first visit that nothing had been seen of the strange machine which Dornfell had discovered in the escritoire. But when they re-entered the drawing-room, Sir Clinton seemed in no hurry to examine it. Instead he walked up to a book-case which stood near the door and began to inspect the volumes on the shelves, reading some of the titles aloud as he went along.

"Sir Thomas Browne's works, three volumes. That's a nice edition. . . . Kipling's *Light that Failed*. . . . Somebody's *History of Art* in four fat volumes.

. . . Helen Keller's Life. I take off my hat to her, and to her teacher as well. A wonderful feat, that. . . . Keats, another nice edition. . . . And Blake, with the facsimile reproductions of *Urizen*. That's not so easily come by, nowadays. . . . *Life of W. H. Prescott*. That's unusual. It's dated 1864. . . . And cheek by jowl with it, some modern stuff. . . . Buchan . . . Aldous Huxley . . . Mason's *At the Villa Rose*. That's a good yarn. . . . Montague. . . She seems to have had a catholic taste."

As he turned from the book-case, his eye was caught by the brown millboard box from *The Times* Book Club, which still lay beside the escritoire where Dornfell had left it on the previous day. The Chief Constable walked over, picked it up, assured himself that it was empty, and then put it down on the floor again. He glanced about the room as though in search of something which eluded him.

"Looking for something, sir ?" queried the inspector.

"I was just wondering what books had come in this box," Sir Clinton answered. "Suppose we look about and see if we can find them. They'll have a little black and gold label on the inside of the back cover."

A search through the bookshelves drew blank. All the books in them bore Hazel's name written on the fly-leaves. Sir Clinton seemed to become more interested after this check, and insisted on having the whole house ransacked for the missing volumes, much to the astonishment of the inspector and the disgust of Wendover, whose curiosity about the machine was thus being baulked. Finally, it became plain that the books were not to be found.

"Difficult to prove a negative," Sir Clinton remarked finally as they gave up the chase, "but in this case I think we've come near it. The things don't seem to be on the premises."

"I don't see what all the excitement's about," Wendover growled. "You didn't expect to find a confession stuck in between the pages, did you?"

"Having got what I want, I'm not a bit excited," Sir Clinton pointed out. "The trouble is that now I've got it, I don't quite know what to make of it, exactly. That often happens in affairs of this sort, so it doesn't discourage me. But I see what you're yearning for. The escritoire, eh? Well, let's have a look at it."

Followed by the others, he went to the writing-desk and, pulling out the top drawer, revealed the machine. At the sight of it, a faintly malicious twinkle came into Wendover's eyes, but he kept his face impassive with an effort. The Chief Constable made a minute inspection of the instrument, fiddled with the keys, watched the carriage move, took the whole thing to pieces and examined it. Then, as he leaned back in his chair, obviously baffled, he heard a half-suppressed chuckle behind him and looked round to find Wendover regarding him sardonically. It was not often that the Squire could catch his host out, and obviously he was enjoying this situation.

"Oh, so *you* know what it is, do you?" Sir Clinton exclaimed, as he saw the smile on his friend's face. "Well, you score. It's beyond me."

"Special knowledge counts for more than cleverness, sometimes," said Wendover with mock sententiousness. "If you'll get up and let me sit down, I'll show you how easy it is."

He took the chair which Sir Clinton vacated, and turned to Dornfell.

"Where did you find that paper?" he asked. "The stuff you took for wrapping-paper, I mean. Manilla paper, it should be."

Dornfell pulled open the drawer and showed him the pile of sheets.

" Ah ! That's right," Wendover declared. " Now observe. I clamp this sheet in the clip at the top of the board—so ! Then I thread the paper through this slit in the carriage—so ! Then I fit the carriage pegs into a pair of these holes on the base-board—so ! And now I proceed to write just as if it were a type-writer of sorts. And, finally, I release the paper. And you'll find the name of the machine neatly inscribed—if you can read it."

He extracted the sheet and handed it to Sir Clinton upside down. On the surface of the paper, a series of pin-pricks had been made which formed an irregular pattern :

" Braille ? " ejaculated Sir Clinton, suddenly enlightened.

" BRAILLE WRITER is what I've written," said Wendover with a wholly undignified grin. " It's a Stainsby machine, the model with the keys arranged to correspond with the positions of the dots in ordinary Braille type. Of course the needles are protected by the base of the carriage ; that's why you see nothing when you turn the carriage upside down to examine it. I saw you were completely stuck when you found nothing but a plain plate. But of course the paper threads in above that plate, just under the invisible needles. It's a most ingenious little affair."

The Chief Constable made a gesture of presentation.

" Your laurel wreath ! There's no doubt you've

beaten us here. But how do you come to know about it?"

Wendover fidgeted slightly. He preferred to do his good deeds without advertising them; but this time he had left himself with no escape.

"Oh, there's an institution called The National Library for the Blind. It supplies blind people with books in Braille type: all sorts of works, classics, history, modern fiction—thousands of volumes. The blind can get the loan of them for nothing. A God-send to the poor creatures! Well, some of the transcribing into Braille—with machines like this—is done by voluntary workers who've passed an accuracy test. I've sometimes got time on my hands. It seemed the sort of thing I could make myself useful at, so I bought a Stainsby machine like this one and started to train myself as a transcriber. Which reminds me that I want a subscription to the Library from you, Clinton, in payment for this bit of assistance."

"Remind me when I've got my cheque-book handy," said the Chief Constable. "I shan't grudge it."

Dornfell's face had been falling by degrees as Wendover made his explanation.

"Then there's nothing in the thing, after all!" he ejaculated. "From what you say, most likely Mrs. Deerhurst's been on the same game—a voluntary transcriber."

"It sounds the sort of thing she would do," Wendover admitted, with a certain triumph in his tone.

"You'd better ring up the National Library for the Blind and make sure if she's on their list, though," Sir Clinton said to the inspector. "I don't see any trace of an unfinished transcription here," he added, as he pulled our drawer after drawer. "Nothing but a blank space which would just hold another set of these Manilla sheets."

"Perhaps she'd just finished the transcription of a volume, and sent it off to the Library," Wendover suggested.

"Well, the inspector will check that up for us," said the Chief Constable. Then, turning to Mrs. Butterswick, he asked: "Did you ever see Mrs. Deerhurst using this machine?"

"No, I never so much as saw the machine, sir, till Mr. Dornfell pulled out the drawer yesterday and showed it to me. I never pried into that writing desk in my life, and the machine was never left lying about the room."

"Adeney had never seen it either?" asked Sir Clinton of the inspector.

"That was the impression I got, sir," Dornfell answered guardedly. "Certainly he seemed just as much surprised by it as I was myself!"

"Well, we may know more about it after you've rung up these National Library people," Sir Clinton said, doubtfully. "By the way, Mrs. Butterswick, do you know where Mrs. Deerhurst kept her cheque book?"

"Yes, sir. It was always in one of these drawers, sir. I've seen her take it out often when she had to draw a cheque."

Sir Clinton glanced at Dornfell.

"You didn't find it when you searched the drawers? We'd better have another look, just in case."

In his search he came across the unfinished embroidery which Dornfell had noticed in the lowest drawer. After a glance at it, Sir Clinton turned to Mrs. Butterswick.

"Was Mrs. Deerhurst clever with her needle?"

"Oh, yes, indeed, sir. You've only got to look at that embroidery to see that. She did beautiful sewing, and she made a lot of pretty things to wear."

Mrs. Butterswick did not particularise, but Wendover

guessed from her slightly embarrassed manner that she meant intimate garments which she could not bring herself to mention in that company. He smiled to himself, but not unkindly. This old-fashioned reticence was decent, by his standards.

"She didn't make dresses for herself, did she?" Sir Clinton queried.

"Oh, no, sir. Just pretty things generally. She had an electric sewing-machine, but of course she did all the embroidery by hand."

The Chief Constable nodded absently and his eye ranged over the escritoire.

"You've looked through the counterfoils in these cheque-book stubs?" he questioned, turning to the inspector.

"Yes, sir. There's nothing of any interest in them, so far as I saw," Dornfell answered.

Then something seemed to be recalled to his mind.

"I'm sorry, sir," he went on, "I should have mentioned this before. I questioned the constable on this beat the night before last, and it seems he saw lights in this room about midnight. But he'd often seen that before, when he passed along, so he thought nothing of it. Somebody was sitting up, reading, he imagined. I asked if he'd noticed anything, later on when he passed again. He can't remember exactly, but he thinks the lights had been put out then."

"We all forget things at times," Sir Clinton conceded. "I meant to tell you to syphon off the petrol in the car's tank and measure it exactly. One can't trust these electric gauges. You'll see to that?"

"Certainly, sir."

Mrs. Butterswick was still lingering, in case her assistance might be needed, but now the Chief Constable thanked her and dismissed her. When she had left the room he made a gesture inviting the others to sit down.

" We seem to have collected a fair amount of evidence amongst us," he observed, as they took their seats. " Suppose we go over it now, and see where it leads. We may as well begin with Deerhurst. What do you make of his affairs, Inspector ? "

Dornfell spent a few seconds in arranging his ideas.

" Well, sir," he began, " I think Deerhurst's case is fairly plane sailing now with what we've got together. It begins with that telegram despatched from the G.P.O. here on the 16th. You remember that it ran : '*Come here at* 11.30 *p.m. Wednesday. Don't advertise yourself. Don't reply. Hazel.*' "

" Have you got the original of that telegram yet ? " Sir Clinton interjected.

" Not yet, sir. It hadn't reached me when I came out to meet you this morning."

" Very well. Go on."

" Well, sir, Deerhurst was released from gaol on the 17th. He got that wire, and I expect he came here in response to it. Most likely he came by train and dumped his luggage, whatever he had, in the cloak-room at the station. We'll get hold of it, sooner or later, but the cloak-room porter who was on duty that night has gone on holiday and we haven't got his address at present. When we get hold of him, he's almost bound to remember Deerhurst leaving his stuff. There's not so much doing at that cloak-room, and Deerhurst was easily recognisable."

" Yes, quite," Wendover confirmed, remembering the photograph he had seen.

" Deerhurst came here in reply to that wire," the inspector continued. " He wouldn't call on the Calbournes or anyone else, because the wire gave him a straight tip that he wasn't to make himself conspicuous; so I expect he came by a late train and walked straight up here from the station. He must have reached here about 11.30 to keep his appointment."

"That sounds reasonable," the Chief Constable agreed.

"He must have been admitted to the house or found the door on the latch," Dornfell went on, "for he never lived here and couldn't have a latch-key. Anyhow, he found his way into this room. He sat here for a while, either alone or talking to someone, for he had time to smoke half a cigar. We know that because a half-smoked cigar stub was in the hearth along with a band corresponding to the bands round the cigars in his case: Flor de Naves, they were. I think that's good enough. It would be too much of a coincidence to happen by chance."

He looked interrogatively at Wendover, who nodded in agreement.

"Then there was a bit of a set-to," Dornfell continued. "Deerhurst was stunned unexpectedly with a sand-bag—made out of red lead, you say, sir."

"Why 'unexpectedly'?" demanded Wendover.

"Because there was no sign of a struggle, no upset chairs, or anything of that sort," the inspector pointed out. "The only thing amiss was an ash-tray upset, and it had been on the arm of his chair and would be knocked over with a touch. Seeing he was a big, powerful fellow, the inference is obvious, I think."

Wendover did not contest this, and the inspector proceeded.

"Once he was unconscious, but still alive, he was dragged on to the floor there and two stabs made through his heart—with a skewer, you say, sir?"

"It might have been a stiletto," Sir Clinton admitted.

" but a skewer's easier to come by. Also, a skewer has been suggested already in one of the best-known of all detective yarns—A. E. W. Mason's *At the Villa Rose*. There's a copy of it on the shelves yonder," he added, with a glance towards the book-case.

If there was any implication in this, Wendover refused to notice it.

" Go on, Inspector," he urged.

" Well, the two marks on the parquet show that he was stabbed here, anyhow," Dornfell continued. " And that finished him. Round about midnight, it must have been, according to the medical evidence ; and that's just when the constable saw the lights in this room as he passed by. It all fits together neatly, doesn't it, sir ? Some blood oozed out of the wound, and it's the same type of blood as Deerhurst's, which seems to put the thing beyond a doubt."

" It's not a certainty. Forty per cent of people have that type of blood," Sir Clinton pointed out. " Still, I agree with you that it's good enough."

" After that came the problem of getting the body away," the inspector went on, avoiding the problem of the murderer's identity. " The wounds were covered with some cotton-wool from the drawer there to prevent any trail being left when the body was moved."

" The presence of that cotton-wool in the drawer wouldn't be known to a stranger," Sir Clinton interrupted.

" No, whoever shifted the body was someone familiar with the house," the inspector concurred. " Mrs. Deerhurst knew about it. So did Adeney."

" So did Mrs. Butterswick," interrupted Wendover sharply.

" Mrs. Butterswick has a perfect alibi," the inspector pointed out.

" So has Adeney," Wendover snapped, and then looked as though he wished he had kept quiet.

" Let's go on," Sir Clinton suggested.

" Before shifting the body," Dornfell went on, " I think most likely the murderer went through the pockets and took away all he saw that was likely to give a clue to Deerhurst's identity. The convict's licence was removed, and any other papers he may have had. The tailor's tag was cut off the coat. The handkerchief was taken. It had his name on it, perhaps. The murderer missed the telegram because it was in an unlikely place—inside the cigar-case. And he was lucky, for Deerhurst seems to have bought himself a complete rig-out of undercloth-ing after he came out of gaol, and none of it was marked."

" Why do you think all this searching was done here ? " Wendover demanded. " Why not in some quiet spot, once he'd got the body away ? "

" Because there was a good light here," retorted Dornfell. " Easier and surer to work here rather than with a flash-light by the roadside."

Wendover conceded the point with a nod.

" The body was taken to the car and driven out to Six Road Ends," the inspector went on. " What you proved about the petrol consumption, sir, is enough to settle that. Then the motor accident was faked and post-mortem bruises made on the body, which was a bit of a slip. And then the car was driven back here and left in the garage. That's how I see the business, sir."

" And where does the clock fit into your tale ? " inquired the Chief Constable.

" Oh, I expect it stopped by accident or something," the inspector answered, rather uneasily. " It's an experimental kind of clock, isn't it ? "

" And yet it had never stopped before," Wendover interjected.

" Well, clocks do generally go until they stop, don't they ? " countered Dornfell. " I mean, it may have gone all right until something went wrong with it, and then it stopped. And then it got started again by some jar or other. Perhaps it was the shake of the body being dragged to the floor," he added as the idea struck him. " It was a self-starter and would go on again if it got the chance. I'm not much bothered about the clock. I don't think it matters, when the main story's cut and dried."

" Well, leave it for the time being," Sir Clinton suggested, to Wendover's annoyance. " Suppose we turn now to the second problem—the disappearance of Mrs. Deerhurst. The last reliable witness we have —Evie Sutton, the maid—saw her, alive and well, shortly after half-past two in the afternoon. The gardener was packed off about three o'clock by young Adeney ; but he didn't see Mrs. Deerhurst before he left. The postman saw young Adeney at the gate at six o'clock, but did not see Mrs. Deerhurst. Young Adeney himself says he left the premises a quarter of an hour later ; but we can't trust his statements unless they're corroborated. You agree with me there, I think, Inspector ? "

" I don't trust him much, sir," Dornfell confirmed with a moderation in words which was quite belied by his manner.

" But wait a moment," Wendover interjected. " There's the circumstantial evidence. The maid left a tray set for afternoon tea, and both cups were used, you remember. She and young Adeney must have had tea together ; and that wouldn't be earlier than four o'clock, and probably later. She must have been on the premises then. And what's more, a cold supper was left for her—set for one person only—and it was eaten. That puts the time on to seven o'clock or so at the very minimum. And at 7 p.m. young Adeney was just finishing dressing for dinner at his lodgings; so she must have been here, alone in the house, up till seven o'clock, at anyrate."

"Oh, I don't doubt she was here at that time," Dornfell declared.

Wendover thought that he detected something faintly sinister in the inspector's tone as he made this remark. It was as though Dornfell had said: "Go on and prove she was here all the time. That's what we really want."

Sir Clinton evidently accepted Wendover's inferences without cavil.

"That carries us as far as we can go, since your inquiries at the station and on the bus routes came to nothing," he said, turning to the inspector. Apparently she was here until after six, at any rate. But she left the house some time after that. The question is: how did she go? I mean, did she go according to a prearranged plan, or did she leave on the spur of the moment, or was she taken away against her will? Or was it one of these loss of memory cases one hears about?"

The inspector permitted himself a sceptical smile.

"Some of them may be genuine," he admitted, "but I don't take much stock in a good many of these affairs where a man vanishes from Wigan, say, and turns up in Truro or Inverness a week or so later. How does it come that the fellow who loses his memory always seems to have enough in his pocket for a good long railway journey and a week's keep? I never could fathom that, I'm free to admit. Dispensation of Providence or something of that sort, perhaps. But I've often wondered . . ."

"So have I," Sir Clinton interrupted. "Have you tried Mrs. Deerhurst's bank?"

"She drew no big cheque lately, sir."

"And her balance in current account?"

"About three hundred pounds, sir, that she could have drawn if she'd wanted money in a hurry. She may have had notes in the house, of course; but the housekeeper says she pays all her tradesmen's bills monthly by cheque and she doesn't think Mrs. Deerhurst liked keeping large sums in the house. I should say that probably she hadn't twenty pounds on the premises, so far as I can guess."

"She had five hundred pounds in Bearer Bonds," Wendover pointed out.

The inspector swung round on him.

"And if you were a young lady, sir, anxious to keep your whereabouts unknown, how would you start in to negotiate hundred-pound Bearer Bonds? *I* might be able to do it. I happen to know people who wouldn't ask questions. But a young lady can't walk into the first strange stockbroker's and ask them to do a deal for her of that sort without having to say more than might be convenient in her situation. No, we're keeping a look-out for these bonds; but you needn't reckon them among her assets for immediate use. I'd be surprised if she's got more than a fiver or two in her possession."

"We can dismiss the loss-of-memory solution on other grounds, I think," Sir Clinton pointed out. "Her wardrobe, for one. I merely mentioned it for the sake of completeness. Try another line. Let's assume she planned her departure well in advance. How do the facts tally with that view?"

"I'm almost certain she hadn't much money with her," Dornfell declared again. "If she'd thought the thing out carefully beforehand, she'd have drawn from the bank. Twenty pounds or so wouldn't keep her for ten days at the kind of hotel she'd stay at, let alone paying her fare."

" You didn't find her cheque-book ? "

" A stranger with a cheque-book isn't always a welcome guest, sir, especially if you can't refer to your banker. And she hasn't referred anyone to her banker, nor have any cheques come in yet."

" Still, her cheque-book's missing. It seems suggestive. But since you don't like it, let's leave it alone. She took her latch key and her bath sponge and her hand-bag. And she left no address."

" There's nothing suspicious in that," Wendover interrupted. " From what we've heard, the last thing she wanted was to have Deerhurst following her."

" So she left in an inconspicuous costume consisting of underclothing and a dressing-gown to escape comment ? " Sir Clinton said with a grave face.

" You can't fit that in with a pre-arranged plan, sir," Dornfell pointed out to Wendover. " I've had inquiries made at all the shops she dealt with, and there's no trace of her having ordered a new dress any time recently. All she had is upstairs, the housekeeper says."

" She might have ordered one from London and got it sent by post," Wendover objected.

" She didn't," Sir Clinton interrupted. " These things are always sent in pasteboard dress-boxes. There's no box of the sort in the house, as you'll remember. And there's been no fire on the premises lately at which a box of that sort could be burned. I asked about that. You can take it that she had no new dress on hand."

" Then in that case," said Wendover reluctantly, " she can't have left here according to a pre-arranged plan. It's nonsense to say she went abroad in a dressing-gown."

"Very well, then," Sir Clinton conceded. "Let's assume she left on the spur of the moment, and see if that fits the facts any better. Can you suggest why she left so suddenly? She'd arranged to meet her husband here at 11.30 p.m. Did she clear out before then, or did she go after she'd seen him?"

Dornfell seemed silently amused by something which he was holding in reserve.

"It's easy enough to account for that, sir. She waited here and saw him. He was murdered in this house about midnight. That's a sound enough reason for her taking to flight on the spur of the moment, surely."

"Simple, specious and summary," Sir Clinton commented, with a watchful eye on the inspector's face. "Elaborate it a little, please, so that we can see its points. 'She waited here and saw him.' Can you prove that?"

"Well, sir, you've just said yourself that she'd arranged to meet him here. She'd gone out of her way to wire him to come. There's no evidence to show she'd changed her mind, is there? Not a scrap that I know of. Oh, no, it's as plain as a pike-staff that she was on the premises when the murder was done."

He paused for a moment as though savouring the sensation he expected to make. Then he added:

"The trouble will be to prove which of them did it."

Wendover sat up suddenly in his chair, to the evident satisfaction of Dornfell. The Chief Constable, however, merely nodded as though recognising a familiar point.

"What do you mean by 'which of them'?" Wendover demanded. "Who was there besides Deerhurst and his wife?"

"Young Adeney, of course," Sir Clinton answered. "He was in the drawing-room after midnight. You'd better explain that, Inspector."

"It's this way, sir," said Dornfell, turning to Wendover. "I was on the premises here before young Adeney appeared on the scene that morning, and I examined the drawing-room and saw the blood-spot on the floor. I'd just finished, and was coming out of the drawing-room when young Adeney turned up with the maid who'd been sent to fetch him. The maid hadn't been in the drawing-room. In fact, she knew nothing at all about the business; so he couldn't have got any hints from her. I questioned him in the hall and mentioned a blood patch without saying where it was, and he let out that he knew it was in the drawing-room. He tried to cover that up by saying he'd seen me lock the drawing-room door after me as he came in. But then he gave himself away again by saying something that showed he had a fair notion of how big the patch was. And he was obviously badly bothered when he found what he'd let out. It's plain enough that he'd seen that patch of blood before I had."

"But he had a perfect alibi," Wendover objected.

"Yes, sir, quite perfect—up to half-past twelve. Nothing after that. And you can't time that murder to the stroke of midnight on the strength of body-temperature measurements. It might have happened between twelve and one sometime; and still the body could have been got to Six Road Ends on time with fast enough driving."

"Then you think young Adeney did it?" demanded Wendover with a faint ring of relief in his tone.

"I'd like to be sure, sir, just as a matter of intellectual satisfaction, so to speak. But practically it doesn't matter a rap. You know as well as I do, sir, that if John Doe and Richard Roe conspire together and John Doe lures Jones to a spot where Richard Roe murders him, then both John Doe and Richard Doe hang together, if the facts are established, even if John Doe never laid a finger on Jones. Mrs. Deerhurst sent that wire to bring Deerhurst here to meet her. After that, whether she did him in herself or whether her cousin did, with or without her help, she'll stand a good chance of hanging as an accessary before the fact, if we can lay hands on her."

"You'd have to prove the conspiracy," Wendover commented sourly.

"I think a jury would be inclined to look at it that way," retorted Dornfell smoothly. "They'd be impressed by the way young Adeney lied to me about his cousin's plans—for he *was* lying there, and we'll prove it before we're done."

"A bit hypothetical," Wendover commented, with a touch of acidity in his voice. "Have you anything else?"

"Yes," countered Dornfell, who was evidently ruffled by Wendover's attitude. "Deerhurst's wounds were plugged with cotton-wool from the drawer of the writing-desk. Only Adeney and the people of the house knew that roll of cotton-wool was there. And that means either Adeney or Mrs. Deerhurst thought of it that night."

Sir Clinton evidently felt that tempers were rising, so he hastened to turn the discussion into a fresh channel.

"Well, for the sake of argument, let's assume that's all sound," he proposed quietly. "And now let's see what it implies. Your view, Inspector, is that Mrs. Deerhurst decamped in a hurry after the murder. That is, well after midnight. Now just imagine yourself in her position and think what belongings you would take with you in your flight. You or I would think first of the sinews of war—money. On the spur of the moment we might grab our cheque-book, though when we'd cooled down a bit we'd realise that it was waste-paper since we couldn't use it without leaving a clue behind. Still, we may pass the missing cheque-book, since we'd probably have taken our own. The missing hand-bag seems reasonable enough, and the latch-key may have been inside it. Some toilette articles, too, don't seem extraordinary in the case of a pretty woman. But what about the bath sponge? Especially when you have to go to the bathroom specially to collect it. I can't swallow that bath sponge, either literally or metaphorically. It sticks in my throat. And yet the bath sponge is quite plausible compared with something else."

"What else, sir?" demanded Dornfell after a moment or two of reflection. "The clothes, you mean?"

"No, something still more curious."

Dornfell glanced at Wendover and found him equally perplexed.

"I can't think of anything else, sir."

"The missing three volumes from *The Times* Book Club," Sir Clinton pointed out with a smile. "Suppose you'd just been mixed up in a murder, Inspector, and were preparing to bolt from the scene. You'd be agitated, no doubt, and feel the need of something soothing. So when your eye fell on these books from the Book Club you'd snatch them up, crying: 'A nice bit of solid reading will take my mind off things for a bit, so let's take these along to while away the time.' Does it sound likely? And yet these books have vanished. I simply can't fit that item into any scheme for a last minute decision to bolt I wish you better luck; for by hook or by crook those books have got to be accounted for."

Wendover saw the inspector was staggered by the importance which the Chief Constable evidently attached to the missing volumes. Now was the time to complete the rout of this cocky fellow, who seemed so certain of putting Hazel Deerhurst into the dock.

"There's another point I'd like to be satisfied about," he said, with a not unsuccessful pretence of impartiality. "If Mrs. Deerhurst was in this house until after midnight, how did she get away without leaving a trace? She didn't use the car; it was in the garage in the morning. How do you suppose she managed to disappear at an hour when no trains or buses are running. Any policeman would have been surprised at the sight of a woman abroad at that time of night and would put two and two together as soon as this affair got bruited abroad. Unless you're going to assume the existence of another confederate with a car. . . ."

He broke off abruptly as a name flashed into his mind. There *was* a possible explanation, after all. There *was* one man who could have no love for Deerhurst and who had every incentive to save Hazel from disaster, now that Deerhurst's death had set her free. And that man was Ferrestone, whose pictures hung on the wall before him. Was Ferrestone the key to the riddle? Had he been summoned to the scene that night to sweep Hazel away into concealment and safety? It might seem improbable; but to Wendover the whole case teemed with improbabilities, on his own reading of the characters of the actors.

The new hypotheses flickered through his mind, half-formulated; and on the instant he decided not to divulge it. If this inspector wanted to bring Hazel to trial, let him find her for himself. It wasn't Wendover's business to hound down a girl whom he believed to be innocent. He covered his momentary hesitation by clearing his throat ; and then, without allowing the inspector time to break in, he edged the discussion on to what he felt was less dangerous ground.

" You've left one possibility yet," he pointed out. " What about Mrs. Deerhurst having been abducted ? That would account for her scanty wardrobe, at any rate. And it's not outside the bounds of possibility. She may have had valuable information about Mandrell's inventions."

To Wendover's relief, Sir Clinton showed no sign of wishing to continue with the previous subject.

" I've asked Mandrell to come here and give us any information he can," he explained. " That should throw some light on the probability or otherwise of an abduction. Frankly, I don't think the wardrobe catalogue is quite complete, so it doesn't appeal to me as an argument in favour of the abduction notion. It's quite on the cards that Mrs. Deerhurst had a dress which Mrs. Butterswick never saw."

" But you said she'd got no new dress by post," Wendover objected. " And the inspector's proved that she hasn't bought one locally."

" I didn't say a *new* dress," retorted Sir Clinton. " If I wanted to play Sherlock Holmes, I might even describe it to you. But I'm not quite sure of the pattern ; so I'd better be cautious, and say " N " or " M " as the Marriage Service puts it. You've got the same facts as I have to go on," he added, turning to Wendover, " but the trail's stone cold by this time."

He paused for a moment and then turned to the inspector.

" None of these nice little hypotheses covers the fact that the mains-controlled clock stopped for three hours forty minutes and then started again. And that's got to fit into the story somewhere."

His eye wandered to where one of Ferrestone's paintings hung on the wall.

" I wish I could see my way through the history of these pictures over there and upstairs. I hate to be puzzled by a thing of that sort."

The inspector, who was no connoisseur, seemed to think his superior was wandering from the point.

" Anything else, sir ? " he inquired.

Sir Clinton nodded rather absent-mindedly, still keeping his eyes on the painting before him.

" Yes. There's a phrase in that telegram which seems peculiar. I won't insult your intelligence by saying which it is."

CHAPTER XI

THE ANTI-SUBMARINE INVENTION

SIR CLINTON'S remark turned Wendover's attention to the picture on the wall before him, and he examined it afresh with renewed curiosity.

" If that fellow had chosen line instead of oils, he'd have come near Beardsley or Phil May," he reflected. " There's a sureness of touch and an economy of effort in every inch of the thing. Even as a monochrome it would tell. It seems a pity he let himself fall into that new style in his recent work. Corot stuff wasn't the kind of thing to bring out his strongest points. That picture upstairs is good enough. I'd be glad to hang it at the Grange. But I don't like it nearly so well as these three down here."

His reflections were interrupted by the Chief Constable, who rose and went over to the writing-desk. He sat down, pulled out one drawer after another, as though checking the list of their contents which the inspector had given in his report. When he came to the drawer containing the boxes of envelopes and note-paper, he pulled it out as far as it would come and sat examining it fixedly as though striving to visualise something which had been removed from the space at the back. Then, evidently still unsatisfied, he slid the drawer back into place and returned to his chair.

" There's one thing I didn't emphasise in my report, sir," the inspector confessed when he saw that the Chief Constable could give him attention. " It's this.

When I questioned young Adeney he was as keen as mustard to give Deerhurst a bad character ; and yet, when I put it to him that Deerhurst might have had a hand in his wife's disappearance, young Adeney froze up at once. Now at that time, of course, I'd no notion that Deerhurst had been murdered. I thought he was alive and at large ; and I couldn't understand why young Adeney shied away from the subject when it would have been easy enough to throw suspicion on him. But if young Adeney and his cousin were the people who got rid of Deerhurst, then it's easy enough to see why Deerhurst's name was the last one young Adeney wanted to bring into the business."

"That sounds like common sense," Sir Clinton admitted. "Thanks."

"There's another point that occurs to me, sir," the inspector went on. "What about these bearer bonds ? They've vanished. They'd be of no immediate use to Mrs. Deerhurst if she's bolted. She didn't post them to her solicitors, for I've had them on the phone about it. And we don't even know that she ever received that letter. It was young Adeney who signed for it, you remember. Did he simply stick it into his pocket and hang on to it ? I have my suspicions about the value of his evidence. It's worth about *that* ! "

Dornfell snapped his fingers in illustration.

"If it's a search-warrant you're thinking of, inspector, I have some doubts about your persuading a magistrate to grant one on that evidence. What do you say, Wendover ? You're a J.P."

Wendover shook his head.

"Reasonable ground for suspicion is needed," he declared. "A Justice can't issue one on mere surmise ; and I'm afraid that's all the inspector's offering us. I shouldn't grant a warrant on that ground, whatever other colleagues might do in the circumstances."

That was another spoke in this cocky fellow's wheel, he reflected, not without satisfaction.

Before Dornfell could reply the door opened and Mrs. Butterswick appeared with a salver on which lay a visiting-card.

"Mr. Mandrell is here, sir, and would like to speak to you," she explained, presenting the card. "He says you asked him to come."

"Show him in, please," the Chief Constable directed.

Mrs. Butterswick retired; and in a few seconds she returned to usher in a stocky, grey-haired man in an old-fashioned reefer suit of blue serge. Wendover at the first glance put him down as abnormally long-sighted, for he wore a pair of highly convex spectacles, through which his eyes appeared magnified to a size out of proportion to the rest of his features. Sir Clinton, playing host, introduced him to the others. Mandrell contented himself with an abrupt nod in acknowledgment. He seemed a person of few words.

"What's this about Mrs. Deerhurst?" he demanded, turning to the Chief Constable. "I've been away. Just back this morning. Your message came in soon after I arrived."

"You haven't seen the local papers then?" Sir Clinton asked. "Mrs. Deerhurst has disappeared, without leaving any address; and we want to get in touch with her. You know where she's gone, perhaps?"

Mandrell shook his head decisively. Even on that brief acquaintance Wendover was struck by his crispness of manner and diction. He seemed to have a natural economy of word and gesture which suited his personality.

"When did you see her last?" Sir Clinton inquired, with a gesture which invited Mandrell to take a seat.

"Last Saturday, about midday."

" That was the fourteenth. She was your secretary, wasn't she ? Was she not at work this week ? "

Mandrell shook his head.

" She took her holiday, starting on last Monday. I give her three weeks usually."

" She gave you no address to write to in case of emergency ? "

" Why should she ? I could write here, if necessary."

" Will you tell us, Mr. Mandrell, how Mrs. Deerhurst came to act as your secretary ? "

Mandrell leaned back in his chair, crossed his legs, and put his fingers together.

" My last secretary died in 1931," he explained. " Double pneumonia ; very sudden. I needed to replace him at once. I mentioned the matter to Mr. Calbourne, of Calbourne, Willoughby & Blunt, my lawyers. He recommended Mrs. Deerhurst to me. She's been most useful. Very efficient."

" Her work has been confidential, of course," Sir Clinton suggested.

" I've found her absolutely trustworthy."

" That wasn't quite what I meant," Sir Clinton explained. " If I'm not mistaken, she must have had opportunities of learning details of the things you were working out, forthcoming patent applications, and business of that sort. You put complete trust in her ? "

" Yes. I knew all about her. She knew a good deal about the inside of my affairs."

" Some of that information would be worth money to other people if they had been able to get hold of it ? "

At this question Wendover noticed a faint shade of surprise on Mandrell's face. It seemed as though the Chief Constable had stirred up something disquieting by his words.

"About some of my inventions, you mean?"

Wendover got the impression that this query was put out merely to gain Mandrell time enough to think over his undisclosed problem in fuller detail.

"Yes, about your patents," the Chief Constable pursued. "She copied your specifications and so forth, I suppose. Information of that kind might give hints enough to allow someone else to forestall you, mightn't it?"

"It might."

Still Wendover had the feeling that Mandrell was really thinking of something else, while he answered Sir Clinton's queries more or less mechanically.

"Have you any idea, Mr. Mandrell, if Mrs. Deerhurst kept copies of any documents of that sort? It's sometimes usual to keep a second copy at your bank, isn't it? Just in case of a fire on your own premises."

Mandrell shook his head with his habitual decisiveness.

"No. There was nothing of that sort."

"So that apart from your office, all she knew she carried in her head? She had nothing in the way of confidential papers in her own possession, so far as you are aware?"

"That was understood. I could trust her implicitly."

"But she had important information stored in her mind?"

Suddenly Mandrell sat upright in his chair, and now Wendover could see that he was plainly perturbed.

"I don't beat about the bush," he said abruptly. "Are you hinting that there's a connection between my affairs and her disappearance?"

"I don't beat about the bush either, on occasion," Sir Clinton retorted. "That's precisely what I'm suggesting. Now what about it? Did she know anything really valuable? If she did, you ought to tell us what it was. We're all officials here, of one sort or another, and we have some discretion."

Mandrell was not the kind of man to yield to a bluff, if bluff had been intended. He sat for a moment or two in silence, evidently thinking carefully over what he should say.

"I see," he said at last. "You think she might have been kidnapped for the sake of the information she has. That's it? Well, unfortunately, the information might be worth the risk. She did know some things. Some very important things. Damn it!" he broke out, "Why did I never think of that?"

To Wendover, he seemed more anxious about his own affairs than about the girl's safety, and this made a bad impression. Here was a man who had used Hazel Deerhurst as a confidant in his money-making schemes; and now, when her special knowledge had led her into danger, he was obviously thinking more of the leakage of information than of the risks which the girl might run when an attempt was made to extract his secrets from her. That was as plain as daylight from his manner; and Wendover hated him for it.

"I never thought of that." Mandrell repeated his thought in almost the same words.

He seemed completely staggered by the idea underlying Sir Clinton's suggestion, which he himself had put into plain English. For some seconds he seemed to detach himself from the company and follow up some train of thought. Wendover could guess what he was after. Did Hazel Deerhurst know enough to give the show away completely to his rivals? That was what was troubling him; and he was evidently going over in his mind the exact range of the information which she had acquired. From his face, she must have known a good deal.

At length Mandrell seemed to make up his mind.

He turned to the Chief Constable and looked him in the eye.

" This is serious," he said bluntly. " There must be no blabbing. Not that I'm going to tell you much. Still . . ."

Sir Clinton glanced at Dornfell. He knew the inspector of old and was quite certain of his reticence. Dornfell, however, had no wish to make any difficulties. He had caught Mandrell's look of distrust in his direction and resented it. After all, if the information came into their hands via Sir Clinton, that was sufficient for official purposes.

" I'll be outside in the hall, sir, if you want me," he explained as he rose.

And with an unfriendly nod to Mandrell, he left the room.

" Just as well," Mandrell commented curtly. " I've perhaps trusted one pair of ears too many already."

He bent forward in his chair and lowered his voice.

" I've been in London this week. At the Admiralty."

He swung round on Wendover.

" I suppose you thought I was worrying about the chance of losing money over a forestalled patent ? " he said, with a touch of contempt. " It's a damn sight more serious ! "

He turned back to Sir Clinton.

" You know what nearly dished us in the last war : the submarines. We had heaps of gadgets : the depth-charges, the ' Q ' ships, the blimps, the hydrophones, the Bragg Loop, the Dover barrage, and these mystery towers that were never used in the Channel. And still the beggars got ahead of us. None of our dodges was a winner. Then we took to convoys, and pulled through. Could we run convoys to-day ? We haven't the ships. So it's plain enough where inventive talent's needed. Something fresh to down the submarine, just in case. Is that enough said ? "

Mandrell closed his lips, folded his arms, and stared at Sir Clinton as though challenging him to push his inquiries further.

" No need to ask for details, if that's how things stand," the Chief Constable admitted in a grave tone. " But how much did Mrs. Deerhurst know ? Had she your whole affair at her finger-ends ? That's the point."

" I've been trying to remember," Mandrell replied, with a gesture of perplexity. " She copied things for me. But they were isolated things. I never gave her anything complete in itself. Question is : did she put two and two together, from what she saw ? I don't know."

" Can you be sure she had nothing on paper ? " demanded Sir Clinton.

" Not to my knowledge," Mandrell answered definitely. " And I'd stake a good deal on her trustworthiness. Besides, she'd heaps of money. She wasn't bribable, I'll swear. If her disappearance has anything to do with this hush-hush business, then she hasn't gone voluntarily. But if she's been kidnapped . . . well, you'd better rescue her before there's any harm done. That's serious. There's something a damn' sight more important than money at stake."

" I understand," Sir Clinton said concisely. " Now another point, Mr. Mandrell. There's something here I'd like you to examine."

He went over to the escritoire and pulled out the drawer containing the Braille typewriter.

" Ever seen anything like that before ? " he asked.

Mandrell came behind him and inspected it.

" Not so far as I remember," he admitted. " But

let's have a look at it. Wait till I change my spectacles."

He fished a case from his pocket and replaced his glasses by another pair.

"I've had a cataract operation," he explained. "You lose the power of accommodation, as they call it. Need special glasses for reading, and that kind of thing. No focusing possible, once they've taken the lens out of your eye. There! That's right now," he concluded as he put his spectacle-case back into his pocket and bent to examine the machine.

After a moment or two, he asked permission and with skilled fingers dismantled the instrument; but even then he was obviously puzzled.

"Never saw that gadget before," he admitted. "What is it?"

"What did you call it, Wendover?" asked Sir Clinton.

"It's a Stainsby typewriter, for writing Braille," Wendover explained.

"Oh, that's it?" Mandrell said, examining it again. "I see. The paper goes in here, eh? Quite so. I ought to have thought of that, but I didn't."

"You didn't know that Mrs. Deerhurst had anything of this kind?" Sir Clinton demanded.

Mandrell shook his head with his usual abruptness.

"My point is this," Sir Clinton explained, shutting the one drawer and opening another. "Apart from the blind, their relations, and some people like Wendover here, very few people can read Braille, though they'd recognise the look of the type if they saw it. So Braille typewriting would make a fairly good system of private communication. Not so good as a cipher, of course; but still enough to keep the man in the street from reading the message right off the reel if it fell into his hands."

"That's true," Mandrell concurred. "And the man in the street wouldn't make much of that brand of typewriter either, if he saw it."

Sir Clinton indicated the out-drawn drawer.

"You see the space left here? It's just big enough to hold the sheets which fit this Stainsby machine. Unless I'm far out, there has been a pile of these sheets in that space. And now they're gone. Does that suggest anything to you?"

Mandrell pulled at his lower lip, evidently puzzled and a little perturbed.

"You mean she might have kept notes in Braille, as a kind of semi-cipher. And somebody's lifted the lot? That's it, eh?"

He ruminated for some seconds before continuing.

"Well, I'd have sworn she was as straight as a die. I'd never have trusted her otherwise. But she'd no business to have any notes about my stuff in her possession. And if she had, and if someone's got hold of them . . . well, you'd better look slippy, my friend. This is damn' serious. You can take my word for it."

"You can't suggest who might have an interest in them?"

Mandrell threw up his hands with a hopeless gesture.

"How many States are interested in submarines? And how many agents has each State got in its Intelligence service? How the devil do I know who might be after it?"

"Not much help there," said Sir Clinton reflectively.

"You'll let me hear if you strike anything?" Mandrell demanded anxiously. "If you get on some track I might be able to put two and two together."

"I'll let you know, certainly," Sir Clinton agreed, rising. "And now, unless you can think of anything else, I won't detain you."

Mandrell pondered for a moment or two; but

evidently he had nothing further to contribute, and he wasted no time in useless discussion, but took his departure. Almost as soon as he had left the room, Dornfell re-entered.

"Very secretive old gentleman, sir," he commented sardonically as he came in. "May I know anything about it?"

"This much," Sir Clinton said seriously. "Mrs. Deerhurst may have had information of considerable value in her possession. She may have made notes of it with that Braille typewriter you saw. These notes may have been in that empty space you noticed in the drawer of the escritoire over there. It's all 'mays' together, you see. Pure hypothesis. Still, these are the possibilities of the affair."

The inspector brought his hand down on his thigh with a slap.

"And she's been kidnapped, sir? That was one of the first notions that crossed my mind when I was called in on the case. And here's how it could have been done. Young Adeney knew she was in Mandrell's employ. He had the run of this house, hadn't he? It's on the cards that he opened that drawer and saw that bundle of Braille stuff that's vanished. Suppose his curiosity got roused a bit. I can't read Braille myself, but if you gave me a bit of Braille typing and a Braille alphabet that you can get in any encyclopædia, I back myself to puzzle out at least what the stuff was about, and that in a fairly short time, too."

"Yes, you could do that," Wendover agreed.

"Well, sir, suppose young Adeney spotted it was important. What is he? Convict on licence, with a nice little lot of friends he picked up in jail. He was seen talking to one of them—a fellow named Sturge, a cracksman—just a day or two back. What's to hinder him from arranging a bit of kidnapping with his pals ? It'd be all right for his cousin, really, with him in charge ; but she wouldn't know that. They might screw the information out of her somehow, once they got their grip on her. And then, when she'd parted, she'd learn that her cousin was in it up to the neck ; and that'd shut her mouth. She wouldn't want to give him away."

" Wait a moment," Wendover interrupted. " You're going too fast for me. You say young Adeney and this burglar fellow were together in prison ? Suppose young Adeney let out to the burglar something about his cousin being employed by Mandrell. Suppose What's-his-name—oh, Sturge, is it ?—well, suppose Sturge took that in. Who was in prison at the same time ? Deerhurst. Suppose Sturge took his news to Deerhurst, and *Deerhurst* arranged the kidnapping of the girl ? That's more credible than that young Adeney had a hand in it, isn't it ? And then suppose that the gang fell out and the rest of them murdered Deerhurst that night. Wouldn't that fit the facts with less straining ? "

" Something in it, maybe," Dornfell admitted with obvious reluctance. " A bit far-fetched, though, I'm afraid."

" It accounts for Deerhurst being here that night, which your hypothesis doesn't," Wendover pointed out tartly.

" Something in that," the inspector conceded, rubbing his chin as he attempted to think of some flaw in Wendover's idea. " They might have coshed her and then gagged her and taken her off in a car . . ."

Then he saw the flaw for which he was searching.

" But that doesn't account for young Adeney knowing about the blood on the drawing-room floor before he saw it," he broke out exultantly. " And you won't tell me that Adeney was working hand in hand with

Deerhurst on any lay. That cock won't fight, if you'll excuse me saying it. I could see well enough how the land lay between Deerhurst and young Adeney. They wouldn't be co-operating—not much!"

It was Wendover's turn to look for fresh light.

"Young Adeney may have come on the scene after it was all over," he pointed out. "His alibi holds good only up till midnight. For all you know, he may have been out-of-doors further on in the small hours. He had a key of this house, and he may have come in, seen the blood-patch, and gone away again."

Dornfell's face showed the disdain of the professional for the amateur's suggestion.

"And there was his cousin kidnapped, and yet next morning he did his damnedest—excuse me!—to persuade me that she'd gone away of her own accord, in the natural course of events. Is it likely, I ask you? Not unless he was in the thing up to his neck."

Sir Clinton had been listening with an expressionless face to this series of thrusts and parries. Now he thought it time to intervene before the discussion grew awkwardly acrimonious.

"Very interesting," he commented. "But I don't quite see how you fit two points into either of these schemes. Three points, perhaps."

"What are they, sir?" inquired the inspector, suddenly cooled.

"Well, there's the fact that the mains-controlled clock stopped for three hours forty-four minutes, and then restarted itself. That will have to be explained somehow or other. And if Mrs. Deerhurst was kidnapped, as you've both assumed, how did she manage to take away those three volumes from *The Times* Book Club? Finally, who got the registered letter with the bearer bonds? Can either of you fit these points into the problem?"

Wendover forestalled the inspector by making the reply which occurred to both of them simultaneously.

"Whoever abducted her might have taken the bonds at the same time."

"It's possible," Sir Clinton admitted. "Even plausible. But what do you make of the stopped clock?"

Before either Wendover or Dornfell could offer a suggestion, the door opened and Mrs. Butterswick reappeared.

"There's a Mr. Granfield here, sir. He's got no appointment, he says; but he'd like to see you, if it's convenient."

"Very well," the Chief Constable directed, after a moment's thought. "Show him in, please."

As Mrs. Butterswick retired, he turned to Dornfell.

"Granfield was Deerhurst's solicitor, Inspector. Mr. Calbourne told me something about him, and it's just possible we may glean an idea or two from him. Obviously he's come to see me about the Deerhurst affair."

CHAPTER XII

PRESUMPTION OF DEATH

WHEN Louis Granfield entered the room, he seemed in no way put out to find three people there. He waited till Sir Clinton had named his two companions, acknowledging each introduction with a slight movement which was more polite than a nod and less formal than a bow. In response to Sir Clifton's gesture, he seated himself comfortably, glanced from face to face without undue haste, as though making sure of the identity of each person before him. Then, crossing his legs, he turned to the Chief Constable.

" I read in the newspapers that the body of Mr. Leonard Deerhurst had been found on the road between Swallow Tail Copse and Six Road Ends. Apparently he died from injuries received in a motor accident."

He paused, as if to allow the Chief Constable to corroborate this, but Sir Clinton merely nodded as though encouraging him to proceed.

" It occurred to me at once," Granfield went on, " that an inquest would be necessary. Also that some-one must identify the body. I rang up the police and offered to do this, if required. I was his solicitor, I'd better explain, and I've known him for many years."

" We may have to trouble you," Sir Clinton answered, " though in this case it's a mere formality. If it's necessary, the coroner will let you know."

Granfield nodded politely, and then proceeded in his even tone:

"When I saw Deerhurst's death in the papers, I looked out his will from my safe, just to refresh my memory. He appointed me sole executor, I may say. Naturally enough, since we were very old friends, and since his relations with his wife and her family in recent years have been—regrettably—not quite cordial."

"Indeed?"

Sir Clinton's tone was mildly interrogatory, but Granfield gave him a sharp glance from his pale eyes.

"I can hardly believe that is news to you," he commented with a faint smile. "The Adeney crash was a fairly notorious affair, not so long ago."

"I'm afraid I was on holiday at the time," Sir Clinton explained innocently. "And, besides, it was outside our jurisdiction. We had nothing to do with it."

Granfield gave the Chief Constable a long look, as though he suspected that his leg was being pulled. If he thought so, however, he betrayed nothing when he spoke again.

"It's common knowledge that Deerhurst and his wife did not get on well together," he said smoothly. "And after the financial crash of Adeney & Sons their differences became acute. You know, of course, that Deerhurst went to prison over that business."

Sir Clinton contented himself with a nod. Granfield leaned forward towards the Chief Constable, as though to emphasise what he had to say next.

"The ill-feeling was mainly on the Adeney side. Deerhurst was quite anxious for a reconciliation with his wife. I had several interviews with him while he was in prison, I may say. He made it perfectly clear that when he was released he hoped to get her to let bygones be bygones."

He paused, evidently to give the Chief Constable a

chance of comment, but Sir Clinton merely repeated his nod.

" There's evidence on that point, in the will I've been speaking about," Granfield continued. " Deerhurst inserted a clause in it, leaving her a small legacy. That was merely a symbolic gesture, you understand, for she was better off in her own right than Deerhurst himself was, after the collapse of Adeney & Sons. It was inserted, as he explained to me at the time, merely as a proof that he bore her no ill-will."

" There were other legacies ? " Sir Clinton inquired.

" Oh, yes, naturally, a few small sums. The estate amounted to very little, as you can guess."

" When was this will made ? " asked the Chief Constable. " You drew it up for him, I suppose ? "

" Yes. I took his instructions and drafted it for him when he was out on bail at the time of the trial."

" And it was witnessed, of course ? "

" Witnessed by my housekeeper and a maid," Granfield explained. " I saw him sign it myself, but naturally I did not sign as a witness."

" Why not ? " demanded Dornfell, who seemed puzzled by this.

A glint of humour crossed Granfield's face as he replied.

" If I'd signed as a witness, I wouldn't be entitled to charge my profit costs," he explained. " Profit costs chargeable by a solicitor-executor are regarded in law as a legacy, and a witness to a will forfeits any legacy to him under that will."

" I see," Dornfell admitted, with something verging on a wink. " Just an ordinary business precaution ? "

" As you say," Granfield confirmed.

" The witnesses were two of your domestic servants ?"

queried Sir Clinton. "Why not two of your clerks?"

"Because he signed his will at my private house one night, and not in my office," Granfield explained.

"Ah, of course, that would account for it naturally," Sir Clinton admitted. "By the way, Mr. Granfield, was a residuary legatee named in the will?"

"Yes," Granfield admitted, "I was named. But he left very little, as you can imagine. I shan't grow rich on it."

He paused for a moment or two, as though expecting further questions; but when none was put, he proceeded with his interrupted narrative.

"This morning, as it happened, I chanced to have some business hereabouts. While I was in this neighbourhood, I took the opportunity of calling on Mr. Calbourne to tell him, as a matter of courtesy, that Mrs. Deerhurst was mentioned in her husband's will."

"You didn't think of informing Mrs. Deerhurst herself?" asked the Chief Constable.

Louis Granfield made a gesture as if to show that he recognised how natural the inquiry was.

"The last time I saw Mrs. Deerhurst—that was on the evening of July 17th—she made it clear to me that if I had any further communication to make to her, I was to do it through Mr. Calbourne. He was acting as her legal adviser, I gathered."

"One moment," interrupted Sir Clinton. "You say you saw Mrs. Deerhurst on the evening of the 17th. That was the day her husband was released from prison. What made you call on her then? A matter of business, I suppose?"

"Yes," Granfield explained. "At least I hoped that there might be a prospect of business. The fact is, I was sorry that these two people didn't seem to hit it off as they might have done. Deerhurst is an old friend of mine, and although I wasn't a friend of Mrs. Deerhurst I had a considerable respect for her character. It seemed a pity not to try to reconcile them, if that were in any way possible. If it couldn't be done, then at least they might be helped to come to some sort of arrangement for the future. Terms of separation might be drawn in such a way as to leave a loophole for a future reconciliation. I'm something of an optimist, you see."

"So you came to see Mrs. Deerhurst on the point?"

"That is so. Unfortunately, I think, I did not succeed in seeing her alone. Mr. Calbourne and his daughter were present, also Mr. Adeney. They made things more difficult. In short, I failed completely to make any progress, much to my regret. So the whole thing fell through and Mrs. Deerhurst made it clear to me that if I had any further communication to make to her I was to make it through Mr. Calbourne. He was acting as her legal adviser, I gathered. So naturally I did not attempt to approach her direct in the matter of her husband's legacy to her. I went to Mr. Calbourne instead. Naturally, in the circumstances, I think."

"Quite naturally," Sir Clinton agreed.

"However, when I called on Mr. Calbourne this morning," Granfield continued, "I found that a complication had arisen, a rather surprising complication. He informed me that Mrs. Deerhurst disappeared from here on the night of July 18th, curiously enough the night on which my client Deerhurst met with his fatal accident. Naturally I questioned Mr. Calbourne about the matter. But Mr. Calbourne, I'm afraid, is not an easy person to extract information from in some circumstances."

Granfield's slow smile spoke volumes as he said this.

"I could get nothing out of him," he admitted,

" nothing that was of any use to me, at least. And at last I began to . . . well, to wonder about the business. Frankly, I was puzzled by his obvious reticence."

Granfield made one of his effective pauses at this point, but the Chief Constable showed no inclination to be drawn.

" I have a natural disinclination to be puzzled," Granfield went on. " I have also a friend on the staff of one of the local papers. Naturally I went to him and asked if he knew anything about this disappearance of Mrs. Deerhurst, which seemed to have closed Mr. Calbourne's mouth. From my journalist friend I picked up a few bits of information, not much, I admit, but enough to throw a little light on the affair. Sufficient to make me want to get to the bottom of things, at any rate. I rang you up at your house and was told that you had come here. So I took the liberty of intruding on you."

" I don't quite see what I can do for you," Sir Clinton pointed out.

" There was one point which I attempted to elicit from Mr. Calbourne," Granfield explained. " Something which he dropped, in the way he phrased it, suggested to my mind the possibility that Mrs. Deerhurst might have come by an accident, like her husband. It was the merest vague suggestion, you understand, and possibly I took it up wrong. But it certainly did enter my mind then that Mrs. Deerhurst might be dead. And as soon as I thought of that I saw that it might introduce complications, unusual complications, into my work as executor of Deerhurst's will. So I asked Mr. Calbourne, point blank, if Mrs. Deerhurst had made a will herself. He, perhaps naturally enough, refused to say anything on the subject, so I am left in a rather awkward position. If she is dead, and if she died intestate, it may make a very considerable difference to the effect of Deerhurst's own will, unless the relative order of the two deaths can be established beyond cavil."

"I'm a child in such matters," Sir Clinton explained gravely. "Would you explain the point?"

"It's quite simple, really," Granfield replied. There are three possibilities before us. Mrs. Deerhurst may still be alive. Or she may be dead, having died later than her husband. Or she may be dead, having predeceased her husband. If she is still alive, or if she made a will before her death, the matter will solve itself in due course. The same holds good if she died *after* her husband, having made no will, for in that case either her property will be distributed under her will or it will go to her personal representatives under the Administration of Estates Act, 1925. Since her husband would be dead, and she had neither parents alive nor issue, her property would in that case pass to the Crown. On the other hand—and this is where the shoe might pinch, so far as I am concerned—if she died intestate *before* her husband's death, then her property would pass into his estate and be distributable under his will."

"In other words," Sir Clinton commented, "unless you know whether or not she predeceased her husband and died intestate, you don't know what property falls to be distributed under Deerhurst's will. If she died first and left no will, then the whole of her estate falls into your hands as his executor, to be dealt with as though it were part of his own estate. Is that it?"

Granfield seemed faintly relieved that the Chief Constable had grasped his meaning so quickly.

"That is it," he confirmed. "And now you see the problem which Mr. Calbourne's reticence has landed me in. I simply don't know where I stand, at the present moment, as an executor. Naturally it occurred to me that you might have information about Mrs. Deerhurst which you have not thought fit to make public as yet. And in these very peculiar circumstances I thought it possible that you might see fit to tell me—in strict confidence, of course—exactly what you have ascertained in the matter. I don't wish to ask anything I shouldn't know. But . . . well, if you can see your way to clear the business up it will make a very considerable difference to me."

Sir Clinton leaned back in his chair and pondered for some second before replying.

"I don't see that I can tell you anything likely to be useful," he said at last.

Granfield took his defeat with perfect good temper.

"I hardly thought you would," he admitted. "Still, it leaves me in an awkward position. I can count on you to tell me what you discover, as soon as you think it safe?"

"Certainly," Sir Clinton assured him.

Dornfell seemed to have been reflecting on Granfield's statements, and now he put forward a suggestion.

"Can't you obtain leave to presume death in some cases? Why not try that?"

Granfield shook his head.

"I doubt if the Court would agree to that as things are," he explained. "So far as I'm concerned, I've no clear evidence that she's dead, nothing that I could produce in Court. In the absence of such clear evidence, I doubt if they would allow any presumption of death before a long period had elapsed since her disappearance. Seven years, or something like that. And of course that's no use to me."

"I was thinking of it from our point of view," the inspector blurted out ingenuously. "If she's in hiding somewhere, the fact that you took action to get her death presumed might be enough to drive her into the open."

"Ah! So you think she's in hiding?" commented Granfield, with a glance at the Chief Constable which seemed to say that the inspector had let the cat out of the bag. "But why should she be in hiding?"

"If you could tell me that, you'd be telling me something," retorted Dornfell ungraciously.

Evidently he recognised, too late, that he had put his foot in it by his intervention, and he glanced uneasily at the Chief Constable's face. Sir Clinton, however, showed no sign of vexation, but he switched the conversation to a fresh topic by his next question.

"When did you last see Deerhurst, Mr. Granfield?"

Granfield considered for a moment or two before answering.

"I was trying to fix the precise date," he explained, "but I'll have to look it up in my diary if you want it. It was some months back, while he was still serving his time. You understand, of course, that while he was in gaol his property passed out of his hands. The Court appointed me as administrator for him, reasonably enough since I was his solicitor and had his affairs at my finger tips. Naturally I consulted him from time to time as to the management of his financial affairs, visiting him in prison for that purpose."

Sir Clinton seemed to have little interest in this point. He nodded perfunctorily in agreement and then put another question.

"You had not seen Deerhurst for some months, it seems, when you called on Mrs. Deerhurst to try to effect a reconciliation. Had you any instructions from Deerhurst about seeing her?"

"Oh, no," Granfield confessed. "I did that entirely off my own bat. Did I not make that clear?"

" Not quite," the Chief Constable apprised him. " So it was pure philanthropy on your part, that move ? "

" Something of the sort," Granfield declared, with just a shade of hesitation. " Of course," he continued frankly, " if anything came of it, I'd probably have got the job of drawing up the terms of settlement, which would have been grist to my mill."

" I understand," Sir Clinton commented dryly.

Granfield became pre-occupied for a moment or two, as though considering whether he should add anything to what he had already said. Then, apparently having made up his mind, he began again.

" There's one thing I ought, perhaps, to tell you," he said slowly. " It's not likely to be important, but it's as well you should know it. It puzzles me a little. I admit. It's this. On the morning of the eighteenth I had a letter from Deerhurst. It was just a short note, written to fix an appointment with me on the following afternoon, so that we could go over his financial affairs. But in it, rather to my surprise, he gave the text of a telegram he had received from his wife, suggesting a meeting between them that night. I mean the night of the eighteenth. In some ways Deerhurst was very business-like, and he gave the date of the telegram's despatch from here. It had been sent off on July 16th. What struck me, though, was the fact that it asked him to come to meet her late at night—half-past eleven, I think—and not to advertise his arrival here."

" You seem to attach some importance to the date of the wire," Sir Clinton interrupted. " What about that ? "

" Well, my impression was that she'd sent that wire with the idea of a reconciliation. What other construction could one put on it at the time I read it ?

Now, it was sent on the sixteenth, and yet when I saw Mrs. Deerhurst on the following evening in this room she showed not the very slightest desire for any reconciliation. Quite the reverse, in fact. When I got Deerhurst's letter next morning I couldn't make it out. I couldn't see what had made her change her mind, as it seemed, from one day to the next. She never struck me as a changeable character."

Again he paused, as though in some perplexity. Then, in a tone of doubtful reluctance, he continued:

"There is a possible explanation, the only one which occurs to me. In sending that wire Mrs. Deerhurst may have been prompted by her feelings, a natural desire to let bygones be bygones and wipe the slate clean. But then a relation or some other adviser may have stepped in and argued her out of her more generous mood. That would account for her turning down my well-meant effort to bring the two of them together. I give it you for what it's worth."

"Let us have this straight," Sir Clinton said briskly. "She sent this wire on the sixteenth. On the seventeenth, without any immediate authority from Deerhurst, you plunged in to bring about a reconciliation between them. You did not learn of this wire until you got Deerhurst's letter on the following morning. Is that it? By the way, where was Deerhurst when he wrote to you? Still in prison?"

"No," Granfield explained readily. "The letter was on the notepaper of an hotel. He must have written it there just after his release, I expect."

Sir Clinton turned to the inspector, who had been busy making notes throughout the conversation.

"You might jot that down," he suggested. Then turning back to the solicitor, he explained. "We're a little puzzled to guess what Deerhurst was doing on the road near Swallow Tail Copse, where the car went over him," he explained. "So we're trying to trace out this previous movements. Can you throw any light on it?"

Granfield's gesture of ignorance was obviously genuine.

"Heaven alone knows," he said. "I can't imagine how he got there at that time of night. I never heard him mention anyone in that neighbourhood, otherwise one might suppose he'd gone to see some friend or other. It leaves me absolutely in the dark."

"I suppose you have that letter he sent you?" inquired Sir Clinton. "I'd like to see it."

Granfield made a movement of vexation.

"That's a nuisance," he said with some annoyance. "I read it at the breakfast table and destroyed it after I'd read it. There was nothing in it that seemed important at the moment. What a pity."

"We shall manage without it, I expect," Sir Clinton reassured him. "After all, you've told us what was in it. Inspector Dornfell has a note of that. The thing itself couldn't have told us any more."

He glanced at Granfield reflectively for a moment or two and then said deliberately:

"I have a feeling that you're not speaking your whole mind to us, Mr. Granfield. Is there anything more?"

Granfield's heavy face betrayed nothing as he apparently considered the Chief Constable's question. At length he made up his mind and spoke with a careful weighing of his words.

"There's a law against slander," he said with a grim smile, "and a solicitor should be especially careful in what he says."

"You needn't worry about that in this case," Sir

Clinton assured him. " Nothing you say will be bruited abroad—unless we happen to want you to repeat it in the witness-box, of course."

Granfield acknowledged this with a slow inclination of his head.

" Very well, then," he said, " I don't mind saying what has crossed my mind. It must have occurred to all of you as well, I expect. Mrs. Deerhurst wired her husband on the sixteenth in plenty of time to be sure the telegram reached him before he left the prison on the seventeenth. He was to come here at an extraordinarily late hour and he was to avoid being seen. That's curious, isn't it ? When I saw the contents of that wire I inferred that she was considering a reconciliation. But next day she wasn't thinking of a reconciliation, quite the reverse. Had she ever thought of getting reconciled to Deerhurst ? If not, the telegram must have been sent merely to bring him here. Why ? She didn't want him back, and behind her was her cousin, young Adeney, who had no love for Deerhurst, to put it mildly. And the next thing is that Deerhurst is found killed in a motor accident, miles away from where he had any reason to be that night, and at a spot he could not have got to between 11.30 p.m. and half-past two, when he was picked up, according to the newspaper report. And now the inspector here drops a hint that Mrs. Deerhurst has decamped and gone into hiding. It doesn't need a Sherlock Holmes to see one possible explanation, considering how easy it would be to persuade a man into a car, get him out of it, and run him down as he stood on the road. I give you it for what it's worth."

" You mentioned young Adeney," Sir Clinton pointed out. " Why do you bring in his name ? "

Granfield leaned his elbow on the arm of his chair

and rubbed his chin between thumb and forefinger, while a slight frown showed on his face.

"I know the Adeneys," he explained dourly. "Young Adeney is a weak character, a useless kind of fellow, I found. But it's just these weaklings who make bad haters in some circumstances. The inferiority complex often takes that turn if they get time to brood over a grievance. And of course young Adeney had plenty of opportunity for brooding," he added, with something like a sneer.

Sir Clinton made no direct comment on Granfield's suggestion. Instead he rose to his feet as a plain hint that the interview was over.

"I'm sorry we can't help you at present, Mr. Granfield," he said courteously, "but beyond what's public property already we have no information available. Later on perhaps. . . ."

Granfield took the implied hint without demur and went away, escorted to the door by the inspector.

CHAPTER XIII

PRINCIPAL OR ACCESSARY?

WHEN the inspector had returned from showing Granfield out, Wendover glanced across at the Chief Constable with a faintly foxy smile.

" Well, do you see your way through it yet ? " he demanded.

Sir Clinton kept a perfectly straight face, pretended to consider for a moment or two, and then answered :

" No, I can't say I see my way through it, as you put it. But the mists seem to be clearing slightly."

Wendover had not expected even so much as this, and his smile changed to an expression of mild surprise.

" You found Granfield useful then ? " he inquired.

The Chief Constable seemed anxious to repay Wendover in his own coin. He made a pretence of pondering again.

" Psychologically, yes," he replied. " In the region of facts, no ! "

" Psychologically ? " queried Wendover. " You're getting too deep for me. You can't put Psychology into the witness-box, on its oath, and convince a jury by its evidence."

" True," Sir Clinton admitted in a thoughtful tone. " But it gets into the box all the same, without kissing the book first. A jury likes a motive if it can find one in a case, and Psychology creeps in on the skirts of the motive, usually. In this affair, for instance, there seem to be two sides : the facts on the one hand,

and the feeling of the actors and actresses on the other. What I'm trying to see is the interplay between the two."

Dornfell had been listening with a tolerant smile to Wendover's queries and his Chief's replies, but at this point he evidently wearied of these refinements.

"The thing seems plain enough, sir," he broke in. "Somebody hated Deerhurst enough to do him in. Question is: Who was that?"

Sir Clinton laughed, not unkindly.

"Our old friend Euclid had an excellent practice of defining what he meant by the terms he used. 'Hate' isn't such a simple idea, when you come to examine it."

"It seems simple enough to me," Dornfell asserted rather downrightly. "Hate's hate. That's clear enough, surely, sir."

"How easy your shopping must be, Inspector," retorted Sir Clinton with an unconcealed grin. "You go up to the counter and say: 'Pound of soap, please.' They hand over a packet, and you see SOAP on the outside and are content. When you get home, and examine it, you may find you've got Dog Soap or Castile Soap or Carpet Soap or Bath Soap. What's the odds? Soap's soap. That's clear enough, surely?"

As Sir Clinton knew, Dornfell was not a touchy person. He could see a joke even if it went against himself, and he laughed as the Chief Constable finished his caricature.

"Plain hate has been good enough for me, sir. But I'm always willing to learn," he declared. "What are all these different brands you seem to have in mind?"

Sir Clinton did not answer immediately, being evidently busy putting his ideas into sequence.

"Two samples will be enough for the present, I

think," he said at last, as though he had discarded some of his illustrations. "Suppose A does B a grave injury and B spends some years with little else to think about than this hurt he has received. Wouldn't he likely come to hate A? That's one specimen of hate; and you'll notice that the injury's over and done with, though the consequences persist. Now take a second case. Suppose that X has got some hold over Y and Y fears an injury in the future. Wouldn't Y hate X? Now I put it to you, Inspector, which of those hates would be the more dangerous?"

"The second one." Dornfell replied promptly,

"Because fear comes into it?" Sir Clinton queried. "I expect you're right. It takes a dash of fear to screw hatred up to its highest notch, so far as my experience goes. Take a man who's been blackmailed and who expects to be blackmailed further in future. I should think his hatred of his blackmailer would be fairly acute, simply because there's a prospect of further injury in addition to what he's suffered already."

"I believe you're right, sir, now I see what you're driving at," the inspector admitted frankly. "And I see what you mean in this Deerhurst business. Young Adeney got his touch and brooded over it, but he'd nothing further to fear from Deerhurst. But Mrs. Deerhurst had got hurt in the past and was afraid of being hurt in the future, when Deerhurst got loose. She was Y in the case you put. She'd more reason to hate Deerhurst than young Adeney had, just because she was afraid of him still."

"Not so simple, after all, you see," Sir Clinton pointed out. "Now there's another side to it. Hate's one thing, affection's the reverse of the medal. Can you pick out the people in this little play who were likely to stand by each other in a difficulty?"

"Young Adeney and his cousin, first of all," the

inspector declared unhesitatingly. " From all I've picked up, sir, they were mighty fond of each other. She's got more brains than he has, I take it ; but I don't think there's much to pick and choose between them in what they think of each other."

" They wouldn't stop at perjury in each other's cause."

Dornfell rubbed his hand up the back of his head.

" Well, I haven't seen her, sir," he pointed out doubtfully. " I want to be fair. But as to young Adeney, lying's nothing to him. He's been lying already, evidently to cover up her tracks."

" And who else do you think would lend a hand if they were in trouble ? " questioned the Chief Constable.

" Calbourne the solicitor and his daughter might," the inspector answered, though much more doubtfully. " They're all very thick, so far as I can gather. But if it's that alibi of young Adeney's you're thinking about, sir, I don't suppose they went off the truth there. No," he added, " I don't believe that Calbourne would go so far as to shield young Adeney if he knew he was guilty of anything really bad. He's not that sort."

He reflected for a moment or two and then continued :

" As to the rest of them, Mrs. Butterswick, the Sutton girl, and the gardener, I put them out of the reckoning. They haven't been trying to mislead me, I'd stake my hat. And in any case, they weren't on the spot. So it really comes down to young Adeney and his cousin. And what's more," he added bluntly, with a side-glance at Wendover, " these are the two that have grudges against Deerhurst, so it fits both ways. They both hate him and they'd stand by each other in a bit of trouble. And Adeney did his best to cover up his cousin's retreat long enough to let the scent get cold. There's no denying that."

The Chief Constable nodded.

"That part of it seems sound enough," he agreed. "But we're not done with psychology yet. Granfield gave us a nice little puzzle not so long ago. On Monday Mrs. Deerhurst wires to Deerhurst arranging a meeting. That looks like a reconciliation, as Granfield pointed out. By Tuesday, he found her quite intractable when he tried to fix up a reconciliation. And yet she hadn't wired to Deerhurst to countermand the projected meeting, although she'd had plenty of time to do that. And on Wednesday Deerhurst turned up here according to plan—the plan of the telegram—and we know what happened to him in this room. Now does the psychology of that satisfy you? Here's a woman who has brooded over her grievance for years and had plenty of time to make up her mind. And yet she makes, apparently, two opposite moves within three days, at the last moment. If we knew her—if we'd met her face to face, I mean, and not just by hearsay—we might find a clue to that *volte-face* of hers; but as it is, it puzzles me. It doesn't seem in 'character' somehow.

"I quite agree with you there," Wendover put in. "All we've heard about her suggests that she's got a fairly strong character, not the kind that gets swayed about one way and another."

"Well, there it is," Sir Clinton confessed. "No doubt it'll be cleared up in time."

"Is that all the psychology, sir?" asked Dornfell slyly. "It doesn't seem to have got us far, does it? What about the facts now?"

The Chief Constable glanced at his watch.

"Time's getting on," he pointed out. "We can't go over the whole of the facts again. But I tell you what I'll do. I'll just mention the ones that seem to me to fit together more or less and to throw some glimmer of light on the affair. But you needn't ask me to go into details just now. It would take far too long."

"Very good, sir," Dornfell acquiesced. "I'd like to hear what seems to you most important."

Sir Clinton began, checking off each point on his fingers as he produced it:

"First of all, there's that stopped clock, three hours forty-four minutes slow. That's Number One. Number Two: the fact that these three volumes from *The Times* Book Club are missing. Number Three: something I heard about Mrs. Deerhurst's early history. Mr. Wendover heard all about it. I haven't time to go into it just now. Number Four: the kind of books she seems to have fancied, to judge from her library—her own library, I mean, not the Book Club. Number Five: the fact that she was evidently acutely afraid of fire, though apart from that she wasn't a nervous type. Number Six: those pictures signed 'Ferrestone' that you see on the walls here, as well as the one upstairs in her bedroom. The dates on them gave me an idea. Ferrestone, I may tell you, Inspector, was an old sweetheart of hers, before she married Deerhurst."

"Oh, is that so?" interjected Dornfell. "Then that's someone else who had a grudge against Deerhurst, maybe."

"Possibly, but I haven't time to go into details now," Sir Clinton reminded him sharply. "Number Seven: something that Mandrell suggested to my mind when he was here. Number Eight: that roll of cottonwool in the drawer. Number Nine: the fact that none of Mrs. Deerhurst's dresses seems to be missing. Number Ten" he checked off his last finger, "that Braille typewriter in the escritoire. Number Eleven: Mrs. Deerhurst's cheque-book is gone. And, to make the round dozen, the fact that young Adeney knew about the patch of blood on the floor here, before he had a chance of entering this room. Finally, a phrase in the wording of that telegram to Deerhurst."

The expressions on the faces of Dornfell and Wendover betrayed only too plainly their anxiety to put questions, but the Chief Constable clearly had no intention of wasting further time.

"We can clear these points up one by one," he said to Dornfell. "Better start with the last but one on the list. Young Adeney's taken up residence here, hasn't he? If he's on the premises, have him in now and we'll try to get to the bottom of this."

"He's out in the garden, sir, I believe," Dornfell explained. "I'll fetch him."

When the inspector had left the room, Sir Clinton got up and stood before one of Ferrestone's pictures; but instead of examining it closely, he seemed to Wendover merely to be musing.

"That's rather good stuff," he commented at last. "I think I must see if I can get a look at some of his other things, if they're accessible anywhere. I'd like to buy one or two, if he doesn't want too big a price for them. See the rush of that waterfall, Squire? You can almost hear the roar of it."

He broke off, glanced at the picture again, and then seemed to change the trend of his thoughts.

"'The sounding cataract haunted me like a passion,'" he quoted. "Does anyone read Wordsworth nowadays, Squire? He seems a bit out of place in the motor age."

"He's full of hints and tips for bemused Chief Constables, though," Wendover suggested with an ironic smile.

"'One impulse from a vernal wood
May teach you more of man,

> Of moral evil and of good,
> Than all the sages can.'

Try a stroll in the nearest spinney, if the psychology of this affair worries you."

" The prescription says ' a *vernal* wood,' " Sir Clinton pointed out. " You can't find that in July. Not in this country, at anyrate. Still, Wordsworth had his points.

> ' Full twenty times was Peter feared,
> For once that Peter was respected.'

For Peter read Leonard, and you get a fair picture of our late friend Deerhurst, from all we've heard of him."

Dornfell interrupted this literary interlude by ushering Adeney into the room. It was the first time that Wendover had seen Nicholas, and at the first glance he was unfavourable impressed. There was something sullen and hang-dog in the young man's air which went rather against the grain with Wendover.

" Just sit down," Sir Clinton requested. " I want you to answer a question or two, if you don't mind."

Nicholas Adeney glanced at Wendover in a hostile fashion, which tended further to lessen the Squire's sympathy for him. He seated himself with evident reluctance and then kept his eyes averted from the three men before him.

" It turns out that Mrs. Deerhurst had a Braille typewriter," Sir Clinton began. " Can you tell us if there was anything wrong with her sight ? "

Nicholas seemed astonished by this opening.

" No, not that I ever heard," he said in a surprised tone. " She had perfectly good eyes."

" There's another possibility," Sir Clinton explained. " She may have done voluntary transcribing for the

National Library for the Blind. Do you know anything about that ? "

Nicholas shook his head.

" I never heard anything of that kind," he said with obvious candour. " Until I saw that typewriter affair yesterday I didn't know she'd anything of the sort. In fact, until you told me what it was just now, I didn't even know it was a Braille machine."

" Then unless she worked for the National Library for the Blind, you can't suggest why she bought the thing ? "

Nicholas shook his head decidedly.

" No, I haven't a notion."

Sir Clinton's opening seemed to have restored young Adeney's confidence. He now looked up and faced his interlocutor squarely.

" I see some of Duncan Ferrestone's pictures on the wall," the Chief Constable continued. " I'd like to see some others. Can you tell me where I could find any more ? "

Nicholas was obviously puzzled by this line of inquiry. He glanced out of the corner of his eye at Dornfell, who was taking notes of the conversation in shorthand. But Dornfell's face betrayed nothing of what was passing through his mind as he took down sentence after sentence.

" I'm afraid I can't help," Nicholas admitted. " I haven't seen Ferrestone for years. For obvious reasons," he ended, with a sardonic twist of his lips.

" He was a friend of yours, at one time, wasn't he ? " the Chief Constable pursued. " I think he was engaged to Mrs. Deerhurst but that was broken off ? "

" That's correct," Nicholas admitted.

" Did he take it badly ? " inquired Sir Clinton.

" Take it badly ? ' 'echoed Nicholas. " Well, I don't suppose he was overjoyed, if that's what you mean.

He cleared out, left the district, if that's any help to you."

"You haven't seen him since?" Sir Clinton asked half carelessly.

"No, never set eyes on him," Nicholas declared boldly.

"That sounds honest, anyhow," Wendover commented to himself. Adeney was anything but a reliable witness, as they had found; but on this point his tone had the ring of truth in it.

Rather to Wendover's disappointment, the Chief Constable pursued the matter no further but switched over to a fresh subject.

"You've been in communication with a man called Sturge?"

Nicholas Adeney seemed taken aback for a moment by this inquiry. He very evidently reflected for a second or two before answering.

"I saw him a few days ago, at the gate here," he admitted, with a sharp glance at the Chief Constable's face.

"You and Deerhurst were in gaol at the same time as Sturge was, I believe?"

"Yes, we were."

"And you found something of common interest when you met him again?"

Once more Nicholas seemed to reflect before speaking.

"Another mare's nest," he said at last, with more than a touch of insolence. "I don't mind telling you what we talked about. His child's got bad eyesight and we spoke about that. Afterwards I interested my cousin in the case and she found the money to send the child to a specialist and get the girl put in the way of regaining her sight. The thing was done through me; Sturge doesn't know where the cash came from."

" And that was all you talked about ? " demanded Sir Clinton sharply. " Deerhurst's name wasn't mentioned ? "

" I don't remember all we said," Nicholas retorted stubbornly. " It was the child's troubles that stuck in my mind."

The Chief Constable probed no further, rather to Wendover's surprise.

" Sturge is an habitual criminal, isn't he ? " he asked, turning to Dornfell. " A burglar, or something of that sort ? "

" More of a sneak-thief than a burglar on the big scale," the inspector corrected. " Lead piping from empty houses is about his mark. But he's known to associate with other criminals. Likely he acts as a spy for them. Keeps watch on houses that they've got their eye on, and that sort of thing."

Sir Clinton nodded his acknowledgment of the information. He seemed to consider his line of action before he spoke again ; and when he did so, it was in the tone of a man who wishes to be perfectly fair.

" Now, Mr. Adeney," he said, " I'm going to put my cards on the table because I don't wish to take any unfair advantage of you. I haven't made up my mind—yet—to bring a charge against you, so that on the basis of the Judges' Rules I could ask any questions I like without going through the formality of cautioning you beforehand. But I'm not going to try to trap you. Anything you say will be noted, just as we've noted what other witnesses have said. And if you answer frankly and satisfactorily, then there will be no question of a charge at all. Now is that quite clear, before we go any further ? "

Nicholas pondered for a few moments.

" I see," he said, in the tone of one who has solved a problem. " The catch is in the word 'satisfactorily,' isn't it? Very neat," he added, with a frown. "Quite straightforward, like all police affairs."

Sir Clinton looked at him in silence for a couple of seconds.

"If you take that line," he said coldly, "you make things more difficult for yourself. The obvious inference is that you've something to hide. Very well, then. Let's get to business. You've accounted for your time up to half-past twelve in the morning of Thursday. What did you do after parting from Constable Goodrich at the door of your lodgings?"

"I went to bed," answered Nicholas, with a return to his original sullenness.

"Obviously, since you were roused later in the morning when Evie Sutton came to fetch you. But at what hour precisely did you go to bed?"

"How do I know?" snapped Nicholas. "I didn't look at my watch."

"Did you come out of your lodgings again that night?" demanded the Chief Constable, speaking slowly, so as to let each word make its impression.

"No, I didn't," said Nicholas, in a tone which came near a snarl.

"Did you come into this room at any time between midnight and seven in the morning?" Sir Clinton asked, with the same deliberation.

This seemed to sting Nicholas into rage.

"What's the use of asking me questions when you don't believe anything I say?" he snapped. "I shan't answer. You can't force me to."

"No, but we can draw our own conclusions. Do you deny that you were in this room sometime between midnight and seven o'clock?"

Nicholas shut his lips and stared malevolently at his interrogator.

"You don't deny it?" Sir Clinton pursued, in the

same chilly tone. " Well, that's a lie saved, at least. Now, another point. Were you a party to any arrangement to induce Deerhurst to come here on the night of the 18th–19th ? "

Rather to Wendover's surprise, Nicholas Adeney's lips parted momentarily as though he meant to answer this question. Then he seemed to think better of his decision and relapsed into impassivity. Sir Clinton frowned slightly at this stubbornness, but he tried once more :

" Had you an interview with Deerhurst in this room ? "

" No," said Nicholas, and then quickly he qualified his statement by adding, " I don't think so."

" Do you want to withdraw that answer ? " demanded the Chief Constable swiftly. " I wish to be perfectly fair. If you've made a mistake, say so."

Adeney considered carefully for some seconds before answering.

" I withdraw it," he said doubtfully.

Sir Clinton made a gesture to Dornfell, and then turned back to Nicholas.

" I'm going to explain how the law stands," he said, in a judicial tone, " because I think you ought to know where you are. A man may be concerned in a murder in one of four ways. He may be a principal in the first degree who actually does the deed with his own hands. Or he may be a principal in the second degree, if he helps the actual offender at the very time when the murder is done. Either of these principals can be hanged on conviction. Then there's an accessary before the fact : anyone who procures, advises, or aids the murderer beforehand, but who is not actually present when the murder is done. And there's an accessary after the fact, who knows that a murder has been committed and yet actively helps the murderer to escape justice. These last two types don't run the risk of the hangman. I've made it quite clear, I hope ? "

Nicholas cleared his throat rather painfully.

" You've made it quite clear," he said huskily.

For a moment he seemed on the verge of adding something. Then he changed his mind and stoically kept silence. Sir Clinton gazed at him with a faintly perplexed look.

" You won't make a clean breast of it ? " he demanded at last.

But Nicholas had evidently come to a final decision. He stared at the carpet and merely shook his head in answer to the question.

" Well, I shall have to detain you for the present until we make some further inquiries, so that we can frame our indictment," Sir Clinton said briskly. " They'll look after you at the police station. And if you change your mind there, you've only to ask for Inspector Dornfell and he'll take any statement you choose to make."

He turned to Dornfell.

" Just ring up the station and get them to send up a couple of men to take him down there, after he's signed these notes of yours. In the meanwhile, you can put him in charge of the constable on the premises. I've done with him."

Dornfell rose, blotted his notes carefully, and then, picking up his papers, he escorted Nicholas Adeney from the room.

As the door closed behind them Wendover turned to the Chief Constable.

" You didn't get much out of him, did you ? " he asked.

" I got what I wanted," rejoined Sir Clinton carelessly.

"It didn't seem very important to me," Wendover confessed.

"That was because you were listening to him instead of watching him as I was doing. Here's the point, Squire. No inquest on Deerhurst has been held as yet, and we've taken the greatest care that, outside official circles, the thing is supposed to be just another of these motor accidents. That rigmarole of mine about principals and accessaries was introduced for one purpose and one purpose only: to see how he'd react to the word 'Murder.' I watched him like a cat; and when it came out, he wasn't surprised in the very slightest. Ergo, he knew long ago that it was a murder case. Well, if he knew that, then he knew just a bit too much for his safety. Obviously he's been mixed up in the affair, and pretty intimately too."

"Then why didn't you charge him?" asked Wendover in some surprise.

"For this reason," explained the Chief Constable. "I can't make up my mind whether he's been a principal or merely an accessary. Now if we charge him as a principal, we can't convict him as an accessary after the fact, on that indictment. So it's safer to find out a bit more, before we start drawing up the precise charge. It's just my usual cautious nature asserting itself. And no harm's done by procrastinating a little in a case of this sort."

"He made a poor impression on me," confessed Wendover, rather irrelevantly.

"Curious how often you and I agree," said Sir Clinton lightly. "Let's try again. Suppose you had to go into hiding, Squire. How would you manage it?"

"Take rooms beforehand somewhere and pretend to be a commercial traveller who was often away. That would build up a second personality ready to step into when I wanted it."

"There's something in that notion," the Chief Constable agreed. "But I can think of a dodge as good as that, for some cases. What about retiring into a nursing home?"

"But if you go into a nursing home you've got to have something wrong with you," Wendover criticised.

"Oh, not necessarily. It could be managed," Sir Clinton declared with a faint twinkle in his eye.

"Through a venal doctor, I suppose?" said Wendover contemptuously. "Morris Finsbury in *The Wrong Box* didn't find it so easy to pick up what he wanted in that line. Or are you suggesting swindling your medico with a set of false symptoms?"

"Not exactly," the Chief Constable retorted, glancing at his watch. "Ah, here's the Inspector. You've got him disposed of? Good! Now we'll need to close this session. There are two things I want you to do for me. First of all, I want the actual form of that telegram which summoned Deerhurst here. You'll be able to square the Post Office people if you go high enough up. The other thing is that I want as much information about Duncan Ferrestone as I can get. That'll take some digging out, perhaps, since he seems to have left the district some years ago. Still, he ought to be traceable eventually. I'll ring up the National Library for the Blind myself. And I've another call to put through as well. That's all we can do at present, I think."

CHAPTER XIV

THE BEARER BONDS

WENDOVER and Sir Clinton were apt to sit late over the chess-board, and it was long past midnight when they were interrupted by the sharp ring of the telephone bell. Sir Clinton went to the instrument, and as he put the receiver to his ear, he recognised Dornfell's voice, speaking in unusually eager tones.

"I'm sorry to worry you at this time of night, sir, but I know you don't go to bed early, so I took the chance."

"Quite right," Sir Clinton encouraged him. "What's the trouble?"

"We've pulled in Sturge, sir, the fellow who was seen talking to young Adeney, you remember. We caught him in an empty house with a lot of brass taps in his bag that he'd sawn off. He was just starting to take out some lead-piping when our man came on him. It's a clean cop."

"Yes, I remember you said he was that sort of person. But why all the eagerness, Inspector?"

"Well, sir, we've been round to his lodgings, and we've got a find. He had the envelope with the bearer bonds in it—I mean the things that went amissing from Norwood House on the night of the murder."

"That's interesting," Sir Clinton commented.

"Yes, but that's not all, sir," the inspector hurried

on. "There's a big packet of papers in Braille. Looks like the stuff which was taken from the drawer in the writing-desk. You remember the empty space in one drawer that we couldn't account for? These papers had been there, and Sturge must have stolen them. Would it be too much trouble if I asked Mr. Wendover to look them over and read them for us? He could do it, and it would save a lot of trouble if he wouldn't mind helping us. It may throw some light on the business."

Sir Clinton glanced at his wrist-watch.

"The night's still young. I'll bring Mr. Wendover down at once. And, by the way, Inspector, we shall want to see Sturge, so keep him handy. You haven't taken any statement from him yet? That's all right. Expect us shortly."

He put down the receiver and turned to his guest.

"I'm afraid the rest of the game's postponed, Squire. *Fiat justitia*, even if it upsets the board. We need you at head-quarters to interpret some Braille stuff which has turned up. You don't mind?"

"Not a bit. But what's all this about?" demanded Wendover.

"Better come to it with a fresh mind," Sir Clinton suggested. "Dornfell has arrested Sturge and found some Braille stuff in his lodgings. We want to know what it's all about. Sorry to keep you out of bed, but duty calls."

Sir Clinton got out his car, and in a very short time he and Wendover entered the police head-quarters, where they found Dornfell awaiting them with the papers on the table before him.

"These are the bearer bonds, sir," he explained, "Arctic & Frigidor Cold Storage Corporation 5 per cent. Bonds, number 515 to 519; and the envelope has the registered number and the stockbrokers' name on it. There's no doubt that these are the missing ones. So we have a second charge against Sturge on their account. And perhaps a third one, later on," he added ominously.

" Let's clear things up as we go along," Sir Clinton suggested. " And that reminds me that I've rung up the National Library for the Blind, and they tell me that Mrs. Deerhurst isn't on their list of voluntary transcribers. So that scores off one possible explanation of her Braille typewriter."

" Here's the packet of Braille scripts, sir," Dornfell pointed out. " Shall we begin by asking Mr. Wendover to glance over them ? Then we'll have some notion how we stand before we tackle Sturge."

He placed a chair at the table for Wendover, who sat down and drew the pile of papers towards him. Almost at the first glance his brow clouded and it was plain that he had little liking for his task. He glanced away from the sheet before him and seemed to be wrestling with some troublesome problem.

" Well, what's the trouble ? " demanded Sir Clinton. " Can't you make it out ? Cipher, is it ? "

Wendover put down the sheet deliberately and faced the Chief Constable.

" I don't feel much inclined to read this," he explained slowly. " It wasn't meant for publication, obviously."

Dornfell was evidently taken aback at this view of the matter.

" What's that got to do with it, sir ? It's evidence, isn't it ? We've got to know what it's all about."

Then, with a shrug of his shoulders, he added :

" It doesn't matter. If you won't read it, someone else will do it for us."

Wendover nodded, as though considering the point in all its bearings. Then he apparently made up his mind.

"I suppose you're right; and in that case I'd rather do the reading myself, though I'm not quite happy about it. You see"—he turned to the Chief Constable—"they're love letters; and I'm not very keen on prying into another man's love affairs. Still, I can keep my mouth shut, and perhaps another reader might be less scrupulous"—this with an angry glance at the inspector. "So if you insist, I'll go through them."

"How do you know they're love letters?" queried Dornfell. "You've only read the first couple of words."

"The first two words are 'My darling'," snarled Wendover, who felt his position acutely. "I suppose that's how you begin your letters when you're ordering soap from your grocer? He must enjoy your correspondence."

Dornfell had taken Sir Clinton's joke about soap in good part, but he obviously resented this variation of it from someone outside the Force. A glance at Sir Clinton's face moved him to take a different line.

"Well, perhaps you'll go a little further," he suggested, in a less rancorous tone. "I see your point, sir. But someone's got to read these things. It may as well be you."

Wendover gave a curt nod and bent over the script, holding the paper so as to get the light at the best angle for seeing the points of the Braille dots. When he came to the end of three sheets he glanced at the bottom of the page which followed.

"It's signed 'Duncan'," he announced, without drawing the obvious inference.

"Duncan?" echoed the Chief Constable, and his tone suggested that he had got something for which he had been waiting for a long time. "Duncan

Ferrestone, eh? That's interesting. Proceed, will you? By the way, are these things dated?"

Wendover turned back to the top sheet and shook his head.

"No date. No address either," he declared. "It starts straight off."

He finished the first letter and went on gloomily with his task without vouchsafing any information until he had finished his reading of all the sheets. Then he pushed them away as though glad to be done.

"There's nothing there that has any bearing on the murder, so far as I can see. No direct bearing, at any rate," he added reluctantly. "They're just love-letters, and rather fine ones. The sort of thing a decent man might write to a girl he's just got engaged to."

"No funny business, you mean?" interpreted Dornfell crudely.

"No funny business, as you put it, Mr. Dornfell," Wendover confirmed icily. "Neither of them was that sort, I judge."

Dornfell acknowledged the snub with a faint sniff, but his vocabulary again betrayed him in his next query.

"Nothing but lovey-dovey stuff in them, then?"

Wendover's only response was a slight shrug. He turned to Sir Clinton, and his expression made it plain that he did not like what he had to do.

"There's something running through the whole series," he said doubtfully. "It's never mentioned explicitly; it comes in here and there as if both of them knew well enough what it was and had no need to put it into words."

He leafed over the sheets as he spoke, hunting for the actual phrases.

"Here it is. '*This horrible affair. . . . One feels it*

creeping on. Every day brings it so much nearer' . . . and so on."

"Easy to see what *that* was," commented the inspector. "It was Deerhurst's release, of course. We heard how *she* felt about it, and naturally this fellow Ferrestone would feel the same if he was gone on her."

Wendover hesitated again, as though his task went sorely against the grain, but he was in a position of trust and he had to do what was expected of him.

"There's one thing more," he continued. "This thing, whatever it was, seems to have brought the two of them together again. You remember they'd quarrelled," he reminded the Chief Constable. "And there's a hint that it isn't insuperable." He hunted through the pages again. "'*With even moderate luck, things will come all right in the end, so don't worry too much about it.*'"

He stopped abruptly, as Sir Clinton noticed.

"What's the next phrase?" demanded the Chief Constable in a silky tone.

Wendover looked chap-fallen, as though detected in a fault.

"I was just going to read it," he said. "'*You will be there, darling, when it's done; and that will give me all the courage I need.*'"

"I thought so!" ejaculated the Chief Constable, in the tone of a man who sees the solution of a puzzle which has long eluded him. "That clinches it."

"Of course it does," said the inspector triumphantly. "She was on the spot when the thing was done, and that makes her a principal in the second degree. They'll both hang now. I was afraid she'd get off for want of some evidence, but that phrase makes it plain enough. All we have to do is to find support for it. Just put a pencil tick in the margin opposite that, Mr. Wendover, please. I want to go over that paragraph myself when I can get hold of a Braille alphabet."

Wendover, the unwilling instrument, sat staring at the sheets of paper before him. Hitherto he had watched the inspector's manœuvres with a certain distaste, but this last triumphant outburst sickened him. The brute seemed to take a pleasure in putting the noose round a girl's neck! It did not occur to him that Dornfell was merely doing, to the best of his ability, the work he was paid to do. The folly of that girl! Another Thompson-Bywaters case, he reflected, where the main evidence would be furnished because some letters were too dear to be destroyed. He bit his lip, cursing his own knowledge of Braille which had dragged him into his present plight. No doubt someone would have been called in to read these cursed letters in any case; but he could not get away from the fact that he was the man who had done it. And having consented, he had to go through with it. He couldn't suppress what he read once he had taken on the task. Damn! Mechanically he took out his pencil and made a tick in the margin as the inspector desired.

"That simplifies matters," the Chief Constable said in a cheerful tone which jarred horribly on Wendover. "We shall be able to lay hands on them quick enough now, I think, and then things should begin to move. In the meanwhile, Inspector, perhaps we'd better interview Sturge and see what he's got up his sleeve. Bring him in, please."

Wendover, seeking to occupy himself, stacked the Braille sheets neatly together and laid them aside on the table. He did not care to look at the Chief Constable as he did so. Criminology was a dirty game after all, when it landed one in fixes like this. The entry of Sturge gave him an excuse for putting the other matter to the back of his mind, and he glanced up at the stunted, unprepossessing figure of the criminal. He noted Sturge's glance of dismay at the papers on the table. Evidently the man had not expected to find this evidence confronting him. However, after the first look, he pulled himself together and assumed an almost perky air.

" You may as well tell us all about it, Sturge," the Chief Constable suggested. " It's what you'd call ' a clean cop,' you know."

" What is, sir ? " inquired Sturge impudently.

The Chief Constable smiled in a friendly fashion, quite unperturbed by the insolence.

" Oh, all this "—he indicated the papers on the table—" and your magnetic attraction for brass taps and lead piping, of course."

" That ? Why, your flattie knows all about it. No need for me to explain when he's got it all down in his penny exercise-book. Apply to him for further perticlers."

The friendly smile faded from Sir Clinton's face.

" Don't strain yourself to be funny, Sturge," he advised. " This is serious. What were you doing in Norwood House on the night of Deerhurst's death ? You needn't trouble to make up a tale, because we can catch you out. The plain truth will do."

The perkiness vanished from Sturge's attitude and was replaced by sullenness.

" Are you a-chargin' me with anythin' ? " he demanded. " If so, you've got no business for to be puttin' questions, an' you know that as well as I do."

" Very well," Sir Clinton agreed. " You'll be charged with stealing certain brass taps, the property of . . ."

He glanced at Dornfell, who supplied the required name.

" And I shan't ask you any questions on that point," Sir Clinton continued. " That charge will let us hold you till we need you on other grounds. But take my advice now and make a clean breast of your doings that night on Mrs. Deerhurst's premises."

Sturge evidently considered the suggestion carefully before speaking again. Finally he glanced malevolently at the envelope on the table, as though it had done him a personal injury.

" No good denying things with these 'ere papers all present an' correct, I suppose," he decided at last. " You've got me fair. But, 's truth, I wish I'd never set eyes on them. A fat lot o' good it's been, pinchin' them. An' yet it looked a bonanza at the time, it did."

" Better leave the moral reflections to the Bench," Sir Clinton suggested. " What we want is a plain tale of your adventures that night."

" Well, I may as well come clean, I s'pose," Sturge admitted. " If I don't, like as not you'll be tryin' for to run me in for bein' an accessary or somethin', and I was absolutely on my own that night. This was the way it was. A week or two back I chanced for to run across an old college chum o' mine, one Adeney, at the gate of Norwood House."

" That's correct," Sir Clinton agreed. " We know all about that. By the way, what took you there in the first place ? "

" That's it, *that's* it," Sturge complained. " Tryin' for to trip me up, ain't you ? Well, you can't, for this is the plain truth, so help me. I went round there to ask after the address of Deerhurst. Some of us would've been glad to get in touch with him just then."

" Why ? "

" Well, he was in stir with us, and he played it low down on some of us over a scheme of sorts."

"Yes, prison-breaking," Sir Clinton interjected.

"It's you calls it that," Sturge declared cautiously, "not me. You seem to know a lot about things, you do. But the fact is, we had a good idea—things gets about somehow, what with one thing an' another—that Deerhurst had a bit o' stuff tucked away quiet in some odd corner, handy for when he'd come out again. An', things bein' as they was, we thought he owed us a bit over that scheme that didn't come off. Sort o' compensation for loss o' wear an' tear in the brain department, see? Anyhow, that's what brought me up to Norwood House; an' there, quite accidental-like, was Adeney. So I had a bit of a chin-wag with him, friendly like, an' we began talkin' about my poor kid with the bad eyes. An' he took my address an' sort o' hinted somethin' might be done about it. He didn't let me down there, Adeney didn't. He forked out the money all right, an' they say the kid's goin' to see well enough to catch a flea 'fore all's done. There's some decent coves in this world, after all."

"You don't know where the money came from, originally?"

Sturge shook his head.

"Not me. Adeney was too close about that."

"Go on."

"Well, that house struck me. Expensive lookin'. Sort o' thing that interests me. So I made a few inquiries, quiet like. It was a fair gift, by the look o' things. Maids sent off after dinner. Only a lone woman left on the premises, an' she was bound to be out seein' her friends some nights, so the place would be left to look after itself. What ho! thinks I, this is the thing I've been dreamin' about for years.

"So I hung about and watched it, night after night, just to see how the land lay. An' that night it was dead dark, not a light showin' at any o' the windows —empty for a snick. So about ten-thirty I hops off to the nearest telephone-box, just for to be sure, an' tries for a connection with Norwood House. Nothin' doin', just as I expected, so the coast was clear. So I hoofs it round again sharp and watches till the coast was clear, an' then I walks up, as bold as brass, to the front door. If anyone *had* have been there I'd my excuse all ready. Ask for Deerhurst's address. But as it was, no one came when I rang the bell, an' after a bit I just gave the door handle a try, an' it opened at the first twist. I was inside in two ticks. Alone in London, eh? Not a soul on the premises but me. What made it a sure thing was that I just pressed the electric light switch for a twink—to make sure—an' the current was off. So I was right on velvet then."

"You're sure the current was off?" demanded Sir Clinton.

"Certain. I remember takin' out my flash-lamp after tryin' the switch."

"Well, go on."

"I went into the dining-room first. Somebody'd been havin' a tuck-in. Lot o' dirty dishes on the table. I turned my flash on to the mantelpiece, and there was that bedamned envelope, with the registered label on it. Registered things is generally valuable, so I pouched it on the chance. Then I went into the drawin'-room an' had a bit o' a look-see there."

"You had rubber gloves on?"

Sturge looked at the Chief Constable with a hurt expression.

"Take me for an ammytyoor, do you? 'Course I had. Well, I looked around, makin' a sort of list of what'd come in handy, an' I come to a sort o' burroo, one o' those things you do your writin' at, you know. I went through it, an' in one o' the drawers I comes across a stack o' paper with Braille on it. As it happens, I know somethin' about Braille—blind writin', you know—because I was tryin' for to teach it to my poor kiddie at one time. So I glances my eye over this stuff, an' plain in sight was a lot o' 'darlin's' an' 'dearests' an' similar small change. An' just out o' curiosity I turns over to the signature, which was in Braille too, as you can see there, an' it was 'Duncan.'"

Wendover scowled at the creature in front of him. It was bad enough that he himself should have read Duncan Ferrestone's love-letters; but when he thought of this obscene thing reading them also he went hot all over.

"Now it crossed my mind," Sturge went on artlessly, "that Deerhurst's name wasn't 'Duncan.' It was Lionel, or Leonard, or somethin' like that, beginnin' with 'L,' anyway. So here was some man 'Duncan' writin' to Deerhurst's moll behind his back an' callin' her 'Darlin'' an' so forth. Reely, the morals o' these rich 'uns is enough to sicken a tom-cat. It struck me Deerhurst might be pleased for to know of these goin's on. He might even be grateful, in a financial sort o' way. So I pouched the lot with the registered letter."

"I suppose it never crossed your mind to blackmail Mrs. Deerhurst?" demanded Sir Clinton.

Sturge held up his hands with a gesture of horror which Wendover found wholly unconvincing.

"Me touch the black!" he exclaimed virtuously. "It's off my beat altogether. I never so much as thought of it, give you my word."

"Well, get along."

"I was just gettin' ready to collect some stuff," Sturge continued, "when all o' a sudden the telephone bell went ‘ kling ! klang ! ’ Gave me a start, I can tell you, in that empty house.”

“ What time was that ? ” Sir Clinton interrupted.

Sturge apparently made some intricate mental calculation.

“ That would be about eleven o’clock,” he announced at last. “ I’d wasted a lot o’ time tryin’ to make out that Braille stuff. I’m not over quick at it. Anyway, that bell give me such a jar that my nerves got a bit askew. I’m apt to get nervous when I’m on a job,” he explained apologetically. “ An’ there was a fair chance that whoever was ringing’ up might drop in when they got no answer to the call. Not likely, mebbe, but you never know your luck. So what with one thing an’ another it seemed best to go while the goin’ was good. Besides, most of the stuff in that house wouldn’t melt down to much—Sheffield plate and things o’ that sort, which ain’t in my line, reelly. So it wasn’t much o’ a wrench to tear myself away. I just opened the front door an’ let myself out like a gentleman, as you might say.”

“ You mentioned the dining-room and the drawing-room,” Sir Clinton pointed out. “ Did you go into any other rooms ? ”

“ Over the whole house,” Sturge amplified. “ Didn’t I say that ? Well, I was, and there wasn’t anything worth notice in any of the other rooms, so I didn’t stay in them long. It was when I was back in the drawin’-room that the telephone went.”

“ And you left the premises . . . ? ”

“ About eleven—ten past eleven at the latest.”

“ You’re sure there was no one else in the house ? ”

Sturge nodded emphatically.

“ Not a ruddy soul. It was empty, and the current was off, as I was tellin’ you. A ‘ dead ’un,’ for all practical purposes.”

Sir Clinton glanced at him curiously.

" Funny that you should have selected the house of the person who helped your little girl, Sturge. Not quite a nice return for her kindness, is it ? "

Sturge seemed completely taken aback.

" Gawd's truth, governor ! You don't mean it ? Why, I'd ha' cut my hand off before I done it if I'd known that."

His contrition was quite unfeigned, and the Chief Constable was satisfied. Obviously Sturge, in telling his tale, had not been trying to shield his benefactress.

" Well, that's as it may be," Sir Clinton said brusquely. " You're sure you were working alone ? Haven't forgotten to tell us about any fellow-craftsman who was with you ? Good. Then you can sign the notes the inspector has made. I haven't made up my mind about you yet, Sturge. We'll have to check one or two things. But if it's any relief to your mind, we may be using you as King's evidence in the matter of the Norwood House affair. The brass taps and lead piping are different. You'll have to go through it in that business."

Sturge seemed in no way cast down by this last item.

" One gets off lighter on one charge than two," he commented in a cheerful tone. Then his face took on a more serious expression.

" Nothin' I've said's going to do any harm to Mrs. Deerhurst, is it ? " he demanded. " If it is, then I don't sign any notes. That's plain."

" Sign or not, just as you please," Sir Clinton said carelessly. " You know we make no promises here."

" I see," Sturge retorted bitterly. " Pumped me dry, you have, an' now you don't care a damn 'cause you've got what you wanted. I wonder what that was."

"Something for you to think about," Sir Clinton assured him unsympathetically. "Have you anything to ask, Inspector? No? Then I don't think we need detain Mr. Sturge, so you can put him back in his cell."

When the inspector had retired with his charge, Wendover turned to Sir Clinton.

"So she wasn't in the house at all at eleven o'clock?"

"Apparently not," the Chief Constable confirmed. "Sturge's tale was obviously somewhere near the truth. He was in a blue funk lest he should be dragged into the more serious business, so he had the sense to give us something near the plain truth about his own doings. And now we must put our hands on Ferrestone and Mrs. Deerhurst as quick as possible."

"You know where to find them?" demanded Wendover, astounded.

"Not the exact address," Sir Clinton admitted "But I think a little telephoning should solve the problem easily enough. It's a very limited choice, on the face of it."

Wendover considered for some moments, and then made a gesture of incomprehension.

"I don't see it," he confessed.

"Well, all the facts are there; you've only got to put two and two together, Squire, and the answer should come out as something between three and five. There's a margin of error, I admit, but it's not enormous."

When the inspector reappeared, the Chief Constable turned to him.

"There's another thing I want you to do. Send round to Adeney's lodgings and have that typewriter he uses brought here. Also any specimens of his typewriting you can lay hold of. I expect he made carbon copies of the articles he wrote for publication, and you may as well bring a few of these also, if you can find them. And you'd better ask him when his cousin first lent him the machine. We may need that information. Do it tactfully, Inspector. Ask him about his literary work, or something of that sort ; and lead up to the inquiry naturally. Don't let him think that it's important."

CHAPTER XV

THE TELEGRAM

"YOU asked for Adeney's typewriter, sir. Here it is," said Dornfell, with a gesture towards a black-covered shape on the table. "And I've brought some of his typescript and duplicates that you wanted. There were any number of them at his lodgings. And here's the original of that telegram to Deerhurst. You asked for that, too. And I've got you some blank typewriting paper and carbons that you ordered when you rang me up. Quarto size. I suppose that will do, sir? Is there anything else I can get?"

"Not at present, thanks," the Chief Constable answered. "These will be enough to go on with. We can get anything else that suggests itself, by-and-by."

Wendover moved forward and examined the telegram form, which was neatly clipped between two sheets of glass to protect its surface.

"You've been testing it for finger-prints, I see," he commented, pointing to sundry black smudges on the paper. "Did you get anything useful?"

Dornfell shook his head ruefully.

"Nothing that suits our purpose," he confessed. "We've identified some of them, made by the post office people after the form was handed in to them over the counter; but there's nothing to take hold of."

In his turn, Sir Clinton inspected the glass-protected paper.

" Very neat," he said critically, with a faint smile. " This is cleverer than usual. It cuts away a good many possibilities of identifying the machine it was written with. Still, we can have a dash at it."

Dornfell looked over the Chief Constable's shoulder to examine the form in the light of this comment, but his expression showed that he had made little of Sir Clinton's cryptic reflection.

" Now let's have a look at Adeney's machine," the Chief Constable proposed, removing the American cloth cover as he spoke. " It's a British Commonwealth, No. 50, as you told me over the 'phone. I've rung up the makers since then, and they tell me that the No. 50 model was put on the market six years ago. Now we'd better see what sort of work it turns out."

He sat down at the table, clipped a blank sheet of paper into the machine, and then tapped out the wording of the telegram, keeping the spacing as it was on the official form. Extracting the paper from the machine, he placed original and copy side by side on the table for the others to examine.

" I took a glance at Osborn's '*Questioned Documents*' before I left home this morning," he explained. " Do you know the book, Inspector ? No ? Then I must lend you my copy. You'll find it invaluable in this kind of case. But let's leave Osborn aside for the moment, and look at things with our own eyes, first of all. Just compare these two scripts and see what you make of them."

Dornfell was obviously eager to forestall Wendover, and his glance had hardly fallen on the papers when he pointed out one difference.

" Your version's clean-cut, sir. The original telegram's lettering seems broader, as if it had got blurred somehow."

" Yes," chimed in Wendover. " Your version's

made with the ribbon, whereas the telegram seems to be a carbon copy. Is that what you're driving at ? "

Sir Clinton made a gesture of agreement.

" I've been waiting for a long time now for someone who would hit on that particular trick," he said. " But why a carbon copy ? It doesn't conceal what both of you must have spotted at a glance—that both versions are printed in the type of the Commonwealth machine."

" Now to drag in Osborn," said Wendover acidly. " That's what you have up your sleeve, isn't it ? "

" It is. Credit where credit's due," retorted the Chief Constable.

He turned to the inspector.

" Here are some of the questions which we've got to answer if we can : Was that telegram written on Adeney's machine ? If so, did Adeney write it ? If not, what machine was used ? And who did the writing ? "

" It seems simple enough if you put it that way," the inspector answered after a moment's thought. " Simple enough to put the questions, I mean, sir. Not so easy to answer 'em, perhaps."

" We can but try," said Sir Clinton optimistically. " Suppose you and Mr. Wendover have a shot at it by comparing these two specimens. Meanwhile I'll have a look at Adeney's own typescript to save time."

" This is hardly a fair comparison," Wendover objected. " We ought to compare two carbon copies, not a ribbon copy and a carbon."

In his turn he sat down at the table, inserted some sheets with a carbon between them, and tapped off a fresh copy. Then, extracting the carbon version, he laid it side by side with the original telegram ; and he and the inspector bent over it with concentrated attention, while Sir Clinton devoted himself to scanning

(Original Telegram.)

Come here at 11.30 p.m. on Wednesday. Don't
advertise yourself. Don't reply. Hazel.

(Fragment of Adeney's Typescript.)

and for several weeks. After this, I was in
of very great depression. I can very well re
one afternoon. It was a Friday, with a dull

(Driffield's copy of Telegram.)

Come here at 11.30 p.m. on Wednesday. Don't
advertise yourself. Don't reply. Hazel.

some of the Adeney typescripts. After a few minutes, Wendover looked up.

"There isn't much to take hold of here," he complained. "Both scripts have been written with a fairly new machine, so there are no obvious defects in the alignment or in the way the letters have struck the paper."

"Adeney's a very neat typist, I notice," Sir Clinton interjected, looking up from the papers before him."

"I see what you mean, sir," exclaimed the inspector triumphantly. "In this wire, the lettering is all off the lines of the form. An accurate typist would have got the lettering exactly on the lines. That's your point, isn't it ?"

"Sorry, Inspector, but it isn't. Just consider how that form was written. The form itself was down under the carbon sheet, completely hidden from the operator. It would have been too much to expect that he should get his type to follow the lines exactly. Have a shot at it on the machine yourself and see what you make of it."

The inspector tried the experiment, and produced something as quite much askew as the original, despite his care. He glanced at the result impatiently, crumpled it up, and threw it into the waste-paper basket.

"It's not so easy as it seems," he confessed, with a cross look at Wendover's graven face.

"The spacing between the lines is the same as on the form, though," Wendover pointed out. "I mean, there's the same distance between lines of type as there is between the separating printed lines on the official form."

"That's so," agreed Sir Clinton. "And if you'll turn the knob of the paper-feed, you'll find that four clicks correspond almost exactly to the shift required to carry you from one line of the form to the one next below. You see, I use a Commonwealth myself," he explained blandly, " and I tried the experiment before I came away this morning. There's nothing in that point. The man who wrote the form simply tried the experiment first of all with the form in sight, found that four clicks corresponded to the spacing between the lines of the form, and screwed up the paper four clicks when he was writing the carbon copy. Try again."

" I can't see why he took the trouble to use a carbon at all," the inspector complained.

" I think that's easily enough explained," the Chief Constable replied. " Suppose you bought two split new machines of a certain make and typed the same message with each. The alignment of the type would be all right, since the machines are new. But it's quite likely that if you compared the printing of two words in the two messages, you might find, by minute measurement, that the letters in each case were not the same distances apart. Take ' the,' for instance. In one case you might find the ' t ' a hairbreadth closer to the ' h ' than it was in the other message. It needs microscopic measurement with a ruled grating to check it, but it can be done if you have the instruments. Then again the ' h,' say, may be quite vertical in one message and just a shade slanting in the other. You wouldn't spot it with your naked eye, but the microscope and grating bring out the error. Further, there might be a very slight defect in the letter on one machine and no corresponding defect on the other machine. It might be so minute that it would appear only under the microscope when the two scripts were compared. And, as a last example, one of the types might be ' off its feet,' as the adjusters say. It might print a shade more heavily on its right side than on its left, or the top of the letter might be just a shade fainter than the bottom, in the typed script. All these tiny defects could be spotted by microscopic examination of the ribbon copy. But if you interpose a sheet or a couple of sheets, of paper and a carbon between your type and the leaflet that you're going to use, isn't it plain enough that most of these little peculiarities will be lost on the carbon impression? The type-impression from the carbon will be slightly coarser than the ribbon copy; and in that coarsening most of the final detail will be lost. So, since there's no obvious reason for using a carbon in the case of that telegram, I infer that it indicates some hanky-panky or other."

"You mean that Adeney wanted to make it hard to identify his machine as the origin of the message?" queried the inspector.

"Well, it's clever, isn't it?" Sir Clinton said, with a twinkle in his eye. "I thought of it myself a long while ago. But that almost sounds like self-praise, doesn't it?" he concluded gravely.

"It does," said Wendover with equal gravity. "But the net result of the cleverness is that we're back at the beginning again; and all we can say is that this telegram was typed on a Commonwealth machine. We can't decide whether it was Adeney's machine or not. A great advance."

"True," Sir Clinton admitted with specious frankness. "Still, to my mind the important point is whether Adeney typed it or not. You agree, don't you? Then we're quite happy."

"Not quite," Wendover corrected, "since we don't seem to have solved that problem either."

"You think not?" said the Chief Constable. "Well, I'm quite sure about the point. No second-sight or crystal-gazing required. It stares you in the face from that table, if you'll only look at the documents."

The inspector pored over the typescripts for some moments, but evidently no light dawned upon him as a result of his examination. Wendover, more cautious, betrayed nothing of his ideas.

"I don't see it," Dornfell confessed at last.

"Typewriting's almost as personal a thing as handwriting, if you know what to look for," Sir Clinton explained. "Osborn gives a list of no less than fourteen points which might serve to identify the writer of an anonymous letter. Unfortunately, in this case, a good many of them don't apply—things like the depth of indention of paragraphs, arrangement of headings, uneven margins, length of lines, and so forth. Further, this trick of the carbon has destroyed some of the most characteristic features, such as the light or heavy striking of certain letters, which might have been clear enough in a ribbon copy. H'm! Do you see it now?"

"No," said Dornfell ruefully. "I don't."

"Certain letters," repeated Sir Clinton. "But there are more than letters on a typewriter keyboard: brackets, the ampersand, the shilling mark, the pound sterling sign—*and the full-stop*."

Dornfell made a gesture of vexation.

"It was staring me in the face, sir, and I never noticed it. You mean that the full-stops in the wire are just a shade bigger than the full stops in Adeney's carbon script and your own? Whoever wrote that wire hit the full-stop key harder than Adeney did? That's it, isn't it?"

"Yes; once you see it, it stares you in the face, doesn't it, inspector? And if you were to turn to the back of the paper, I'm pretty certain you'll find a regular Braille dot at the back of the full-stop. This fellow, whoever he was, came down bang on his period keys. Now Adeney's script, all through, shows the period neatly and lightly marked. Adeney didn't write that wire, so far as this evidence goes."

"But he might have thought of that tip, sir, mightn't he? And pressed hard on purpose when he was writing out the wire?"

Sir Clinton smiled, partly at the inspector's eagerness, but partly in view of what was coming.

"He might," he admitted. "But if he did, then he must have borrowed another typewriter to work with. Just take a good look at the letters 'r' in the wire. Now compare them with the letters 'r' in Adeney's typescript and in my own copy of the wire. See the very slight difference between the right-hand top twirls in the two cases?"

Wendover and the inspector verified this carefully.

"Now this point gives us something worth having," Sir Clinton went on. "Typewriter manufacturers quite frequently change minute details in the design of their types when they bring out a new model. The Remington, for instance, made a change in 1927. The Underwood people changed the design of their letter 't' from time to time. And so on. Now when I rang up the Commonwealth people, I asked when the last change in type-design had been made by them. It was in 1933. The wire was typed with the latest type-design. This No. 50 machine of Adeney's has the older type."

"So whoever typed this wire owns a new model Commonwealth?"

"A good many people fit that description," the Chief Constable pointed out dryly. "It's a popular make."

The inspector pondered for a moment or two with knitted brows. Then a fresh idea occurred to him.

"I wonder what machine Mrs. Deerhurst used in Mandrell's office."

"The same notion crossed my mind," Sir Clinton explained. "I rang up Mandrell and asked, just to have the information handy. His machines are all Rolands ; he hasn't a Commonwealth on his premises."

"Oh," said Dornfell, in a disappointed tone, "so that's that."

Wendover turned again to the typescripts scattered about the table, but they suggested nothing fresh to him.

"You seem to have make it unlikely that the wire was typed by either Mrs. Deerhurst or Adeney," he observed, turning to the Chief Constable. "But that doesn't seem to get us much forward. Is that the most you can infer from this stuff ?"

"One might go one step further," Sir Clinton suggested in a cautious tone. "If this wire was meant to deceive, then it was typed by someone who knew that Mrs. Deerhurst owned a Commonwealth machine and who wanted to throw the onus on her. Or it may have been done by an extra clever fellow who wanted to deceive Deerhurst as to the origin of the wire and yet wished to make it possible to exonerate Mrs. Deerhurst if she came to be suspected. The wire was to bring Deerhurst to the rendezvous, but if we got hold of the original form—well, it wasn't typed on Mrs. Deerhurst's machine and so we can't prove her connection with it. By the way, Inspector, have you managed to find out anything about Ferrestone and his movements ?"

"We have, sir, up to a point. He left the district where he used to live before the Adeney crash, and went off to a place called Cheetham Parva. It's a good district for a painter, they tell me. He used to pay occasional visits to his old haunts, mostly to see a man Leverington. He went there a fortnight ago, for the day, and called on Leverington. Then he went back to Cheetham Parva, sir. And," the inspector's voice quivered a little with excitement—" he vanished completely. Disappeared almost on the spur of the moment. No letters to be sent on. No address. Nothing. And the date of his disappearance was the very same day as the Deerhurst murder, Wednesday, the 18th ! "

Dornfell evidently felt that he was sure of his little sensation, for he glanced round at Wendover as if to say : " There ! What do you say to that ? "

Sir Clinton failed to react quite as Dornfell had expected.

" Leverington ? " he mused, as though the inspector's bombshell had failed to explode. " We must look him up in the telephone directory, just to make certain. But I've a pretty fair idea of the trade he drives, without having to go so far."

He glanced at Wendover's incredulous face and added with a laugh :

" Think I'm bluffing ? Well, I'll jot it down for you and you can put it in your pocket for future reference, if you'll promise not to read it till I give you leave. It's as plain as a pikestaff, I think ; and you ought to have guessed it yourself, you know."

He picked up a piece of paper, scribbled two words on it, sealed it up in an envelope, and handed it to Wendover.

CHAPTER XVI

FERRESTONE

"AND now, Squire, you can take a peep into that envelope, if you like," said the Chief Constable. As he spoke he drew up his car in front of a big, solidly-built five-storied house forming part of a terrace, the kind of house which, not so long ago, must have been occupied by a man who reckoned his income in thousands. There was no plate on the door nor any other indication of the present occupier's identity.

But Wendover had no immediate interest in things of this sort. He pulled the envelope from his pocket, tore it open, extracted the sheet of paper it contained, and read: "EYE SPECIALIST." Then he followed Sir Clinton up the steps. A tall, clean-shaven man in a white jacket opened the door in answer to the Chief Constable's ring.

"I have an appointment with Miss Barclay."

The doorkeeper had evidently been primed.

"Yes, Sir Clinton. If you'll come this way, please. . . ."

He led them along a corridor, past a roomy lift, and ushered them into what was obviously a waiting-room, with comfortable easy-chairs, tastefully-arranged flowers, and an assortment of the week's periodicals neatly stacked on a side table.

"Miss Barclay will be free directly, sir," the attendant informed them as he withdrew.

Wendover, enlightened by Sir Clinton's scribbled note, glanced about him.

" A nursing home ? " he guessed without difficulty.

" Splendid ! " said the Chief Constable, in ironic congratulation. " I'm glad you didn't mistake it for a dentist's anteroom, Squire. Yes, it's a nursing home, as you opine, and a very good one, too, they tell me. Now don't let me interrupt the chain of your reasoning. ' Eye-specialist—nursing-home—operation —patient, all complete. . . .' That's how it goes, doesn't it ? Masterly, my dear fellow. My congratulations ! The only defect in it," he added slyly, " is that it leaves out the principal character in the drama."

Wendover smothered his retort as the door opened to admit Miss Barclay, the controller of the establishment. She was in hospital uniform. Wendover was somewhat surprised to find that she must be in the thirties, for he had expected an older woman to be in charge of what was evidently a first-class establishment. He liked her manner, which seemed to blend efficiency and kindliness in just the proper proportions.

" Miss Barclay ? " queried Sir Clinton. " This is my friend, Mr. Wendover. I hope we haven't come at an inconvenient time. I can guess that you've no sinecure in running a Home on this scale."

Miss Barclay invited them with a gesture to take their seats.

" We're both busy people, I expect," she said with a smile, " so I mustn't waste your time on trifles. We can take the weather for granted, can't we ? You want to see Nurse Adeney ? "

Wendover was taken aback by the name. In all that he had heard of the Adeney family there seemed no room for another girl. Light slowly dawned on him, however, as Sir Clinton arrested Miss Barclay's movement to rise.

"Just a moment, Miss Barclay. I'd like to ask you a question or two. First of all, is Nurse Adeney on your normal staff?"

Miss Barclay reseated herself and gave the Chief Constable a quick glance as he put the question.

"No, she's not on our regular staff," she replied. "She's on special duty here, merely temporarily. We bring in outside nurses for that particular work. The regular staff couldn't do it without dislocating our arrangements."

"May I ask how you came to bring her in?" asked Sir Clinton.

"Dr. Leverington recommended her. It's his case."

Wendover pricked up his ears. "Dr." Leverington? Most surgeons, he knew, preferred to be called "Mr." to distinguish them from the ordinary medical men; but some of the old school didn't mind being termed "Doctor."

Miss Barclay put a question to the Chief Constable.

"You're friends of Mr. Ferrestone's?"

"Not personal friends," Sir Clinton admitted. "I'm an admirer of his work, and naturally when I learned that his eyes had gone wrong I was anxious. It's not anything permanent, I hope."

"Not if it goes normally. He's doing very well indeed," Miss Barclay reassured him. "It's cataract. The lens of the eye gets obscured by the infiltration of water-globules into it, and the sight goes eventually. The defective lens is taken out in the operation. After that, the patient has to lie absolutely still for a few days, and he needs a special nurse to watch over him at night for fear he gets restless in his sleep and does himself harm. Nurse Adeney is doing that."

"The operation was on the 19th, wasn't it?" asked Sir Clinton, without showing any great interest.

" And so in a day or two he should have his sight again ? "

" Of course only one eye's done at a time," Miss Barclay explained. He'll have the other eye done as soon as this one is quite well again."

The word " cataract " had enlightened Wendover. He felt angry with himself for not having put two and two together long before this.

" Nurse Adeney has been very careful of her patient, I expect," Sir Clinton went on in a casual tone.

" Indeed she has," Miss Barclay agreed. " She's done her part admirably. Kept him soothed when he felt restless, you know, and watched over him most carefully."

" So I should expect," Sir Clinton declared. " She's on night duty, you say. Where does she sleep in the daytime ? "

" Usually these special nurses make their own arrangements," Miss Barclay explained. " But we have a sort of hostel near-by for our regular staff. One of our nurses is on holiday now, and Dr. Leverington suggested that we might give Nurse Adeney her room for a day or two. She's a stranger in the district, and that saved her the trouble of hunting for lodgings."

" Obviously. A very convenient arrangement for her. And she came on duty, I suppose, about eight or nine in the evening and went off duty about the same hour in the morning ? "

" Yes, the day and night staffs change over at 8 a.m. and 8 p.m."

" She wouldn't see much of the other nurses, I suppose," Sir Clinton inquired, as though merely trying to widen his general knowledge.

" No," Miss Barclay confirmed, " except perhaps at meals. I really don't know."

Sir Clinton shifted his inquiries back to the patient.

" Was Mr. Ferrestone quite blind before the operation ? "

" Practically," Miss Barclay said, with a ring of sympathy in her voice. " Usually one eye goes quicker than the other, so the worst one can be put right before the other fails completely. But in his case both eyes went simultaneously. A dreadful state of affairs for an artist who depends completely on his sight."

" One could trace the advance of the trouble by his change in technique," Sir Clinton said. " I noticed that, but it puzzled me till I thought of eye-trouble. I suppose, when cataract comes on, things get gradually more and more blurred, and the colour-values alter bit by bit as time goes on. He painted as he saw; for I noticed that his handling of detail grew vaguer with each successive picture in later days. His colours went a trifle off, too."

Miss Barclay laughed pleasantly, as if at some happy recollection.

" He was nearly thunderstruck when the bandages came off for the first time. He told me he'd been living for months in a world of greys and browns, and suddenly the whole flood of colour came back at once. He never seems to get accustomed to it. Of course, as an artist, it strikes him more vividly that it would most people, I suppose."

" Well, that's good hearing," Sir Clinton said heartily. " He's too good a painter to lose. By the way, when do you expect to let him out of the Home?"

" About a fortnight after the operation, usually, we let them go. The first three or four days are the worst. In a week or less he should be sitting up and smoking, if he wants to. Of course it will be some weeks before he can be fitted with glasses. After that, his one eye should be as good as ever, if he's lucky. And so far as one can tell, his case is a good one.

"I'm delighted to hear it," Sir Clinton said with every appearance of frankness. "And now, Miss Barclay, I've kept you longer than I meant to do."

He rose and opened the door for Miss Barclay.

"I'll send Nurse Adeney," she said as she went out. "If you want to see me again, just tell her. If not, I'll say good afternoon now."

"I've taken up too much of your time already," Sir Clinton apologised.

He closed the door and came back to his chair.

"I'm rather puzzled to know what we're pretending to be," said Wendover. "There wasn't much of the official about you in that interview."

"I'm not pretending to be anything," said Sir Clinton lightly. "I'm an interested admirer of Ferrestone's work, and naturally anxious about him. I don't need to put on false whiskers to assume that part, Squire. It's second nature to me."

The door opened, and a hazel-eyed girl came quietly into the room. Obviously she was rather puzzled, but Wendover could detect no signs of distrust or apprehension in her manner. She was not exactly like the picture he had conjured up in his mind; but in her own way she was quite as attractive.

"My name's Driffield," the Chief Constable explained. "This is my friend, Mr. Wendover, Nurse. Miss Barclay's told us something about your patient. He's doing very well, I'm glad to hear."

"Yes, he's been a very good patient."

Wendover liked her voice.

"I'm so glad he's practically out of the wood, now," Sir Clinton went on. "Won't you sit down, Nurse? I'm one of his admirers, and it would have been a terrible thing if he's been crippled in his work. You know his pictures, perhaps ? "

" Oh, yes, I know his work quite well," the girl answered as she took a chair. " I'm glad you like it too."

Sir Clinton in his turn took a seat. Then he turned to the girl with a kindly smile which took any edge off his question.

" Why have you gone back to the name Adeney, Mrs. Deerhurst ? "

The girl was obviously taken completely aback ; but what Wendover read in the hazel eyes was astonishment, not apprehension.

" It suited me to do so," she said, in a tone which betrayed a faint resentment at the question. " Is it anyone's affair but my own ? "

" You haven't seen anything in the newspapers ? " queried the Chief Constable, still in the friendliest tone.

" No, I've hardly looked at a paper for the last few days. Why ? "

Her surprise was obviously quite genuine, and it dawned upon Wendover that she knew nothing whatever about the Deerhurst tragedy. Then he remembered that it had received very little notice in the newspapers, since to the outside world it had been presented as a mere matter of a road accident and an adjourned inquest. It had been given no scare headlines in the local papers, merely a little paragraph tucked away in an odd corner.

" Well," Sir Clinton explained in aneasy tone, " your rather abrupt disappearance from home naturally made people anxious about you. My friend, Mr. Calbourne, for one."

" Oh, so Mr. Calbourne's a friend of yours ? "

Hazel's tone indicated that she thought she saw some light. Wendover guessed that she had been trying to " place " Sir Clinton and had not been able to account for his visit. So obviously he had not mentioned his Chief Constableship when he rang up Miss Barclay. What sort of game was this ? Wendover asked himself, rather uncomfortably.

" Yes," Sir Clinton explained, still in the same easy tone, as though the whole thing was commonplace. " He came over specially to see me, one night, just after you vanished. He couldn't understand it. Can you wonder ? It looked a bit mysterious, didn't it ? "

" I suppose it must have done," Hazel confessed with a smile. Then the smile vanished and she added : " I had a reason for it."

" I think I can guess it," Sir Clinton answered. " Mr. Calbourne relied on my discretion, I may say, and told me the story. He guessed that you had gone off to avoid meeting your husband."

" Oh," Hazel rejoined. " He told you that ? "

Sir Clinton looked at her appraisingly before he spoke again.

" Can you stand a shock, Mrs. Deerhurst ? Not altogether an unpleasant one, I suspect ; but still, a shock. You needn't trouble about meeting your husband in future."

" You mean he's going to gaol again ? " Hazel demanded, in a hard tone.

Sir Clinton shook his head.

" No, something that will free you from him for good. He's dead."

" Dead ? " ejaculated the girl. " Are you sure ? It's not a mistake ? How could he be dead ? I can't believe it. You're not playing a cruel trick on me, are you ? He's really dead ? Really ? No, it can't be true."

But Wendover was not surprised to hear no trace of

sorrow in her tone. It sounded rather as though the news were too good to be credited. These quick, staccato phrases gave him a deeper insight into Hazel Deerhurst's married life than he had gained from all Calbourne's long narrative. How she must have hated the dead man, he reflected. It must have been far worse than even Calbourne guessed.

"There's no doubt whatever about it," Sir Clinton said, soothingly. "You're quite free now, Mrs. Deerhurst. He'll never trouble you again."

He felt in his pocket and extracted a newspaper cutting which he handed across to her: an account of the preliminary proceedings at the inquest, Wendover assumed. She took it, read it through with almost painful attention, turned back and re-read it from start to finish. Then, for a moment, she sat silent as though still she could hardly credit the news. Her face betrayed a final struggle with disbelief in which it was finally conquered.

"I suppose I look a perfect beast," she said at last "but it's good news. You can't guess how good." She gulped with a touch of hysteria, which she fought down with evident effort. "Everything seems coming right all at once. It's—it's wonderful! Oh, I know what it looks like. I ought to pretend I'm sorry. But I'm not, not a bit. I'm glad. I'm so glad. . . ."

Sir Clinton let her enjoy her emotions for a minute or two. Then, still in the same tone of sympathy, he spoke again.

"We quite understand, Mrs. Deerhurst. You see, Mr. Calbourne told us enough to make things clear. Frankly, I'd have thought less of you if you'd pretended to be sorry. There was no need of that with Mr. Wendover and me."

He paused, and then in a lighter tone continued:

"But I think you owe us something, since we've

brought this news. You've given us some anxiety by your doings. I think you might clear the business up. Your vanishing trick has caused a lot of trouble. Even the police have been called in. . . ."

"The police?"

"Yes. Mrs. Butterswick was in what she would call 'a fine state' about you when she found you'd gone like that. She set the Force to work at once. We've spent quite a lot of energy in tracking you down. I'm the Chief Constable, so I speak authoritatively on the point."

Hazel thought she saw a faint twinkle in his eye, and took her tone from his. Probably, Wendover reflected, she was glad to have the opportunity of obliterating the impression her emotion had made.

"Poor Mrs. Butterswick!" she exclaimed. "I never thought of that side of things. She's a dear old thing really, but inclined to be fussy, you know. I'm sorry she's been put about like that."

She considered for a moment, and then suddenly her face cleared.

"Of course, there's no need to keep it quiet any longer," she continued, as though speaking half to herself.

Wendover guessed that she was thinking of Deerhurst's death.

Hazel looked up suddenly at Sir Clinton.

"What exactly do you want to know?" she asked. "Where do I begin?"

"Better begin with Mr. Ferrestone's eyes," Sir Clinton suggested. "That seems to be the origin of the whole affair, I gather."

Hazel nodded, and then paused for a few seconds as though putting her thoughts into shape.

"So Mr. Calbourne told you about Mr. Ferrestone?" she began. "That makes it easier then. And you know all about my marriage—what a fool I was!—and the trial, and all that? Duncan and I parted. Neither of us was the kind of person to . . . well, to do anything underhand, you understand? And the Adeney family had enough already in the way of scandals. I wouldn't have another, even for Duncan's sake. So for some years I saw nothing of him. We didn't even write to each other. But I had to have *something*. I bought some of his pictures—through agents, for I didn't want to let him know where they had gone."

"I saw them in your house," Sir Clinton interposed, "and I saw something in them that caught my attention."

"The change in his painting? You saw it, too? I used to pore over them, you know; and I couldn't help wondering what it meant. And then, one day, I got a dreadful idea. . . ."

"That his sight was failing?"

"That *something* had gone wrong. And then my good resolutions broke down. I couldn't help it, when he might be in trouble. I wrote to him."

"That was in 1933, wasn't it?" Sir Clinton queried.

Then seeing the surprise in her face at the question, he explained. "I noticed that 1933 was the latest date on the pictures. It was on the one in your own room."

"Yes, that was the last thing he painted," Hazel answered. "I kept it apart from the others on that account."

"So I suspected," Sir Clinton rejoined. "You mustn't mind if I ask a question here and there. When we were called in I made some guesses about what had happened, and I'm interested to know how near the mark I came. I'm sorry I interrupted you. You wrote to him, you said?"

" Yes, we began to correspond. I met him once or twice—not often. I didn't want any risk of scandal. Not that there was the least ground for that. Still . . ."

Obviously she had meant to say that she was resolved to give her husband no pretext for even an unfounded charge against her.

" People might talk ? " Sir Clinton supplied. " You were very wise. But of course you could correspond. You learned what the trouble was. That reminds me of something. I'm told that cataract operations can be carried through at a reasonably early stage of the trouble nowadays. They don't stick to the time-honoured rule of letting the patient go completely blind, as they used to do in the old days. Why didn't Mr. Ferrestone get his operations over long before this ? He was quite blind, wasn't he ? I judged that from the fact that you and he corresponded in Braille with the Braille typewriter."

Hazel made a gesture of suppressed vexation.

" Of course the operation could have been done earlier if he'd gone to another oculist. Mr. Mandrell had his done at quite an early stage. But Dr. Leverington was a very old friend. Duncan relied on him implicitly. And Dr. Leverington wouldn't undertake to do the operation until the eye was quite ' ripe ' as they call it. In other words, Duncan was to go blind and to stay blind until Dr. Leverington decided he could do the operation safely. You can guess what blindness meant to him, an artist.

" I made inquiries from Mr. Mandrell and other people and found out all about the newer methods. And I tried to get Duncan to go to someone who was *au fait* with them. But he was stubborn. He believed in Dr. Leverington so strongly, you see ? I couldn't sway him at all. And I was in a difficult position. Suppose I got him to go elsewhere, he might have no confidence in the other surgeon, and confidence counts for a lot in a cataract case. Dr. Leverington was always stressing the risks which he thought were probable under the newer technique, you know. And if anything *had* gone wrong and Duncan lost his sight permanently I'd never have been able to forgive myself—never. So I gave up trying to persuade him and let him go his own way."

"Well, it's been a success so far," Sir Clinton reminded her. "I can imagine what you both went through; it must have been a ghastly strain. But it's over now, fortunately. By the way, I had an idea that the books in your library pointed to something of the sort: Axel Munthe, Helen Keller, and the others. You were trying to put yourself in his place, weren't you? I mean trying to realise what blindness meant to a sufferer?"

"Yes, that was it," Hazel confirmed. "You must be clever to have thought of that."

"Well, there was your interest in another eye-case, you know. That little girl of Sturge's, the one with conical cornea. You financed her cure, I learned. And your Braille typewriter. It all pointed in the same direction. By the way, you lent your Commonwealth machine to your cousin, didn't you? Before that, I suppose, you used it for correspondence. And that reminds me of one question. Did you use it when you wrote to your husband? I'm asking that to confirm another guess of mine."

"I didn't write much to my husband when he was in jail, as you can guess," Hazel retorted with a flush. "I did write him one or two typewritten notes, though it went against the grain. But that was a couple of years ago. I had no desire to keep up any communication with my husband. None whatever. I think you'll understand how I felt about it."

She was obviously vexed by the introduction of the subject, and Sir Clinton hastened to make an apology.

"I was merely trying to confirm a guess," he said. "I'm sorry. I know it's a painful subject, Mrs. Deerhurst. Now may I go on to another point? Mrs. Butterswick went through your wardrobe and gave us a list of the things she found missing. What made it look a bit queer was the fact that apparently you'd taken no outdoor dress with you. So I inferred that you'd gone off in some costume which you'd made yourself"—he pointed to her uniform—"because so far as we could see, you hadn't bought any new out-of-door clothes. I put that fact along with the indications of eye-trouble in Mr. Ferrestone, because I remembered that before you married you took a training as a nurse. You could easily make yourself a nurse's uniform, for I learned that you're clever with a needle. Now I wonder how far it's safe to push that? Am I right in saying that you left by train and that you helped an old lady into her carriage at the station?"

Hazel thought for a moment or two.

"I believe I did," she admitted, "though I'd forgotten all about it till you reminded me."

"You didn't buy a new dress, but you bought a new suit-case to take with you?" Sir Clinton asked.

"Yes," Hazel explained frankly. "My own suit-cases had my initials on them, and I was coming here as Nurse Adeney. Naturally I didn't want to arrive with luggage stamped with a wrong initial."

"It might have raised talk? Really, Mrs. Deerhurst, I didn't give you credit for such a mastery of detail, so I missed the point there. I guessed you were coming to look after Mr. Ferrestone, but that was all."

"Wasn't it natural?" Hazel asked with a smile. "The critical time is after the operation, especially when the patient falls asleep. Someone has to be at his side all night to see that he doesn't unconsciously turn or twist or do anything else that might put a strain on the eye before it's healed up. Who was likely to look after him better than I would? Do you think I'd have let another woman come in then, when I had the training that was needed?

"And naturally you didn't want to come under your own name? So you fixed it up with Dr. Leverington? He stood sponsor for you with Miss Barclay?"

"Yes. And of course I kept to myself when I was off duty in the daytime."

"Quite so. And now another bit falls into the jig-saw puzzle, I think. While you were sitting by his bedside, you had to occupy yourself. So you brought some books with you—from *The Times* Book Club?"

Hazel laughed at this, a pleasant little laugh.

"You seem to know everything!" she exclaimed. "Yes, I had a shaded light behind a screen and I spent part of the time in reading."

"Another point," Sir Clinton went on. "You took your cheque-book with you in case of emergency? You could always get Dr. Leverington or Miss Barclay to cash a cheque if you needed money urgently, so you wouldn't have had to go near a bank."

"Yes, that's exactly what I meant to do."

"Now there's another point," Sir Clinton pursued. "Can you remember exactly what you did just before you left home?"

Hazel sat a little forward in her chair and smoothed her cheek in her hand as though thinking hard.

"Let's see," she said at last. "I was rather flurried

at the last moment. The post had come in, I remember. I opened a letter from my stockbrokers, with some bearer bonds inside. I meant to take it with me and put it on the mantelpiece meanwhile. Then in the hurry at the last I forgot about it. Was it there all right ? "

" It's in safe keeping," Sir Clinton returned evasively. " And now, can you remember the last thing you did ? "

" Oh, yes, that's easy. I pulled out the main electric switches, both the power and light, to cut off the current in the house. I'm always very nervous about the risk of fire. Silly, perhaps, but I can't help it."

" Better to be on the safe side, certainly," Sir Clinton said seriously. " People are a bit careless in leaving big fires going when they go to bed. You'd think, sometimes, it was a case of arson. By the way, when did you leave your house that night ? "

" About twenty to eight, roughly. I know, because I was going to catch the 8.5 train, and I left myself plenty of time."

Wendover pricked up his ears. If the current at Norwood House was switched off at 7.40, and remained off for three hours and forty-four minutes, then the electric clock must have been restarted at 11.24 p.m. Sturge, according to his own evidence, had left the premises about 11 p.m. when he heard the telephone bell ring. If his tale were true, then someone else had entered the house twenty minutes after he had gone, and had turned on the current.

" Just one other point," Sir Clinton said, rather apologetically. " I'm afraid I'm giving you a lot of trouble, Mrs. Deerhurst, but I'd like to know if you sent off any wires recently to anyone ? "

Hazel shook her head decidedly.

"No, I haven't sent a wire for ever so long. Why should I when I'm on the phone?"

Sir Clinton saw that she was on the verge of asking the meaning of his question, so he swiftly interposed with a final subject.

"When you vanished like that we were rather troubled by one possibility," he explained frankly. "Mr. Mandrell gave us to understand that as his secretary you had access to a lot of very private information which might be coveted by . . . well, some people who might not be scrupulous when so much is at stake. It worried us, I admit."

"Oh, I see what you mean," Hazel said, with a slight frown. "I certainly have a good deal of confidential information, though I never thought of it in that light. No wonder poor Mr. Mandrell was in a state about it. I ought to have thought of that. Stupid of me, wasn't it? But it never crossed my mind. I had my own worries, and they pushed everything else out. I must write to him."

Sir Clinton rose to his feet and Wendover followed his example.

"Thanks for helping us to clear these points up, Mrs. Deerhurst," he said, holding out his hand. "And now I mustn't keep you any longer. I hope your patient will soon be quite out of the wood. If this eye is a success, it'll be a tremendous weight off both your minds. The second operation won't be anything like such a strain as this one, since at the very worst he'll have one sound eye, won't he? But I hope he'll have both back again in a few weeks from now."

They took their leave, and it was not until they were back in the car that Wendover thought fit to make the comments which had been stifled during the interview.

"You didn't tell her anything about the real state

of things," he pointed out. " I know your methods, Clinton. But do you think it was quite fair to lead her on like that, without giving her the least inkling of the importance of her evidence ? It'll be a fearful shock to her when she learns that young Adeney is in jail. It's a blue look-out for him, since she's completely exculpated. I think you might have played fairer than that with her."

" We've amended the old tag, Squire. 'All's fair in love, war, *and* detection.' But calm yourself. No, need for meeting trouble half-way. Difficult, too. when trouble doesn't happen to be on the road at all It may surprise you to hear that my first move will be to turn young Adeney loose again, so the shock to her will be slight. She's in the seventh heaven just now over Ferrestone's operation. Even you must have seen that. Why introduce a jarring note at this moment ? "

" But Adeney was in the house after Sturge left," objected Wendover. " Why are you letting him loose ? "

" Consider three points, Squire," retorted Sir Clinton. " First, that wire was handed in on a form, over the counter. If Adeney had sent it, wouldn't it have looked ever so much better to have phoned it to the exchange from Norwood House ? He could easily have done that, couldn't he, without raising suspicion ? Isn't it clear that the fellow who sent the wire hadn't access to Norwood House, or he'd have added that neat little bit of circumstantial evidence."

" There's something in that, perhaps," Wendover admitted grudgingly.

" Second," pursued the Chief Constable, " the mains-controlled clock re-started itself at about 11.25 p.m., as you'll find by adding three hours and forty-four minutes on to 7.40 p.m. Therefore, somebody must have been in the house and switched on the current before half-past eleven. Adeney's alibi covers the time up to half-past twelve. Ergo, whoever switched on the current, it wasn't Adeney; so there's 'some person unknown' in the field."

"I saw the point about the clock," Wendover declared, "but I forgot to put it alongside Adeney's alibi. You're right. Though that doesn't exclude the chance that Adeney had a hand in the affair all the same."

"Quite true," admitted Sir Clinton. "In fact, I'm pretty sure he had a hand in it. Whether we can frame a charge against him, is another question. If I'm right, it would be a very queer charge indeed, and I'm not sure it would be good in law. But I've only the psychology of the people to go on, here, and I may have made a mistake."

"And your third point?" demanded Wendover.

"My third point's plain enough. Someone rang up Norwood House at 11 p.m. and disturbed Sturge at his work. Why? Obviously this unknown person was simply repeating Sturge's own trick—trying to find out if the house was empty. But that unknown person couldn't have been Adeney, for two reasons. First, because Adeney was at Calbourne's house at that moment, talking to Mrs. Latchmere. Second, because if he *had* wanted to know if the house was empty, all he had to do was to walk in and see. He had his latchkey. He didn't need togo ringing up."

"Well, I hope you're right," Wendover commented, "for it would hit that girl pretty hard if her cousin was found to be mixed up in the business."

"Oh, he was mixed up in it, all right," Sir Clinton rejoined. "You needn't fret about that, Squire. He was in it. But what exactly he was 'in'—well, *that's* something I've never struck before in my experience."

" I'm not supposed to understand that, of course," Wendover suggested sardonically. " You like being cryptic, don't you ? And your jokes take some thinking over, sometimes, before one sees the point. But at least I see one of them now, Clinton. When you were humbugging me about the sort of dress Mrs. Deerhurst wore when she disappeared, you talked about the pattern being " N. or M. as they say in the marriage service." I suppose you meant that the uniform might be a Nurse's or a Matron's ? "

" Really, Squire," Sir Clinton declared in mock admiration. " You hang on my lightest word ! But that's what I did mean."

CHAPTER XVII

PARTICEPS CRIMINIS?

"NOW I'm going to put my cards on the table, Mr. Adeney," said Sir Clinton bluntly. "We've traced Mrs. Deerhurst; and she's made a very full statement about her doings on the night of Deerhurst's death. She was perfectly frank about it all."

Wendover saw a sudden look of dismay cross Adeney's face at this news. Then, with a violent effort of self-control, he regained his surface composure.

"Indeed?" he said, in a colourless tone.

"Yes. She was very wise," the Chief Constable said deliberately. "And if you have any sense, you'll follow her lead and tell us the plain truth about your own manœuvres that night. We'll consider your—h'm!—fairy tales as wiped out, and start afresh."

Nicholas brooded for some moments, with an ugly expression on his features. When he spoke again it was in a sneering tone.

"Some old game, isn't it? 'Now, Smith, we've had the whole story from Jones, so you may as well make a clean breast of it!' And all the while, poor old Jones has never opened his jaw, eh? Well, it won't wash this time. 'I know your methods, Watson,' as they say."

Sir Clinton was betrayed into a slight gesture of impatience.

"If you only knew what an unholy mess you're making with your supposed cleverness," he said acidly, "you'd go hot all over, Adeney. I'll do you the credit of saying that this attitude of yours—'Gallant lad, he'll die before he speaks!'—isn't just a pose. I'm taking it at its face value. And now let's get down to brass tacks. I'm not thinking of bringing any charge whatever against Mrs. Deerhurst. Does that alter your perspective?"

Adeney considered for some moments in silence, but at the end of his consideration his face still had its ugly-sceptical look.

"Will you put that down in writing?" he demanded, with a cunning glance at the Chief Constable.

Sir Clinton made a half-genuine gesture of despair.

"Really, you are an ass, Adeney," he pointed out. "Suppose I did put it down in writing, would it be worth the paper it was written on? Somebody else could bring the charge. The plain truth is that no charge will be brought, because there are no grounds whatever to base one on. Is that good enough for you? There isn't a scrap of evidence against your cousin. Mr. Wendover heard her story and he'll tell you that, if you don't take my word for it. The fact is, you've been on the wrong tack yourself, all through, and by your 'cleverness' you've simply helped the real murderer by mixing up the trail."

Nicholas was obviously shaken by this view of the case. He glanced from the Chief Constable to Wendover, and then again from Wendover to the Chief Constable. Finally he turned to Wendover.

"Is that really so?" he demanded.

"It's the whole truth and nothing but the truth," Wendover assured him, and the Squire's manner seemed to carry conviction. He, at least, had nothing to gain by lying, and he did not look the sort of man to lie in any case.

Seeing Adeney wavering, Wendover thought it well to go a step further.

" She has a perfect alibi for the time of the murder," he volunteered. " She was in a nursing home when Deerhurst came by his death."

Nicholas looked up swiftly in obvious amazement and concern.

" In a nursing home? What's wrong with her? "

" Nothing whatever," Wendover assured him. " She was nursing your friend Ferrestone after an operation."

The tense muscles of Adeney's figure went suddenly slack. It was plain that this news had come to him wholly unexpectedly and that he was trying to fit it into the information which he already had. At last he looked up again, with a different expression on his face.

" Well, that's a relief! " he ejaculated. " I *was* a fool to think she'd any hand in an affair of that sort. Still . . . it looked damned black to me, after what she'd told me about her plans."

He broke off abruptly with some return of his old suspicion. Evidently he was afraid that he might say too much.

" Now, if you're satisfied on the main point," Sir Clinton suggested in an ordinary conversational tone, " you might as well follow her lead and tell us a plain tale. I'll say straight out that I'm not thinking of charging you with anything; and I think I can make a guess at the story. If it's what I think it is, you've nothing to be afraid of. You were trying to shield your cousin, weren't you? "

Adeney nodded sullenly.

" Then, with no mental reservations, I don't see what I could charge you with. Is that plain enough for you? "

" You mean it? " demanded Adeney.

His tone showed that conviction was almost complete.

" I mean it. You can't hurt Mrs. Deerhurst, since she had nothing to do with the business in any way. And I'll tell you something more, Adeney. The fellow who murdered Deerhurst did his best to throw suspicion on your cousin. He might have got her into a very bad fix, if he hadn't made a slip or two. We want to lay hands on him, and your evidence may help. Does that alter your views ? "

" Oh, he did, did he ? " commented Adeney with a vicious twist of his mouth. " That alters my views considerably. I don't care what happens to myself, now ; so I may as well give you the whole yarn. But who is this skunk ? "

" Tell us your own tale and leave him to us," said Sir Clinton sharply, seeing that he had gained his point at last. " And tell us everything you can think of. We don't know what may be useful. Wait a minute. I'm going to get your evidence taken down."

Adeney obviously suppressed a sarcastic comment on this, and gave a nod of agreement. Sir Clinton summoned a constable and gave him instructions.

" Now, we're ready," he intimated. " Start at the very beginning, wherever you think that is. And don't spare details, remember."

Adeney sat hunched up in his chair for a minute or two, evidently thinking hard over the various points which he had to bring in.

" You know about our affairs, of course ? " he began.

" Mr. Calbourne told me about the firm's collapse and about your cousin's unfortunate marriage," Sir Clinton explained. " You can take that for granted. I'll ask you any questions that occur to me, later on, if necessary."

Adeney nodded and continued.

" So long as Deerhurst was in prison, my cousin had

some peace," he pointed out. "But when he got out. . . . What then? Ghastly prospect for a girl like her, wasn't it? But she'd thought it all over, and seen a loophole. She told me about it. She meant to goad Deerhurst into making an aggravated assault on her when he came back; and then she was going to get a judicial separation on the strength of it and be rid of the beast once and for all. She told me her plans. Of course I objected; anyone would, in my shoes. But she convinced me that her plan was the only one that would satisfy her, and I had to stand aside. After all, she was the one who would suffer, either way, and it was for her to decide. Not very nice for me, and I hated the idea, for she was all alone in that house at night, and things might get more serious than she intended. But I owed her a lot, one way and another, and I could see her point of view."

He paused and scanned the Chief Constable's face for a moment as though to make sure that he had established his point.

"She wouldn't let me stay with her in the house. That would have cut across her plans, obviously. So I agreed to stay on in my lodgings. But, without telling her, I made up my mind that as soon as Deerhurst was released, I'd keep some sort of watch on Norwood House in the late evening. If anything looked ugly, I could intervene; and I'd be a witness on her side. But naturally I kept that dark so far as she was concerned, or she'd have forbidden me to do even that."

"The night Deerhurst was killed, I was at the Calbourne's, and I got home after midnight. I was uneasy, because Deerhurst had got out of gaol on the 17th, and he might turn up any minute, so after I'd said good night to Goodrich, the constable on the beat, I came out of my lodgings again, meaning to take a turn up to Norwood House and see that nothing had gone wrong there."

"You knew nothing of Mrs. Deerhurst's plans for going away?" Sir Clinton demanded.

"Nothing whatever," Adeney admitted frankly. "All I told you about that was lies; I was fighting for time, to give her the best chance of getting clear away, as I thought."

"So I supposed," Sir Clinton said. "Go on."

"I went up to Norwood House," Adeney continued. "That was about a quarter to one in the morning. Everything was quiet; no lights on or anything of that sort. Still, I wanted to make sure, so I walked up to the front door to listen, for I was anxious, naturally. When I got up to the front door, I found it ajar, and that brought me up standing; a front door standing open at that hour of the night and all the house dark.

"I thought I'd better take a look round. So I went in quietly and switched on the light in the hall. And that gave me a bit of a start—when the light went on, I mean—because Mrs. Deerhurst never forgets to switch off the current in the house when she goes to bed. She has a special switch in her room for that very purpose: to switch off, last thing at night, for fear of fire."

"So naturally it took you aback when you found the current on at that time of night? But didn't it occur to you that Mrs. Deerhurst msight be out late at a bridge-party or something of the sort?"

"With the front door ajar?" parried Adeney. "Besides, I'd seen her a few hours before, and she hadn't said anything to me about going out that night. Usually she told me if she was going out, in a case of that kind."

"Very well," Sir Clinton admitted. "You know

best yourself what you thought about it. It made you suspicious. What next ? "

"I walked along to the drawing-room and opened the door. The place was dark. When I opened the door, I smelt cigar smoke. I'd been in the room shortly before I left, round about a quarter past six that evening, and there had been no cigar smoke then. That made me a shade more worried, for obviously some man had been on the premises—and not so long before, for the smoke wasn't stale. So I switched on the lights and went into the room. Then I saw Deerhurst's body on the floor. It gave me a fearful jar. . . ."

"Naturally," said Sir Clinton dryly. "But we needn't bother about that side of your psychology just now. It suggested something to you, didn't it ?"

Adeney paused for several seconds, glancing from the Chief Constable to Wendover with more than a trace of suspicion in his expression. Evidently something of his mistrust remained, in spite of all the assurances he had been given.

"Come, come," Sir Clinton pointed out impatiently. "You needn't stumble over that point. We know that Mrs. Deerhurst used to have a quick temper when she was younger, an uncontrollable temper. When you saw that body and remembered her plans about goading her husband into a passion, you thought that she might have lost control of herself completely in her excitement and killed Deerhurst ? That was what you imagined ? "

"Something of the sort," Adeney admitted with sulky suspicion in his tone.

"Well, it wasn't beyond possibility," Sir Clinton commented. "But as a matter of tact, it didn't happen. Still, you acted on that basis ? "

The Chief Constable's words seemed to have lifted Adeney's suspicions again.

"Yes," he admitted. "I thought she might have been driven to do it, in defending herself against him. He was a brute, Deerhurst. I wouldn't like to put limits to what he might have done if he'd lost his temper with her. And, physically, she would have been nothing in his hands if he set about her. I thought she might have snatched up something to defend herself with, and killed him before she knew what she'd done."

"And then, when she realised he was dead, decamped in a panic?"

"Yes, that's what I thought," Adeney continued. "I stood and looked at his body for a time; probably it was only a matter of seconds, really, but it seemed ages; and all the while I was thinking hard how I could get her out of this hole she'd got into. All I could think of was two things. To get the body away, somewhere, and to give her as much time as possible before a hue-and-cry started—if it did start at all. Once the body was out of the house, there was a chance that she wouldn't be associated with his death at all. That was the foremost thing in my mind then."

"So you thought of the car in the garage?"

"Yes. I must have made a muddle of it somehow, evidently, since you seem to know all about it; but I did my best in the hurry of the moment. The thing was to get the body clear away as quick as I could and to leave no traces in the car. He'd been bleeding, I saw. So I got some cotton-wool out of a drawer and made a pad to put over the wound in his back, and fastened it with some twine. That made sure that he wouldn't leave blood-traces on the back of the car-seat when I got him on to it. And I went through his pockets and took everything that might identify him. Then I carried him—and that was a stiff job, for he was heavy—through the house and out into the car. I propped him up in the back seat and then went back into the house to switch off the lights. I shut the front door, too. But I was in a state of nerves by that time, and I forgot the most important thing of the lot——"

"You forgot to clean the blood off the parquet ?"

"Yes, that was it. If I'd kept my head better, I'd have wiped it up, and then there wouldn't have been anything left to suggest foul play of any sort. But I forgot it, in the flurry I was in."

"And then you took the body away in the car ?"

"Yes. I began to think of quiet places where I could dump it, and the road to Swallow Tail Copse seemed as good as any. Then, as I was driving along, a fresh idea struck me. Why not fake a motor accident ? That would cover the trail completely, or so I imagined. So I thought that over as I was driving along, and when I got to the place I'd fixed on, I bundled him out on to the road and ran the car over him. Then I came back the same way I'd gone out. I suppose I ought to have come back by some roundabout route, but I was desperate to get the car back into the garage again. It seemed to me the one remaining link between him and the house, after what I'd done. I was in a blue funk lest someone should happen to see me putting the car back into the garage ; but there was no one about at that time of night. And then, instead of going into the house for a last look round, I felt I'd got to the end of my nerves, and I went off to my lodgings and let myself in as quietly as I could. They were all asleep in the house, and no one knew I'd been out after I came back from the Calbournes' house. It seemed a perfectly sound scheme, for I'd forgotten about the blood on the floor."

"You must have been surprised when you were routed out, first thing in the morning, by the maid ?"

"Yes, that was a staggerer," Adeney admitted, with

a wan smile. "All of a sudden, I remembered about that pool of blood. I'd clean forgotten it till then. That was a bad oversight. Once the police got on to that, I knew, they'd begin inquiring about this and that and the other thing, and Heaven alone knew what would come out. All I could see was that I'd have to spin things out if possible, and give my cousin the best chance I could of hiding herself before the hunt for her began. I did my best to bluff your inspector, but he was too many for me; and the blood patch was so much in my mind that I gave myself away about it straight off, like a fool."

Sir Clinton made no comment for a second or two after Adeney had come to the end of his narrative. Then he asked casually, as though reminding his witness of something which might have slipped from his memory:

"There's no telegram in your tale, is there?"

"Telegram?" demanded Adeney in obvious surprise. "No, there's no telegram that I can remember anything about. What sort of telegram?"

"The less said about it the better," cautioned the Chief Constable. "You didn't send it, evidently. But someone did send it, with the idea of implicating Mrs. Deerhurst. So keep your mouth shut about it, please."

"And you've nothing against my cousin? Or myself?"

"I've nothing against your cousin, Mr. Adeney. She'll be home again any day now. And, by the way, I didn't tell her any more than that Deerhurst had met with an accident and the inquest on him was adjourned. So when you see her, you can take your own line. It's on the cards that your part in the affair may never come out officially; so perhaps 'least said, soonest mended,' might be your best guide in talking to her. I'll say one thing. Nobody could have stood by your cousin better than you've done. . . ." He smiled a little, and then added : " But your intentions were better than your practice."

" Well, I owed her a lot, and I was grateful," Adeney confessed awkwardly.

" That was my reading of the psychology of the affair," Sir Clinton admitted. " It was one of the threads that led to a solution of that part of the business."

" And you've nothing against me ? " Adeney demanded.

" I don't think it's likely that there will be any charge brought against you," the Chief Constable declared frankly. " You're free to walk out of here now. And I've no doubt you'd like to get in touch with a razor as soon as possible."

Adeney rubbed his unshaven chin and smiled.

" Might be a good scheme," he agreed, rather ruefully.

The Chief Constable held out his hand.

" No grievance, I hope ? We had to detain you, because if you'd bolted before Mrs. Deerhurst was cleared, it might have been awkward. And I was afraid you might bolt—to make it appear that you were the villain of the piece."

" No grievance," Adeney confirmed, as he shook hands. " One might almost think the police had their good points, after all."

When he and the constable had gone, Wendover turned to Sir Clinton.

" I don't quite get this," he confessed. " Surely, on his own showing, young Adeney was an accessary after the fact. He helped the murderer by removing the body, didn't he ? "

" He did, undoubtedly, to some extent. But it's a question of definition, Squire. An accessary after the fact is one who, knowing a felony to have been committed by another, receives, comforts or assists the felon."

"Well, isn't that exactly young Adeney's case?"

"Wait a moment, Squire; there's another point. To constitute the offence, it is necessary that the accessary at the time when he comforts or assists the felon, should have notice, direct or implied, that he had committed a felony. Now the person young Adeney assisted was Mrs. Deerhurst. But she committed no felony. So how does your indictment lie?" Sir Clinton demanded with a quizzical look.

"Well, whether he thought he was assisting her or not, he did assist the murderer by his manœuvres, didn't he?"

"Perhaps he did," retorted the Chief Constable. "But it's clear he doesn't even yet know who the murderer was, or he'd have given us the name as soon as I let out to him that the murderer had tried to throw suspicion on Mrs. Deerhurst. That's elementary psychology. So you've got this tangle: X committed the murder; Adeney helped X; but Adeney doesn't know who X is. Can Adeney be said to have known that X in particular committed the felony? I've thought it over, and it would take a Schoolman to find a satisfactory solution. And, as a practical business, no jury would look at it, if we did bring young Adeney up before them. Of that I'm quite convinced, and I don't propose to present myself to any jury as a stickler for etiquette of that sort. So far as I'm concerned, young Adeney's out of it."

"There's something in what you say," admitted Wendover. "It might be too refined a point to carry much conviction in the mind of a juryman. And, to tell the truth, I like young Adeney better now than I did before. He always put his worst side foremost in the other interviews, and I didn't think much of him."

"And now, of course, he's the young hero, since he took risks for a pretty girl?" said Sir Clinton sardonically. "Personally, I've found him a damned nuisance in the way he confused the trail."

"That reminds me," Wendover said, avoiding the point; "you said you'd got some light from something Mandrell suggested to your mind when you interviewed him about his inventions. What was it?"

"He'd had cataract," Sir Clinton pointed out. "I was sure by that time that something had gone wrong with Ferrestone's eyes. Cataract was the very disease that might fit the case. At least it was the only one I knew that seemed likely."

"All along you seemed suspicious of that telegram," Wendover pursued. "Why? You mentioned something in its wording, when you were going over the list of things you had in mind."

"What struck me—and I wonder it didn't strike you also, Squire—was the phrase: 'Don't reply.' Why should Mrs. Deerhurst spend twopence in saying that? What would it have mattered to her whether Deerhurst replied or not? But if Mr. X wrote it, then there was value to be got for the twopence. If Deerhurst *had* replied, the case would have been quite different. Mrs. Deerhurst would have got a wire in answer to a telegram she'd never sent. And that would have been a pretty kettle of fish, wouldn't it? Even the least intelligent Chief Constable might have lifted his eyebrows a bit if that had come to his notice. Hence, obviously, the lavish expenditure of the extra twopence."

"Lucky that Adeney overlooked the telegram in the cigar-case when he went through Deerhurst's pockets, or you'd never have known about it."

" Even if he had destroyed it, Squire, we'd have come across it in another way when we began to make fuller inquiries about Deerhurst's doings at the time of his release. Somebody must have delivered that wire to him; and once we learned that, we could easily have got the original form. As a matter of fact, we've come across something fresh."

" What's that ? " demanded Wendover, pricking up his ears.

" We've tracked down the suit-case which Deerhurst left in the station cloak-room when he arrived there on the night of his death. In going through the contents, we found some documents. One of them was a will which he'd made in prison, just before his release. It's all quite in order and witnessed by a couple of officials."

" Then it's different from the one Granfield has ? "

" It's a very ordinary will. He leaves £5,000 to one cousin of his and £3,000 to another relation—people we've never heard of before—and some odds and ends elsewhere. There's no residuary legatee, and he's left nothing to Mrs. Deerhurst. Not even kind regards."

" There seems to be a lot of changing of minds in this affair," Wendover said thoughtfully. " Is Granfield nominated as executor this time ? "

" No," Sir Clinton explained. " He's made Calbourne executor, of all people. We've handed the will on to him."

" That reminds me of something," Wendover said doubtfully. " When Calbourne came to see you that night, it was plain enough that he was trying to put you off the track of Mrs. Deerhurst. What made him take that line, do you suppose ? "

" Try something more difficult, Squire. That's child's-play. Young Adeney had gone to him, you remember, and told him his version of things. Well, I don't suppose he put his ideas into plain words, but Calbourne was sharp enough to see what was in his mind. And what *was* in his mind just then ? That his cousin had murdered Deerhurst. So I expect Calbourne had more than a suspicion that Mrs. Deerhurst was in a bad fix, and he came to me to do his best for her. Sounds likely, at any rate."

"Something in that, perhaps," Wendover admitted. "And what are you going to do next ? "

"I've given Dornfell inquiries enough to make. They'll keep him and a staff more than busy for the next few days, unless they're lucky. But it's more or less pure routine work. I'm not by any means in despair. Would you care to stay on with me for a day or two longer, Squire, and be in at the death ? I think I can promise you that pleasure, as things look at present."

CHAPTER XVIII

THE STAMPS FOR THE HOSPITAL

"THIS insistence on irrefragable proof may be the palladium of an accused man," Sir Clinton remarked as his car came out into the open country, "but there's no denying that it's an accursed nuisance to a hard-worked constabulary. Think how nice it would be, Squire, if all I had to do was to kiss the Book and swear: 'I'm satisfied that So-and-so is a murderer.' Instead of a simple procedure like that, I've got to waste time running after clues to-day; and meanwhile my office work gets behindhand at an appalling rate. I see myself sitting up with strong coffee for the next two nights, trying to catch up on my routine."

The uniformed constable in the back seat of the car smiled to himself at his Chief's sentiments. So far as he himself was concerned, this trip meant a release from more irksome duties as well as a pleasant run through the country.

"It would save the Crown a lot in expenses of prosecution, too," Wendover suggested, entering into his friend's mood. "Something in your notion, Clinton. It might help to bring down the income tax. And that would be a relief to some of us. But what are you hunting for to-day, if one may ask?"

"Like to enter for the nursery guessing competition?" asked the Chief Constable. "I'm looking for somebody. He bought a cycle inner tube when he hadn't a bicycle; he got a letter that was never written; he bought paints, though he isn't an artist; and he sold bonds that he'd never bought. And the answer is: A Murderer."

"And he's got a newish Commonwealth typewriter, hasn't he?" supplemented Wendover. "I see. But how are you going to prove that about the inner tube? It sounds like hunting for a needle in a bottle of hay."

"That's done. Dornfell has had a squad combing every cycle shop in the neighbourhood, each man with a portrait of the suspect; and we've managed to prove the purchase. Not very exciting work, but patience tells in the end. Same with the paint. It's 'dogged that does it,' Squire, even if it seems a bit slow. The bonds were the easiest part of it. Two visits to stockbrokers did that for us."

"And the letter?" demanded Wendover.

"The letter's a nuisance," Sir Clinton confessed. "So difficult to prove a negative, you know. One can but try. And now, Squire, I want to think, so have a look at the pretty scenery till we get to our destination. It's only twenty minutes ahead."

Wendover kept silent until the car reached the suburbs of a neighbouring town. Sir Clinton evidently had its geography in his mind, for he took several turnings and finally pulled up before a small villa standing in an unkempt garden, at which Wendover glanced disparagingly. Obviously the owner took little pride in his abode.

"You stay by the car till I want you," Sir Clinton ordered the uniformed constable. "You'd better come with me," he added to Wendover, as he pushed open the garden gate.

Wendover followed him up to the front door, where the Chief Constable rang the bell. After a few moments the door opened and a stout woman confronted them.

"Very pleased with herself," was Wendover's mental verdict. "Probably a cook-housekeeper by the look of her. Garrulous, most likely, if one gave her a chance."

He noticed that, as she opened the door, she gave a sharp glance at the uniformed constable on the pavement at the gate.

"Mr. Granfield in?" inquired Sir Clinton.

"No, he's out," was the reply. "He's never here in the morning. You'll find him at his office."

Evidently the housekeeper was a person who was prepared to go further than merely answering the questions put to her, Wendover noticed as a confirmation of his initial surmise. Granfield's name had been no surprise to him, for already he had more than a suspicion about the solicitor. But, as Sir Clinton had pointed out, suspicion and proof were two different things; and he wondered how the police were going to get conclusive evidence in a case of this sort.

The housekeeper's reply seemed to have taken the Chief Constable rather aback, to judge by his manner.

"Not in? But I have an appointment with him," he said sharply. "I expect he'll be back shortly. We'll come in and wait."

He stepped forward confidently, and the woman, after another quick glance at the uniformed man by the gate, gave ground easily enough. Obviously the sight of the policeman had lulled any suspicion she might have been harbouring.

"If you'll come this way," she invited, leading them to a room at the back of the house.

Wendover moved over to the window and looked out upon another stretch of unkempt garden. Some flowers struggled for existence here and there in the beds, the lawn served as a washing green, and an arbour seemed to be sinking into decay. Wendover's eye was caught by a decrepit potting-shed in one corner, for its freshly painted red roof made a bright spot in the dullness.

"What a place!" he reflected contemptuously.

Sir Clinton meanwhile had detained the housekeeper.

"Have you been long in Mr. Granfield's service?" he inquired. "I don't remember your face."

Wendover had difficulty in suppressing a smile. He could not help admiring the neat way in which the Chief Constable had hinted that he was an occasional visitor at the house, an acquaintance of Granfield's with whom it was necessary to stand on ceremony.

"I've been here for over five years now," the housekeeper replied.

"Ah, then it must have been the maid who opened the door."

"That might be it, sir," the housekeeper concurred, evidently not ill-pleased to find that Sir Clinton seemed to put her in a superior class. "She's been here almost as long as I have, five years come Michaelmas."

"Old retainers, eh?" said Sir Clinton in a friendly tone. "Then perhaps you can help me. I'm the head of the police in the next county, and we're trying to find out something about Mr. Deerhurst. He was killed in a motor accident lately. Perhaps you saw it in the papers?"

"Oh, I knew Mr. Deerhurst, sir, very well indeed by sight. He used to be a great friend of Mr. Granfield's, sir, and in the old days he was often about the house, calling on Mr. Granfield. It was a great shock to us when we heard about his being arrested; I can remember it just as if it was yesterday. It struck me all of a heap seeing someone sent to prison that I'd known, so to speak, personally, like him. It made a very deep impression on me, sir, as you can well understand," she added solemnly. "And now he's dead. These motors are dreadful things, I always think, rushing about the way they do. One's hardly safe to cross the road in these days, with them whirling down on one at express speed like a lot of mad things. It oughtn't to be allowed, indeed it oughtn't."

Wendover's eye was caught by a typewriter which stood on a little desk in one corner of the room. Cautiously he moved over towards it. A Commonwealth machine, sure enough, but of a model later than Adeney's as the gold figures "51" on the base proved. What a fool Granfield was not to have got rid of it. But then, he reflected, it would have been even more suspicious to buy a new machine and scrap it almost immediately. Perhaps, after all, Granfield had chosen the wiser course in keeping his Commonwealth.

Wendover's reflections were interrupted by Sir Clinton's response to the housekeeper.

"There's far too much reckless driving," he agreed. "I'm quite with you there . . ."

The interrogative pause extracted what he wanted.

"My name's Stebbing, sir—Mrs. Stebbing."

"Thank you. Well, I quite agree with you, as I said, Mrs. Stebbing; but it's a difficult problem. No one knows that better than the police." He dismissed the subject with a gesture. "Now I wonder if you can cast your mind back to the time of Mr. Deerhurst's trial. He was about this house a good deal then, wasn't he?"

"Yes, indeed he was, sir. You see, Mr. Granfield was mixed up in the case in a way, giving evidence and that kind of thing, and I expect they had a good deal of business together. I remember the last time he came here the verdict was to be out next day, and I just looked at him when he came in and I wondered when I'd see him again, for the way things were going it seemed pretty sure that he'd have to go to gaol. I was sorry for him in a way; he looked so worried and put out, though it was a bad business, that was, and there's no denying it."

Sir Clinton seemed struck by a sudden idea.

"Did you ever witness his signature by any chance?"

"I did indeed, sir, and it was on that very night, as I remember well. I can see it as if it was yesterday, because I was so interested in the trial, and naturally anything about Mr. Deerhurst caught my attention just then. Mr. Granfield called me in to see them signing a lot of papers. Emma was there too."

"Anything about Mr. Deerhurst interests us just now," Sir Clinton explained. "Just tell us what happened, Mrs. Stebbing. You seem to have an excellent memory."

The compliment evidently put the housekeeper on her mettle, and she gathered herself together to do justice to the subject. Wendover was faintly amused to see her draw a long breath at the start.

"This is exactly how it happened, sir," she began. "It was latish in the evening, and we were just thinking about going to bed when the bell rang and Emma went up to answer it. Down she came again, and says she: 'You're wanted in the study, Mrs. Stebbing. Something about signing some papers. And I've got to go too.' So in we both went—into this very room, sir—and there on the desk were a lot of papers, big things, most of them, about as long as this." She indicated with her hands something that Wendover recognised as foolscap size. "And Mr. Granfield, he motioned us to come forward, and says he: 'Mr. Deerhurst and I want you to witness our signatures to some documents, Mrs. Stebbing. Do you mind?' So of course I said 'Certainly.' And then Mr. Deerhurst put his hand to one paper after another, us watching him all the time till he was finished, and then Mr. Granfield he told me to come and sign my name and write 'Witness' after it. So I did that on all the papers and Emma did the same, with Mr. Granfield's own fountain pen. And then Mr. Granfield said to me: 'You'd better witness my signature to another paper,' and he pulled out from the desk two or three sheets clipped together and took up a pen from the desk and signed his name and then we signed ours as witnesses, and that was all over. Mr. Deerhurst he thanked us for our trouble, and then we went away."

"I wish my memory was as good as yours, Mrs. Stebbing," Sir Clinton complimented her. "By the way, did you notice anything about these papers, anything that struck you?"

Mrs. Stebbing hardly hesitated. Evidently the whole scene had graven itself in her mind owing to its association with Deerhurst and the coming verdict in the Court.

"Some of them had little red dots on them at the side, and some of them were just plain typewritten things. I remember that."

Wendover surmised that the "little red dots" were the sham seals on stock and share transfer forms. So apparently Deerhurst at the last moment before his conviction had been transferring some of his shares to Granfield. Wendover did not know enough of the law to feel sure whether such transfers would be legal in the circumstances of the Deerhurst trial. It seemed rather too simple a method of evading Nemesis.

"There's another point where you might be able to help us, Mrs. Stebbing, since Mr. Granfield isn't here to tell us," Sir Clinton went on. "Did you know Mr. Deerhurst's handwriting?"

But here he drew blank. Mrs. Stebbing was a truthful

witness, and not even her obvious desire to pose as infallible could get her to diverge from accuracy.

" No, sir," she admitted reluctantly. " I can't say as I'd recognise it if you showed me it."

" Well, let's try another way," Sir Clinton suggested, with the air of collaborating with her. " What happens to the morning letters after the postman delivers them ? "

" I always take them myself and put them on the breakfast-table beside Mr. Granfield's plate, sir, along with the newspaper. He reads his letters first and then goes on to his paper, always."

" He gets a lot of letters, I expect ? "

" No, sir, he does not. Circulars, bills and that sort of thing he does get plenty of, but very few letters. All his business correspondence goes to his office, you see, sir."

" I just wondered if by any chance you noticed where his letters came from—locally or outside the town, I mean. But you'd never pay any attention to postmarks, of course."

He made a gesture as though giving up the point as hopeless, but to his surprise Mrs. Stebbing broke into a smile of self-gratification. Once again she was going to astonish this visitor.

" Postmarks, sir ? I don't notice them, as you say. But I could show you them if it's important."

She beamed with pride as she saw how her proposal took the Chief Constable aback.

" This is the way of it, sir. I'm interested in the Trelawney Hospital for Sick Children in Stanway Street, because my cousin's a Sister there. I often go to see her and walk through the wards. They're very hard up for money, she tells me, and though of course I can't subscribe much, still there's other ways one can help. One of them's by collecting old postage stamps. You see, what's an ordinary stamp to us is a foreign stamp if you send it abroad, so we collect old stamps, halfpenny, penny-halfpenny and what not, and we hand them over to the hospital and the hospital sells them to dealers at so much a pound, and then the dealers send them abroad, where they're foreign stamps, you see? That's how it was told to me by my cousin, the Sister. So when I heard this I asked Mr. Granfield if he would be so good as to give me all the stamps off his letters, and he said he would, so he always leaves the empty envelopes on the table after he's read his letters, and I collect them and tear off the stamps to keep for the hospital."

"And doesn't he ever forget?" asked Sir Clinton.

"He did often at first," Mrs. Stebbing explained, "and then he told me to count the letters that came in and remind him if the stamps didn't tally with the number of letters he got, so I always do that now every post, just to make sure. But nowadays he never forgets; he just leaves the envelopes for me, and they always tot up exact to the number of letters that come by the post, for I still keep count in case he forgets. So, you see, I can show you the stamps for this month, for I always hand in a parcel once a month to the hospital."

"That's very fortunate indeed," Sir Clinton assured her. "You're doing a good deed twice over with your stamps this time—helping the hospital and saving me a lot of trouble. May I see the parcel you have?"

Mrs. Stebbing, much delighted with her cleverness, went off in search of her stamp collection. When she had closed the door Sir Clinton turned to Wendover.

"A gift from the gods, that, Squire. We could have got at it otherwise, probably, but not nearly so conclusively. That woman's a bit of a gas-bag, but she's an excellent witness for all that. Perfectly guileless, and yet with sharp eyes and a fine memory."

" Save me from a closer acquaintance," said Wendover. " She'd talk the hind leg off a duck if one gave her a chance."

" Quaint, these old phrases are," commented Sir Clinton. " Has a duck a foreleg by any chance? You live in the country, Squire, and know better than I do."

" A poor joke," said Wendover with a shrug. " I'll show you a better one."

He walked over to a bookshelf and picked out a volume which he held out to the Chief Constable for a moment before putting it back on the shelf.

" Mason's '*Villa Rose*'? I hardly expected to see it," Sir Clinton confessed. " Our host isn't clever, or he'd have got rid of that book once he'd borrowed the trick of the skewer from it. That's one of the neatest weapons in detective fiction—deadly, and yet almost untraceable, since skewers are so common."

" You've made yourself quite the old friend of the family here, Clinton. Very neatly done, I admit. But aren't you afraid of the Big, Big Bear coming home suddenly and surprising you like the girl in the fairy tale? "

The Chief Constable shook his head.

" One takes a precaution or two. Dornfell wrote to Granfield asking him to make an appointment at a local police station just now. Pretext: the handing over of Deerhurst's cigar-case and other things, since Granfield claims to be the executor for Deerhurst. If the proceedings don't last long enough for my purpose, then some innocent constable will loosen a couple of Granfield's tyre-valves and when he comes out again he'll find two flat tyres, which will take a few minutes to pump up. And in the meanwhile I shall be notified by telephone. We have still time in hand, Squire, but I'd better hurry Mrs. Stebbing a little, perhaps, for the rest of the act."

The housekeeper returned with a large envelope, out of which she shot on to the desk a fair number of postage stamps still attached to fragments of the envelopes.

"That's the lot, sir, from the first of the month up to this morning."

Sir Clinton rapidly sorted out the three-halfpenny stamps from the pile and subjected them successively to a careful scrutiny. Then he passed them to Wendover, who searched through the series without finding any bearing a postmark outside the local radius. When he finished, Sir Clinton shuffled the stamps back into the envelope; but instead of returning it to Mrs. Stebbing he laid it negligently down on the desk and glanced at his watch as though rather pressed for time.

"Mr. Granfield seems to have forgotten his appointment," he said, as though giving up hope. "Perhaps I'd better write him a note. If I had a sheet of paper, I see you've got a typewriter there."

Mrs. Stebbing produced a sheet of letter-paper, and the Chief Constable walked over and clipped it into the machine. But after writing a few lines he unclipped the sheet and put it into his pocket, as though he had changed his mind.

"Perhaps, after all, I'd better ring him up," he said. "May I use this telephone?"

Taking consent for granted, he consulted his notebook and dialled a number.

"Sir Clinton Driffield speaking. Will you tell Mr. Granfield that I'm waiting for him at his house? Thanks."

Wendover saw that Mrs. Stebbing was duly impressed

to find that she had been entertaining somebody with a title.

"That'll impress *this* interview on her mind," he reflected with a suppressed chuckle. "And I suppose when he telephoned he was using a pre-arranged code to the police station. She didn't notice what number he dialled, of course."

Sir Clinton turned back to Mrs. Stebbing.

"Mr. Granfield doesn't go out much at night, does he? Glad to sit by his own fireside?"

"That's quite true, sir," Mrs. Stebbing agreed. "I don't remember his being out except once in the last fortnight."

"A Wednesday, wasn't it? The eighteenth?"

"That's right, sir, for I remember it was Emma's night out."

"Yes. He had some business with me that night," the Chief Constable explained.

Wendover had little difficulty in guessing that "business with me" was a synonym for the Deerhurst murder. Certainly, he reflected, that was undoubtedly part of "the business" of a Chief Constable. Very neat to give it that twist and use it to persuade this housekeeper that he was a friend of her master. It would have been clumsy to draw her attention to the coincidence in dates.

"Well, many thanks, Mrs. Stebbing. You've been of great help to us," Sir Clinton assured her as he skilfully but courteously edged her to the door. She retired, leaving behind her the envelope containing the stamps, which still lay on the desk.

Sir Clinton opened one or two drawers, and finally secured a large envelope into which he thrust the packet of stamps.

"Better write your name across the flap, Squire," he suggested, after sealing the envelope. "You examined these things, and we may as well observe all proper forms."

Wendover did as he was asked. Then he looked up and inquired:

"I suppose that phone message was the cue to arrest him?"

"Oh, no," the Chief Constable explained. "I want something out of him before we arrest him formally."

"But suppose he smells a rat and bolts?"

"What does a rat smell like? I never tried," said the Chief Constable lightly. "No, rat-smelling won't help him now. Dornfell is going to ask him for a lift in his car up here, on the excuse that he wants to see me. So he'll be well watched and he'll have to come here. Besides, why shouldn't he? We haven't made a move that would rouse his suspicions. I expect he thinks he's got away with it all right. By the way, I suppose you noticed the nice new paint on that shed out there? Red lead, by the look of it. He had to give some excuse for buying the stuff."

"I saw you found an excuse to try his typewriter," Wendover observed.

"Yes," Sir Clinton answered, taking the half-finished sheet from his pocket. "Look, Squire. Same kind of letter 'r' as you saw in that carbon writing on the telegram form, and quite different from the one on Adeney's machine. Every little helps. But that seems to be our friend at the door. Try to look innocent, will you?"

In a few seconds Granfield entered the room, closely followed by Dornfell. Sir Clinton, who was giving a good imitation of a man bored by waiting, turned to him with apparent relief.

"Ah, here you are," he greeted his involuntary host. "I'm sorry to have had to ring you up so unceremoniously. I happened to be in this district and it occurred to me that we might as well have a copy of Deerhurst's will. Nothing in it, I expect, but we have to collect odds and ends of that sort in a case of this kind. You've not sent it in for probate yet, have you ? "

Granfield made his habitual pause before answering ; but so far as Wendover could see, it was not due to any suspicion.

" I happen to have it here," he explained, moving across to a safe which stood in one corner and fishing out a bunch of keys from his pocket. " Deerhurst signed it here, and for some reason I've never removed it to my office safe."

He searched through the contents of the safe for a moment or two and then drew out an envelope from which he extracted the required document.

" That's it," he said, handing it to the Chief Constable.

Sir Clinton opened it out and read through its clauses slowly.

" Not much help to us, on the face of it," he confessed. " Still, it was as well to inspect it."

Wendover noticed that he exchanged a glance with Dornfell as he said this, and the inspector edged imperceptibly a little nearer to the solicitor. As he did so, Sir Clinton pulled a long envelope from his pocket and gave it a peculiar shake. Then he breathed hard on the will, at the spot where Deerhurst's signature was placed. Granfield's face betrayed nothing, but Wendover could see that he was watching the Chief Constable's manœuvres with almost painful concentration.

" That ought to do," Sir Clinton decided, after giving several slow exhalations.

He drew out his cigarette-lighter, snapped it into flame, and then carefully ignited a corner of the envelope he had taken from his pocket. Mingled with the usual paper smoke, Wendover saw a violet vapour, and he felt a peculiar tang in the air.

" Sorry to give a display of parlour fireworks," said the Chief Constable apologetically to Granfield. " But one has to try these experiments at times."

He held the signed place of the will in the violet vapour for a short time and then scrutinised the sheet carefully.

" That seems to have done it," he declared in a satisfied tone, with another warning glance at Dornfell which prevented the inspector from coming forward to examine the paper.

Wendover had no reason to hold back, so he came to Sir Clinton's side and looked over his shoulder. On the paper, in ordinary ink, he read " Leonard Deerhurst." But that was not the only writing; for under the heavy inked letters of the signature, another faint and elusive series of letters had appeared: " Louis Granfield."

Puzzled by this, Wendover glanced across at Granfield. It was plain enough that he had no need to examine the sheet. He knew, without seeing it, what Sir Clinton had unveiled. But he made no sign. Wendover admired his self-control; for although he himself could not do more than guess at the explanation, he could see that the Chief Constable's discovery evidently went to the root of things.

" I'm not sorry I took chemistry at school," Sir Clinton said with satisfaction as he tossed the burning envelope into the fire-place. " It turns up usefully now and again."

He swung round to look Granfield in the face.

" Louis Granfield, you will be charged with the murder of Leonard Deerhurst. Do you wish to say anything in answer to the charge? You are not obliged to say anything, but whatever you say will be taken down in writing and may be given in evidence."

Granfield's features remained completely under his control and his voice was perfectly normal as he answered:

"I have nothing to say at present."

Sir Clinton turned to Dornfell.

"You'd better handcuff him and put him in charge of the constable. There's some work for you to do here. Then you can take him to the station and charge him formally."

"Very good, sir."

Granfield made a movement as though to object to being handcuffed, but evidently thought better of it, and submitted to the indignity without verbal protest. Dornfell called in the constable from the gate and put the solicitor in his charge in another room. When he returned he was evidently burning with curiosity to know what was on the last sheet of the will.

"It may have faded a bit," Sir Clinton said, as he handed him the paper, "but we can always bring it up again if necessary."

Dornfell examined the will carefully, but when he looked up again it was plain that he was not much enlightened.

"Some jiggery-pokery here, evidently, sir," he said. "But I don't quite see what it's all about."

"You'll perhaps understand better when you've heard the housekeeper's evidence," Sir Clinton suggested. "Ask her to tell you the same story as she told to me a few minutes ago, and take it down in writing. Then get the maid, Emma, on the same tack. Make them sign their statements, of course, when you've finished. After that, you can collect that typewriter as an exhibit, and this book"—he took down the copy of Mason's "*Villa Rose*" from the shelves—"and when you've taken Granfield to the station and charged him formally, you'd better come back here with a search-party—I've made it all right for you with the local police—and see if you can pick up the remains of the inner tube of a cycle tyre. But I doubt if you'll find any remains. He's not quite such a fool as to leave that about!"

"You've got him, you think, sir?"

"I shouldn't arrest him unless I felt fairly sure. You see, Inspector, we've got the motive fairly plain at last, I believe. A jury likes a motive."

CHAPTER XIX

METHOD AND MOTIVE

"I CAN see my way through some of your manœuvres, Clinton," said Wendover, as he and the Chief Constable were driving homeward, "but this extract from *The Boy's Own Book of Chemical Magic* left me standing. So did some other things," he admitted honestly. "What made you suspect Granfield in the first place?"

"You're content with the elimination of Mrs. Deerhurst and young Adeney from the business?" said Sir Clinton, giving question for question. "Quite right. I think their share in the affair is plain enough now. H'm! What turned my suspicions on to Granfield? Well, I got my first inkling when young Adeney blurted out that story about Granfield getting a tip in time and selling out his Adeney shares before the crash. It suggested that he and Deerhurst had been pretty thick at that time; for obviously Deerhurst was the only person likely to know that the crash was imminent!

"That wasn't much to go on," criticised Wendover.

"No, it wasn't. But almost immediately after that came old Calbourne with his wholly independent story of how the trial went. You remember he told us that Deerhurst did his best to cook young Adeney's goose, whereas he seemed bent on exculpating Granfield, even at his own expense. Seeing that Adeney was a relative of Deerhurst's by marriage, one might have expected the converse procedure. That made me sit up and take notice, when I coupled it with the other point. It might have meant nothing, but it was worth noting as we went along."

"And after that?" pressed Wendover.

"Then out came the story of Granfield's visit to Mrs. Deerhurst, the night old Calbourne was at Norwood House. On the face of it, Granfield's excuse for calling then was the thinnest sort of fake. What had he to do with Mrs. Deerhurst's family affairs? Nothing. And nobody but a child would have been deceived by the pretence that he hoped to make a fee out of drawing up a scheme for an amicable separation. Granfield really isn't a clever fellow, Squire, or he'd have invented something better than that."

"Then why did he go there?" demanded Wendover. "Surely his game was to keep completely in the background and not appear on the scene at all."

"That's quite true," agreed Sir Clinton. "But you overlook one point, Squire. Granfield had never been inside Norwood House. If he hoped to commit a murder on the premises, it was a wise precaution to have a look at the geography beforehand. Further, he wanted to learn if there was any chance of Mrs. Deerhurst being out of the house on the night of the 18th, for that was going to affect his plans. If she was at home, then he'd have to do his murder in the garden which, if you remember, was nicely screened from both the road and the house. On the other hand, if she was to be out of the house on the 18th, then the obvious thing was to do his little crime inside four walls so that no one could interrupt. By the merest bit of luck for him, he learned that she was not going to be in the house that night. Calbourne mentioned that, if you remember, when he was trying to persuade us that she'd just gone off on an ordinary holiday."

"Yes, I do recall that; but I thought it was rather like eyewash."

"You took good care not to say that at the time," Sir Clinton retorted, with a grin. "It would have jarred a bit with your arguments in her favour, just then, wouldn't it?"

"I was always sure she'd nothing to do with it," Wendover claimed, with a slight flush of vexation. "But go on. What was the next thing?"

"The next thing was the call that Granfield insisted on paying me. Again his excuse was simply paltry, some rubbish about Mrs. Deerhurst's death and his duties as an executor. Obviously what he really was after was to find out, if he could, how we were getting on with the good work. And while he was at it, he tried to do a stroke of business for himself."

"What?" asked Wendover. Then, after a momentary pause, he added, "Oh, you mean the telegram?"

"I mean the fact that he told us the wording of the telegram, more or less. And the telegram was obviously meant to inculpate Mrs. Deerhurst, wasn't it? And that meant diverting any suspicion from friend Granfield himself, obviously. I found his move interesting when one put it alongside the other evidence."

Wendover had been thinking, as he listened to this.

"By the way, haven't you overlooked one clue?" he inquired. "I mean the way the period key punched the paper of the telegram form?"

"No, we haven't overlooked it, Squire. Didn't I tell you that Dornfell wrote to Granfield, asking him to make an appointment at a local police station this morning? He wrote to Granfield's private address and friend G. fell into the trap and answered with his own typewriter, punching his periods through the paper quite neatly. So that was that."

"How did Granfield know that Mrs. Deerhurst used a Commonwealth machine?" asked Wendover. "She told us she wrote to her husband, but I don't remember that she wrote to Granfield."

"Granfield saw her letters to Deerhurst when he went to visit his dear client in jail. After a sight of the typescript, it was easy enough for him to identity the machine as a Commonwealth. Perhaps he took one of her letters away with him on some excuse or other. But that was where he came a cropper, Squire, for he didn't know she'd lent her machine to her cousin."

"No," said Wendover, with grim satisfaction, "he slipped a cog there. By the way, I suppose that the ring on the phone that startled Sturge was Granfield ringing up to be certain the house was empty?"

"Certainly. But we can't prove that. He must have used a public call box. My own impression is that he had been watching the house from about six p.m. onwards, and followed Mrs. Deerhurst to the station. After seeing her into the train, he'd be pretty sure the coast was clear; but still he rang up to make certain. But that's only surmise. We can't call definite evidence."

"Then I suppose he went into the house and waited for Deerhurst? Probably he meant to break a window, but the open door saved him the bother?"

"That's how I read it. And he manufactured a 'cosh' out of a bit of cycle inner tube and some red lead. Naturally, when he put the 'cosh' down on the floor after striking the blow, it leaked a little. I admit my guess at the inner tube was a wild one, but what else would fit the bill ?"

"But why didn't he use an iron bar or something of that sort ?"

"Because it might have meant a splash of blood over his clothes, and blood was the thing he very wisely wished to steer clear of. Hence the skewer trick, since a wound of that sort wouldn't bleed much. And, obviously, his 'cosh' had to be a small weapon. He could hardly meet his old friend with a stocking filled with sand in his hand. Hence the red lead, to give a nice heavy weapon of small size."

"Well, then, let's get back to the telegram," Wendover suggested. "He said he'd got the text of it in a letter from Deerhurst."

"Which he read at the breakfast-table," Sir Clinton threw in. "That meant that if he ever got such a letter it must have been at his private house. Hence my inquiries about the post-marks of any letters he'd received recently. As you saw, none came from outside the local radius. But if Deerhurst had been in the vicinity he'd have rung Granfield up, obviously, instead of wasting time with the post. Ergo, 'there never was no such letter.' And that made the thing pretty certain; for if Granfield knew the text of that telegram without communication with its recipient, then he must have sent the wire himself."

"Yes, he *did* give himself away there," Wendover commented with some exultation. "And have you anything more against him ?"

"Well, we've tracked his purchases of the inner tube and the red lead. Also, the poor fellow had a bit of hard luck, one must admit. You've seen one section of it, Squire, already. The way we were able to clear up the motor affair. I told you we were running a kind of traffic census that night, didn't I ?

Well, naturally, we've been looking into the records of car numbers which were taken as part of the routine. And we find that Granfield's car was on the road from the station just after Mrs. Deerhurst left, and it brought him to his house half an hour later, say a quarter to nine or so. His car reappears on the records again about 10.30 p.m. and we can trace it on its road to Norwood House. Then it appears once more on its road home, between midnight and 12.30 a.m. He'll find it hard to explain all that running up and down the country-side, I think."

"That still leaves the will business," Wendover pointed out. "And your chemical conjuring trick."

"Just cast your mind back to the interview Granfield forced on me," Sir Clinton said. "By his story, Deerhurst had made a will just before he went to prison. He told us how Deerhurst, good fellow, had left his wife some property as a sort of symbolic gesture to show he bore no malice. That didn't sound to me like the Deerhurst character, as we'd heard it described from other quarters. Also, Granfield took care to emphasise that Deerhurst and his wife were at daggers drawn before that, and he also threw out a few suggestions tending to implicate Mrs. Deerhurst in the murder."

"Yes, I remember that," Wendover interrupted angrily.

"Then do you also remember that when I questioned him first, he accounted for not witnessing Deerhurst's signature by telling us that if he'd done so he'd have lost his profit costs. It was only when I pressed him with a straight question that he was driven to admit that he was the residuary legatee under that will, and so would collar everything that was left over after the specific legacies had been paid out of the estate."

" Yes, I remember that now. But he said the estate amounted to very little, in any case, didn't he ? "

" ' Very little ' is a matter of comparison, Squire. I remember in the old days, one of the American multi-millionaires talked about ' a poor man with only $100,000.' Suppose that friend Granfield had ideas on this scale, then what he'd call ' very little ' might be a nice round sum to a person like myself."

" Yes, there's something in that, perhaps," Wendover agreed.

" There's another advantage in being both executor and residuary legatee," Sir Clinton pursued. " As executor, you pay out the various specific legacies mentioned in the will ; and then you take the remainder. And it's no one's business—except the Death Duties officials—to inquire how much the residue actually amounted to."

" You think there's a lot of capital in the estate, then ? " Wendover asked swiftly, for he thought he saw his way through the problem.

Sir Clinton's reply dashed him, however.

" No, I don't think there's a lot of capital in the estate. In fact, I know there's next to nothing left of the estate. But there was a fair amount when Deerhurst went to prison—£8,000, at any rate."

" How do you know that ? "

" Because that's the total of the legacies which Deerhurst put down in figures in his latest will, so he must have supposed he had at least that amount of capital in hand."

" Yes, I remember that now," Wendover confessed. " It had slipped out of my mind. Well, £8,000 is a fair sum."

" If the legatees expect to get it, I'm afraid they'll be disappointed," said the Chief Constable. " The stuff was there when Deerhurst went to prison. We've gone through his stockbroker's books, and through the books of Granfield's broker too. And we find, as I told you, that somebody has been selling a lot of bearer bonds that he never bought. Now then, pull yourself together, Squire, and elucidate that for me."

"I see," Wendover declared. "Deerhurst embezzled a lot of the firm's money just before the crash, and used it to buy bearer bonds. To conceal that he had these bonds, he handed them to his confederate, Granfield, to keep for him safely, on the quiet, while he was in prison. And Granfield went back on him, sold the bonds, and . . . Did he lose the proceeds in speculation, Clinton ?"

"I'm pretty sure he did," the Chief Constable confirmed. "Now, go a bit further. What would happen when Deerhurst got out of jail and asked Granfield for his money ? "

"It would be gone, I suppose."

"Yes. And Deerhurst, being a nice, gentle, forgiving sort of fellow, would just say: 'Forget about it, dear old man. Don't worry further.' H'm! Would he ? Or would he be inclined to say: 'All right! You've embezzled the money I trusted you with, the money I've been counting on all the time I was in prison. I can't touch you for that, I suppose, seeing the way I got it myself. But I can touch you in another way, and now I'm going to put you through it. *I've* served my time for the Adeney swindle. They can't bring me up again on that count. But I can turn King's evidence and give away your little part, which I kept quiet about at the trial. And you'll get your touch, my friend!' That's what Deerhurst would have done if he'd lived to find out how matters stood; and no one knew better than Granfield that he *would* do it, when he found his money gone."

"So *that* was the motive ? " ejaculated Wendover.

" That was the motive, so far as I can see. But the method was not quite so simple as all that, Squire. This is a long-planned affair. Our friend Granfield was thinking of it before Deerhurst went to jail. He hadn't decided to murder him—not settled it, perhaps, definitely. But he'd thought of the possibility, and he drew up his scheme to be ready in case of accidents."

" What do you mean ? "

" I mean that he took precautions to provide himself with a wholly fictitious will, in which he himself figured as residuary legatee. Then, if he lost the money and had to kill Deerhurst, he could produce this will, pay over a few small legacies which he had put into it, and then sit tight on the residue. As he was executor, and a lawyer, he would have the whole thing in his hands, and no one would learn that Deerhurst's money had been embezzled. Deerhurst was the only person who knew about the hidden assets of the estate ; and Deerhurst wouldn't be there to talk."

" I begin to see light now," Wendover admitted, " and I ought to have seen it a lot earlier. But put it into words, Clinton, and let's hear how it went."

" To begin with, Deerhurst never made any will before he went to jail. It never crossed his mind to do so, I'm sure. Now Granfield needed a pair of sound, unimpeachable witnesses to Deerhurst's signature. So what was he to do ? My reading of it is this. He made some fuss about getting Deerhurst to sign a lot of legal documents—I've no doubt he faked up some plausible yarn to account for this—and some share certificates were also hauled in to be signed. The whole point was to have Deerhurst signing often in front of the witnesses, so that Mrs. Stebbing and the maid wouldn't bother to look at one paper more than another, but would just sign where they were told, time after time. Then, apparently as an after-thought,

Granfield pulled out another paper—his faked will for Deerhurst. Most likely it was prepared so as to look like some of the other papers, the ones Deerhurst had signed. Anyhow, Granfield brought out this fake and got his maids to witness *his own signature* to it. They'd witnessed so many things that night that they'd never remember which was which. And now we come to the crucial point, where Mrs. Stebbing proved herself an invaluable witness. I wonder if you noted that point in her evidence ? "

Wendover cudgelled his memory for something significant, but had to admit at last that he must have missed the point.

" Don't you remember, Squire," Sir Clinton reminded him, " that Granfield handed his fountain-pen to the witnesses to sign with ? But when it came to his own signature, he didn't bother to take back his own pen. He picked up an ordinary pen from his desk, dipped it into his ink-pot, and signed the faked will with that ! And then the two women signed with the fountain-pen and wrote ' Witness ' after the signature, just as they'd been doing for the last ten minutes or so. And there was half the trick done."

" I don't see how," protested Wendover. " If this paper was supposed to be Deerhurst's will, what good was there in Granfield signing it ? "

" This is where my schoolboy chemistry comes in," explained Sir Clinton with a chuckle. " If you add a drop or two of iodine solution to a solution of starch, you get a blue colour very like the tint of blue-black ink. That was what Granfield had in his ink-well, all ready. *That* was what he wrote with when he put his signature to the document. Then he got his witnesses to sign *with ordinary ink* in his fountain-pen. See the point of the second pen now, Squire ? The witnesses didn't know what the document was. They just signed as they'd signed already a dozen times over. And they were quite sound, unshakable witnesses—at least Mrs. Stebbing was, as you heard yourself. Deerhurst, of course, hadn't the faintest idea that this document purported to be his will. He would take it for some business stuff of Granfield's own."

"Still I don't see it," Wendover confessed.

"No? You should have taken chemistry at school, Squire. The point of the thing is this. Starch-iodine blue doesn't last. It fades fairly quickly; and if you want to get rid of it completely, all you need do is to expose it to the fumes of burning sulphur in a moist atmosphere. The iodine is bleached by that, and the blue colour vanishes. In other words, once he was left by himself, Granfield could bleach out that signature of his and leave no sign of erasure on the paper. He did that, at his leisure. Then he forged Deerhurst's signature to the 'will' instead of his own writing. And there was a nice little will, duly authenticated by perfectly honest witnesses. If Mrs. Stebbing had been unobservant as well as honest, the thing would have been lock-fast. Luckily she has good eyes and a good memory. But I wasn't depending entirely on her, as you saw."

"You mean your bit of parlour magic? How was that done?"

"It was safe enough to try, once I'd heard Mrs. Stebbing's evidence. But actually I'd thought of a disappearing ink myself, in conning over the whole business, and I'd come provided with some iodine. The point is, Squire, that when a writing done in starch-iodine fades out, it's the iodine that goes, while the starch remains behind unchanged. So on that paper, though Granfield overlooked it, there was his own signature written in a solution of starch. And when I moistened it by breathing on it, and then let iodine vapour come in contact with it—hey, presto! out came the letters in starch-iodine blue, just as they had been when he wrote his signature at the start. That starch-iodine blue test is an amazingly delicate one for either starch or iodine, as I learned at school by doing thiosulphate titrations."

"That was certainly neat," Wendover admitted, referring to both the crime and the detection of it. "Now let's see if I can work out the rest for myself. Clinton. Deerhurst's dead and Granfield produces this faked will. That's the theory of it, isn't it? Who can contest the signature, with those witnesses to support it? Granfield drew up the will himself, and he's executor and residuary legatee. If he's lost Deerhurst's secret hoard—gambled it away or what not—who's to know that it ever was part of the estate? He's the executor and has every means of covering his trail. There would be no documentary evidence of the transfer of the bearer bonds to him. That wouldn't have suited Deerhurst any more than it would suit Granfield. On the other hand, if there is anything left of Deerhurst's money—why, Granfield gets it as residuary legatee. I suppose he took good care, in drawing up the 'will,' that there were only a few odd little legacies elsewhere, to give it verisimilitude. The main bulk would go to the residuary legatee—himself. That's how it ran, didn't it?"

"More or less, I expect," the Chief Constable agreed. "And, of course, if he shirked the murder, he could burn the faked will any time that suited his book. No one knew of it except himself."

"So if he didn't lose the Deerhurst assets in his gambling, he was on safe ground; and if he did lose Deerhurst's money and had to eliminate Deerhurst, he could produce the 'will' and lament the smallness of the estate. Very neat, indeed. You may say he wasn't clever, Clinton, but he had some sparks of ingenuity, I must admit."

"Sparks in the wrong place lead to trouble," Sir Clinton pointed out rather grimly. "And I expect that Granfield will find it so."

THE END

››› If you've enjoyed this book and would like to discover more great vintage crime and thriller titles, as well as the most exciting crime and thriller authors writing today, visit: ›››

The Murder Room
Where Criminal Minds Meet

themurderroom.com

www.ingramcontent.com/pod-product-compliance
Ingram Content Group UK Ltd.
Pitfield, Milton Keynes, MK11 3LW, UK
UKHW022319280225
455674UK00004B/379